A DARKER
SHADE OF RED

A Novel

LLOYD PYE

Π

BELL LAP BOOKS
www.BellLapBooks.com

A DARKER SHADE OF RED

For information contact:
Bell Lap Books, Inc.
38 Blue Angel Pkwy.
Suite 210
Pensacola, FL 32506
www.BellLapBooks.com

ISBN: 978-0-9793881-2-5
LCCN: 2007905645

Printed in the United States of America

DEDICATION

To my father, "Doc," who as a boy in the Depression had to work after school and couldn't play football, but who would leave his optometry practice early to watch every high school practice and game I ever participated in.

To my mother, Nina, who never allowed me to practice or play a game in any sport in a dirty uniform, even if she had to wash and dry them after midnight.

And to my wife, Amy, without whose steady encouragement this story might have stayed a fading memory in the hearts and minds of a goodly number of aging men.

ACKNOWLEDGEMENTS

The Redshirts (1965): **Bob Dawson, QB. **Weldon Russell, FB. **Lloyd Pye, TB. Gayle Owens, WB. **Turk Evans, WR (D). Gene Goode, C. *Bruce Young, LG. Rich Brue, RG. **Tom Nosewicz, LT. **Bob Rue, RT. *Ken Tanana, TE.

The Mid-1960s Team (in alphabetical order): John Anderson, *Paul Arnold, **Bill Bailey, *Warren Bankston (P), Tom Barrows, Jim Besselman, *Mack Brabham, *Bill Brown, Charles Browning (D), **Buddy Caldwell, *Mike Cammarata, *Lou Campomenosi, Bob Capan, Don Capretz, *Fred Carpenter, Butch Coco (D), **Jerry Colquette, *Tim Coughlin, Carl Crowder, *Jim Darnley, *Dan Dembinski, *El Donaldson, *Bobby Duhon (P), David East (P), *Vic Eumont, Mike Findley, **Mike Fitzpatrick, Calvin Fox, Bill Goss, *Roger Green, Bruce Guidry, *Scott Haber, Blake Hamilton, **Steve Hartnett, *Lee Haynes, Dwight Howell, Jim Hutchinson, *Jim Jancik, Pete Johns (P), Dennis Krause, Jack LaBorde, Chuck Loftin, *Joe Melancon, *Conrad Meyer, Larry Mikal, Jeff Miles, Howard Moore, *Schott Mumme, *Lanis O'Steen, Ernie Parker, *Nick Pizzolato, Bobby Picou, Uwe Pontius, Richard Redd, **Hershel Richard, Billy Roberts, Dean Smith, *Don Smith, George Smith, John Snell, Pat Snuffer, *Mike Sontag, *Jim Spring, Dick Steigerwald, Jim Trahan, *Nat Toulon, David VenTresca, Leon Verriere, *Jim Wallace, Jim Wright, Tom Wright, Bill Zimmerman.

* Reunion attendee
** Regular reunion attendee
(P) Played in NFL after college
(D) Deceased as of 2007

A DARKER

SHADE OF RED

PREFACE

In September of 1964, I was among forty-four young men who enrolled at Tulane University in New Orleans with the hope we could survive four or five years as Green Wave football players. We were no different from thousands of other eighteen-year-olds reporting to football programs at campuses around the U.S. Nor, for that matter, were we different from hundreds of thousands before us who played the game after it took root in millions of hearts throughout the Heartland. Nor would we be different from the four-plus decades of players who have followed us from then until now. We were *typical.*

It is often said football players are a breed apart. This manifests in grade schools everywhere, when a select few boys begin to demonstrate on playgrounds that they have a special skill, or a special desire, to excel at the game.

By junior high, their natural positions have become apparent. By high school, they are solidly tracked. Those with enough ability to move up to the next level, to the college game, will almost universally do so. Then, if fate and fortune continue smiling on them, they become pros.

Because football players start so young, they end up heavily indoctrinated in the game's totems and rituals, to the exclusion of much else in their lives. Football becomes their primary interest, and they will play until they reach the limit of their ability, or they physically can't do it any more. Very few leave the game willingly or without regret, and after they do leave, they tend to become avid fans.

It is the first great love of their lives.

So it was with the Tulane group in 1964, no different from thousands of others before or since—except that I was among them, and the second great love of my life, writing, gave me the ability to tell our story by wrapping it in the accessible format of a fact-based novel.

My novel's events, while based on experiences unique to me and my teammates, are not substantially different from what many others might have written if they were so inclined. We all played the same game in the same way.

And then there is this astonishing fact:

Every year, in the first week of December, a core group of those who came to Tulane in 1964 return to New Orleans to enjoy a weekend of reminiscing and reconnecting.

Reunions of old football teammates are not especially noteworthy, but what sets our Tulane group apart is that we have sustained our yearly gatherings *for the past 25 years!* Nothing has stopped us, not even the massive devastation caused by Hurricane Katrina in 2005.

This, clearly, we do *not* have in common with football players who preceded us or who have followed us. In fact, I doubt if our record has ever been matched, and because it seems destined to continue until the majority of us are permanently benched, it will almost certainly never *be* matched. (Most who attend our seasonal get-togethers were born in 1946, making us 61 years old in 2007.)

The fact that we hold our reunions every year is, among other things, a testament to what we all endured in the two, three, four, or even five years that we played football together. It forged a ferociously tight bond between us, in the way wartime experiences bond young soldiers.

Our bonds were forged in blood, pain, fear, and anguish, the same witch's brew that turns soldiers at war into bands of brothers. Yet, despite all that, we found ways and means to have a helluva lot of fun, too. This is also the fate of soldiers, as are the wounds inflicted on their bodies, and the often more painful ones that fester in their minds.

We football players also had wounds inflicted on us in various zones of conflict, and like the old soldiers who survive their wars, when asked we will readily discuss our physical injuries. We proudly display them as symbols of achievement, knowing they represent something exceptional we accomplished in those long ago days at Tulane.

Our emotional injuries are another matter. As with war survivors, we tend to hide those away, ashamed to have them, to feel them, to carry them to our graves. We seldom if ever get to unburden ourselves from them. They are as permanent as the scars that show we once were warriors, fighting for what we believed was a good and noble cause.

My hope is that this book will help at least some of us come to grips with the emotional baggage we all carry. The scars on our bodies can't be erased, but the wounds in our hearts can be salved, I think, by giving our battles—our dark and often shocking experiences—a shape and a form we can share with those we love, and who love us.

INTRODUCTION

A Darker Shade of Red is based largely on real experiences I had during my four-year career as a college football player at Tulane University in New Orleans (1964 to 1968). The story's core revolves around my "redshirt" season in 1965, and my purpose for telling it was to provide a clear picture of what being a redshirt was actually like for any player who endured a year or more of it.

To outsiders, or even to the many "never-a-redshirt" players, some of the scenes described might sound implausible or even unlikely. However, they will resonate as fundamentally true with every player who endured the same kinds of indignities, insults, and physical abuse.

Despite being set in the middle 1960's, this book is surprisingly contemporary in the "feel" of what was happening with the team, on the field and off it. Football is football in any era because the basics of throwing and catching, blocking and tackling, and winning and losing have always been the same. However, some aspects are indeed unlike the modern game of football.

There are no African-American players in it. They did not make inroads into college football teams in the Deep

South until a few years after I graduated in 1968. There are no "social" drugs being used by anyone. Those were not really widespread until 1970, when the film "Woodstock" sent millions of us merrily traipsing down that path. For our time and place, alcohol was always sufficient.

We were part of the testing process that led to the invention of Gatorade, so that is covered in detail. Weight training, which today is mandatory for football players, still had not made sufficient inroads among teams to warrant serious interest from most coaches. It was made available to us, but participation was not encouraged.

Unlike today, freshmen were not eligible to play in games as varsity members. They practiced with the varsity, but were not allowed to participate in more than games against other freshmen at other schools.

Most important to understand is that players had no intrinsic value apart from what they could contribute to a team. Because scholarship numbers were unrestricted in those days, player value was cheap. Most teams would sign 50 new freshmen per year, then they'd pinpoint the 20 to 30 who could play well enough to suit them. That meant getting rid of the rest by making their lives so miserable they would give up their scholarships, which would then be given to new freshmen with more potential.

That "getting rid of them" process is a large part of what this book is about. It provides extensive details regarding the whys and wherefores of the process, which is still in effect today. Inevitably, football teams will grant scholarships to players who are eventually deemed "wrong" for that team. They have to be removed, one way or another, and methods used when I played are still needed today.

For a much more detailed analysis of matters of historical significance relative to football, please read the extensive Epilogue, which follows the end of the story.

With that said, let's now meet the Fightin' Crawdads of Cajun State University, and get ready for some football!

***

A DARKER
SHADE OF RED

This book is a novel, although not entirely a work of fiction. The author participated in, witnessed, or was privy to information regarding many of the events depicted in it. Nevertheless, the recreations of those events are not necessarily accurate, and the characters who participate in them are never portraits of real people, living or dead.

It is, always, a novel, employing approximations, composites, and fabrications to enhance clarity and continuity within the story, and to establish and maintain compelling characters. It is a painting in words, not a photograph.

WAKE-UP

My position as senior manager of the Cajun State Fightin' Crawdads football team required keeping to a few basic commandments, one of which was: *Thou shalt not interrupt or try to influence the natural flow of events on the team.* Consequently, even though Jimbo Wheeler was a good guy and a friend, I left the chiding note tacked to his door when I went in to rouse him and his roommate.

The dormitory's fluorescent hall lights flushed dawn from the left side of the narrow, evenly divided room. As usual, Wheeler's immaculate, military-style bedding tucks barely loosened during the night. From the clothes in his closet to the books above his desk, everything in Wheeler's half of the room was neat and tidy. Even his hair seemed to stay combed when he slept.

I glanced right to check Quink Thompson, his roommate. Equally asleep. I moved along the middle aisle between their beds and leaned first toward Wheeler, shaking his shoulder firmly. "Jimbo, it's time."

His eyes creaked open and focused on me.

"Okay, Sage . . . thanks."

As always, no problem. He accepted what had to be done and got on with it. I turned to deal with the Quink.

Technically, a *quink* is someone short enough to fart in a bathtub and break the bubbles with their nose. This Quink was a shade under five-nine, but dense, knotty muscles widened his frame to create the impression of a shorter man. Those overly taut muscles projected a bristling physical intensity that stayed with him even at rest.

Waking the Quink during two-a-days was not my favorite task. At his best, he was surly and difficult to rouse in the morning, but these two weeks of double practice sessions put him at his absolute worst. Without my fifty pound size advantage over him, he was one sleeping dog I'd be safer avoiding. I reached for his shoulder and heard Wheeler's sleep-slurred voice behind me.

"Wait! Is another note stuck on the door?"

I turned to shrug apologetically. "Sorry."

"That damn Everett!" he groused. "What does it say?"

"Stoner's freckles have muscles."

I heard a kind of snort, then, "They probably do."

Three days earlier, it became obvious that junior Jimbo Wheeler had rolled senior Sandy Hancock as the starting center on our team. They engaged in a stirring battle for the job, but Hancock was bigger and slower while Wheeler was lighter and quicker. Because centers were the heart of the offensive line, quickness off the ball was paramount.

Barring injury, in nine days Wheeler would make his first start for us against the defending National Champion Texas Longhorns. He would be head-up against the man considered by most knowledgeable fans to be the toughest middle linebacker in all of college football—a heavily freckled mass of speed and power named Kevin Stoner.

As a junior last year, Stoner was elected to nearly every All-American team in the country. He was 6-4, 240, and fast and aggressive, which made him certain to be a high first-round pick in the pro draft. However, much of his future worth depended on how well he performed in this, his final year. He would be at his best for the first game of the season, especially against a weak team like ours.

Wheeler was 5-11 and weighed 200 soaking wet, so even if he was as quick as a lightening bolt, he didn't have a hope in hell against an agile, mobile, hostile monster like Stoner. Everyone connected with the team accepted that grim reality; everyone, that is, except Wheeler. He doggedly refused to confront, much less accept, his fate, which was a primary reason he was starting.

Successful self-delusion was a skill of immense value among football players, and Jimbo Wheeler had mastered it. That brought the first note taped to his door two mornings ago. It was a good-natured attempt to reconnect him with reality: *Stoner is God.* Yesterday morning's said: *Stoner eats nails and shits bullets.* Wheeler would endure those reminders of impending doom until game day, and by then he'd be strung out tighter than a piano wire.

"Just do your best against him, Jimbo," I said matter-of-factly. "That's all anyone can expect." It was all anyone *could* expect. He was going against a true stud hoss.

I stepped across the thin strip of white tape that ran the length of the floor, dividing the room into halves. Shortly after Quink and Wheeler became roommates, they discovered that while they got along fine in everyday activities, they were completely unable to live together comfortably. On our team roommates were assigned instead of chosen, so they had to make the best of their situation.

Since a wall was out of the question, their only recourse was the strip of tape. It did little more than symbolically isolate them from each other, but they found it comforting and sometimes useful when resolving territorial disputes.

Quink lay in a twisted heap of sheets, dirty clothes, crumpled skin magazines, food crumbs, and one lone shower sandal. The entirety of his side of the room looked as if a tiny cyclone passed through in the night, and he looked, as the saying went, like death warmed over.

On any other morning, I would assume he had a few too many at one of the campus watering holes, but not during two-a-days. Nobody had any energy for anything but the practicing, rehydrating, eating, and repeating that cycle; then—most precious of all—sleeping.

During two-a-days, I tried to wake all the players gently because they tended to sleep poorly. They'd toss and turn all night in an effort to find comfort for their aching bodies. Fear kept them checking the clock whenever they woke up enough to remember who and where they were. Most discovered the inevitability of time watching phosphorescent hands sweep darkness toward these particular dawns. Some had a difficult time accepting it.

I shook his shoulder. "Rise and shine, Quink."

He jerked his arm away, turned his back to me, and crammed the bare pillow over his head.

"Wake up! I can't waste time coddling you."

He lay unmoving. I reached out and shook him again, harder. Without warning he swung a vicious backhand that barely missed my left knee. I was on him in an instant, rolling him over so I could press my right knee onto his chest and pin his shoulders with my hands.

"Listen to me, you little pissant! I can put the air horn against your head tomorrow morning and blow your goddamn eardrum out! *You hear me?*"

He went limp in my hands. No matter how angry and retaliatory he might have felt, not even Quink would risk a return to the more traditional way of waking a team on two-a-day mornings. That was walking from one end of a dorm hall to the other, blasting everyone out of bed with a hand-held, high-compression air horn that rattled teeth.

That method took twenty seconds per dorm wing, while mine took twenty minutes for the whole team, so I had no time to waste on laggards. For the two weeks of two-a-days, my first responsibility was to get everyone checked in for breakfast by 6:45 am, and this was the next-to-last day of that obligation. Nobody had been late during my two seasons of seniority, and I was determined to prove decency as effective as that godawful horn.

I glared at Quink and shook him again. "Well?"

He was bold and reckless, and it wouldn't be beyond him to fight back. However, it was hard to be reckless with 230 pounds of strong-armed threat kneeling on your chest.

"All right . . . I hear you."

"You better!" I snarled, giving him a last hard shake before pushing up off him and turning to leave their room.

I closed their door and waited a few seconds. When Quink felt I was out of earshot, he started in on me.

"What's *his* problem? He doesn't have to go out and get his ass kicked through every practice the way we do! He's going to school on a goddamn *laundry* scholarship!"

Wheeler set him straight. "You almost hit his bad knee."

I heard a long, low whistle, then, "Ho-lee shit!"

Laundry scholarship. . . .

That hurt nearly as much as the shot I took that blew out my knee because it was a truth I couldn't deny. A lot of my responsibility as senior manager involved making sure junior managers properly handled all the parts of players uniforms, dirty and cleaned. In my year as a junior manager, I picked up and washed and rolled up thousands of socks, jocks, and the half T-shirts that went under shoulder pads, not to mention the jerseys, pants, and redshirt tank tops that were part of every practice.

Soiled uniform pieces were a huge part of my life during that year, as they would be in this coming season. So Quink's put-down was painfully accurate. I *was* attending college on what amounted to a laundry scholarship.

BREAKFAST

Players shuffled to breakfast wearing variations of the same basic costume: sandals, cut-off jeans, and a T-shirt of some kind—seldom anything different. Enormous density bore down on them, a pressure they couldn't escape, and their outfits were an outward attempt to lighten the load. It was as if coolness and brevity before practice could balance out the heat and weight of what came during it.

Their destination was Seward Cafeteria, "the sewer," a dining hall midway between the dormitory and stadium. I checked them all into the sewer by 6:45, and by 7:00 most were finished nibbling or sipping whatever they chose to try to eat in those taut minutes preceding suiting up for practice. Then they went to the dressing rooms beneath the stadium's west side: varsity to the south or "front" end, freshmen and redshirts to the north or "back" end.

In the dressing rooms they started the agonizingly slow rituals of preparing for a hitting practice. It was called "quantum time" because it was like the slowdown that supposedly occurred as you approached the speed of light. The faster you went, the more time slowed for you relative to everything around you. It could get to a point where it slowed so much, the air around you felt like clear syrup.

To fight the slow grind toward practice, everyone found ways to stretch the tiniest actions into major projects: a sock had to fit exactly right; a loose screw had to be tightened; shoulder pads had to be adjusted a dozen times; every strip of tape had to be perfectly applied with no wrinkles—anything to fight that excruciating wait.

The only thing lightening the mood today was that it was the last day of double sessions. There was still an important scrimmage tomorrow that officially ended two-a-days, but today would put the worst behind them. Each player wanted only to get through the day unhurt, but they all knew it was unlikely everyone would.

Every practice during two-a-days seemed to bring injuries, as summer-softened bodies slowly adjusted to the power and velocity of full-speed, college-level collisions.

***

After breakfast, we walked to the stadium and I went into the equipment room, located exactly opposite the varsity's "front" dressing room, where my assistant, Chris Stanton, and I would "pull" equipment for practice.

We'd gather up canvas bags of towels and of footballs, and a case of medical equipment like moleskin for blisters and ammonia caps for rung bells. Another case held spare parts like chinstraps and mouthguards, and tools like the screwdrivers needed to tighten face masks. Then came blocking and tackling dummies, big heavy things with weighted bottoms that required both of us to lift them up into the bed of the battered old equipment truck.

That dark green pickup was new before World War II, and it was on duty at the stadium when a couple of our team members' fathers played at Cajun State. It had over 80,000 miles on it, all racked up driving in and around the stadium complex. So far as anyone knew, it had never been off campus, and the rumor was that a few children had been conceived in its spacious rear bed. I didn't know that to be gospel truth, but I had no reason to doubt it.

Once the gear and dummies were in place in its bed, we set about a duty that started for us the previous season. We began filling two 10-gallon metal canisters with water and the salty tasting concoction we were asked to test on the players. It had no name, so we dubbed it "green gold" because it was pale green in color and was so precious to a player during a hard, dehydrating practice.

All the teams in our league had been asked to test the stuff for scientists at the University of Florida, who were trying to find a way to prevent the two dozen heat-related deaths that occurred during two-a-days throughout the blistering Deep South and Southwest each summer.

Up until now, and certainly when I could still play, there was no such thing as drinking during a practice. It was absolute gospel that if you drank anything during the intensity of a typical two-a-day practice, you'd get stomach cramps and your muscles would seize and your practice would be over. That was as certain as knowledge came in the world of football that I grew up in.

It was so certain, in fact, that nobody ever even thought to challenge it. It just *was*, like the sun or moon. But now, incredibly, coaches at selected colleges all over the south were permitting fluid breaks in the middle of practices.

A lush oasis had opened up in the middle of our humid Sahara, for which we all were profoundly grateful.

Stanton and I stirred in and dissolved the two packets of green powder sent to us by the Florida researchers. Once the canisters were ready, we loaded them into the old green truck and moved everything out to the field.

Nobody ever drove the truck *on* the field. That would risk sinking its wheels into the well-groomed turf, making turned ankles a certainty. Instead, we drove around the eight-lane, quarter-mile cinder track that circled the field, on which track meets were held during the spring track season. By pausing the truck at various places on the track, we could transfer everything we carried in it to where it all needed to be during practice.

Because the canisters went into the bed last, they came out first. They were quite heavy, so we moved them one at a time, each of us holding one of the thick metal handles. We carried them to two large tables set up on the other side of the track, in the shade cast by the three-stories of Holt Field House, closely abutting the track complex.

Later, after practice began, an old assistant equipment manager named Soupbone would fill 150 large paper cups with the green gold. Those cups would be on the tables and waiting for players, coaches, and staff when the mid-practice break whistle blew. It was served cool, hence the shade, but without ice, as the Florida people instructed.

Our players wouldn't balk if we served it hot with dung balls as a chaser. They'd guzzle the green gold and smile munching the dung. That needed break, and that precious cup of liquid, had become all-important. Now nearly all of them got through every practice without entering the first stage of heatstroke. Before green gold came into their lives, that would have been all but impossible.

Not every round we prepared was equally successful. The Florida technical people asked us to report on the formulas that worked best for our players. Each packet was a distinct color with a number followed by a letter, which facilitated charting the impact of each solution.

Sometimes a packet made a solution too salty, resulting in "cotton mouth" among the players after they drank it. Other times it was too diluted, which had refreshing water in it but left the players susceptible to leg cramps. Most of the time, though, it was within a wide range that provided refreshment while preventing dehydration.

When all was said and done, green gold was probably the greatest thing to happen to football since the forward pass became legal. During each two-hour practice of two-a-days, I used to drop 20-25 pounds, while skinny little backs and ends lost 10 or more. Then, in the several hours between practices, we all had to furiously rehydrate those lost pounds. Now, at worst, everyone lost 5-15.

To call it a lifesaver could never do it justice.

After Stanton and I finished with our field chores, he drove me back under the stadium so I could go to the training room, while he parked the truck outside so it would be handy in the event of a serious injury like a broken limb or a blown knee or shoulder. I was carted off the field in that truck bed with my blown knee, and I couldn't imagine how many hundreds were in it before me.

The training room was always a steady swirl of muted voices and slow movements. Players, trainers, and occasionally coaches passed in soft eddies of sound that were felt more than heard in the hushed, intense atmosphere.

Whirlpool baths located in the rear produced a background white noise as a few injured players tried for a last-minute loosening of knotted muscles and bruised joints. Others sat or stood on tables with jockstraps on beneath towels around their waists, waiting to be wrapped or rubbed or treated in whatever manner was necessary to get them through another hitting practice.

Senior managers were experienced enough to care for minor injuries, so I often spent time taping ankles and covering abrasions. I worked at a rear-corner table, away from the front-wall tables of the team trainer, Cedrick Hanson, who loathed his first name and demanded to be called "Trainer Hanson." He, along with his two assistants, Bud Ross and Ray Trent, cared for most varsity players and all serious injuries, while redshirts, freshmen, and routine tape jobs like ankles and wrists usually came to me.

We could talk safely at my isolated table if we kept our voices low, which provided some relief against the inescapable grimness of what was playing out all around us.

"Heard anything about Prosser today?" Quink asked, as I taped his ankles. "He looked good yesterday."

I shrugged. "He looks good every day."

Our wake-up confrontation was forgotten, being little more than the kind of jawboning two players might do after a late hit or a block in the back in the heat of competition. Your hackles raised and you shouted at each other a bit, then you both dropped it and moved on.

"He didn't rise on the depth chart . . . I checked it."

Quink was obsessed with Pete Prosser, a new player on our team with singular football ability but an impudent attitude. He was also the current redshirt tailback, where he had been mired since the start of two-a-days.

"He won't move up," I said. "Don't worry."

Redshirts existed outside the varsity's three offensive and defensive units. They were no longer freshmen, but they hadn't been able to achieve varsity status, so they were expendable. At practice, they imitated each week's upcoming opponent, which made them little more than cannon fodder for the varsity. Their life expectancies as players were the shortest of any sub-group on the team.

Quink's thick black eyebrows pinched in toward a nose splayed by a forearm in junior high. "The rumor is that Teekay Junior said the coaches might move him up if he has one more good day today. You think they might?"

Quink was running at third team tailback and knew he was fortunate to be there. Tailbacks carried the ball more than any other runners, so the redshirt slot was a highly vulnerable position. All third teamers who lived on the bubble at any position dreaded getting rolled down to the redshirt squad, which in Quink's case would happen if Prosser moved up into his far more desirable slot.

"They could go back to the single wing or even the flying wedge and it wouldn't surprise me."

Quink's hot temper flared. "Dammit, Sage!" he hissed, "I want to know what you *think!*"

I felt sorry for him, but he couldn't handle a straight answer. Irrefutable generalities were what bubble riders needed to hear when they were as anxious as he was.

"Things almost never make sense around here, Quink, they just happen. Nothing can be predicted, so why worry about it? Just take it easy, man . . . take it as it comes."

He knew that was true, so he changed the subject. "What about him?" He nodded toward where Don Slade stood on Trainer Hanson's table. "How's his knee doing?"

I glanced over at the heavy, crisscrossed tape job being applied to Don's right leg from mid-thigh to mid-calf. It was wrapped that way before every practice to prevent licks like the one he took yesterday from buckling it.

Don's knee was torn up almost exactly a year ago, and everyone was amazed at how well he was playing on it. I still had trouble walking comfortably on mine.

"Bruised," I said. "Back like it was in a few days."

Quink smiled slightly. "That's the end of his shot at the Bull, though. He couldn't afford to lose even one step."

The Bull—Ken Rowley—was Quink's best friend and the team's starting fullback. Don Slade had challenged him for supremacy since the start of two-a-days.

Ken went at football and life in general "like a bull in a china shop," and his superior size and strength made him our best all-around back. Don's bruised knee would slow him just enough to remove what little hope he had of rolling the Bull off first team, but Don would be okay with that. He knew he was damn lucky to still be playing.

"That's true," I agreed, "but second team is a helluva lot better than where he was last year at this time."

It happened at the start of last year's two-a-days, and he'd worked like a fiend to rehabilitate it. Looking back, that's where I may have screwed up with my own knee. I didn't rehab it worth a damn. On the other hand, I maintain a strong suspicion that my surgeon came in hung over the day he operated on me. I haven't been free of pain for a single day since it happened, so I can't help thinking he must have left something wrong inside it.

I was finishing Quink's ankle when he spoke up again.

"What about Prosser, though? Could he move up?"

I gazed into his pinched, worried expression. Prosser would be a heavy millstone around Quink's neck until the coaches got rid of him, which would be any day now.

"He deserves to move up, doesn't he?"

"Well, ahhh. . . ." Quink knew the truth if anyone did.

"Then he probably won't, so relax."

I slapped the sole of his foot to indicate I was through, and he walked off looking and feeling measurably better about the threat Prosser represented to his position.

MORNING PRACTICE

At precisely 8:15, Stanton blew a shockingly loud air-horn to signal our team to take the field and spread out across the south end-zone for warm-up calisthenics.

BRRRRAAAAAAAAKKKKKKKKKKK!!!!!

Whooping like madmen, a hundred green-helmeted Cajun State Fightin' Crawdads poured out from under the stadium and crossed the track to take warm-up positions. They all wore white practice pants, with the offense in white jerseys made of thick cotton that would stand up to a season of hard use and daily laundering. The defense was in green, and redshirts wore a red singlet over their white jerseys, an extra layer of heat to battle against.

Both the field and the track were bounded by the baseball field and stadium to the north; a field house, tennis courts, and racquetball courts to the east; and, to the west, a tall chain-link fence that separated the track and the football area from a long row of residential homes.

The airhorn woke everybody in the neighborhood who might still be asleep. Those unfortunate people tried to complain when the airhorn was first introduced, but they quickly learned it was impossible to go against the power of the coaching staff. Besides, the coaches argued, if their incessant whistles were tolerable for decades, what was so bad about an occasional blast from an airhorn?

The sun was up and sweat was pouring when the players broke into position groups at 8:30. Each specialized group went off with its respective coach to its particular area, while freshmen and redshirts avoided cluttering the practice field by running plays against each other over on a small portion of the adjacent baseball outfield.

Surveying it all from atop his portable coaching tower near midfield was head coach T. K. Anderson, Senior.

Coach Anderson was a bona fide enigma. He was starting his second season as our head coach, after spending many years as the top assistant at Auburn. He brought a big-time reputation and attitude to this job, so none of us could understand why he would decide to come to a school like Cajun State. A team like ours could do nothing but put a big-time drag on his big-time career.

***

I walked over to my usual position near the south end of the west sideline. From there I could survey each drill at a glance and be ready to assist anyone who might need, say, an equipment fix. I was so absorbed with what was going on in front of me, I didn't notice Randall Webber come from behind to put a friendly hand on my shoulder.

"How's it going this morning, Larry?"

I looked down into his round face and smiled. We'd met at a couple of preseason press functions for the team and hit it off fairly well. He was my age and just starting out as a junior sportswriter on one of the city's newspapers.

He was built like a troll, short and squatty, with the kind of bowed-up, bristling energy more expected in a boxer than a reporter. Only black horn-rim glasses and a notepad in his hand gave away what he really was.

"Going good," I replied. "Last morning workout of two-a-days, so everyone is cranked up. How have you been?"

After the first day of practice, Randall wrote an article about our widely acclaimed status as a "breather" on the schedules of powerful teams. Our value, he wrote, was that we were good enough to be a spirited opponent, but bad enough to always lose against superior teams. Randall hadn't been around since then, and I knew why.

"Ahhhh, my asshole boss got a call from your asshole boss suggesting I make myself scarce for awhile. I've been covering a bowling tournament and a ladies' golf match."

I couldn't help smirking. "Sounds about right for you."

"Bullshit," he said sourly.

We gazed at the action on the field for several seconds, then I asked him, "To what do we owe the honor?"

"I wanted to get a look at Prosser. He's all I've been hearing about down at the office during my 'suspension.' Prosser this and Prosser that. Hell, they make it sound like he could run through a rainstorm and not get wet."

I grinned at the cliché, which in Prosser's case was close to the truth. The day after checking in, everyone was timed in a 40-yard dash, a 100-yard dash, and a mile run to check stamina. Prosser ran a 4.3 forty and a 9.6 hundred, with nobody else close to his times. And he was near the head of the pack when backs and ends ran the mile. If there was one thing he could do, it was run.

"Is he really as good as they say?"

"He's the best pure runner I've seen here, or anywhere else, for that matter. He's in a class by himself."

"Then *why* is he only a redshirt?"

"His attitude is atrocious."

"In what way?"

"He lets the coaches know what he thinks of them."

"Lowbrow pricks," Randall grumbled.

"It's part of the job description. But players—and I guess reporters—are supposed to pretend they don't notice it."

"So the best runner on the team is a redshirt because he won't play kiss-ass? Is that what you're saying?"

"In a nutshell."

"But isn't the object of the game to *win*? Don't they play their best people no matter what?"

It suddenly struck me that this was no longer a sideline chat between friends. I was being quizzed by a reporter who could quote me verbatim in tomorrow's paper. If that happened, I could end up as exiled from practice as he was. I decided to take out some insurance against that.

"Everything I'm telling you better be off the record, Randall . . . waaaay off. Understand?"

He bowed up like a bantam rooster. "I'm offended you'd even suggest otherwise. We're friends, Larry! Besides, it's not you I'm after. It's those idiot coaches who won't play their best people to try to win games. That's insane!"

"It's not insane, it's human nature at work, that's all."

His head shook. "Not the humans I'm familiar with."

I thought about trying to explain it to him, about how the difference between the top three or four players at any one position was often very slight, that one could fill another's role as easily as yet another. Injuries proved that on every team every season, when a starter went down and his substitute turned out to be a better player overall. Stories like that were legion in football.

Coaches were people, with likes and dislikes, and blind spots and prejudices, and emotional tangles that often prevented them from making the best decisions possible. Choices of who played ahead of whom were often capricious and arbitrary, based on nothing more than simple likes and dislikes. Some players were a lot more likeable than others, and in any situation where the talent differential between two was not dramatically wide, the likeable one always played ahead of the not-as-likeable one.

To have a system of such importance based, at bottom, on little more than individual whims, it made those doing the whimming, so to speak, easily vulnerable to abusing their positions of authority. In fact, abuse of that power was inevitable and, without a doubt, rampant.

Not every coach, but certainly most, were ex-players who did not have admirable careers at the high school, college, or even pro level, so their lives became a perpetual "do-over" of a failure they could never quite remedy. That left a majority of them angry, unfulfilled, frustrated men trying to somehow become stars in a different aspect of the system they didn't shine in the first time around.

Seen in that light, it was hard to feel much for them except pity, but I didn't think Randall could understand that, much less write sympathetically about it. More importantly from my viewpoint was that, as in the military and government, coaches avoided having to defend stupid or petty decisions by making those decisions—and, by association, themselves—as far beyond question, doubt, or reproach as they could arrange it.

As in the military or in government, the worst breach of football protocol was to even obliquely question any coach's absolute authority and/or scintillating brilliance, so even a washed-up ex-player like me could not afford to be quoted criticizing them because the consequences would in all likelihood be dire. I didn't want to risk it.

That left me no choice but to be evasive with Randall, which I intended to do if he asked me anything else about why our coaches didn't always start their best players.

HALF-LINE DRILL

Stanton blew the drill-change signal and the half-dozen specialty groups immediately broke up, the players scurrying to their new areas in order to avoid punishment laps for failure to hustle. I led Randall across the field to a spot near where the half-line drill would take place.

"You'll get to see Prosser in action now," I said as we walked. "It's a half-line drill. Half of the redshirt offense goes full-speed against half of the varsity defense."

The left side of the varsity defense—linebacker, nose guard, tackle, end, cornerback, and safety—were joined by the freshman offense on the twenty yard line's far hash mark. The redshirts joined the varsity's right side defense on the hash mark nearest us. Only half the offensive lines would go on each snap, and the ball would always move toward the short side of the field. Since the varsity was defending the short side in both halves of the drill, things were heavily stacked against the offense, but practice wasn't held for the benefit of redshirts and freshmen.

"Which one is he?" Randall asked.

I nodded at the slender figure standing to one side with his arms folded across his chest, motionless. The other redshirts seemed typically nervous about the impending contact, squirming and fidgeting as the drill set up.

Randall studied him. "He doesn't look like much."

That was true. At close range the uniform's illusion of size dissipated and you could clearly see how slight Prosser was. Not only that, he was very blond, a few shades away from albino, giving him a ghostly aura of fragility.

"He's big enough," I replied. "5-11, 170, but tough as a hickory knot, and quick as anyone you'll ever see. Plus, when he wants to, he can hit like a train. Don't make the mistake of judging him by how he looks."

Randall nodded, then mentioned the obvious. "Why is he dressed different from the others?"

Because of his pale skin, Prosser avoided the sun as much as he could. He wore his own special long-sleeved thin cut-off T-shirts under his shoulder pads, and thin white knee-length socks over his calves. When he practiced, all he exposed to the sun was his hands and his face, which he liberally covered with bootblack under his eyes. It gave him a distinctive, very noticeable look.

"He has some skin problems," I replied to Randall's question as Teekay Junior, Coach Anderson's recently graduated son, stepped in front of the redshirt huddle and assumed the position of the signal caller while Tom Everett, the quarterback, stood respectfully to one side.

Part of the humiliation dumped on redshirts was not letting them call their own plays, or even giving them credit for enough intelligence to remember called plays. It was still worse that Teekay Junior was a total incompetent who got his job through flagrant nepotism, which he tried to justify by imitating T. K. Senior whenever any opportunity arose. He was a sad, even pathetic case.

Before each snap, Teekay Junior would produce notebook-sized laminated sheets with basic plays diagrammed on them and say, "This one, on two. Got it? Break!" The redshirts would check their assignments on that schematic, the huddle would then break, and they'd shuffle up to the line of scrimmage to take their positions.

Texas ran an I-formation offense, with their running back usually lined up behind the fullback, quarterback and center. The redshirt fullback, Dave Duggan, got down in a normal football stance, while Prosser assumed a semi-upright position with his hands on his knees, to maintain a clear view of the line of scrimmage.

Tom Everett stepped behind center, barking out signals. The lines clashed together as he handed off to Prosser on a dive over left guard. Bill Hopper, a stout tackle, threw his man aside with a loud grunt and smothered Prosser.

Randall winced. "Not much there."

"Not much anywhere."

The next play was a power sweep snuffed when cornerback Andy Ferragino stripped away Duggan's lead block and left Prosser naked against the backside pursuit.

"Can't those guys block any better than that?" Randall asked. "Prosser's getting creamed!"

"They're just following their motto."

"They have a *motto?*"

"Do it wrong the first time."

His confusion amplified. "*What?*"

"If redshirts run a good play, it means someone on the varsity screwed up. When that happens, coaches make them run it over until the varsity gets it right. Getting it right means creaming the redshirts, so it's to everyone's advantage—varsity and redshirts alike—to make sure the redshirts do everything wrong in the first place."

While I talked, Prosser got smeared on an inside trap, but Randall didn't notice. He was muttering to himself, "Do it wrong the first time, eh? I bet there's a story in that."

"You better forget that one if you don't want Anderson to ban you permanently."

Randall kept silent until after Tom Everett handed off to Dave Duggan on a cross-blocked fullback dive.

"Why should I pretend redshirts don't exist?" he finally said. "They're an important part of the team, aren't they?"

"Yeah, they are, and every season someone like you writes a nice story about how much their selfless dedication helps the team prepare for its opponents. What I'm saying is that you can't get into what it means to actually *be* a redshirt. And you sure as hell better not tell the truth about what happens to them. If you do that, it'll be the end of your career on this campus."

Randall stood silent as Everett ran an option left, then he shrugged and said, "We'll see."

Twenty minutes later Randall sighed with disappointment. "I guess it isn't his day. I'm going back to the office."

The redshirts had run a couple dozen plays, and Prosser carried the ball on half of them, showing nothing of his true talent. I'd half expected him to respond to the rumors Quink heard about him moving up if he had a good practice this morning, but he was giving the standard redshirt performance of into the line and onto the ground in the most direct way possible. Everyone on the field knew he was sandbagging, but that was exactly what the coaches expected—and wanted—redshirts to do.

Prosser knew his personal die was already cast, so he didn't have a chance in hell of moving up no matter what he did, no matter how good he looked. I did admire the fact that he hadn't fallen for Tom Everett's latest ploy.

Tom was our team's main prankster, which put him behind the string of chiding notes on Jimbo Wheeler's door. He'd also be behind Teekay Junior allegedly saying Prosser might move up, a rumor he would have planted to get under Quink Thompson's extremely paranoid skin.

"Why don't you stick around a bit longer?" I suggested. "You might see something interesting when they bring the defense back together after the break."

His blunt face grimaced. "Naaah, I've had enough. I'll come back this afternoon to see if things pick up then."

"I can't blame you. Mornings are usually routine."

Just then Randy Colter, the right safetyman, came tearing upfield to help stop a sweep. He speared Prosser much harder than necessary, which could only mean Wade Hackler, the head defensive coach, had decided to stir things up by ridiculing Colter in the defensive huddle.

Colter was a square-jawed Alabama redneck who would

respond with a vengeance to Hackler's prodding. That was a major reason he was a starter. Coaches loved guys with insecurities large enough to manipulate easily.

Prosser normally didn't respond to late hits or any of the other garbage the coaches laid on him, but I'd seen him tangle with Colter twice already since he got here.

A quick glare from pitch-smeared eyes told everyone he took umbrage at that flagrantly cheap shot.

Colter took a threatening step toward him, but Prosser just turned and jogged back to his huddle.

"Better hold up on leaving," I said to Randall. "I think we're about to see something here."

PAYBACK

Randall moved back beside me as Tom Everett barked out the next snap count. It was an end run, shallower than a sweep, but still leaving Prosser plenty of room to maneuver. He took Tom's short pitchout and headed left behind Dave Duggan's fullback escort. Will Jensen, the defensive end, sensed what was coming.

Jensen shed his blocker outside to force Prosser to cut back inside, but as soon as Jensen stepped in to fill the hole, Prosser jumped back left with a quick hop. Jensen hit the ground empty-handed, and Corky Ames, the linebacker who joined Jensen anticipating the inside move, found himself tangled up in the interior double-team that neutralized the defensive tackle.

Prosser's move left only two people with decent shots at him: Ferragino at cornerback and Colter at safety. Ferragino had outside responsibility, which left him no choice but to take on Duggan's block. That left Prosser and Colter one-on-one in the defensive secondary.

Prosser stuck his nose straight upfield for his first two

strides beyond the line of scrimmage, but then he inexplicably swerved toward the sideline. That move exposed his right side to Colter's unbeatable angle, and Colter, like a shark sensing blood in the water, accelerated for the kill.

Three yards away from contact, he lowered his head toward Prosser's knees—and the instant his eyes went down, Prosser reacted. He pivoted directly toward Colter and lowered his own head, stepping full force into the blow. Their helmets made a sickening crunch that drew startled glances from all parts of the field.

Colter, totally unprepared for that kind of blow, dropped like a wet rag and lay stunned. Prosser drove on through the contact point, touched his free hand to the ground to regain his balance, and then, as was required, jogged several yards downfield until he crossed the goal line.

"God-dammit-to-hell, defense!" Hackler raged at them. "Get back on the line and run that one over!"

He stomped over to Colter's still-prostrate form and kicked him hard in the butt.

"He made you look like drizzleshit, Randy! Get your lazy ass up and pay him back this time! *Stick him!*"

Colter staggered to his feet and weaved to his position, while Hackler grinned behind his back. Hackler was a grossly overweight ex-substitute defensive tackle with the jowls of a blue-ribbon hog and the disposition of a constipated rattlesnake. He was an obese, ugly, mean-spirited, socially inept slug of a man, which made him the most important coach we had after head coach Anderson.

Every coaching staff needed at least one blatant asshole to attract and focus player animosity the way a lightning rod grounds electricity. They were usually men who channeled deep shame at having been mediocre, unaggressive players into success as vicious coaches. Hackler fit that to a "T," because it was more than a rumor that he played without talent or courage at a Midwestern backwater.

No defensive player acknowledged Prosser as he made his way through them toward his own huddle. Even his redshirt teammates weren't sure how to react. Their football instincts applauded the beauty of his run, but their survival instincts feared how the defense would respond.

"What now?" Randall asked.

"They run it over until Prosser gets creamed."

"How many times?"

"Depends on how pissed off the coaches are."

The redshirts assembled at the line. There was no need to huddle; everyone knew the play. The defense waited eagerly because they knew who was coming at them and from where. They didn't have to play the usual position football, so they could afford to tee-off on their opponents. The redshirts hesitantly took their stances.

The ball was snapped. Prosser took the short flip from Everett and went left. The defense instantly reacted and hurtled themselves after him. After four steps Prosser hit brakes and then cut back inside over tackle. The entire defense had over pursued, and Prosser blew by them all. He quit running twenty yards downfield.

"God-damn-shit! How many times do we have to tell you turds—*don't over pursue!* Now get your stupid asses over here and do it again, and this time *do it right!*"

The defense held their ground and waited for a hint of Prosser's same inside move. When he gave it they all froze, so he had no trouble changing direction back outside. In five steps he turned the corner and showed them his heels. In two plays he hadn't been touched.

"Christ on a bleeding crutch! You look like a bunch of limp-dick pussies out here! Can't you hit? Can't you pursue? That's a fucking *redshirt* over there doing that to you! Now get up on the line and stop his ass! *Stop him!*"

The air crackled and adrenaline gushed. Everyone was on edge. Even Randall began breathing in short gasps.

At the snap, the defense fired out and stopped every redshirt charge at the line. After being burned every way possible, they weren't going to fall for anything else. Prosser must have seen it because he cut into the hole without a fake. As the defensive line sagged in on him, he leaned into their waiting arms. They were heading for the ground and the play seemed all but over.

Suddenly, Prosser executed a violent spin that twisted him out of their relaxing grips. Standing clear, he found himself face-to-face with Ames, the linebacker. Ames lunged and made solid contact with Prosser's right thigh, but as he slid his arms around to lock the tackle, he found himself holding air and falling. Prosser had given him a classic limp-leg and was now pointed as before, straight at Colter in the secondary.

Colter had learned. He came up in full control and maintained a perfect hitting position—head up, feet apart, tail low. Prosser didn't even bother with a fake. He lowered his head five yards away and left Colter no choice but to do the same or risk getting pancaked backward.

One stride away from contact, Prosser suddenly straightened back up. Colter was fully extended with his head down and didn't see the move, so he dove through the contact point and continued onto the ground. Prosser, meanwhile, had jumped straight up, hovering for a brief instant with his cleats above the small of Colter's back.

It seemed certain Prosser would stomp Colter into the turf, which he had every right to do, but at the last second his feet spread and landed on either side of Colter's kidneys. Staggering more than striding, he jogged the required extra yardage. Exhaustion was beginning to show in him, but his mastery of the moment was complete.

BRRRAAAAAAKKKKKKK!!!!

Stanton blew the water-break signal just as Prosser turned to head upfield for the fourth straight time. Usually, when that signal came all football activity stopped, and everyone went directly to the break area. Not this time.

"Goddammit!" Hackler roared, yanking his baseball cap off to throw it on the ground, revealing a sweaty bald head glistening in the morning light. *Nobody move!*"

Everyone stopped dead in their tracks.

"I'm gonna find someone who can tackle that sonofabitch if it takes all day! I want every last one of you turds to get after his ass, and nobody stops till he's down! *Move!*"

The six men on the right-side defense began running full tilt at Prosser. I don't know if he was being defiant or was simply too winded to run anymore, but he made no effort to get away. He tossed the ball aside and crouched in a hitting position to absorb the blows coming his way as fast as they could run toward him.

Colter was closest to Prosser when Hackler shouted his instructions, so he reached him first and the two men hit head-on once again. The five others piled right into them, creating a cordwood stack of exhausted bodies.

Suddenly, a loud whistle blew from the tower positioned at midfield, Coach Anderson's incontrovertible signal to end the work period and start the water break.

Subdued players jogged past Randall and me toward the break area. Randall stood in a kind of shock, staring at the spot where Prosser was plowed under.

"Wow!" he muttered. "I've never seen *anything* like that."

"Prosser's talent or Hackler's assholery?"

"Both . . . together . . . I mean . . . shit!"

WATER BREAK

We started toward Soupbone's handiwork. Soupbone was the team's assistant equipment manager, an old black man with ash-white hair and a diligent work ethic. He was the one who, during each practice, filled 150 large paper cups with the green gold Stanton and I made and moved out to the tables where the cups now rested.

Randall tugged at my elbow as we headed toward the tables. "Prosser *is* as good as everyone says!" he rasped.

"Yeah, but you also saw what's wrong with him. He can play the hell out of football, but he won't play the *game*. He's waaayyy too hard to handle."

"You mean he aggravates the coaches?"

"Not just them, everyone. When a player won't kowtow properly, that impacts on his teammates, too, because in their heart of hearts they'd all like to behave the same way. They all want to stand their ground and not take crap from coaches, or anyone else. But almost nobody has the balls to do it, to actually live like that. So who wants to be reminded of that shortcoming every day? Nobody on this team, and nobody on any other team."

We took a place outside the gaggle of players crowding around the tables, reaching for their cups of green gold. We'd get one, too, but only after all the players had theirs.

"Are you serious?" Randall went on. "These guys will be glad to see him gone, even though he could help them?"

"He makes them feel like cowards. Hell, he makes *me* feel like a coward. Nobody likes to feel like that—nobody."

Soon all players had their cups, so it was okay for us to take a couple of spares, which we did. Then we threaded our way back through the sprawled, gasping bodies, careful to avoid being spit on. When players were dehydrated, a phantom layer of cotton seemed to cover the inside of their mouths, which they cleared out by hacking repeatedly.

Prosser squatted on his helmet near the outside edge of the track, head hanging down, sides heaving for air, sweat dripping off the end of his nose. All you could see of his face was the dark smears of bootblack he put on his cheeks to help protect his eyes from the glare of the sun.

He held the precious cup in both hands, at the ends of extended arms resting on his upraised knees. That was a common position for players to take. Some guzzled their cupful in one long pull. Others nursed it, gulp by gulp. The guzzlers tended to drink up and then sprawl on the ground. Gulpers did like Prosser, sitting on their helmets or on the ground, nursing it along, making it last.

Randall and I took a position near him, but out of hearing range if we kept our voices low.

"Looks like he's in bad shape," Randall said. "He hasn't even had any of his drink yet."

"He's too winded to drink now . . . he'll get over it."

Randall sipped his drink before saying to me, "What can you tell me about him? What kind of guy is he?"

"Is this off the record, or on?"

His head shook vigorously. "Off! I'm not trying to get you in trouble, Larry, I'm just trying to figure him out."

I decided to just go ahead and trust him. I couldn't imagine him shafting me for trying to help him out.

"He's unusual, to say the least; certainly not a typical football player. Of course, I only met him two weeks ago, when the team came together to start two-a-days. I still don't know him well. I don't think any of us do. It's been the typical two-a-day blur for all of us since we got here."

"All right, then, tell me what you do know."

PROSSER

Check-in at the athletic complex was two days before two-a-days began. I signed everyone in and gave them their playbooks, adding the usual caution to guard them like their family jewels. Then I gave them their dorm room keys, told them who their roommates would be, listened to the complaints of those who didn't like whoever they'd been assigned to live with, then I left the veteran players to fend for themselves because they all knew the drill.

I focused on the new guys, the freshmen and walk-ons, to be certain they were clear about where to go, when to be there, and what was expected of them.

Today would be check-in, tonight would be the "team social," tomorrow morning would be medical exams and fitting for uniforms, and tomorrow afternoon would be a timed 40-yard dash, a timed 100-yard dash, and then a mile run to determine who had arrived in shape and who hadn't. The day following that one would be what they all came for: two-a-days would officially begin.

New guys—freshmen, walk-ons, and transfers—were required to first visit the coaches' complex so coaches and administrators could assure their extremely proud Pappas and inevitably weeping Mammas that their sons were being turned over to good, nurturing hands, which could hardly have been further from the truth.

The coaches then sent them to me for check-in. I well remembered how stressful and disorienting it all was when I did it, so I tried to minimize that for them. However, there was no way around the fact that, as of today, their lives were changing in ways they couldn't begin to imagine.

Late in the process, late in the day, I was alone in the office beneath the stadium that was used for the check-in procedure. By then we were down to the final few names on the list, usually the handful who got cold feet at the last second and decided not to report for duty.

Suddenly, I noticed the muffled rumble of a motorcycle engine drawing closer. I rose from the table and went to the window to look outside. There was only one name left on the list that anyone really cared about—running back Pete Prosser—and everyone cared about him.

While checking in, all the veterans asked me if he'd shown up yet. I had to tell them "No," so seeing this guy pulling up outside caused conflicting emotions in me.

Everyone wanted things to go smoothly with Prosser, and if this was him, it would be a great relief for us all. On the other hand, in the world of football, motorcycles were not cool. Only thugs and hoodlums rode them, the kind portrayed by Marlon Brando and his gang in *The Wild One*. The image that movie established was poison, and image was all-important to our coaches and staff.

There were plenty of wild guys on our football team, and several owned motorcycles they kept at home or off campus, but nobody flaunted them openly. They were scorned by coaches as accidents waiting to happen, which was much truer than of any other mode of transportation.

This wasn't just any motorcycle, either. The seat was low-slung and the handlebars arched up and over so the rider had to reach shoulder-high to control the grips. At first glance, all I could tell was that he didn't look big.

We knew Prosser wasn't big, but I expected more than what I saw. And the way he sat on the motorcycle—slung back, low to the ground—made him seem even smaller. Or maybe it was the mound of gear piled behind him, a big wad of travel bags with a bedroll and sleeping bag strapped to a brace bar anchored to the rear fork. Whoever he was, wherever he came from, it looked as if he camped out along the route. That was a hard way to get here.

He wore black riding boots, blue jeans, a long-sleeved denim shirt, riding gloves, a red bandana tied around his neck, and a black crash helmet with a dark shield in front of it. Not an inch of his skin was exposed to the sun, and when he took off the gloves, bandana, and helmet, I saw why. His hair was blond and his complexion very pale, neither compatible with the intensity of Louisiana sunlight.

With skin like that, if he was coming to play football at Cajun State, our relentless summer sun would be only one of many physical challenges he'd face.

He put down the kickstand and climbed off the bike as I walked to him, saying, "Here to check in for football?"

He nodded as he turned to put the helmet on the seat. He then pulled a pair of dark shades from a pocket in his shirt, so when he turned back to me, I couldn't see his eyes. But everything other than his pale color and his blond shock of sweat-matted hair seemed normal enough.

His face was solid, with a strong chin and an aquiline nose that didn't look as if it had ever been broken, though

I'd seen a few fixed so you couldn't tell. Double-bar face masks were the norm everywhere, protecting mouths and teeth well enough, but still leaving noses open to forearms and shoe edges, so breaks were fairly common.

"I'm Pete Prosser," he said, in an accent I couldn't place. Not from the south or midwest, but it didn't sound northwest or northeast, either. It had an unusual twang.

"Sorry I'm late, but predicting travel times on a motorcycle can be tricky. Are you Larry?"

I smiled and stuck my hand out. "Yeah, but only the coaches and staff call me that. To the team, I'm Sage."

He returned my smile, showing perfect white teeth. "Would that be the seasoning sage . . . or the bush?"

"According to Websters, I'm 'a venerable man of sound judgement.' The guys here think I know what's going on."

He cocked his head to one side. "Do you?"

"I've been here a while, that's all. It's my last semester."

He paused to scan this part of the campus, which was the eastern side of the south end of the stadium. As he did, I pointed to the coaches offices on the west side.

"You've seen the coaches, I presume."

He nodded. "Yeah, sure. They seemed like a nice enough bunch. Told me to come see you over here to check in."

"Which ones did you meet?"

"Just a few. I think most already left. But I met Coach Marshall, the offensive coach, and Coach Anderson and his son. Those I'm sure of. The rest, I'd be guessing."

"Did they say they were worried you were late? I think everyone was starting to think you changed your mind."

He smiled again and I noticed how dry his lips were. Even under the helmet, the wind got to him. "No, all they said was they looked forward to seeing me on offense."

"With stats like yours, where *else* would they put you?"

Pete Prosser was a rarity for our team, a transfer from another school. We were the kind you transferred *from*, not *to*. Making it more unusual was that in his freshman and sophomore years, he tore through a junior college league in Washington State and Oregon. He set so many records it was mind-boggling, but because it was junior colleges, we assumed his stats were skewed by weak competition.

When first hearing about those phenomenal stats, one of our crustier coaches said that Proser must have played so far in the sticks, they used billy goats for safeties.

Billy goats or not, he ran around and through all of them, and everyone figured he'd go to one of the many football powers recruiting him. But he didn't. One day, out of the blue, a letter from him arrived in Coach Anderson's office, asking if Cajun State would be interested in him.

Coach Anderson checked him out by talking with his head coach in Washington. That coach said Prosser was "eccentric." When Coach Anderson pressed for something more specific, Prosser's coach reportedly said, "Just give the boy his head, Coach, and he'll do fine for you. Don't try to corral him in any way, just give him his head."

Coach Anderson heard the words, but he didn't focus on the underlying drift of what he was being told. He figured Prosser was an acclaimed talent, he had the stats to prove it, and any "eccentricities" could be worked out after he became part of the team. They sent him a scholarship sight unseen, based on his statistics alone. They didn't even call him up or ask to see film of him.

"How was your trip?" I asked as we neared the office door. "Biking from Washington must have been rough."

"From California, actually. My mother lives there, in San Francisco, so that's more or less my home base."

That might explain the unusual twang in his voice, and almost certainly the James Dean/Marlon Brando style.

I paused at the door, turning to him. "I know you don't know me, and you don't have to answer if you don't want to, but everyone on the team is wondering why you came *here*? You could play anywhere else, so why here?"

"Scott Brown."

"A relative?"

It was surprising how often the choice of college for an athlete was dictated by the fact that a close relative lived within an easy reach of the campus. Those guys were usually from badly broken homes, so they wanted to get away from Mom and Dad's belligerent bickering, but not so far away that they didn't know anyone at all. Settling near a relative often solved that problem.

A wry grin cracked his dry lips. "You're not a philosophy major, are you?"

"Nope, business," I said, opening the door. "I want to go where the money is and then make a lot of it."

"My background is mostly in eastern philosophy, but I want to learn as much as I can about all aspects of it while I'm in college. Scott Brown is one of the best teachers of classic philosophy in this country, and he's here."

Now it was my turn to smile wryly. "Let me amend my question, then. What the hell is *he* doing here?"

"His mother lives nearby."

"Figures. . . ."

CHECKING IN

We settled into chairs in the office, him across the desk from me. I gave him his key and his playbook and told him his roommate wasn't checked in yet. If he didn't show up, as might well happen, then Prosser would have the room to himself until the end of two-a-days.

Twenty to thirty guys would quit during two-a-days, and when that dust settled, the remaining roommates would be paired up like everyone else for the start of the school year and of the regular season. Naturally, some would quit during the season, too, but far fewer than during two-a-days or spring practice.

Most who left would be homesick freshmen unable to go for long without easy access to their high school sweethearts. Others would be walk-ons who found football at the college level was vastly more rigorous than in high school. It was a good thing for all of them to figure out early that they didn't belong in this crucible.

The saddest cases were always the second-year redshirts, the guys starting their junior year in college and finding themselves looking at a second year on the cannon fodder squad. That was when most of them gave up their scholarship by quitting. They had to find a way to pay for only two more years of school, which was a lot less intimidating than three or four years.

If you were a redshirt facing a second year of it, the time to quit was when you realized you were likely to be a permanent redshirt for two more years, *if* you could survive the physical attrition rate, which was highly unlikely.

Only maniacs attempted that.

As we finished up, Prosser said, "The team social thing you said we have to attend tonight—is that mandatory? I had a long ride today and I'm beat. Can I skip it?"

"No, it's prime time for the coaches because it's their first chance to address the team about the new season. But they also have to introduce the new guys to their real selves, to who they really are, not wearing those candy-assed PR masks they put on when parents are around."

He stifled a yawn. "Sorry, no offense . . . the humidity around here always tends to sap me."

"You've been here before?"

"I've been just about everywhere. An Army brat. My Dad moved us all over the world. Actually, I've lived overseas more than I've lived in the States. The day I graduated from high school—that was in Germany—my mother left him and moved the two of us back home to San Francisco. I never realized she hated military life as much as I did. She stuck with it, and with him, for my sake."

That felt like a little more personal information than I needed to know. "If you lived overseas so much, how did you learn to play football?"

"Every big base has leagues of different kinds. Lots of flag leagues, but some tackle. Baseball and basketball, too. It's easy to play anything in the American compounds where we all lived. Plenty of sports of every kind."

"Where did you live the longest?"

"Overseas? Okinawa."

I knew about Okinawa. It was the home of karate, something I dabbled with a bit when I was in high school.

"Ever get into martial arts while you were over there?"

"Sure, it was everywhere. In fact, that's how I wound up in Washington. One of my favorite instructors emigrated to the U.S. and settled there, so I checked where he was and found it had the junior college. I called their football team and asked to walk on, and things worked out."

"Was your teacher a philosopher, too?"

"Not formally, but if you get heavy into martial arts of any kind, you'll be exposed to a lot of eastern philosophy and meditation techniques. I enjoy all of that."

"I didn't," I said. "My teacher was an asshole masquerading as an oriental disciplinarian. A colossal jerk."

Prosser winced. "Those give all martial arts a bad name, but what can you do? Put every asshole away somewhere so they have only each other to make miserable?"

"You sound like you know your assholes."

He winced again. "My Dad was world-class."

Here, again, it was more than I needed to know, so I shifted to a lighter mood. "You know, most guys come here out of high school trying to figure out which end is up. A helluva lot of them leave that way, too. But you sound like you're on the exact track you want to be on."

He smiled easily, and I felt myself genuinely liking him. There was just something *solid* about him, like he was perfectly grounded and nothing could ever fluster him.

"So far, so good. . . ." he agreed.

I checked my watch. "Okay, it looks like you're the last guy to check in today. Five no-shows; about average."

He rose to indicate he was taking my hint.

"It's almost 5:00 now," I went on. "Dinner is served at 6:00, the social starts at 7:30. If you get settled in your room right away, you might have time to catch a nap."

He motioned toward his motorcycle. "I have to put away my stuff. Can't leave it sitting out. Too tempting a target."

He extended his right hand while lifting his left to the corner of his shades. He pushed them up to his forehead, and I found myself staring at the palest blue eyes I'd ever seen in my life, just the barest hint of color in them, like certain Blue Tick coon hounds. It took my breath away.

"It's been a real pleasure meeting you, Sage," he said, shaking my hand. "I feel I have a friend here already."

"You do, Pete . . . you absolutely do."

With that he dropped his glasses back down onto his nose, picked up his dorm key and playbook, and left. He was nothing like I imagined, but I sure liked what I saw.

TEAM SOCIAL

The team social was a get-acquainted meeting for old members of the team with new members, and also a means for the coaches to start establishing the "team" concept of doing what you're told when you're told with no questions asked. That was the basic bottom line of all teams—to put group welfare ahead of any notion of self-interest—and for us this was where it all got started.

Prosser arrived wearing his motorcycle boots, jeans, a white T-shirt under his open denim shirt, and his dark shades. He wasn't in the room five minutes before head defensive coach Wade Hackler noticed him and came waddling over as rapidly as his porcine girth would allow.

How a gross schlubb like Hackler ever managed to become a reasonably well-regarded football coach was simply
beyond those who knew him. There had to be good reasons,
but whatever they were, they stayed behind the doors of
the coaches' offices. The reason his players gave was caus-
tically blunt: "He must be sucking someone's dick."

Hackler put himself right in front of Pete's face, as close
as his bulging midriff would allow, and spoke to him with
as much strained civility as I'd ever heard him attempt.

"Pete, I'm Coach Hackler. Coach Anderson told me you
wore those shades indoors when you checked in this afternoon. Maybe that's 'cool' out west where you come from, I
don't know, but it's damn sure not cool here, so from now
on take them off when you're indoors. Understand?"

Prosser didn't seem fazed. "I always wear shades, Coach,
indoors or out. My eyes are sensitive to light."

Hackler was not used to having a direct order dismissed
like that, even for good reason.

"Then how the hell," he snapped, "do you play football?
You can't wear shades under a damn helmet, can you?"

"No, of course not. I wear dark contacts and I use a lot
of bootblack on my cheeks."

The whole of Hackler's gelatinous body quivered at the
insult of being talked back to like that. Suddenly, he lifted
his right hand toward Prosser's face, moving faster than
he should have. What happened next is open to debate.

Hackler swore he was only trying to pull the shades
off Prosser's face to see if his eyes really were sensitive to
light. Prosser said he thought Hackler intended to swat
him upside the head in an attempt to knock them off. In
either case, what resulted is beyond dispute.

Prosser's left forearm shot up, fingers tight together,
like a blade, and firmly deflected Hackler's reach. From
that epicenter, an eddy of silence swept across the large
room in a matter of seconds. No player was allowed to
touch a coach for any reason. Coaches could slap the
hell out of any player, punch them, kick them, absolutely

anything they felt like doing, and if the player retaliated
in any way, even in personal defense, it was grounds for
dismissal from the team and revocation of scholarship.

Prosser hadn't been on our team for three hours, and
technically he was already off it.

The two of them stood toe-to-toe, as close as Hackler's
spilling gut would allow, for three or four seconds that
seemed like a minute, then Prosser said something very
softly so that no one but Hackler could hear it.

With that, he turned away and left the social.

Hackler's faced flushed red with rage, but he didn't respond with his usual cursing. Fists clenched, trembling,
he grimaced and walked in the opposite direction from
Prosser, over to where the other coaches were gathered.

It took several seconds for the room's buzz of chatter to
begin returning to its normal level. However, things would
never return to normal for Prosser, not on this team, not
as long as Hackler was a member of our coaching staff.

Prosser had fouled this nest about as badly as it could
be done. He'd made a very dangerous, very capable enemy
that he didn't need. Now his time at Cajun State wouldn't
be counted in seasons, it would be counted in practices.

Bets were being laid on how many he'd last when Tom
Everett sidled over to me to ask the obvious question.

"Could you hear what Prosser said to him?"

"No," I admitted. "I think only Hackler could hear it."

"Whatever it was, I bet he wishes he had it back now."

I shook my head. "Not the guy I met this afternoon."

A THREAT MADE GOOD

Before I could begin telling Randall what I knew about
Prosser, I noticed Hackler breaking away from the coaches

clustered inside the track near the standing dummies.

Coaches never stopped playing the game of trying to prove one man's worth at the expense of another—especially among themselves. Ridicule was the method most frequently used, and Hackler had apparently had enough of their needling about what just happened to his defense. He stormed toward Prosser with a flushed scowl and both fists clenched into white-knuckled hammers.

"Uh-oh," I muttered. "Trouble on the way."

"Listen, you little cocksucker!" Hackler shouted as he neared Prosser. "Don't you *ever* pussy-out on me again! When I tell you to run, goddammit, *you run!* Don't stand there like a fucking *statue!* Statues belong in parks, and we play *football* out here! You understand me, boy?"

Without breaking his stride, Hackler kicked the cup of green gold from Prosser's outstretched hands. Prosser glared up at him, his anger obvious but not making any move to openly retaliate. Hackler then reached down with his left hand and grabbed a fistful of sweat-soaked blond hair, snapping Prosser's head up and back with a vicious jerk as he thrust his ugly red face down to almost level with Prosser's smoldering, lens-covered eyes.

Prosser said something to him, again softly so no one nearby could hear. Infuriated, Hackler's face went from red to white, and he cocked his right fist back to swing a roundhouse. Prosser saw it coming and ducked to his right, which pulled his wet hair from Hackler's grasp as he fell onto his side. As he went over, his left leg lifted so that his foot caught Hackler behind his right knee.

Prosser later insisted it was an accident, but everyone could see it wasn't. Whatever it was, it made Hackler's knee buckle, which threw him off balance as his bloated body followed the violent arc of his arm. As he keeled over, he flailed out for support with his right arm. His wrist smashed into the raised concrete edge of the track, and we all heard the familiar sound of bone breaking.

***

Coaches hurried to aid their stricken comrade, who was rolling on the ground and squealing like the stuck hog he resembled. Even Trainer Hanson, who normally took immense pride in the stoic way he reacted to other people's injuries, hustled over at twice his usual leisurely pace.

Everyone's attention was focused on watching the assistant coaches pull and push Hackler to his feet so Trainer Hanson could drive him to the infirmary. As that played out, I noticed Prosser move over to blend into the crowd of nearby gawking players. A figure stealthily moved behind him to slip a fresh cup of green gold into his hand.

As Prosser drained it, I checked to see who dared such a gamble. It was his erstwhile rival, Quink Thompson.

With Hackler on his way to the infirmary, Randall said to me, "Serves the bastard right."

"Lighten up!" I groused at him. For as much as I didn't like Hackler, injuries always rattled me. Since my own, three years earlier, I couldn't get a bad paper cut without getting upset to my core. "As bad as he is, he's just doing his job. Somebody has to get rid of Prosser, and the sooner they do that, the better off everyone will be."

"What a callous, jerky thing to say! How can you *be* so callous? I don't understand any of it."

"You can say that again. For someone who's supposed to be a hot-shot sports reporter, you don't know a helluva lot about football, do you? Where did you go to school?"

He mumbled something indistinctly.

"Where?"

"Vanderbilt."

I smirked down at him. "They get rid of their unwanted players, too. You couldn't have gone to many practices."

He stiffened a bit. "Okay, I admit it. I'm short and dumpy and I have bad eyes, so I was never an athlete. And, yes, I didn't give two hoots about football until I got this job."

That floored me. "Why would you take a job reporting on something you don't even understand?"

"I understand *journalism!* That's the same wherever you go. My focus in school was on political coverage, but I learned the mechanics of sports coverage, too. Just show me the inside workings of this game and I'll do the rest."

"This isn't city hall."

"Dirty laundry is dirty laundry, wherever you find it."

Just then Stanton blew the airhorn to signal the water break's end. BRRRRAAAAAKKKKKK!!!

"Excuse me now, Randall. Gotta go earn my keep."

When anyone got singled out for abuse the way Prosser was, player reaction was usually no more than, "Thank God it wasn't me." Verbal and physical abuse from the coaches was an inevitable—and they would insist it was an integral—part of the game, so no one thought much about it. This instance, though, was an exception. Prosser was scourged for doing well, not for screwing up, and it was hard to justify such a blatant miscarriage of justice.

Even though Hackler reaped what he sowed, the water break episode caused an immediate deflation throughout the team. Practice became peppered with fumbles, dropped passes, missed assignments, and poor execution.

Anderson could see that as well as I could. He called me over to his tower twenty minutes before the scheduled end.

"Everyone's gone flat," he called down to me. "They look like a bunch of dead-legged dogs. Let's go ahead and give them a reward for the good early work."

"Yes, sir!"

I signaled Stanton to blow three quick blasts on the airhorn, which meant practice was over.

Team members jogged from various work areas to the middle of the field to surround the tower's south side. Anderson had climbed down to the ground, and now he looked out over a hundred-and-few sweaty, flushed faces.

"Take a knee, men," he said, then waited for everyone to get down and settled.

"Men, we had a good workout for the first half of this morning," he resumed, "but we got a little sloppy after the break. I can see we've lost some zip in our legs, so we're going in early this morning to try to get some of it back."

A halfhearted cheer went up. Everyone knew the real reason behind cutting this one short was Hackler's abortive attack on Prosser and the injury that resulted.

"So let's head in and take care of any injuries. Get some rest so we can come out this afternoon and have a solid final practice to end two-a-days. What do you say, men?"

The standard cheer went up followed by:

"*Craw*-dads! *Craw*-dads! *Craw*-dads!"

"Hit the showers!" Anderson shouted.

One last cheer and the players took off at a fast jog, slowing to a walk only after clearing the practice field's end zone back-line. Football tradition allowed no walking on the field itself, as if walking on it at ordinary times would create an uncontrollable urge to walk during a game.

Stanton and I moved to different parts of the field to begin gathering stray equipment into piles beside the track that we'd retrieve later in the pickup when Trainer Hanson returned it from the infirmary.

As I worked, Randall approached me. "Listen, Larry, I want to apologize for snapping at you a while ago."

"That's okay, Randall, we all blow up on occasion."

"I have to go now to file a story about Hackler having an 'accident' at practice. I don't think anyone will get mad at me for that. But I would like to talk with you again at this afternoon's practice. I mean, you're dead-on right about me. I have a *lot* to learn about covering football."

Before I could respond, I saw Paul Marshall, the head offensive coach, walking our way. I had a good idea of what he wanted, and it wasn't good.

"Get lost!" I muttered. "Here comes trouble."

Randall turned to where I glanced, he saw Marshall, and then said, "Right, gotcha . . . see you later."

He passed Coach Marshall with a cheery greeting, as if nothing at all were amiss, while I resumed dragging a heavy tackling dummy over to the side of the track.

COACH MARSHALL

Coach Marshall was Hackler's opposite number in most every way imaginable. He was a lean, craggy-faced man with alert, darting eyes and a voice like a belt-sander. He had fashioned that raspy marvel through two decades of screaming at people who couldn't possibly play football with the skill he displayed as an All-SEC end at Ole Miss. Unlike Wade Hackler, his toughness was bred-in-the-bone authentic, and he was widely admired and respected for it.

Like the genuine abiding asshole every coaching staff needed, every staff also needed at least one genuinely good guy who was a topnotch coach and an ex-player of unquestioned credentials that everyone could respect.

That person was the interface for players with legitimate problems or gripes that needed to be addressed by someone on the staff. Nobody took problems directly to a head coach, and a head coach never stooped to doing the dirty work involved in getting rid of players who were no longer useful. Those jobs belonged to the good guy and the asshole, and on our team it happened to be the chief offensive and chief defensive assistants.

"How's it going, Larry?" Coach Marshall asked.

I looked up from the sand-filled dummy. "Fine, coach. Hard to believe it's the last of two-a-days."

"Here, let me help you with that."

He grabbed one of the two handles from me, which made sliding it go twice as fast. In just a few seconds we moved it all the way to the edge of the track.

"It's a heavy sombitch, ain't it?" he said with a grunt.

"Lots heavier than the ones we used to hit. Ours were so light, they could dodge you if you weren't careful."

"Yes, sir, I sure do believe that."

He winked at my complicity with his joke. "Are you all finished now? That was the last one?"

"Yes, sir, that was it."

"Good. Let's head on in, then."

We started walking toward the dressing room, and I knew what was coming. My only concern was the depth of the hot water I was now in with the coaching staff.

"What'd that new boy from the paper want?" he asked, as offhandedly as he could manage. "You and him seemed to be talking an awful lot today."

"He was asking about football fundamentals, sir, very basic stuff. He never played or followed the game before now, so he doesn't know enough to write about it intelligently. I also assume that after the story he wrote about us being a schedule breather, he doesn't want to get into any more trouble. He's trying to feel his way along."

His relief upon hearing that lie was almost palpable.

"Hah!" he rasped. "It figures. Most of those damn reporters are ignorant like that. But listen, Larry, in the future, don't be so friendly with him. You know we like to let Coach Anderson do all our talking and explaining for us. Next time he comes around asking you any questions, send him over to the tower. Okay?"

"Yes, sir, I understand."

My own level of relief easily matched his. Normally, it would be Hackler's job to set me straight about Randall, and I shuddered to think how he might have handled it. I now owed Prosser a favor for keeping him off my back.

Coach Marshall winked again. "I figured you would."

We walked in silence until it was time for us to part, then he stopped and looked at me. "I sure am sorry you're not able to play any more, Larry. With an attitude like yours, I know you'd have been a really good one for us."

I felt myself flush. "Thanks, coach, I appreciate that."

He gave me a pat on the shoulder and turned away.

I couldn't help feeling great in the glow of praise he didn't have to offer. It showed yet again that all the emotional hot buttons that brought me into football and kept me going in it were still in place, as functional as ever.

Precious moments like that made it all worthwhile.

The "back" dressing room was two separate rooms sharing a common shower and toilet area. The large room was for the thirty-plus freshmen who were still with us, and another room half its size was for fifteen redshirts still hanging on. I always checked there right after each practice session because those two groups got shorted first, especially when the schedule was disrupted.

"Did you all get oranges?" I shouted from a central spot near the showers. No complaint from anyone. "Ice?" Still no reply. Everything seemed in order.

I moved into the redshirt room, where Tom Everett spoke quietly to me. "What do you think, Sage? Will this morning's confrontation impact this afternoon?"

Though mired as a player at redshirt quarterback, Tom was an authentic natural leader. Blessed—or cursed—with a choirboy's innocent face, he inspired trust and confidence with little effort. As the redshirts' man-in-charge, he did his best to sustain their physical and emotional welfare, which was especially precarious now.

"I don't think so. They need to get work done, but I can't see them exhausting everyone. Their top priority will be getting good film of the varsity in tomorrow's scrimmage."

He nodded, then raised his voice to the room. "Listen up, everyone!" The postpractice hubbub quickly faded.

"Sage and I talked it over, and we think it will be an easy one for us this afternoon. There might be some hitting somewhere along the line, but mostly they'll want to save the varsity's gas for tomorrow. That means we can all relax and look forward to surviving two-a-days!"

A cheer went up and several eyes were cast toward Prosser's locker space. He was already in the shower, but everyone knew how unlikely it was that he'd survive this far. But now, with the break at the break. . . .

"What about Hackler's 'accident'?" Tom asked as the room's drone of conversation resumed.

"I don't want to jinx Prosser, but I don't think they'll let him get away with it. That thing at the social, he got lucky there. It was Hackler's word against his, and they didn't know the kind of guy he is. Today, though, that was too much. It looked enough like he hooked Hackler's knee and took him down. They have to get rid of him."

Tom's dark eyebrows lifted with surprise, or doubt, or maybe some of both. "Quit drills?"

"You said it, not me. But don't be surprised."

Quit drills were a special kind of hell reserved for when a player's dogged determination, or fear of returning home to face a disappointed family and community, wouldn't let him quit even after the coaches made it abundantly clear that his services were no longer needed. Quit drills were how they made the message *crystal* clear.

They were designed to injure players—to injure them seriously. If a player survived his first session of quit drills and still wouldn't take the hint, everyone assumed they were terminally stupid and deserved whatever happened to them in the next session. Quit drills were a grisly, and sometimes ghastly, aspect of scholarship retrieval, but in certain cases they were simply necessary.

I'd seen it twice in my time at Cajun State, and I didn't want to go through it again. Unfortunately, Prosser was now on a fast track to it . . . unless he quit while he could.

Before going into the varsity dressing room, I stopped at the equipment shed for a chat with Cap'n, the team's senior equipment manager and my immediate superior.

Cap'n was an intense, orderly little man who had been at his job for fifteen years, during which he established a direct pipeline to the secretaries in the football offices. The secretaries told him in advance of most everything that came down from the coaches. I'd picked up my nickname, the old Sage, because of inside scoop he often gave me about the inner workings of the coaches' offices.

"You hear what Prosser did today?" I asked.

Cap'n replied without looking up from tightening the cage on somebody's helmet. "Yeah, Soupbone saw it. I don't know what they gonna do about that boy. They want him gone before reporters start hangin' around every day."

"Any word on quit drills for him?"

"Not yet, but I expect it any time now."

I went in the varsity dressing room and looked around. By then most players were undressed, with several already showered. I noticed Don Slade, the second team fullback, having trouble cutting the heavy bandage off his knee.

"Let me get that for you," I said, reaching down for the tape cutter. "I have a better angle than you do."

Don winced as the blade passed over the still-pink scars on opposite sides of his right kneecap.

"Sorry," I said, "it can't be helped."

"I know, I know . . . just get it off."

Twelve months had passed since his knee was injured, but swelling was still evident. Of course, yesterday's bruise added to it, though blown knees never really looked the same. Mine was still puffy after thirty-six months.

With the bandage off, Don leaned back in his cubicle and closed his eyes. Relief swept over his broad, deeply tanned face, which suited the image of the farm boy he was more than the doctor he was studying to be.

"Thanks, Sage. You still clear for Sunday?"

Don and his wife, Annie, had invited several of us to lunch Sunday to mark the end of two-a-days. "Miss a meal of Annie's? They don't make stupid on that scale."

He laughed. "Annie's psyched out of her mind for it. She's gonna lay out a hell of a spread. Wait and see."

"Tell her we'll redshirt her if she doesn't."

I headed across the room to Quink's corner locker. He sat in front of it picking tape flecks off a bare ankle.

I reached down to rumple his dark, sweat-soaked hair. "I saw you slip Prosser that green gold. A damn fine gesture. I thought you were worried about him rolling you."

"I don't want to get rolled by him or anyone," Quink replied, "but I can't stand the crap-ass way the coaches treat him. Why can't they just give the guy a break? Get off his case and let him do what he knows how to do?"

"You know why," I reminded him. We all did.

DOWN TIME

After practice a good many players spent time in the campus University Center, called "the U.C.", a three-story complex of offices on the top floor, a cafeteria, bookstore and swimming pool on the second floor, and a bowling alley and pseudo German beerhall on the ground floor.

Players gravitated to the spacious cafeteria so they could perform one essential function and exhibit a basic tendency. They replaced lost body fluids with various soft drinks and milk shakes, while eyeballing any attractive females who happened to wander anywhere near them.

During two-a-days, heat and humidity sapped five to fifteen pounds from each player per practice session, so the need to replace lost fluid was almost constant. Luckily, few females were on campus during the summer break, so temptations were scarce and easy to resist.

Now that two-a-days were ending, the pattern would reverse. Practice would become tolerable and curfews would be extended at precisely the right moment. The summer drought would end with the following day's class registration for the fall semester, so it seemed part of a grand design to have girls return to campus exactly when the players could begin to take advantage of them.

"Jesus!" exclaimed the Bull. "Would you look at the wheels on that one? Nine-fives at least."

"No way!" Quink shot back, being argumentative more than deliberative. "Nine-seven, tops."

I sat with Quink, the Bull, and several other players at the main counter as they graded female calves, a criteria they knew well and judged themselves by. Under their system, women were rated by the projected speed at which their sons might run a 100-yard dash. It was all based on a seat of physical power that each player understood and could relate to. Muscular, well-developed calves—male *or* female—commanded immediate, sincere respect.

Just then Tom Everett strolled into the room.

"Aw, geeze," Wheeler said softly, in a mixture of annoyance and caution. "Who's he gonna stick it to this time?"

No one on the team ever wanted to say anything that might annoy Tom and draw more than his passing attention. Despite his choirboy looks and demeanor, Tom was the brain and the nerves behind a number of memorable hoaxes, cons, and practical jokes on our campus.

He was a virtuoso schemer with a seemingly unlimited capacity for mischief. His notes to Wheeler were far beneath the apex of his skills, but that was only further testimony to his craftsmanship. He could see possibilities everywhere, and he never hesitated to exploit them.

"Howdy," he said, sliding into a seat on the other side of the counter, facing us with his back to the main room.

"Wheeler was wondering who's next on your hit list?" Quink said, gigging his roommate for our amusement.

"I was not!" Wheeler snapped. "I don't care."

Tom shrugged, unperturbed. "Rabbit again. We have a big one worked up for him this time. Goes down Sunday afternoon around 5:00. Be in the dorm to check it out."

We laugh/moaned anticipating impending havoc, but we also made mental notes to adjust our plans accordingly.

"Dat purr baastid," said Johnny Jenkins, an end from a part of New Orleans called the Ninth Ward. People there had an accent that was amusing to me, more like a Bronx dock worker than someone from the Deep South.

Rabbit was Prosser's mirror image. His football talents were mediocre, yet he somehow managed to stay on the varsity at third team wingback. He had a bad habit of dropping passes when he heard defender footsteps coming his way, which earned him the nickname "rabbit ears."

Rabbit was basically harmless and totally unhindered by any accurate perception of the reality he lived in. He thought of himself as a good football player, and he seemed to believe that everyone on our team wished him well.

In short, he was an ideal—perhaps deserving—victim on whom other players felt free to take out frustrations. And now, only three days ago, the coaches added to that frustration by announcing the incredible decision to put Rabbit at safetyman on our kickoff team. It wasn't a vital job, but we had many better players who deserved it.

Tom Everett's pranks often challenged a fundamental aspect of my role on the team. One of my strongest mandates was to never interfere with the natural flow of events, to let them unfold as fate decreed. If I did interfere, I would forfeit my impartiality, and if I lost that, nobody would trust me any more. I'd no longer be a friend and confidant any player could be honest with, I'd be just another factotum in the hierarchy of power they had to deal with. Not a friend, not an enemy, just someone useful and necessary, like shoulder pads, shoes, or a helmet.

It was important to me, personally, to remain "one of the guys," which meant I'd go along, willingly and uncritically, with whatever hijinks any of them got up to. So even though I seldom approved of what was done to Rabbit, I justified my acquiescence by telling myself he asked for it by staying on in a world where he simply did not belong.

***

From the U.C., we went to lunch at the sewer's athletic training table. At lunch, players gobbled everything in sight because few ate much for breakfast. Lunch and dinner were the major meals on any team during two-a-days.

After lunch, almost every player went to their dormitory room for an hour or so of sleep that was as restless and uneasy as at night. In this case, I was nervous too because when practice shifted from group work to unit work, my responsibility increased significantly. I played an important role in certain aspects of unit work, and to do it well I had to prepare myself mentally, like everyone else.

Well, not quite like everyone else. I could be virtually certain I'd still be walking at the end of the day.

AFTERNOON PRACTICE

As it turned out, by the time that afternoon's practice neared its conclusion, only a freshman guard named Dirk Hatfield was seriously injured. He broke his right collarbone during the first tackling drill of the day, so he was long since removed to the infirmary.

Hackler heroically returned to the battlefield, stomping about as always, shouting and brandishing his elbow-length cast like a shiny new toy. He gave no indication of how he intended to retaliate for it, making it seem possible that Coach Anderson's, or Coach Marshall's, sense of fair play might spare Prosser an immediate reprisal.

Except for Hackler's appearance and Hatfield's injury, this practice was uneventful. The varsity went through the tedious routine of polishing its offensive and defensive sets, so the redshirts could easily maintain a low profile.

Tom's prediction of a relatively easy workout for the redshirts came to pass. The toughest drill of the day was saved for last, and it didn't include redshirts or freshmen. It was a twenty-minute goal line defense drill, which would be an abbreviated version of tomorrow's two-hour scrimmage. Since this drill often determined who ended up with the most playing time in goal line situations, contact along the line of scrimmage tended to be fierce.

I noticed Randall Webber walking my way as the drill was setting up. "I'm late," he said, stating the obvious. "Sorry about that. Did I miss anything good?"

"You missed me getting my butt gently chewed out by Coach Marshall for spending so much time with you."

He winced. "Dammit!"

"You're the Prosser of sportswriters around here. He said to tell you to spend more time at the tower, sucking up to Anderson. That's good advice, too; you should take it."

"Will you talk to me later, away from here?"

I considered the implications of what he was asking. The coaches would discipline me—maybe even fire me—if they found out I was fraternizing with someone they told me to stay away from. On the other hand, they'd never find out unless Randall shafted me, and I couldn't imagine him doing something like that.

"All right, I'll fill you in, but it'll be strictly off the record unless I say otherwise. If you tell anyone what I say, or if I see a word of it in print, you'll he sorry. Understood?"

His round face split in a big grin. "Understood," he said, turning toward the tower. "Thanks!"

I supervised ball placement on goal line drills because quickness and accuracy were essential. The ball was centered on the ten yard line, and the offense had four plays to take it in for a score. The first team offense went against the second team defense, then the first team defense faced the second team offense. The rivalry between those top four units—and their respective coaches—was never more spirited or intense than during this drill.

"First and goal, at the ten!" I shouted, then I blew my whistle to signal that the action was under way.

I took my position straddling the line of scrimmage ten yards outside Loop Watson, the second team left defensive end. From there I could control the ball and call offside if necessary, but the coaches invariably beat me to it.

"So-and-so, you turd!" they'd shout at whoever jumped a snap. "Get your head out of your ass and listen to the damn count!" Many players heard that shout so often, their name followed by "you turd!", some worried that it would follow them into the real world as a nickname.

The first team offense hustled into position over the ball, and the second team defense dug in. The first play was a dive by the Bull over right guard, and he got three tough yards going directly through a linebacker.

"Way to hit in there, Bull!" came a shout from Quink, somewhere along the sideline.

Then, smirking across the line at a furious Hackler, Coach Marshall yelled, "Way to run hard, Ken!"

Ken the Bull was our best short-yardage runner, and we all liked to watch him work. Coach Marshall, though, was always especially appreciative of his toughness and drive. Birds of a feather, it seemed, did indeed flock together.

"Second and seven!" I shouted.

Ronnie Davis, our starting quarterback, rolled left on a keeper behind a block by the Bull, picking up five more.

"All right, Ronnie! Way to work!"

And from the other side, "Dig in, defense!"

"Third and two!"

The Bull slammed into the line and the defense pinched in on him, but it was only a fake. Davis pulled it back and pitched it wide to John Lawrence, the tailback, who came steaming around end toward me. It was all I could do to get out of the way as Watson, who didn't take the fake, swept upfield to cut Lawrence down for no gain.

A groan went up from the offense while the defense cheered, and Hackler grinned across the line at Marshall.

"Fourth and two!" I called out. It would be the offense's last chance to score in this series.

Anticipating a fullback dive, the inside linebackers disguised a stack against it. They were waiting when the Bull hit the line, pinching him high and low in a vicious cross-tackle. There was no sound of ligaments or bones snapping, but everyone heard him scream.

Dead silence fell over the field as I rushed in to help untangle the pile. I found the Bull on the bottom, writhing in pain, holding his left ankle with both hands.

When practicing goal line defense, the action stopped for injury because it was too time consuming to reassemble at the other end of the field. In all other instances, the ball was simply moved away from an injured player, a gesture that illustrated how quickly the unfit were isolated.

No one looked at him, and he was automatically replaced by his substitute with hardly a beat missed in the continuity of practice. His existence was thoroughly ignored, and his value as a player was immediately discontinued.

In football, when your function ceased, *you* ceased.

Trainer Hanson removed Bull's shoe and sock to check his injury. He didn't need long to reach a conclusion. "Not broken, but a bad sprain. Get him to the infirmary."

Stanton handed Hanson an ice pack kept in a cooler on the sideline for just such occasions. Hanson taped it to the ankle as Stanton went to fetch the truck, while two redshirt linemen stood by to carry the Bull to it when it came as close as it could to where the injury occurred.

Seeing the truck rolling toward an injury put a knot in every player's stomach, as they wondered if or when their turn might come to take that very long short ride in it.

"All right, men!" Anderson boomed through the megaphone atop his tower. "Get back to work."

The squads huddled uneasily, watching the Bull being carried to the truck while Marshall glared across the line at Hackler, who wouldn't look back. Marshall was pissed off because he knew those linebackers wouldn't call that stack on their own. We never used it against ourselves in goal line drills because it elevated the risk of injury.

Hackler called for it to make sure his defense didn't get scored on. He protected his recently stung ego at the expense of our team's best runner, and I expected Marshall would find a way to pay Hackler back for it—in spades.

It took only one series of downs before the Bull's injury seemed forgotten. Don Slade moved up to first team full-back, while Roger Johnson took over the second team spot. The injury was a golden opportunity for both substitutes, who ran hard and acquitted themselves well.

The Bull would be sorely missed, but on any football team no one was irreplaceable.

"Men," Coach Anderson said at the end of practice, "we had a good workout this afternoon. We had some injuries, one of them key, and that's unfortunate. But it only means the rest of us have to tighten our belts, suck up our guts, and get after the other team that much harder.

"Now, we have an important scrimmage tomorrow that will be the last chance for some of you to show you can contribute this season. You'll all get a chance to play, so you all should do everything you can to be at your best.

"Be sure to get a good night's sleep, and remember: there'll be fans out there, and reporters, and the Big Eye will be watching every move you make. Give a hundred and ten percent effort on each play and you'll have no problems; loaf and we'll all know about it. The ones who stand up to that pressure are the ones we want to put on the field against Texas next Saturday night.

"Lastly, tomorrow morning is class registration, so I want all of you in front of the registrar's office at 9:00 a.m. We've arranged for you to have the first shot at every course in the catalogue, so I don't want any excuses for having afternoon classes. If it looks essential that any of you cut into practice time with a lab or something, see Dr.

Westrum and let him try to make other arrangements. We've been assured full faculty cooperation in scheduling around practice, so I don't expect any problems.

"Questions?"

That was a cue for silence.

"All right, then, hit the showers!"

A cheer went up as the players broke for the dressing rooms, and Stanton and I stayed behind to gather up equipment for when the truck returned from the infirmary.

I had just started working when I noticed Richard Biggs running through an after-practice lap around the track. Two days ago he pulled a hamstring slightly, and now he was testing it out. Biggs was a second team cornerback with the inevitable nickname, "Big Dick."

He was an innocuous looking guy who wore granny glasses most of the time and contact lenses whenever he played. But despite his looks, he was what we all termed a "heavy hitter." He was as tough a tackler as we had, and only frequent injuries kept him off the first team.

I drug the last tackling dummy into place as he puffed up to me looking pleased with his spin around the track.

"How's it feel when you run on it?" I asked.

"Not bad," he said between breaths. "Be ready Monday."

We walked toward the stadium as he caught his breath, then he said, "Terrible luck losing the Bull like that."

"Yeah, he's our biggest gun."

"Can Slade and Johnson take up the slack?"

I shrugged. "They have to now."

"You think Duggan will move up off the redshirts?"

"No need for that. The Bull will be back soon enough."

"In a way, you know, I'm glad for Don. Not to take anything away from the Bull, but anyone who works as hard as Don deserves a chance to play. Of all the runners out here, Prosser included, I hate going against Don."

Coming from such a hard-nosed defender, that was high praise indeed. "Why?"

"He's so determined. He never stops driving for those few extra inches. The Bull can juke you, and Prosser can make you look like a fool, but Don tries to run you over."

It was true. The Bull had the most natural ability, no question about that, but Don had the fiercest heart. Maybe this would be the chance he needed. Even a decent game against Texas would be remembered and valued.

I went to the back dressing room to check things out. Everyone had oranges and ice, and many had already showered. I headed for Tom's cubicle. He glanced across the room at Prosser, sitting at his locker, half dressed.

"When Anderson said they'd play everyone tomorrow, you think he meant you-know-who?"

Tom was probably Prosser's biggest booster. He hadn't had time to get know him any better than the rest of us because of the torrid pace of life during two-a-days. However, he worked with him every day on the field, and had come to appreciate his spectacular football ability. Also, like many others on the team, he greatly—and vicariously—admired Prosser's consistent defiance of Hackler's excesses.

"What did you expect him to say? *Everyone will play tomorrow . . . no, wait, scratch that . . . everyone except Prosser. My fault, men . . . slip of the tongue.*"

Tom cracked up at my impression.

THE INFIRMARY

I went into the freshman room to clean out Hatfield's cubicle. Hatfield was the guard who broke his collarbone in the early part of practice. Whenever players were injured enough to go to the infirmary, I was responsible for getting their clothes and personal belongings to them, so I was usually the first team-related person to visit them.

They were invariably scared and upset over their injury, and worried sick about how their team status would be affected, so I had to do my best to be calm and reassuring with them. That nearly always required deception.

Fortunately, today's visits would be minor problems. Hatfield was a cocky kid who was a good player and knew it. He'd be down but not devastated. As for the Bull, anything short of a compound fracture wouldn't faze him. If anyone knew where they stood on our team, he did.

I was picking up the Bull's gear in the varsity dressing room when Helmut Moedle approached me. "Helmet" was our German-born, soccer-style placekicker, the only certified star on our team. Although we managed few drives sustained enough to exhibit it, his kicking leg was known as the best in the Deep South, if not the whole country.

"Sagely," he said, in his distinctive accent, "are you and your lovely Carla with plans tomorrow evening?"

He was referring to Carla Andrews, my de facto fiancee. She was starting her second year as a mathematics instructor at Cajun State, only a year older than me but already solidly tracked on her career path. We had been together for a year and a half, and were steadily working our way toward marriage. I loved her deeply.

"No, we don't have plans to go out," I replied.

"Good! You must excuse this brief notice, but there is a party arranged only today. It is a small affair for a Belgian diplomat at the home of a friend. Will you and Carla wish to join with me as my companions for the evening?"

Helmet was the son of a wealthy German diplomat, and his courtly manners and Teutonic good looks made him a favorite on the local social circuit. As might be expected, he was the object of much female admiration, but often they were underage or married. In potentially awkward situations, he liked to have "chaperones" tag along.

I shook my head. "Carla's math department is meeting through most of the weekend to get ready for the start of classes on Monday. I won't even mention your invitation to her so she won't feel bad about missing out on it."

Helmet smiled with his usual good humor. "This is as I expected; arrangements of the last moment always create difficulties. But tell me, Sagely, do you care to come alone? Surely Carla does not wish you to sacrifice for her."

"Sorry, not tomorrow. I want to hang around campus."

Tomorrow night would be my last "First Saturday" as a student, and while I hadn't planned to do anything specific, I didn't want to miss out on its special energy. Also, Carla was one of those magic people who fit well into any social situation, but I wasn't always comfortable with the people who circulated at Helmet's level of sophistication. I hoped to get better at that after I became a stockbroker.

"Some other time, perhaps," Helmet said.

"Absolutely," I assured him, and I meant it.

Hatfield was even less of a problem than I expected. He grew up within a mile of the stadium, so his parents were already in his room when I arrived. He was still in considerable pain, so I just delivered his clothes and offered encouragement to him and his parents.

The Bull, on the other hand, was alone in bed when I got to his room, his ankle propped up on two pillows and packed with ice. "How's it going, champ?" I asked him.

"Sage! Great to see you, man! I have a problem that I'm gonna need your help solving."

I could guess what it was.

"They're keeping me here overnight so they can keep it iced and elevated."

"But you need some beer. . . ."

I knew he didn't like being so transparent, but it was an open secret on the team that the Bull, and a few others, were already developing serious drinking problems.

"You don't need me for that. I saw four candy stripers on my way in. You can take your pick."

"Really?" he said, genuinely amazed.

He was darkly handsome and went through women
like a chain saw through balsa, but he never seemed to
appreciate his own attractiveness. Carla said that was
the secret of his widely renowned success with women.
What Helmet had in quality, the Bull had in quantity.

"There's a redhead out there who'll have to be put on a
leash as soon as I leave, so beer is the last thing you'll need
tonight. Besides, you know the rules. If we got caught, I'd
be right in here alongside you with my ass in a sling."

He forced a grin, obviously wanting beer more than he
could dare let on, even to me.

I changed the subject to get his mind off it.

"What's the word on your ankle?"

"Bad sprain," he said without emotion. "Looks right
now like I'll miss two or three games . . . three at most."

"Then you're a lucky Bull. The word from Texas is that
Stoner wanted to pick his teeth with your bones after he
goyaed Wheeler and the rest of the line."

We both laughed at that. Several years ago, well before
our time here, a player came across a print of Francisco
Goya's famous painting of *Saturn Devouring One of His
Children*. That grisly picture of the monster holding the
half-eaten human quickly gained fame as the winner's
reward in the team's "Goya of the Week" contest.

The player voted to be head-up against the opposing
team's toughest individual had to keep that print above
his locker for the week before the game. In time, the name
"Goya" came to mean the act the painting represented.

In games or at practice, you'd hear, "Goya that sonofabitch!" or "The bastard goyaed me!" It was dying out now
only because Coach Anderson banned the picture when
he took over as our head coach, but old hands like the
Bull and myself could still get a kick out of it.

Suddenly, the Bull's smile faded. "How about some beer,
Sage? If I'm gonna be out two weeks, what can it hurt?"

"Please, Ken, don't put me on that kind of spot."

"Okay, forget I asked. I made it this far; I can go one

more day." He said it smiling, but he didn't look pleased.

I kept a room in the dorm for occasional sack time, but I'd lived with Carla for over a year in her apartment four blocks from the stadium. Actually, I lived "off" her more than "with" her, since she worked and paid all the bills.

Luckily, she was great at protecting my feelings about that, never making me think of myself as "kept." Besides, I had every intention of making an honest woman of her after this semester, when I'd finally graduate. The engagement ring was already picked out and half paid for.

The best part of coming home was the way Carla would always greet me. No matter how her work went, no matter how lousy she might feel, she made it seem like the highlight of her day was when I walked through the door.

"Hello, my handsome darling!" she gushed in her resonant, husky voice, coming over to hug and kiss me.

Carla Biscotti was an imposing young woman, five-nine and built like God's little sister, but she was as warm and open as a puppy. Her voluptuous figure, long black hair, olive skin, and delicate facial features made her a treat I never got remotely tired of looking at or being with.

"How did it go today?" she asked.

"Not so good. We lost the Bull with a sprained ankle. He'll be out for a couple of weeks."

She leaned back in my arms and seemed upset for a moment, then she broke into an unexpected smile. "Well, it's a tough break for Ken, but it means Don gets to play."

"Honey, I like Don as much as you do, and I love Annie, but this is business. The Bull is a damn sight more valuable to the team than Don is, no matter how you cut it."

"But you've been saying it's a good competition between them. Besides, Annie's been dying to see Don play ever since they moved him up from third team to second."

Arguing with Carla about such things was hopeless. When it came to football, her Mediterranean blood easily boiled because she let herself get emotionally involved.

It happened again over dinner when I told her about the series of incidents between Prosser and Hackler. Her usually cheerful expression faded into despair.

"They'll get rid of Prosser soon, won't they?"

"Probably quit drills early next week.

"Why can't those damn coaches correct their mistakes without hurting people? Why are they so . . . *barbaric?*"

"It's a barbaric sport, honey, and Prosser is just more than they can deal with. To them, he's like a Martian."

Carla looked across the table at me with a familiar glint in her eyes. "Why do you stay in football, Larry? It's not you any more. It's not even close to who you really are."

She'd asked that question many times before, and each time I tried to make her understand my addiction.

"Football has been the major part of my life since I was ten years old, Carla. It's the thing I know best and feel most comfortable being a part of. Can't you see? I know how bad it is sometimes, but I love it anyway. I get a satisfaction from being in it that I just can't explain."

Her luminous dark eyes held mine. "What will you do after this season, when you're no longer a part of it?"

"What's for dessert?"

REGISTRATION

Wakeup was at 7:30, so I had no difficulty getting them going. Most took Anderson's words to heart and went to bed early. I read the new Wheeler note, then went in the room to find Quink awake, sitting cross-legged amid the madcap jumble of his bed, while Wheeler slept on.

Quink was one of several smokers on the team who daily proved that there was nothing to the homily that you couldn't smoke and play football at the same time. A butt was in a corner of his mouth and four in the ashtray by his knee. He had obviously been at it for a while.

He was poring over a class schedule catalogue, which was entirely typical of him. He was planning his semester class schedule less than two hours before it was due.

"I need a super-easy crip philosophy course, Sage," he explained. "Any suggestions?"

"Yeah, stay away from a professor named Scott Brown. Prosser says he's death."

"Prosser?" He squinted through a puff of smoke. "What does *he* know about philosophy?"

"That's his major . . . he's very heavy into it."

"His major, eh? That's good news. If Prosser's into it, any course I take is a crip. He can just coast me through."

"Don't count on Prosser. He'll be gone soon."

"I've been hearing that since the social, and he's still here. I'm not betting against him. He's got sticking power."

I shrugged, then turned to Wheeler. "How about it, Jimbo? You think Prosser can stick?"

"Like a two-ton tick," Wheeler said sleepily.

"Hey!" Quink grinned through another drag. "You're a poet and don't know it!"

Wheeler fanned the smoke away and said, "The note?"

I went back to the door to read it because it was long and I wanted to get it right.

"It says 'Look! Up in the sky! It's a bird! It's a plane! It's Stoner! Yes, Stoner, strange visitor from another planet who comes to Cajun State with powers and abilities far beyond those of mortal men. Stoner, who can leap tall buildings at a single bound; change the course of mighty rivers; bend steel in his bare hands; and who, disguised as an All-American linebacker for the University of Texas Longhorns, fights a never-ending battle for fame, big bucks in the pros, and the annihilation of Jimbo Wheeler'."

Wheeler was a high gradepoint English major who could appreciate a clever turn of phrase. He smirked and said, "Speaking of . . . I didn't think Everett could wax poetic."

Quink glanced up from his scheduling. "Wax *what?*

That Superman thing? It isn't even a poem. . . ."

I grinned at Wheeler, then turned to resume my rounds.

Quink's voice came at my back. "Honest opinion, Sage; you figure Prosser will play much today?"

Prosser's mercurial ability still haunted him.

"He won't get in at all."

"I hate it that it has to be like that," Wheeler cut in. "We could really use him if they'd just let him play."

"He's a pain in everyone's ass."

"Pain or not," Quink said, "he looked good again yesterday. Even breaking Hackler's arm can't change that. So how come he won't get in for at least a few plays?"

"Because it's okay if he looks good at practice in front of local reporters who live and work under the coaches' thumbs. It's another matter entirely if he cuts loose in front of a few hundred fans watching a scrimmage."

"And the Big Eye, too," Wheeler said. "Don't forget that."

"You're right," I agreed. "They wouldn't want him on film, either, doing what he's been doing in practice."

"Why not?" Quink asked.

"Evidence."

Everyone was in front of the registrar's office by 8:50, and most were frantically discussing ways to eliminate obstructions from their paths of least resistance.

"Listen, I'm telling you, it's a tough course and he's a tough instructor. I had him last year."

"C's, he only gives C's, never D's or B's."

"*Physics*? Hey! Did you guys hear that? Moron Wisner here thinks he can handle physics!"

During any week of football season, if you added together all practice time—pre, during, and post—and time spent in meetings, and time spent watching film, and then added most of each weekend consumed with games, football cost each player fifty to sixty man-hours.

As a result, challenging academic courses that normal students sought out were avoided by most football players.

There simply wasn't enough time—much less energy—in their busy weeks to deal with hard courses or professors.

I sat on a bench with Tom Everett, waiting for the doors to open. "How does it feel," he asked, "to have only one final semester before you graduate? Is it a relief for you?"

"No, not at all. It scares me. I keep wondering if I'll be able to handle whatever comes next in my life."

"Really? I thought you'd be stoked blind. The night Danny graduated, he blubbered like a baby."

"After what he did, who could blame him?"

Danny was Tom's older brother, a high school All-American who went to Duke as a highly rated drop back passer. Unfortunately, a coaching change at the end of his freshman season brought in a winged-T, option-based offense, and they found out Danny wasn't quick enough to manage the roll outs that make an option offense work. The new coaches put him on the redshirt squad to get rid of him, but he managed to stick it out for three years.

Being a three-year redshirt is as rare as being a three-time All-American, except you get no credit for what you've done. It's certainly a much harder thing to accomplish, because the physical and psychological battering is unreal. It's no wonder Danny cried when it was over.

"Do you ever think about just quitting and being done with it," I asked, "instead of going through what he did?"

Like Danny, Tom brought to Cajun State fine credentials as a drop back passer because we ran that offense then. No drop back passer would ever sign with a roll out school, and vice-versa. But then, exactly as in Danny's case, Coach Anderson and his crew took over after Tom's freshman year, and they installed a roll out offense.

Just like Danny, Tom didn't have quick enough feet, so now he was starting his second year as the redshirt quarterback, and he couldn't realistically expect more of a college football career than his brother endured.

"Sure, I think about quitting a lot. In my place, who wouldn't? But because of what Danny went through, I think I have this whole football thing in proper perspective. I came here for the education. If I never take a snap in a real game, I'll still end up with my diploma, and in the long run I can accomplsh a helluva lot more with that on my resume than that I took snaps in games."

"Geeze, Tom, you sound like the coaches when they're out recruiting some poor schnook."

"Yeah, I guess I do. But, you see, when my recruiter sat in our living room telling me and my parents that my education would always be the team's foremost concern, it was all we could do to keep from laughing out loud at him. We held on, though, and just plain old out-lied him. We made him think we believed all that bullshit."

"Your father's a successful rancher, isn't he? So why not let him put you through? If my family was well off, I think that's what I'd do. But, really, even working full time to put yourself through night school would be easier on mind and body than what you go through now."

He smirked at me. "That's a pot calling a kettle black! You're as hooked on this stuff as I am!"

I grinned back. "Yeah, I guess I am."

We could see activity behind the registration doors, so we knew they'd open up momentarily.

"I probably know this system as well as you do, Sage," Tom resumed, "which is saying a lot. I know I have a good idea of what it can do to me . . . of what can go wrong. Even so, I want to stay with it as long as I can. Let's just say that, at this point in my life, quitting would be a heck of a lot tougher for me than sticking with it."

I thought back to three years ago, when I made my own decision to quit. I was a scared nineteen-year-old with a shredded knee and no older brother to measure myself against. I was so ashamed, I could barely face my family.

"What if you get hurt, or never get to play?" I asked. "Could you live with that all your life?"

"I think so, because I know the football only matters to me. A lot of guys think it matters because of someone else—family, friends, hometown people, you name it. So I know I'll carry scars from it if I get hurt, or even if I never play in a real game. But mine won't be as deep as for those who go through it all because it matters to other people."

I looked at my own scarred knee and felt a pain in my gut. *Everything* about football still mattered to me.

The athletic department smoothed out registration for all scholarship athletes for two reasons. First, it was a nightmare of confusion and frustration for an ordinary student, especially one unfamiliar with the process or the professors. Second, it gave no excuse for missing practice because of class-scheduling conflicts.

When scheduling problems did come up, they were handled by Dr. Keith Westrum, a small, ferret-faced man who was the team's academic counselor. The coaches called him our "brain coach" when assuring a prospect's parents that their son would be well-looked-after, mentally and physically. The fine print was that his help was given selectively, according to status on the field.

"I need a three-hour humanities elective at ten o'clock every Monday-Wednesday-Friday," a starter might say to Dr. Westrum at registration. "What's available?"

Westrum had "flexible" morals, and he knew who signed his checks. He'd pull his class files and say to the starter, "History of Western Civilization, H-203, Dr. Clarkson."

Once, when we played Virginia, Clarkson accepted a ride on the team's charter flight to Charlottesville. His mother was sick and he wanted to visit her. So while redshirts, freshmen, and the injured stayed on campus to hear away games on radio, empty seats on the team plane were filled with assorted alumni jock-sniffers, and a few people whose influence the coaches considered valuable.

Professors like Clarkson, who sold out for a favor like that flight, would thereafter find a clutch of athletes in their classes. But only the top-level athletes.

Say that a redshirt approached Westrum with the same

problem. "I need a three-hour humanities elective at ten on Monday-Wednesday-Friday. Can you help me out?"

Westrum would again go to his files. "Sure, I have just the thing. Psychology of Interaction, P-300, Dr. Blandings."

When we played Georgia Tech, Westrum offered Bland-ings a free flight to his hometown of Atlanta. Blandings knew the drill and told him to stuff the trip up his ass. Unfortunately, that tart reply only alerted the coaches to his animosity, which they used to their own advantage.

They sent nothing but marked players into his classes, and he obliged by making life miserable for those unfor-tunates. As a result, Blandings helped the coaches get rid of their unwanted athletes while thinking he was getting back at them. That made him as valuable to the athletic department, in his own way, as Dr. Clarkson.

No matter how carefully the athletic department struc-tured registration to prevent it, occasionally someone *had* to take an afternoon class. It was usually a once-a-week lab, which presented unique difficulties for players with brains enough to qualify for them. The first difficulty was keeping the decision making out of Dr. Westrum's hands.

"Sage, I need some help deciding on a class, and I know Westrum will screw me over if I ask him."

I sat at one of the long tables set up in the gym so stu-dents could complete class-confirming computer cards. I looked up and saw Sir Henry the Wolf, a redshirt tackle with a large head and thin face. Deadly serious about life, it was a major event when he cracked a smile. His somber expression betrayed more than his usual degree of angst.

"What kind of help do you need, Hank?" I asked, not sure I could do him any good. Sir Henry was extremely bright and planned to become an engineer, which meant I knew next to nothing about the courses he would need.

"I have an option between a fluid mechanics lab on Tuesday afternoons and a hydraulics lab on Thursday afternoons. The mechanics professor doesn't like football, the hydraulics one does. I have to take one or the other, and there's no way Westrum can rearrange it. I also have to make a B or better in either one. What do you suggest?"

His was a classic scheduling problem. During football season, Thursday was a fairly easy practice day because the hard work of the week was tapering off in anticipation of Saturday's game. In contrast, Tuesday was the toughest day by far. It was usually wall-to-wall hitting for the redshirts because the coaches would run them ragged trying to mimic the upcoming team's offense.

Logic dictated that Sir Henry should take the Tuesday lab to avoid that tough practice day. However, a professor with a grudge against football could make a hard class even harder, and possibly put a critical dent in Sir Henry's grade-point average. No wonder he was concerned.

"The object of the game for redshirts," I said, "is to try to stay healthy and get through the season in one piece. So take the fluid mechanics on Tuesday and hope for the best with the hard nosed professor. They'll get rid of you a lot quicker on the field than in the classroom."

"Thanks, Sage," he said as he turned away. "I knew I could count on you to make sense."

Lunch followed registration, so we all made our way to the sewer. I found myself leaving the gym at the same time as Prosser. He was just ahead of me. "Hey, Pete! Hold up!"

Out in daylight, he always wore a rakish wide-brimmed hat favored by Australian cattlemen. I asked him about it one morning when I woke him up before practice. He told me they were called Akubras, and he developed a fondness for his when he lived in that part of the world.

He said once you broke it in, there was nothing better to keep the sun off your face and neck and ears. And, of course, there were his ubiquitous dark shades, along with light khaki chinos, a thin long-sleeved shirt, and his cycle boots. He never wore shorts or short-sleeved shirts. As was his "look" in practice, here too he was distinctive.

"Hi, Sage," he said. "Registration squared away?"

"Yeah, my last time through as an undergraduate, so I know the drill. I lined myself up for grad school next year."

"It's different here than it was at junior college. There are no real crip courses. Everything looks worthwhile."

"Did you get any classes with Scott Brown?"

"Oh, yeah, two for credit and I'll audit his introduction to classic philosophy. That's the one I really wanted, but my junior college credits leave me overqualified for it."

I didn't know what to say. He spoke as if he planned to be here through the semester, as if he didn't understand he was on his way out as soon as it could be arranged.

"That, uhh, thing with Hackler yesterday," I said, awkwardly changing the subject. "Can I ask you about it?"

"If you won't repeat what I tell you, then sure. You're a friend now; I believe I can trust you."

"Was it really an accident?"

He turned as we walked, flashing white teeth below his shades. "Only the breaking his wrist part. I knew I could take him down if he swung at me. It was a perfect set-up for a knee hook. But the wrist thing was a nice bonus."

"What did you say to him to make him swing?"

"I reminded him of what I told him at the social."

"Which was. . . ?"

"That if he ever put a hand on me in anger, *ever*, I'd drop him like a sack of shit."

The sheer staggering effrontery of that must have been evident on my face, because Pete smiled and resumed.

"If you look at it in that light, he had it coming."

The sewer loomed ahead, only a minute or two away, so I dove in with what was on my mind.

"Do you understand that Hackler won't let you get away with what you did to him? Or that the coaches can't tolerate the way you are . . . that constant insubordination?"

"Sure they can, they just don't *want* to."

"Okay, they don't *want* to. Put it however you like. The bottom line is, you have a bullseye on your chest, on your back, on the top and sides of your head. You're a target for them now, and they won't rest until you're gone."

He stopped walking and his dark lenses looked up at me. "Gone from the team, or gone from this school?"

"The team, for sure, but most guys usually have to leave school when they have to leave the team."

"I won't have to go. I can do what I came for."

"You have the financial resources to stay?"

"I can teach martial arts and get through anywhere in this country. I'd have to take a reduced class load, but I can get through four more semesters. No problem."

"Then why not quit now and be done with it? Why go through what they'll put you through?"

Just then Quink came striding up behind us, oblivious to the intensity of our conversation. He clapped an arm around Pete's shoulders. "Just the guy I was looking for! I signed up for an introduction to logic course, part of the philosophy department, and I need your advice. . . ."

Quink moved him away, leaving me to follow a step behind. I didn't worry about it, though, because I knew I could find another time to complete our conversation.

I had no business interfering in such a deeply personal matter, but I could tell Pete needed help to see the train wreck barreling his way. And when he finally did see and accept it, he'd be wise to drop football and get his degree studying under a man he wanted to learn from.

He would certainly have no business transferring to another team elsewhere. Anyone with his attitude would be as intolerable there as he was here. That he managed to play two years in junior college was coming to look more and more like a miracle. His coaches there must have been vastly more desperate to win than ours were, more than coaches on any other team I was aware of.

A headstrong guy like Pete was not tolerable because he'd cause internal rot on any team dedicated to the idea of absolute obedience to any and all orders issued by any and all coaches. It was the classic wartime mentality of strict, unquestioning, immediate obedience to orders, no matter how stupid or self-defeating they might be. Football had adopted "teamwork means obedience" as a bedrock that now was so entrenched, it couldn't be otherwise.

Pete needed to quit and establish a life away from football. It could never accommodate him on his own terms.

THE WAIT

After lunch, everyone endured "the wait," the period that had to be filled before reporting to the stadium to dress out. It was like quantum time, but in the opposite direction. Now it ran faster than normal, and the struggle was to slow it down by filling it with activity to keep your mind off what was looming ahead.

Helmut Moedle filled his waiting time doing whatever he felt like, without a care. Practice was never a problem for him. He had mastered his skill so well, coaches didn't allow him to be hit for any reason. It was even dangerous to jostle him in the dressing room. Helmet was magic.

Rabbit didn't worry about practice, either. The coaches never said a harsh word to him, and his existence as a football player of very modest talent seemed every bit as charmed as Helmet's. Rabbit spent his wait time sleeping.

Everyone else sweated it out.

Sir Henry would close the heavy black drapes he had hung over the window in his room, then in the dark he would listen to medieval organ dirges on his stereo.

Tom usually concocted hoaxes and scams during the waits before practice, but this time he was busy arranging the details of Rabbit's weekend fate. I had no idea what it would be, but if Tom said it was good, it would be great.

Wheeler would perfect his half of the room: sweeping,

dusting, shining shoes, ironing clothes, filing hand and toenails, doing crosswords—nervous work, busy work.

Quink and Big Dick and several others would take seats at the long counter in the U.C., jawboning, wise-cracking, checking out the calves on women walking by.

No one was sure what Prosser did. He sometimes took off on the motorcycle he kept parked and chained behind the dorm, but nobody knew where he went because, for the most part, his teammates stayed away from him.

He was a *doppelganger* existing among them—there, but not really present. Everyone was uneasy about being seen with him, fearful a coach would stigmatize them by association. Nothing quieted a dining table like Prosser taking a seat at it, which was yet another reason most guys would be glad to see him gone. He was bad juju.

Because Don Slade was married, he lived in a separate dorm for couples. "The wait" left him with no particular place to go. He solved that problem by visiting from room to room in our dorm, a practice which had built him the widest circle of friends on the team. Don was probably our best-liked and most respected player because of the injury he overcame and how hard he played the game.

Whenever he felt like sack time, he'd come to the fifth-floor room I shared with Stanton. Chris and I lived primarily off-campus with lady friends, so we nearly always had an unoccupied bed available. We'd given Don a key, and I woke up to the sound of it scratching in the lock.

"Oh, I'm sorry, Sage. Didn't mean to wake you. I thought you'd be home with Carla this afternoon."

"She's busy today," I replied through a yawn. "Getting ready to teach the new semester. Come on in."

"I wanted to take the pressure off my knee for a while," he said, stretching out on Stanton's empty bed. "Today's a big day for me, so I want to give it my best shot."

I wasn't fully awake, so I asked the all-time cliche question. "How's it feel to be first team?"

"Great!" he answered, with the same enthusiasm he'd probably been asked to show a hundred times by then. "Even if only for a few days."

"Only a few days? The Bull told me the Doc told him that he'd be out for at least two games."

Don's head shook. "They iced it so quickly and got it elevated so soon, the swelling is a lot less than expected. Now they think he'll be able to run on it by next Saturday night. He won't be able to cut well, but he'll be able to fire out straight ahead. He'll be able to play."

"I don't know whether to feel glad for him or sorry for you. You sure have come a long way."

"The best athlete at any position ought to play it in games. I've always believed that."

That was exactly what I'd expect Don to say. He was so decent it hurt, which hurt all of us when he blew his knee out. After it happened, I helped load him into the truck bed, and when he saw the tears leaking out of my eyes, he broke down, and soon both of us were bawling over it.

His injury was actually a fairly common one. He was fighting for yardage with a tackler draped across his back, which was typical for him, when another tackler hit him from straight on. He'd just planted his right knee at the moment of impact, so it had no chance to hold together. It buckled backward, tearing the posterior cruciate ligament and badly stretching the anterior cruciate, medial collateral, and lateral collateral ligaments.

His surgeons told him that if he rehabbed it like a madman, he could come back this season, which was all he needed for motivation. And now he'd be starting—or playing a lot—against the defending national champions in one of the biggest games Cajun State ever lined up in.

The best man ought to play. . . .
Those words rang in my head as I recalled my injury. I was heading into a pileup of bodies, so my trunk got twisted as my cleats stayed stuck in the turf. Everything

inside my knee was torn to-hell-and-gone, all four major ligaments, like a chicken leg twisted from its socket.

I was told I'd be lucky to walk comfortably on it, much less play again. Hearing that crushed me, and it gave me no motivation to try to rehab it as hard as I should have. Looking back, I wish they had lied to me and told me I had a chance to come back. If they told me that, I know I would have worked a lot harder to recover from it.

I looked at Don sitting on the other bed and felt deep admiration for his effort. "You've come from a helluva long way down, and you did it in almost record time. No matter what, you'll always have that to be proud of."

He nodded somberly. "I didn't have much choice, did I?"

I knew what he meant. His story was a common one for ten to twenty players on the team in any given year. After signing his scholarship during his senior year of high school, he got Annie pregnant. Both were devout Catholics, though Catholics with all the typical teenage hormones. Rather than abort it, they decided to get married and do their best to make the most of it.

That one they lost to an eventual miscarriage, probably due to the stress Annie's family put her through because she got pregnant. Luckily, she and Don found they loved each other even more than they imagined, and they were very happy as a young couple. In fact, Annie had recently found out she was pregnant again, and sometime next spring several of us would be delighted godfathers.

"What's the fluid situation since the bruise?" I asked Don. Fluid buildup was something I knew a lot about.

"Hanson thinks it's five or ten cc's," he said through a tight-lipped grimace. "They'll drain it in about an hour."

My stomach flipped. Draining is a grisly procedure in which a fat hypodermic needle is jammed into an injured joint, then moved around in search of fluid pockets to suck dry. The pain reduces even hard-bitten pros to screams of anguish, so I knew what Don had to be feeling. In fact, revisiting those memories flipped my stomach again.

"Hang in there, man, you've been through it before."

He grimaced again. "Yeah . . . I know."

"The wait" morphed into the slowed-down, syrup-aired "quantum time" on the walk over to the stadium. And before any big scrimmage, the dressing room tension was only slightly less than before a big game. The quality of varsity scrimmage performances sometimes determined who started in regular season games, so the top-level players prepared religiously to give an all-out effort.

The lower echelon third teamers and the redshirts were under even more pressure to perform well. Their playing time was mostly a matter of luck and coaching whims, and it was never as much as they wanted. Nobody had it easy.

"What are you doing back here now?" Tom asked as I walked into the redshirt dressing room. "Aren't you supposed to be up front taping ankles?"

I shrugged. "They're draining Don's knee."

He patted the bench beside him, indicating I should sit down. "That stuff still freaks you out, eh?"

I nodded as I sat down. "It always will."

"So, how's it look outside?"

"Tough day for it. No clouds, ninety-plus heat."

"You figure we'll play much?"

"Hard to say. If the varsity is sharp early, and execution is crisp, you ought to play a lot later on. If they drag around in the heat, the coaches will probably work them into the ground. Remember, tomorrow is an off-day."

He nodded, then glanced over at Prosser, leaned back against his cubicle, eyes closed. He had already smoothed bootblack across his cheekbones, which meant his dark contacts were in place. Contacts had to go in first.

"What about him?" Tom asked.

I shook my head. "Not a chance."

"Doesn't it just suck that the only way to get off the redshirts is to look better than people above you on the depth chart, yet everything is rigged to keep that from happening? What's a guy like Prosser supposed to do? Hell, what are *any* of us supposed to do?"

I noticed Sir Henry trying to struggle into his shoulder pads, so I got up to go help him.

"Hope for a miracle," I said to Tom.

On the second day of two-a-days, Hank Wolf bruised his sternum, one of the most painful injuries you can get. From a coaching standpoint, it's a perfect redshirt injury because it's not crippling and the victim can be made to play in excruciating pain. The only way out is to quit.

Hank survived by designing his own protection: a foot-square sheet of foam rubber that covered his entire chest. The fist-sized hole over his injured breastbone reminded Tom of a jousting target, so ever since, except when we addressed him directly, he'd been Sir Henry the Wolf.

"Let me help, Hank," I said as I began squeezing the foam sheet under the breastplates of his shoulder pads.

He offered a rare smile as thanks.

It was an extremely tight fit, difficult to adjust properly, but once everything was in place, all pressure was directed away from the weak spot over his heart. It was an ingenious, functional design, fitting for the engineer Hank intended to be. Trainer Hanson had already stolen it to treat a varsity guard with the same problem.

Thanks to Sir Henry the Wolf, there would probably never be another Cajun State redshirt unwillingly leaving the team because of a bruised sternum. And, in time, word of it would spread throughout the football world. In ten years it would be everywhere, on every team at every level, from pee wee to pro, and its unheralded inventor would never see a dollar from it.

Dat purr baastid. . . .

I banged my fists on the tops and sides of his shoulder pads to make sure they were set properly on the foam.

"Thanks, Sage. That feels exactly right."

His normally deadpan face seemed amused.

"What are you looking so smug about?"

"I have a good feeling about today, that's all."

"Great!" I said with a wink. "*Somebody* back here ought to get a break once in a while."

"As long as it's not a bone!" he quipped.

Next, I stopped to have a few words with Prosser. It wasn't a time or place to pick up where we left off before lunch, but I felt I needed to make contact with him again so he'd know I didn't intend to let it rest where Quink ended it.

"Now, where were we?" I said as I sat down beside him.

He smiled wryly, opened his eyes, and his dark contacts gazed back at me above the bootblack. "You were telling me I should quit while the quitting is good."

"You should, but it doesn't have to be today."

"Yeah, I know, I won't be getting in today."

"Anderson did say everyone would get in," I reminded him. "So who knows? You may get to show your stuff."

He smirked sourly. "They've seen my stuff."

"I meant to the crowd. There'll be several hundred people in the stands . . . maybe a thousand. It's a beautiful day to watch football. Not to play, but to watch."

He closed his eyes in a gesture that told me he'd heard enough. "They won't put me in."

I stood up to leave. "No, probably not."

As I headed toward the varsity dressing room, Cap'n motioned me over to the equipment shed.

"Little fat guy in a white shirt and tie came by lookin' for you a while ago," he said.

Randall. "What'd he want?"

"Didn't say. He did say he'd be in the press box during practice, and he'd talk to you after."

"Okay, thanks."

***

Everything seemed ready inside as quantum time got screwed down one more turn. Last-minute dumps and whizzes were audible in the toilet area. Helmets were spun nervously by taped and padded hands; mouthpiece ends were chewed to shreds; fist-and-jaw-clenching psych-ups were scattered all around, as were endless finicky equipment adjustments. All of it seemed to be in slow motion.

"How do you feel, Quink?"

He looked up at me with a faint smile, the best he could manage under the circumstances.

"How about it, Jimbo? You doin' okay?"

Wheeler's heels were bouncing up and down in a nervous frenzy, but his face was a mask of calm resolve and purpose. "I'm ready, Sage . . . ready to go."

Don and the Bull sat together talking, the Bull's new crutches laid between them. Their rivalry was a friendly one, based on genuine ability and mutual respect.

"Good luck, Don," I said. "Have a good one."

Don glanced up. "Yeah, Sage, you too."

Under the pressure, he was humorously distracted and forgot that I wasn't a player.

I wished I could do the same.

SCRIMMAGE

Most fans thought scrimmages were held in the stadium for their viewing comfort. Actually, it was easier for the "Big Eye," what everyone on the team called the filming camera, to do its job. Of course, what fans didn't know couldn't hurt them, or their enthusiasm, which was considerable when the team hit the field at 2:30.

I stood to one side watching calisthenics with Big Dick, the Bull, and other injured players dressed out in shorts.

"What's the crowd size?" the Bull asked me.

"About a thousand . . . maybe more."

Packed, the Cajun State stadium held fifty thousand, but it was almost never full, and only a thousand or so were easily swallowed up in it.

"The Crawdad's lonely," Big Dick said wryly.

Looming beside the scoreboard in the south end zone was a 30-foot-tall wooden cutout of our team's famous mascot, the most famous thing about our entire athletic program. A giant red crawfish stood upright on its tail, with its two large claws lifted up in a muscleman pose, flexing human-like biceps and snarling defiantly with a human-like expression on its distinctly crawfish face.

That was Cajun State's Fightin' Crawdad, which everyone in Louisiana had on a T-shirt or a cap or a poster or a coffee mug or a bumper sticker. LSU might have been the state's one true college football power, but our Fightin' Crawdad trumped their Mike the Tiger at every turn.

The crowd was the usual mix of friends of players and our few die-hard fans, but this last Saturday scrimmage always brought another contingent—newly arrived students drifting between bouts with registration's madness to sit in the sun for a while, check out this year's team, and then prepare pom-pom analyses to relate to their friends at fraternity rush parties later that night.

Coach Anderson stayed in the press box during scrimmages so he could be with reporters assigned to cover them. Public relations was a crucial part of a head coach's duties, and none of them shunned it. Coaching itself was a questionable skill—you either had enough studs to win, or you didn't—but there was no substitute for a man who could manipulate the press. During his career, our Coach Anderson had developed quite a fine touch for that.

Coach Marshall was the acting head coach on the field. At 2:45 he blew his whistle to start the scrimmage, and the field rapidly cleared of players other than the first team offense and the second team defense.

Zebra suited professional refs were hired to officiate,

which left me watching with the remaining players scattered along the sideline below the press box.

"First and ten at the twenty!" an official yelled.

Scrimmages had no kickoffs, and the offensive coaches stood behind the offense and the defensive coaches stood behind the defense. Otherwise, game conditions were in effect, except that players knew the coaches were looking right up their backsides, taking note of everything they did on every play. The theory was that if you couldn't stand up to that kind of pressure in practice, you had no business being in a pressure-packed game.

Because game conditions were more or less in effect, there was no stopping to run plays over. That was fortunate, because the first play was a trap up the middle that made the defense look ridiculous. Jimbo Wheeler drove the nose guard well off the ball and then pancaked him, allowing Don Slade to roll fifteen yards up the middle.

"God-*damn*-it, defense!" Hackler roared, brandishing his cast so everyone could see it before throwing his cap down with his good left hand. "You turds better hit somebody!"

"All right, big offense, way to roll!"

"C'mon, defense! Dig in! Hold 'em!"

That sideline chatter would go on for the next two hours. It was an important part of the game.

"First and ten at the thirty-five!"

The offense kept its drive alive for two more first downs, then had to punt from the defense's forty-two. The punt ended in a touchback, so the second team offense took over on its own twenty against the first team defense.

The action was crisp and fluid. Marches went up and down the field, good runs were followed by crushing tackles, long completions led to fumbles, and all gains seemed balanced by equal losses. Suddenly, a player was down, rolling in pain, holding his left arm.

"Who is it?" someone on the sideline asked.

"Looks like a lineman," someone else answered.

Substitute linemen tensed and their stomachs knotted.

One of them would be going in as the replacement for the injured player when his identity was determined.

"It's Smathers!" someone finally shouted.

Ralph Smathers was the second team offensive right tackle, and his right forearm looked to be broken just above the wrist. Luckily, it wasn't a compound fracture.

"Jennings!" Marshall shouted from the cluster of offensive coaches on the field. "Where the hell is Jennings?"

Rick Jennings was the third team right tackle, so he was automatically next in line to move up into Ralph's spot. He promptly did what he had to do, stepping forward from the sideline to call out, "Right here, Coach!"

All eyes turned his way, and there he was—wearing shorts because he was injured. It was always a first-rate disaster for a player to be called to emergency duty while injured and wearing shorts. Jennings knew the unwritten rule as well as anyone: there was simply *no* acceptable excuse for not being ready when called upon. The coaches would remember this for a long, long time.

"*Goddammit!*" Coach Marshall's raspy voice bellowed, "Jennings doesn't want to play! Give me a tackle who wants to get out here and *play* this game!"

Sir Henry was sharper than most, so he immediately grasped the situation. Smathers' spot was being thrown up for grabs to the first man with nerve enough to take it. Sir Henry's helmet was on and his chinstrap secured when he broke away from the sideline at full speed. Two other reserve tackles made bareheaded moves, but Sir Henry had too much of a jump on them.

"All right, Wolf!" Coach Marshall yelled at the sideline. "Wolf wants to play! Get in and show us what you can do."

A thrill of anticipation ripped through every redshirt's heart. Coach Marshall was hard but fair, so he'd give Sir Henry a decent chance to prove himself. If he did well, he'd take Smathers' place on the varsity. It wasn't often a redshirt managed to rise out of the mire like this, so his shirtmates hoped he could maximize his opportunity.

The next few plays went away from Sir Henry, so he couldn't show much, but they finally ran his way on a cross-buck. He got under his man in perfect position and drove him cleanly out of the hole.

"All right, Sir Henry!"

"Way to block, Hank!"

Redshirts knew coaches couldn't see everything occurring on every play, so they often listened to sideline shouts to determine who was doing well. The noise was a way of sticking Sir Henry's name in the backs of their minds.

Later, coaches might say, "Hank Wolf did pretty well out there today," not having particularly noticed his performance, but remembering all the yelling. And afterward, when they graded the films, they might be inclined to give him their benefit of doubt on any questionable efforts.

As scrimmages go, this one was about B-plus. The heat drained everyone into puddles of sweat, so the coaches began to substitute liberally after the first hour. Don scored two touchdowns on short plunges and gave every indication of being able to fill a large part of the Bull's big shoes. Helmet kicked three medium-range field goals, which showed that he had lost nothing since last season. Sir Henry hung tough and gave a good account of himself. Even third teamers and redshirts got their promised chance to show what they could do—all except Prosser.

As expected, Prosser hadn't been called as the scrimmage neared its end. But then, without warning, Quink popped through the line on a dive and blew past the linebacker. He shot into the secondary and tried to run over the safety, hitting him at top speed in a violent collision.

Quink's aggressive, head-down attack on the safety was a move that frequently produced injuries to running backs, but it always won high marks from coaches.

"All right, Thompson!" Coach Marshall yelled at him. "That's the way to run the damn ball! That's the way to stick it in somebody's earhole!"

Every coach—especially aggressive ones like Marshall—in his heart preferred savage contact over long, untouched runs, so he beamed as Quink wobbled back to the huddle.

"That's the way to hit in there, little stud," he said, patting Quink on the rump as he went past. "You left him blowing snotbubbles. Take a break and clear your head."

Then, without thinking about what it meant, Marshall turned to the sideline and shouted out the routine call in that situation: "I need a tailback for one play!"

Quink was the third team tailback, so that meant Prosser was next on the depth chart, his right to be the substitute clear and undeniable. There was no way to avoid using him after Coach Marshall called for him and he promptly responded. The protocol had to be followed.

As Prosser headed onto the field, Hackler left his defensive position to waddle across the line of scrimmage for a heated word with Marshall. He needn't have worried. Marshall realized his mistake, leaned into the huddle to call the next play, and was behind the huddle smoothing Hackler's ruffled feathers, when Prosser jogged into place.

We knew who *wouldn't* carry on the next play.

Coach Marshall took no chances, calling a simple fullback dive over left tackle. Roger Johnson took the handoff and plowed into the line, while Prosser swung behind him, faking a pitchout run around left end.

Chip Martinson, the defensive tackle at the point of attack, shed his blocker and threw himself at Johnson. His helmet hit squarely on the ball, which squirted from Johnson's grip into the backfield. Prosser was about five feet from where it hit, and as he took off after the bounding ball, everyone realized what could happen next.

"Fall on it!" the coaches shouted.

"Pick it up!" the rest of us screamed.

Prosser picked it up and surveyed his situation. The flow of the defense had pursued left with Johnson, leaving nothing straight ahead. He had no choice but to swing back to his right to reverse his field, moving back to where the play started and toward the cluster of coaches, who were obliged by more protocol to scatter out of his way.

All of them did—except Hackler.

Hackler had stayed with the offensive coaches for this one play, and he stood his ground as Prosser streaked toward him, head turned upfield to survey the defense.

With admirable focus, Hackler waited to move until the moment when he could do so and pretend an awkward stumble while sticking his foot out.

It was as clean a trip as you could ask for, and the surprise of it should have dropped Prosser in his tracks; but he staggered like a wino for about five steps, barely keeping himself off the ground with his free left hand, then he finally regained his balance enough to stand upright.

What he saw then was worse than what he found on the other side. The defense had pursued with him to his right, while most of his own men didn't know what had happened behind their backs. That left him on the right side of the field facing most of the defense, while his own men were to the left side facing each other.

That left him no choice but to head back to his left, and this time as he went, he kept a wary eye out for Hackler.

Hackler gave up all pretention of accidental interference, taking a healthy swipe at Prosser's head with his cast, but that was like trying to swat a turbocharged wasp.

Prosser left Hackler screaming obscenities behind his back as he turned his attention upfield. He was getting behind some blockers by then, and they were starting to knock holes in the back-pursuing wall of defenders.

Suddenly, as Prosser neared the left sideline, he planted his left foot hard and hesitated for an instant. Because it was Prosser, and because every defender knew what he was capable of, they avoided overpursuing by throttling down in anticipation of what he might do next.

That slight drag on their momentum gave him all the opportunity he needed. He darted into a gap as if someone jabbed him with a hot poker, and from there he ran like a scalded cat, zigging and zagging through open spaces among the strung-out defenders.

Thirty yards downfield, he was in the clear, and he simply coasted the rest of the way to the end zone.

Fans in the stands went crazy as Prosser wearily jogged back to the sideline. It was a sixty yard run from scrimmage, but he traveled well over a hundred yards to do it.

"Hot *damn!*" the Bull shouted above the noise. "Can you *believe* how that guy can run?"

Prosser ignored all the back slapping and congratulations, gazing upfield as he looked past those around him.

"Hank Wolf," he said, "took a bad hit on a block."

We looked for Sir Henry and found him still down on the turf, back near the line of scrimmage. Trainer Hanson was already bent over the familiar ugly angle of his right arm.

"Dislocated!" I muttered, feeling sick inside. "Dislocated and twisted." That meant surgery, for sure.

The scrimmage ended right after Prosser's run. Hackler called his entire defense onto the field and berated them loudly, then he ordered them to run ten punishment laps around the track outside so the fans wouldn't see them.

Not to be outdone, and perhaps feeling guilty about his mental error, Coach Marshall made the offense join in the laps. That included the redshirts, too, so Prosser returned to his pariah status as quickly as he became a hero.

The coaches left me to supervise the penalty laps, so I let everyone go in after five. What the hell? I knew that by then the coaches were long gone from the stadium, off to whatever they'd be doing on Saturday night, and not one of the lappers would ever mention me cutting it short.

Gloom, as they say, hung heavy in the redshirt dressing room when I went in to get Sir Henry's clothes. Many vicarious hopes rode on his broad back, and now those hopes were as crushed as his shoulder. His injury also meant he was now on a level with Prosser as far as the coaches were concerned, which depressed us all.

Whenever it became obvious that a player was doomed, others would react as if he were already gone. With "guilt by association" so common among coaches, today's friend was tomorrow's liability. Even a marked player's best buddies would break away rather than risk what the coaches might think about it. Their capricious natures kept everyone in a constant state of stress, trying to outguess them.

"Just when he had it in the bag!" Tom exploded.

"Easy, Tom," said Gene Skidmore, the other redshirt tackle. "It happened, it's done. Try not to think about it."

"Mind your own damn business, Skid!" Tom snapped, as righteous anger spilled out of him.

Skid wouldn't react to Tom's harsh words. He was a gentle, lumbering giant who always tried to cool hot tempers. Besides, everyone in the room felt as bad as Tom did about what happened. Even Prosser showed it, sitting at his locker with his head hung down in dismay.

"It's the luck of the draw," I offered to them all as I picked up Sir Henry's clothes. "Today wasn't his day."

When I left the back dressing room, Randall was waiting in the shadows under a stadium ramp. That meant he understood my concerns about being seen by the coaches talking to him. Cap'n must have told him where I was.

He motioned me over. "Man, you look like hell."

"I have to take these clothes over to the guy who hurt his shoulder on that last play. He's a good friend."

Randall winced. "Tough part of the job, eh?"

"The toughest. . . . So what's up? You told Cap'n you wanted to talk to me about something?"

"What I came to tell you originally was that two assistant coaches from Texas flew in this morning to scout the scrimmage. They spent the whole time up in the press box with Anderson and the reporter pool, which included me."

The fact there were only two was a bit of a surprise.

Because our campus was so close to New Orleans, scouting us was a plum assignment for assistants, and we were often scrutinized by whole flotillas of them. Only two meant that others were at the final scrimmages of other teams Texas would face early in the season.

They were clearly serious about defending their national championship, and just as clearly no more than moderately serious about us. And who could blame them?

"You should have been up there," he went on, glowing with delight. "Prosser started running loose and one of the Texas coaches said, 'You told us he wouldn't get in, T.K.!' Then we reporters started whooping and hollering, but Anderson shouted at us, 'Shut the fuck up!'

"After that we stayed quiet, even when Hackler made those two stupid moves to try to knock him down. But listen, all of us up there *knew* what we were seeing, *knew* how special it was. And when it was over, the other Texas coach gripped Anderson's arm and said, 'You told us you were gettin' rid of him. What the hell happened?' Those two were *not* happy about it, and Anderson was livid."

"Coaching is a cutthroat job, Randall. They can never stop being paranoid about what others will do to win."

"Okay," Randall resumed, "so Anderson turned around and gave a halfhearted laugh for everyone up there, then he spoke to us reporters first. 'Listen, fellas, I know how that run looked, but the boy's just a redshirt on our team. He got lucky, that's all. It's late and the defense is tired.'

"Then he took the Texas coaches aside to where we couldn't hear, and let's just say he *energetically* explained his position to them. When they came back to where the reporters were, it was all smiles and good humor, and Prosser wasn't mentioned again—not by them, not by us."

"He's being 'disappeared,' like what communists do to their dissidents," I explained. "Texas would have taken Prosser if he wanted to play there. Hell, *any* major school would have taken him based on his stats and grades in junior college. But he came here, and now our coaches have found out the truth about him. They'll spread that word to coaches everywhere, and that will end his career. There just isn't a place for a guy like him in football, so they'll all just pretend he doesn't exist."

"But he *does* exist!" Randall yelped. "He's right there in that locker room!" He pointed at it with disgust, rightfully frustrated by his inability to alter this grim reality.

"He won't be there long," I assured him. "He sealed it for himself today. He embarrassed the entire coaching staff in front of all those fans, and he humiliated Anderson in the press box. They'll get rid of him for sure now. During two-a-days they were hoping he'd take the hint of being stuck on the redshirts. Now they'll make damn sure he understands that he has no place here."

"Why can't he be accommodated? He's so talented!"

"He's not afraid of them!" I hissed. "This whole system, the whole game of football, it all operates on *fear!* Fear of authority, fear of the coaches, fear of screwing up, of letting the team down, of being the one person who botches a play at the wrong time. Fear keeps the whole thing going, so any guy without fear of all that is a guy that can't be a part of it, no matter how well he plays the game!"

"That's *wrong*, Larry," Randall fumed, "and you know it! I want to try to change that, or at least some of it. I want to do a headline story for tomorrow's edition: 'Prosser Shines In Last Cajun State Scrimmage.' What do you think?"

"Your editor won't print it, and it will tell him you're not properly fearful, either. But even if he would print it, it wouldn't help Prosser. The coaches will stick with their 'lucky-break' excuse and get rid of him anyway. You understand what I'm telling you? You can't *win* against these people! They're entrenched, they're ruthless, and their power is absolute. Forget about it."

"But Larry!" he sputtered. "The public has a right to know about Prosser! They have—!"

"The public doesn't give a damn!" I rasped, struggling to keep my voice down. "They don't want to know these things. Go stop ten fans on the street and try to tell them the truth, the actual real truth, about what goes on in this back dressing room, and they'll turn on you."

His head shook slowly, as if I'd just punched him. "No, you must be wrong . . . I don't believe it."

"You're not a reporter, Randall, you're a fan, no different from any of them. Until you decide to be a reporter and stop being a fan, you can't really cover this team."

Still looking stunned, he mumbled, "I'm not a fan, I'm a reporter. I have a degree to prove it."

"You're an idealist, which you have to drop if you want to cover football in any depth. You also have to drop the idea of doing a story about what Prosser did here today. That will be completely erased in short order."

"But how? How can they erase something like that, something so many people witnessed?"

"They'll make him quit. Now, I have to leave. I have to get these clothes over to the infirmary."

INFIRMARY

I went to the varsity dressing room to pick up Ralph Smathers' clothes, too, then headed for the infirmary, which was only a quarter mile from the stadium. Not a long walk under normal circumstances, but tortuously long when bringing clothes to friends who'd been injured.

I dropped Smathers' off first. He was in the usual good spirits of someone with a major injury that was minor.

"If I had to break something," he said, "this is as good as I could ask for." He nodded at the cast already applied to his right forearm. This infirmary was used to handling football injuries quickly and cleanly.

"I just don't want to blow a knee," he added. "Let's face it, knees never heal worth a damn."

He noticed my expression.

"Sorry if that brings up bad memories. I'm just happy to get this, that's all. It could have been *so* much worse."

"You're right, Ralph, it sure could have."

Sir Henry was anything but cheerful. He sat propped up in a bed with the entire right half of his upper torso covered with tape. Because his injury occurred on the last play of the scrimmage, the work on his shoulder had only recently ended, and it was purely stopgap.

Surgeons would have to check him to assess the degree of damage he suffered. If ligaments were torn, which was likely, he'd need surgery and extensive rehabilitation. In their own ways, blown shoulders were as bad as knees.

He'd been in his room five minutes when I arrived, and he was still in serious pain, physically and emotionally.

I asked the required question regarding how he was feeling, and he answered through tightly clenched teeth.

"Every . . . breath . . . hurts."

It figured. With a blown shoulder added to his bruised sternum, his whole torso would be aching. "Just try to take it easy, Hank. The pain-killers should take effect soon."

"I hope so. . . ."

"I'll go now and let you rest," I said, turning to leave. "I'll come back later to see how you're doing."

"Wait! . . . don't go . . . I want to ask . . . something."

I knew what it would be and dreaded hearing it.

"What will . . . happen . . . to me now?" he forced out through his pain. "What will . . . they do . . . with me?"

I stepped back beside the bed and decided it was best to give it to him straight. Another player I might have lied to, but he was too smart for any subterfuge.

"Your shoulder is blown. For a lineman, that's almost as bad as a knee, and both joints are hard to repair properly. Don Slade got a good repair job on his knee, so he's managed to come back on it. I had a bad repair job, so I couldn't come back. It's the same with shoulders.

"But even if your surgeons manage to fix it well, it'll always be a weak spot on you. That makes it vulnerable, so you tend to start favoring it. If that happens, you never play well again. You may as well hang it up."

"But I . . . can't quit!" he groaned. "I just . . . *can't!*"

The most gut-wrenching part of my job was helping terminally injured players through the initial rejection stage of adjusting to a loss that, at bottom, was monumental.

To most guys the worst aspect of their loss was football itself, because that was the only thing they felt they really knew how to do. For most of them, it was all they could ever remember doing or being. It felt like they were born, then they became a football player. Nothing in between.

Losing so much of yourself was always tragic.

"*Why* can't you quit, Hank? Are you afraid of what your family will think? What your friends will think? What your girlfriend will think?" It was usually one of those.

His strained expression softened a bit. The pain pills had to be kicking in. Soon an ambulance would arrive to take him to the hospital downtown, where a surgeon probably playing golf right now would operate on him later tonight. He'd be brought back here tomorrow, so he could recuperate where his friends and teammates could visit.

"I'm poor, Sage . . . I come from a poor family. I want to be an engineer . . . my parents can't help. Football is my ticket . . . into the world. I really *can't* quit . . . I *do* have to stick with it . . . if I possibly can."

My heart went out to him because three years ago I was lying exactly where he was, in exactly the same shape, poor and broken and scared to death. Someone took pity on me then, so it was time for me to pass along the favor.

"Would you consider becoming a manager?"

His eyes widened. "You mean . . . like you?"

"Yes, like me. This is my last semester. At spring training, Stanton will take my place, and he'll need an assistant. Cap'n will need some help. It's a laundry scholarship, but it's a scholarship. Would you be interested?"

Tears welled in his eyes. "Yes . . . I think I might be. What would I have to do . . . to apply for it?"

"Nothing, really. I think I can set it up for you the same way someone set it up for me. Okay?"

Now tears rolled down his cheeks. "It can't be . . . that easy . . . can it? And if it is . . . why me?"

"For one thing, Hanson is ga-ga over that pad you made for your sternum. But beyond that, you're the kind of guy they like to help. You have a good attitude, you're a hard worker, and everyone will remember the effort you were giving when you got hurt. Your block on Gorman was the one that sprung Prosser, and he went through the rest of 'em like coatin' oil through a widow-woman!"

That was dumb for me to say because it was bound to make him laugh, but it was perfectly appropriate. Last year we had a freshman linebacker who grew up as far in the North Georgia backwoods as was possible to get.

He had a thick hillbilly accent, and the widest array of down-home country sayings any of us ever heard. Every time he popped out a new one, we'd all crack up at it, but he blew us away with that one. Just the way he said it, it *sounded* funny, but none of us actually knew what the "coatin' oil" was. He shrugged and said, "Says 'castor oil' on the bottle, but we always called it coatin' oil."

It was a laxative!

Everyone hated to see him go because he was hilariously funny *and* a tough linebacker. But he got homesick after a couple months and went back where he belonged.

SATURDAY NIGHT

After a long hard day of faculty meetings getting ready for the start of the new semester, Carla was going to bed early. I still had a lot of gas left in my tank, so I decided to go visit the dorm to see what might be happening there.

The First Saturday night with all students on campus was always frantic. Rush parties were held in every fraternity and sorority house. Football players let off a lot of pent-up steam with the end of two-a-days. Everyone was anticipating the start of classes and actually having to buckle down to the work part of being at college. This was always a special night at almost any university of appreciable size, and it would be my last time to partake in it.

As I walked across campus enveloped by the warm, sweet air of a late-summer evening, I hoped we'd have the same kind of weather next week at this time. Then I checked my watch and realized that in exactly one week from that moment, it would be time for the second-half kick-off of the first football game of the year.

That, too, would be another last dance for me.

My first stop for a social visit at the dorm was usually Tom Everett's room because it was always such a hub of activity, and because Tom was so enjoyable to be around. For as addicted as he was to pranks and practical jokes, he was also one of the most mature guys on the team.

Sure enough, Tom and two of his many henchmen were operating when I got to his room. I stepped inside and nodded silent greetings to Gene Skidmore and Wizard Burke.

"That's right, sir," Tom was saying on the phone in his *Joe College, Freshman Honor Student* voice, "I'm certain it was fireworks. Yes, sir, right in the quadrangle, sir. Right in the middle of it. Yes, sir. I hope you do catch them, sir."

Tom hung up and turned around to face the room. He always worked turned toward a wall so onlooker expressions wouldn't crack him up in the middle of a routine.

"Hey, Sage! Good to see you, man. You're just in time to catch a little dipthong action."

Dipthongs was what we football players called our campus police. Years ago, well before my time here, a football player taking a German class was introduced to the word "dipthong," which he found funny. Later, at the U.C., he was with a group of his teammates when a trio of campus cops came in for some lunch. He smirked and said, "Look at the three dipthongs!" and everyone immediately realized how well it worked as a euphemism for "dipshits."

Dipthongs were a favorite and deserving target of Tom's scheming because they were often petty and incompetent. He stood and walked to the room's picture window, facing out onto the large open quadrangle five stories below.

"Come check this while I tell you what we have set up."

The quadrangle was faintly illuminated by lights from the men's dormitories that bordered two of its adjacent sides. A darkened ROTC building and an even darker parking lot formed the other sides. The quadrangle was about a hundred yards long by seventy-five yards wide.

"We have fifty—count 'em, *fifty*—cherry bombs scattered around out there," Tom began. "They're on cigarette fuses timed to go off randomly for twenty minutes. You heard me call the dipthongs pretending to be a squealer who saw some guys with fireworks out there, right? And you know how badly they want to catch the Mad Bomber? So we figure they'll be there inside of five minutes, easy."

They'd be there sooner if it was humanly possible. In his deep bag of tricks, Tom favored explosion stunts of all kinds, but he was especially fond of cherry bomb routines, and the dipthongs were determined to collar the person the campus newspaper called *The Mad Bomber.*

"Swede is out laying down the last series." Tom went on. "He'll finish just about the time the dipthongs arrive."

Swede Olson was a third team end who was also Tom's roommate. I peered into the murk below and saw a tall, light-haired figure near the ROTC building. It was Swede.

"Here they come," Wizard Burke said as a dipthong car pulled into the parking lot. "Right on schedule."

Wizard was a second team wingback with a knack for orchestrating Tom's projects with hit-team precision.

"Timing?" Tom asked, tension clipping his words.

Wizard checked his watch. "So far, so good." From here on it was his show. He glanced up for a quick assessment of the situation below. "Uh-oh . . . they're being careful."

Two dipthongs had left their car and, flashlights in hand, cautiously approached the darkened quadrangle.

"Will they even be *on* it when the first one goes off?" Tom pressed. Everything was out of his hands now, and his frustration was evident.

Wizard's eyes were back on his watch as he shrugged. "Only thirty more seconds."

"That's not long enough," Tom said. "They won't be anywhere near the middle by then."

"With so many people back on campus," Wizard said, "most of the cigs in the area were cleaned out. I could only find menthols, and they burn a few seconds quicker."

Wizard Burke was a born experimenter and statistician who had test-burned dozens of cigarettes of every major brand, timing how quickly or slowly they burned, perfecting cherry-bomb fuses. Now he knew the exact burn time of any length of any cigarette you could name. Last Christmas he cut a string that played "Jingle Bells" with cherry bomb explosions out on the quadrangle.

"Where's the first one supposed to go off?" Tom snapped. "Maybe we'll get a break there."

Wizard quickly rifled through the notes he compiled for each major operation. "Skid laid that one," he said matter-of-factly. "Where did you put it, Skid?"

"Over near the—"

Boom!

A bright flash and noise finished his reply.

"Perfect!" Tom exulted. "Right near Swede!"

The two dipthongs got a good look at the tall figure lurking across the quadrangle near the ROTC building and took off across the wide expanse after him. Swede stepped behind the building's corner and disappeared.

The dipthongs were ten yards from dead center when

Wizard spoke, eyes on his watch.

"Four more, starting . . . now!"

Boom!   Boom! Boom!   Boom!

With explosions ringing all around them, the dipthongs had no choice but to stop running.

"Got 'em!" Skid said with satisfaction.

Looking at this watch, Wizard said, "Three more."

Boom!   Boom!   Boom!

The dipthongs were stranded, unable to move safely. Even using flashlights, they couldn't be sure of not stepping on a hidden live cherry bomb. They could only stand helplessly in the center of the quadrangle, waiting for the explosions to stop. It would be a twenty-minute eternity.

Students in the two adjacent dorms heard the noise and began raining insults down from open windows.

"Hey, ya big cowards, get the hell outta there!"

This was the purpose of the exercise, to welcome all students back on campus with a bang, so to speak, though it was also for Tom to establish that the Mad Bomber's prank creating ability hadn't lost a step over the summer.

"Wassamatta, chickenshits, scared to leave?"

Tom's crew never heckled their victims. All they cared about was the operation's high degree of complexity, and their precise control of it. That, and gaining a measure of release from the special build-up of anxieties and frustrations in college football players everywhere.

When the kick began to wear off, Skid asked if I'd care to join him for a snack at the University Center. Something in his tone told me I should go, so I agreed and we left.

Skid was the other redshirt tackle with Sir Henry, but his was a special case. Like Prosser, he was a transfer this season, but he enrolled here only because his previous school decided to drop football to focus on academics. He *had* to play out his transfer season as a redshirt.

This year he was a junior, and on his other team he was a starter at tackle as a sophomore. At 6-5, 250 pounds, he probably would have started for us, too. He was the biggest man on our team now, and a very good player.

When we ordered our burgers and settled at the counter to eat, Skid opened up. "I'm new here, so I don't really know who to talk to about this; but everyone seems to turn to you when they have a problem, so I figured I would, too."

"Sure," I mumbled, chewing my burger. "Fire away."

He fingered a saltshaker for a few moments, then his words poured out. "I think I'm losing my desire or ability or something. It's been downhill for me ever since they made me a redshirt, and now I'm getting worried about myself. I'm not sure, but I think it has to do with always having to hold back, always doing less than my best. I'm picking up bad habits now, and regularly dodging work."

"It's the universal redshirt dilemma," I said, offering the safest platitude I could think of. "It happens to all of you because you have to gear your game down to play it that half-assed way the coaches want you to play. But you'll get over it next year when you move up to the varsity."

He took a deep breath, then let it squeeze out slowly. "Problem is, I'm not sure that's what I want anymore."

This was serious. Once players—redshirts or varsity—started to question the system itself, and their place in it, the process of decay was practically irreversible.

"You see," he went on, "wherever I've been, I've never been less than a starter, because of my size if nothing else. I saw and received only the good things football has to offer, and there are great rewards when you're on top. But, Christ, man, looking from the bottom up like I've been doing . . . that gives you a whole new perspective!"

"Redshirts aren't as bad as you thought, eh?"

His big shoulders shrugged. "Some are, but I used to be convinced they *all* were a bunch of lazy screw-offs who didn't want or deserve to play because that's what the coaches always said about them. But that's not the way it is at all. Some of them want to play as bad as anyone, and several of them—especially Prosser—have more than enough ability. But someone got down on them at some point, for whatever reason, and they're just screwed."

"I know what you mean. Nothing sticks harder or longer than a bad rap on a football field, even if it's all wrong."

His head hung in silence, and I could see he was wrestling with more than what he'd already said. "Last year, before I transferred, this hot-shot high school tackle came in as a freshman. Big kid, and cocky, so the first thing the coaches did was put him in the chutes with me to see if he could back it up. I blew him out about ten times in a row, and it got easier and easier each time. The easier it got, the more I punished him, and by the end he was dodging like a squirrel on a rifle range. It was pathetic."

Skid paused to look off into the distance, visiting a blot on his record that he still hadn't come to terms with. "He was an eighteen-year-old kid, away from home, probably scared to death, going against an older, bigger, tougher guy at a really important moment. And sure enough, the coaches judged him once and forever on that first day's performance. He never got another chance, and he never got his confidence back. He might have been great if the coaches handled him right, but we ruined him and he quit a few weeks later. I'll always feel bad about that."

Skid stared hard at his Coke glass while I said nothing, knowing he had to find a way out of that one by himself.

"Anyway," he went on, "It's bad enough that I believed he was weak just because the coaches said so. Now I realize it's what I *wanted* to believe. I *wanted* to feel superior to him because it made me feel like a winner. But now I'm in that kid's shoes, stuck behind the redshirt eightball, and I can see how wrong it was, what I did to him."

"*You* didn't do that to him, Skid, *they* did. They used you to serve their own screwed-up ends."

He shrugged and nodded, but I knew no platitude from me would ever let him off that particularly painful hook. It was one of those things he'd have to learn to live with.

***

We were returning to the dorm when we met Tom, Swede, and Wizard on their way out.

"We were coming to the U.C. to find you guys," Tom said without breaking stride. "Time Bomb just called to say he needs some jocks to help juice a Kappa Sig rush party."

"Do you owe him a favor?"

"No, but now he'll owe me one. Can you come?"

Fraternities used rush parties to entice rushees to become pledges. Willing coeds were recruited to provide companionship, and fraternity members did their utmost to convince rushees that their frat was "the wildest, raunchiest, goddamnedest frat in the whole friggin' universe!"

With enough hard liquor in their bellies and pretty girls on their arms, most rushees came to believe that about one fraternity or another, which kept the system going.

Kappa Sigs were known for being deep into debauchery, and their rush parties sometimes reached postmidnight depths later marveled at in hushed tones. We were understandably expectant as we approached their frat house.

"Sage, Everett, all of you, come in!" Time Bomb said, welcoming us. Time Bomb was an injured-out running back from my own class who was now the Kappa Sig president.

"Hey, everybody!" he called to the fifty or more people nearby. "Look who's here! The jock brigade!"

Frat members were always glad to see us during rush week, the theory being that we lent an air of potential menace to parties. Football players were known far and wide as the true hell-raisers on any campus, so our presence made the rushees think Kappa Sig was where bad-ass action *really* went down. Of course, our group of bad-asses was bent on trashing no more than a few beer cans.

We stepped inside and began to drift around, enduring introductions to various rushees. That was the price we all paid for having the run of the house and free booze any time we wanted it. I finally made my way to the backyard bar for a beer, and as I turned around, I got hit with a question I always hated to deal with.

"You came in with the football players," a good-looking coed said with a smile. "What position do you play?"

"I'm, uhh, not really a player," I answered, unable to suppress the shame I always felt when I had to admit that to any stranger. "I'm the team manager."

She looked shocked. "You're the water boy?"

"That's another way of putting it, I guess."

"But you're so *big!* Why don't you play?"

"I used to," I said, a little too quickly.

"Well, what happened?"

"I got hurt."

"Oh," she said, turning away.

Well before midnight, Tom and I decided to leave.

Tom was that rare bird on a football team, a guy who was invariably faithful to his girlfriend back home, while I had Carla, the best thing that ever happened to me. So with no regrets, the two of us left the others to their fun.

"Are you in any hurry to get home?" Tom asked as we headed from fraternity row back toward the campus.

"Not really. I told Carla I'd try to be in before midnight, but I'm sure she's asleep by now. Why?"

"I have to check out the Rabbit action that's going down tomorrow. Want to come along?"

"Sure," I said, without hesitation. Tom seldom offered sneak previews to coming attractions.

At the dorm, Tom put his hand on Rabbit's doorknob and told me to brace myself. I did so and he swung it open.

"Oh, for God's sake!" I yelped. "What a mess!"

Big Dick, who was also Rabbit's roommate, calmly looked up from his seat on the floor. "No shit, Sherlock."

The room was filled with every manner of automobile parts and pieces, which could have come from only one car in the entire world—Rabbit's pale blue Triumph TR-4.

"That's right," Tom said as he read my mind. "Rabbit's little baby has come to pay him a visit."

"You mean you're planning to just *leave* it like this?" I

asked unbelievingly. "Completely torn up?"

Grant Heape scratched his curly brown hair. "It was a toss-up after we broke it down and got all the parts up here. Man, that frame was tough!"

Heape was the redshirt wingback, and his labor in this was more than simple loyalty to Tom. If not for Rabbit's charmed existence at third team wingback, Heape would be on the varsity with a good chance of lettering. He made no effort to hide his negative feelings toward Rabbit.

"Now we think we can reassemble it by the time he gets back," Butch Colley said, finishing Heape's sentence.

Colley was the other second team safety along with Big Dick, and also Heape's roommate. The three of them were our team's top mechanics bonded by their intrests in cars and motorcycles. Heape and Colley kept Colley's very old bucket-of-bolts MG running, while Big Dick could disassemble a motorcycle as fast as many Hell's Angels.

Big Dick was as close to a buddy as Prosser had developed on the team. He told me they'd talked about motorcycles a few times, when Big Dick was sure no coaches were around—or any of their stoolies.

Stoolies were players who would snitch on anyone doing anything wrong, or outside the myriad rules, in the hope it would curry favor and improve their positions.

"Why isn't Prosser here?" I asked. "He would have been handy with a job like this."

Big Dick shrugged. "I invited him, but he had plans to meet with some professor he came here to study with."

"Scott Brown," I said. "A specialist in classical philosophy. Prosser told me he's very well known in that field."

"Yeah, whatever. . . ." Big Dick replied. "We can do it without him, so no big deal."

"Will the whole thing fit in here?" I asked.

Heape smiled. "Like a glove between the beds.

"We measured it to the millimeter," Colley added.

"Then do it," Tom said. "But get some sleep first, okay?"

Big Dick nodded. "We'll be back on it bright and early."

"And the girl?" Colley asked Tom. "You're still sure she's good until 5:00 tomorrow afternoon?"

Tom smiled. "Don't worry, she's an old friend of Swede's from high school. It's all taken care of."

"She was *your* doing?" I said delightedly.

"None other than," Heape said on Tom's behalf. "You don't think a bozo like Rabbit could score something as hot as her on his own, do you?"

I didn't see it happen, but I heard about it at the rush party. When Rabbit left the dressing room after the scrimmage, a stunning blonde no one had ever seen before walked up to him, threw her arms around his neck and laid a deep, soulful kiss on him. Then she turned and led him by the hand to a waiting red Corvette.

Everyone who saw it agreed that Rabbit seemed stunned by her actions, but she supposedly acted like he was her long lost love. Rabbit came from money, so it was easy for him to talk girls into a date. However, his track record showed that few made the same mistake twice.

"Do you mean to tell me that a dish is sleeping with Rabbit tonight just so you can have the time to do this?" I couldn't imagine such a sacrifice, even for an old friend.

"In a way," Tom said. "She'll pull the 'having my period' routine. But he'll sleep at her place tonight and stay with her all day tomorrow, even if he has to sleep on the floor."

"He'll do it because he'll want us to believe he scored with her," Big Dick said. "He'd sleep in her yard tonight if she wouldn't let him stay in her apartment."

Heape nodded. "Sounds locked in all the way."

SUNDAY

I was so used to getting up early, I couldn't sleep past 6:00, so I left Carla sleeping and went to the U.C. to get some breakfast, and to see if anyone on the team was up and about that early. As I reached the front entrance, I noticed the Bull being let out of an unfamiliar sedan. He was having difficulty staying upright on his crutches.

"Who's that?" I asked as the car pulled away.

"Someone named Shirley," he said woozily.

Up close his looks explained everything. He was snockered. "Quite a night, huh?"

"I'm not sure . . . I don't remember much of it. You seen Quink? He may know what happened."

I doubted it. Quink and the Bull were equal in drinking capacity, and neither had an edge in drunken rationality, but Quink was the driving force behind their escapades. If the Bull drank himself into a stupor, Quink set the pace.

"I haven't seen him, but I'm going inside for some breakfast. You should join me for some coffee, too. You wouldn't believe how your eyes look."

"Feels like the sandpaper fairy paid a visit."

The Bull struggled up to a counter seat while I went to get some eggs and grits and toast, and a couple of coffees. When I put the tray down on the counter, it made a bit of clatter, the sound of which caused him to wince.

"Sorry," was all I could say.

I let him take a few sips before I asked what happened. He took another sip, then began speaking in the slow, modulated tones that distinguish a true hangover victim.

"It began like usual . . . at Las Ramblas."

Las Ramblas was a five room downtown bar heavily trafficked by students and would-be swingers.

"Quink and I had a few beers that turned into boilermakers. After a while, we started talking to this table full of really raunchy-looking babes, six or seven of them.

"Quink started shining them on, saying we were a pair of thieves planning to steal Plymouth Rock to hold hostage for millions. It was all just in fun. They were so bad, everyone else was ignoring them, so we moved in for a few laughs. I'm sure we didn't intend to pick up any of them."

"Or get yourselves picked up?"

"Whatever. All I remember is going to their table and talking for a while. Beyond that, pretty much a blank."

I felt myself starting to get angry, which I promptly throttled back. I'd never been able to understand why quality guys like Quink and the Bull would risk so much for so little, but it wasn't my place to be a parent to any of them.

"You know," I said offhandedly, "getting so wasted is dangerous. I know God is supposed to watch over all drunks, but shouldn't you meet Him halfway on the deal?"

"Yeah, I know . . . it worries me sometimes."

Unlike Quink, who attacked life even more like the bull in a china shop that gave Ken his nickname, the Bull had the capacity to consider consequences of actions. His problem was in judging his limits—or admitting them.

Feeling sorry for him, I spoke without thinking. "You want something to eat?"

He looked stricken and almost gagged.

"Never mind," I added, changing the subject. "Was that one of the boilermaker girls who brought you here?"

"I don't think so," he said with a gentle shake of his head. "She was good-looking . . . wasn't she?"

I nodded. "What did she have to say about last night?"

"She was sure she started at Las Ramblas, too."

"No need to go any further, you sound like a perfect match. Where did you sleep?"

"In the front seat of her car. It looked like we'd been trying to get it on when we passed out. You know how it is when you're drunk and you lay down—you just drift off."

We noticed Wheeler enter the room, which was starting to fill with other students looking like they'd gone through wringers similar to the Bull's. For all of them it seemed to be a First Saturday back to remember, but Wheeler was smiling and whistling cheerfully as he joined us.

"How goes it, sports fans?" he asked, then got a close-up of the Bull's haggard features. "Ohhhh, you too, huh?"

The Bull looked up. "Quink's in already?"

"About an hour ago."

"Did he know what we did last night?"

"He said he couldn't remember. Said he woke up on the hallway floor of a girl's dorm, with a big pair of blue panties stuck in one front pocket and a small pair of pink ones in the other. He has no idea how they got there."

All that talk about sex, consummated or not, drove me back to rejoin Carla in bed at our apartment. Besides, I didn't need to be anywhere until the lunch being prepared for a few of us by Annie Slade.

At 12:30, I met Tom and Wheeler at the dorm so we could walk to Don and Annie's apartment and arrive by 1:00. However, one of our party was missing in action.

"Did the Bull have to cancel?" I asked.

"Not that I heard," Wheeler said. "But he should if he still looks anything like Quink. Those two are morons."

Wheeler was one of those guys who tended to swallow everything the coaches said about how to achieve success in football, so he went along with their black-and-white mentality. Gray areas and contradictions confused him. People who could flagrantly break rules and still play well were more than his narrow view could accommodate.

"Speak of the devil," Wheeler said, as the Bull hobbled shakily from the elevator. "We thought you'd bagged it."

"Annie would kill me," the Bull said, "and I'd expect all of you to kill anything she didn't get to."

"We better get a move on," I put in.

We set off with the Bull grimly swinging like a pendulum between his crutches. Halfway there, Tom asked Wheeler about Stoner. "You think you're ready for him?"

"Yes, no thanks to your little inspirational messages!"

"How do you plan to handle him?" I asked.

"Just like I'm taught. I'll fire out hard and stick my cage in his numbers, then slide my helmet up into his chin."

"If you pull any cheap shots on him, he'll tear your head off and shit down your neck stump," Tom warned. "He's All-American, don't forget. You better show respect."

"The coaches say no one comes at him straight up and hard anymore because they're all afraid. So I might get him off balance and make him less sure of himself."

"It'll only piss him off," Tom countered.

"All I can do is play the game the way I know how to play it," Wheeler insisted. "I plan to go all out on every snap, and I'll take it to him as hard as I possibly can. If I do that, I'll do all right. I mean, the guy's not Superman, for Chrissake! He puts his pants on the same way I do."

"Yeah, but his are about twice the size of yours," the Bull reminded him.

"So is his ego," Wheeler countered. "All I have to do is make it a point to expunge his ersatz hubris."

"*What?*" the Bull croaked.

English major Wheeler smiled. "Look it up, Einstein."

ANNIE'S LUNCH

Annie opened the door and flashed the huge smile that lit up everywhere she went. She was a blond pixie with the energy of a giant, and we didn't even have time to say hello before she was chattering at us nonstop.

"I knew it was you guys, so I beat Don to the door! Come on in and let me fondle you!"

She gave us all a big hug and then a kiss on the cheek. "What men!" she crowed. "What men I have in my house! I love it! If the girls back home could only see me now!"

We hung our heads and scuffed at the rug like bashful boys. Annie invariably humbled us while delighting us.

"Come on, guys, take seats. Especially you, Ken. You look like something the cat drug in."

"I feel like something the cat wouldn't *have*," the Bull said, hobbling to a chair with a footrest.

"Big night, huh?"

"Don't ask."

"I have just the thing for you," Annie assured him. She hustled over to the refrigerator and pulled out a six-pack. "A little hair of the dog for the Bull!"

"Hey, Annie," Wheeler said, "where's Don?"

"Powdering his nose, dear," she replied, then lowered her eyebrows mock-serious. "But don't go in after him without a *box* of matches. We had chili last night, and I swear, Don's farts can actually make your eyes sting!"

Annie lacked pretension on a grand scale. No phony modesty or any other cutesy behavior. She was a straight-on, up-front, full-grown woman at nineteen. We loved her.

"No, seriously," she went on about Don's toilet habits. "You know how most people slip farts around and then out?" She made a swimming motion with her hands. "Don drives 'em right on through!" She drove a left jab at us for emphasis, which practically put us on the floor.

Don picked just then to walk into the room to join us. "Hey, guys, what's all the laughing about?"

We laughed harder and then began pointing at him. He grinned sheepishly, then he, too, began to laugh. We laughed even harder at him laughing with us laughing *at* him, and it got totally out of hand in about ten seconds.

We started holding our noses and waving imaginary matches at Don's rear, in general acting like huge grade-school children. The whole time, Annie stood behind the kitchen counter, grinning hugely between slugs of beer.

"God, I love you guys! I really, truly *love* you guys!"

The meal itself was Annie's version of Thanksgiving dinner for ten: baked turkey with giblet dressing, cranberry sauce, fresh green beans, fried cauliflower, cornbread, yams, bean salad and enough beer and wine to have us weaving over our plates by the time dessert came.

"Baked apples a' la mode." Annie beamed.

"Jesus, Annie," the Bull moaned, "I can't eat any more. Honest, I'm about to pop. I was queasy when I got here."

Annie looked down at him and said, very sweetly, "Ohhhh, you think you've had too much? Well, then, we'll just take it right away so you won't even be tempted."

The rest of us began to hoot as Annie took his dessert, and a blushing Bull turtle-headed into his shirt collar.

Annie quickly turned about and sprang to his defense. "You boys stop making fun of Kenny!" she snapped like a teacher. "He can't help it if he's a candy-ass."

Ahhhh, Annie. . . . The Crawdad was the Crawdad, but she was our unofficial mascot.

Naturally, Don came to witness Rabbit's reaction to finding his car in his room. We arrived there just before 5:00 to find Big Dick, Heape, Colley, and a couple dozen others loitering in open doorways along the hall.

"How is it?" Tom asked chief mechanic Heape.

"See for yourself. We finished an hour ago."

It was all there, jammed between the beds, a completely assembled TR-4. Crammed into that small room, it looked like a whale in an aquarium.

"Oh, Christ," I couldn't help muttering. "He's gonna turn purple when he sees it like that."

Looking guilty, Colley held up a canvas gym bag and rattled it for emphasis. "We, ahhh, couldn't find places for a few parts. He'll turn purple about that, too."

We all laughed, then Tom focused on Big Dick. "You know what to say to him, right?"

"I have it down cold."

We waited for Rabbit while exchanging accounts of the previous night, some believable, many not. Quink finally got around to asking Helmet what he did. Every player was well aware of the quality breeding Helmet's dates displayed, and there was a never-ending effort to find out where and how he found such refined women.

"I go to a party with friends," Helmet replied, which I knew was true because he invited me to it.

"Was it an orgy?" Peso Rodriguez asked.

Peso was a third team nose guard from El Paso, a guy who grew up dirt poor but with plenty of smarts and enough football talent to get to Cajun State. He maintained the enduring belief that wealth and style assured unlimited decadence, which was one of many reasons he wanted to become rich, and probably would.

"No, never!" Helmet said indignantly. Then, to me, "What gives him this idea always?"

"Jealousy," I suggested. "Pure jealousy."

That was only partly true, but if anyone deserved to be envied, it was Helmut Moedle.

His father was a diplomat posted to several different countries while Helmet grew up. That rearing gave him fluency in five languages and a social development light years beyond anything the rest of us could ever hope to achieve. On top of that were his good looks, matched by unshakable inner confidence, all of which he carried without giving offense to anyone—except our coaches. To them, Helmet was nothing more than a Prosser who had been gifted with one lucky break.

Two years ago, Helmet transferred to Cajun State from Heidelberg University to take advantage of our topflight Latin American Studies program. One fall afternoon, he happened by a football practice session and watched our inept crew of placekickers flailing away from forty yards out. He marched right up to our kicking coach and boldly announced to them all, *"This,* I can do."

He proceeded to lace five in a row through the uprights from forty yards out—in street shoes! Three days later, Helmet kicked a forty-seven-yard field goal in the first American football game he ever saw. He also kicked two shorter ones, and from that day to this he was the most publicized and valuable member of our team.

Unfortunately for the coaches, that debut put Helmet above criticism and retribution before they fully understood who and what he was. In addition to his wondrous right leg, developed during years as a soccer whiz in Europe, he came with a fully developed sense of himself. Also, his foreign upbringing left him with utter disregard for the sanctities of American football tradition.

The coaches had no leverage over him because they needed him badly, and he didn't need them at all. If they had any notion of the problems that turnaround would cause them, they would have handled him like Prosser and others who don't fit—they'd have dumped him before knowledge of his talent expanded beyond their control.

Now, though, Helmet was well established as our best player, and the coaches had no choice but to appear to accept him. They took full advantage of their eccentric "Krauthead" prodigy's skills, but otherwise ignored him as much as possible. They also tried to save face by insisting he was a specialist who in no way could be considered a "real" football player. After all, a real player could never hope to be successful with his kind of carefree attitude.

That rationalization was understandable because Helmet was living proof they based their professional lives on fabricated bullshit. He was also a prime reason our coaching staff, of all staffs in the country, would be skittish about taking on another "problem" like Pete Prosser.

HIGHS AND LOWS

At 5:15, Rabbit came bopping down the hall, snapping his fingers, beaming happily, filled with the joyous energy and false pride of his faked accomplishment.

"Where you been?" Big Dick snapped at him.

"With a babe!" Rabbit gloated. "All night and all day!"

Big Dick pointed dramatically to their room, raging at him: "Explain *that,* asshole!"

Puzzled by his roommate's inexplicable fury, his steps became halting as he uneasily edged toward their room.

"Go on!" Big Dick commanded. "Take a look!"

Rabbit stepped into view of the room and his jaw flew open in thunderstruck shock, dismay, and disbelief.

Big Dick was all over him. "Listen, Darryl, I know you love that car, but you can *not* keep it parked in *here.*"

Rabbit could only stare, goggle-eyed, as his hands slowly lifted to cover his gaping mouth.

"Can't you see there's no room now?" Big Dick went on, as if this were merely an argument between roommates. "We can't even pull our beds away from the wall! Where are we gonna *sleep?* Did you stop to think about *that?*"

"But . . . but. . . ."

"This is the *last* straw! Either park that thing back outside, or get a new roommate! I'm not gonna live with your damn car in here as a four-wheeled third wheel!"

Big Dick stormed down the hall and out the door at the end of it, followed by the rest of us. Rabbit didn't even notice. When the last of us left the hall, he was still rooted to the same spot as when he first laid eyes on his car.

"But . . . but. . . ."

When Rabbit's moment was duly honored by hilarious reenactments and mimicking of his walleyed reaction, we said our goodbyes and went our separate ways. I swung by the infirmary to visit Sir Henry, knowing he'd appreciate seeing someone who would sympathize with his raw deal.

Only a few, if any, of his friends would have dropped by to see him this soon after the surgery on his shoulder. An important part of being able to play football is keeping the possible consequences well out your mind. It doesn't help much to see a buddy lying broken in a bed.

***

When I arrived at Sir Henry's room, his parents were there. Some parents could drop everything when something like this happened, but others worked at jobs that required arranging an emergency leave. That's how it was when my knee went. My parents couldn't get off until the following weekend. Hank's parents, though, were farmers, so they could manage their schedule enough to come be with him for a while at this difficult time.

Sir Henry introduced us and we exchanged the usual polite phrases for a while. Finally, I asked Hank how he was feeling, and if there was anything I could do for him.

"Yeah," he said in a grieved tone. "You could explain to my parents why I have to quit because of this."

"Now, son," his father interjected, "there's no need to air our dirty laundry in front of anyone."

"Sage isn't just anyone, Dad. He's one of my best friends in this place. Please . . . just listen to him."

"Now, now, Hank," his mother added, "this is a family matter and we'll settle it ourselves."

"What's to settle? I'm quitting and that's that."

"But, son," his father said, "how can you throw away all the sacrifices we had to make to get you on this team?"

Sir Henry flinched at his father's words.

"And what about our friends back home?" His mother pleaded. "What can we tell them?"

"Listen, I told you and now Sage can tell you: my career as a football player here is *over.* My shoulder is wrecked, so I'll never make the varsity, or ever even play again. I might as well become a manager and try to be happy with that."

His father turned anguished eyes toward me, while his mother silently pleaded for support I couldn't give.

"He's upset about his shoulder right now," his father said. "He'll change his mind when it gets better, won't he?"

I glanced at Sir Henry. It was clear he wouldn't.

Quitting is always a two-part process that first involves the player, and then his parents. Players come to think of themselves as among the chosen few, and parents get hooked on the reflected glory. All three have to give up some powerfully addictive status, and one of the saddest parts of a miserable process is that for as hard as players take it, their parents often take it even harder.

"I'm afraid there's no going back, Mr. Wolf," I said. "Once you quit, you quit. That's it. Over."

"But it's such a waste!" his mother groaned.

It was time to deliver an exit speech I'd given several times before, in one form or another.

"Mr. and Mrs. Wolf, please try to accept and understand that Hank is going through two traumatic experiences right now. His injury is bad enough, but he also has to face up to quite a few failed expectations. Please don't make it any harder on him than it has to be.

"You both should be very proud of him and of what he accomplished here, but now he's going to need your help and support like never before. Trust me, he gave all he had trying to live up to what everyone back home expected of him. It would be nice if you could do the same for him."

Sir Henry couldn't speak just then, but tear-brimmed eyes eloquently expressed his thanks.

"I'm going to recommend that he be kept on as a manager like me," I told them. "To replace me, actually."

"My son is a *football* player!" his father barked at me, "just like I was! He ain't no goddamn water boy!"

Like I said, parents often take it the hardest.

Carla and I had dinner in the apartment because, in addition to her stunning good looks, she could rival Annie at cooking. In fact, I think Annie's lunch spurred her to extra effort in retaliation. She laid out a beautiful Italian spread built around her incredible lasagna.

During dinner I told her about Tom's prank with Rabbit's car, complete with me mimicking Rabbit's gobsmacked expression as well as I could match it, which had her almost choking with laughter. Then I leavened that with Sir

Henry's sad tale, which she saw as a positive.

"He's a lot like you, Larry, so he'll become an excellent manager for the team. And downstream he'll make the absolute most of his free education."

"It's not exactly free," I reminded her.

"You know what I mean."

Later, cleaning up the kitchen, the phone rang. It was Tom with news from the team's always-active grapevine.

"The Bull was in the training room getting his ankle worked on. He overheard Hanson tell Cap'n the coaches ordered quit drills for Prosser tomorrow. It's definite."

Even though I had expected this for days, my stomach still flipped at the finality—and potential horror—of it.

"You've seen it before, haven't you?" he asked.

"Yeah, twice. When I was a freshman, a flanker on our squad had ability and an attitude like Prosser. Another Army brat, actually. In the second drill they broke a rib that punctured a lung. The other guy was a jerk nobody liked, a troublemaking bully of a linebacker. He had something coming; if not quit drills, then something else."

"What happened to him?"

"Broke his tailbone. As long as he lives, he won't sit comfortably, and I'm not sorry for him. The guy was psycho."

There was silence on the other end of the line for several seconds, then Tom said, "It's time to have a heart-to-heart with Prosser. I'm doing it. Will you come with me?"

Even though I was not supposed to get involved in cases like this, I was thinking along the same line. Something about Prosser drew involvement out of me. His talent was so incredibly special, I wanted to protect it if I could.

"Absolutely. I'll be there in twenty minutes."

I hung up and Carla asked, "What's wrong?"

"Quit drills for Prosser tomorrow. Definite. I'm going with Tom to try to talk him into quitting."

Carla didn't say a word. She knew what would happen if the coaches found out I'd interfered so blatantly, even if it served their ultimate purpose of getting rid of the thorn in their side. But she'd also heard me talk about Prosser enough to know this was the right thing for me to do.

ROCK AND HARD PLACE

If Prosser was in his room, he'd be alone because he and Helmet were assigned as roommates to start the new semester. The coaching strategy behind that was to keep rotten eggs in the same baskets. What it actually meant was that Prosser had a roommate in name only, because Helmet, like Stanton and me, primarily lived off-campus.

Helmet's fortunate circumstances allowed him to live in an elegant townhouse apartment several blocks away, He used his dorm room for occasional naps and such, but for the most part his roommate had exclusive use of the room assigned to them by the athletic department.

Now Prosser would be gone soon, and when he went, the room would be empty until someone else quit and created a player without a roommate. So Helmet's room was a kind of dumping ground for the lower rungs of the team ladder, the guys with the absolute poorest prospects.

It was ironic that the most famous Crawdad of all— though nowhere near the best football player—always had to room with guys on the way out. It was a good thing Helmet never got to know any of them very well. The constant loss of so many friends might have put a different slant on his otherwise positive outlook.

Tom and I had a vague plan of attack. We meant to double-team Prosser with the news about the quit drills being arranged for him tomorrow. If we could make him understand the absolute futility of trying to resist the will of the coaches, he'd quit now while he was still in one good piece. What he did after that would be up to him.

Tom knocked on his dorm door.

"Come in! It's not locked."

Tom opened the door to reveal Pete and another man sitting opposite each other on the two trundled beds that filled the bulk of space in dorm rooms. Along each wall was a closet, a bed, shelving above the bed that the bed tucked under, and a large study desk against a window.

Dorm rooms didn't provide much comfort, but they were functional and could be made more than bearable if you worked at it. Some of us made them downright homey.

In Prosser's case, the only major alteration he seemed to make was putting low-watt bulbs in the room's two study lamps. It was odd to see him dressed in shorts and a T-shirt without his shades on. I'd forgotten how eerie his pale eyes were, even in light that was dimmer than usual.

"Sage! Tom!" he said, with what sounded like genuine enthusiasm. "Nice to see you guys. What's up?"

"We, ahhhh. . . ." Tom gazed at the man on the other bed, who rose with Pete to greet us.

". . . we don't want to butt into anything," I finished for Tom. "We can come back later."

"No problem," Pete said, turning to his companion. "Guys, I want you to meet Dr. Scott Brown. He's the reason I'm at Cajun State. I think I told you that already, didn't I, Sage? The day I arrived for check-in?"

I nodded, then reached out to shake his hand, and Tom followed right behind me. "Pleased to meet you."

Scott Brown didn't look at all like like a philosophy professor. He had a square face with blunt, rough features and long hair frizzed around his head in a dark corona. It was a wrestler's face, complete with cauliflower ears, and the wild hair of a beatnik poet like Bob Dylan, resting atop a solid body that seemed like it could still win a match. He looked to be in his middle forties.

"Please feel free to join us," Dr. Brown said. "We were actually talking about football, not philosophy."

He said the last part with a wry grin to put us at ease.

"I'm a philosophy professor here," he said as an aside to Tom, so he would understand the unusual reference.

Pete motioned us to take seats at the foot of each bed, while he and Dr. Brown resumed seats near the pillows. I sat on Pete's bed, Dr. Brown and Tom sat on Helmet's.

"What part of football were you talking about?" Tom asked as we all got comfortable.

"Quitting," Pete replied. "Yesterday Sage said things to me that got me thinking about quitting, so I asked Scott if he'd drop by tonight and we'd try to kick it around a bit."

"What's to kick?" Tom asked. "No offense, but I don't see anything philosophical about quitting. When your turn comes, it comes, whether by injuries or just a bellyful of the crap coaches dish out when they want you gone."

Dr. Brown's frizzy head shook. "I disagree, Tom. When a football player quits, it's a pivotal moment in his life; not just in his life as a player, in his *real* life, and that life is something he knows nothing about until he finally quits."

He could tell that comment confused us.

"From the time you put on a helmet for the first time," he continued, "until you take it off for the last, everything that comes in between, all the highs and all the lows, provides a window dressing for your football life that makes it look wonderful to someone looking from the outside in. However, your inside perspective tells you it is, at its heart, without long-term substance."

He paused to gaze at Tom and me, making sure we were hearing and understanding him.

"So the bottom line is, everything you do prior to quitting is merely a prelude to the rest of your life. When that helmet comes off for the last time, *then* your actual real life begins. Thus, choosing to quit—if indeed you get to choose—is a decision that skews your life into an entirely different direction, into unknown territory. That's a primary reason quitting scares you so badly and keeps you hanging onto football long after you should give it up."

I assume Tom and I both looked as rattled as I felt. It wasn't often we heard our lifestyle dissected so expertly by someone who wasn't even one of us. *Or was he. . . ?*

"You sound like you played football," Tom guessed.

Dr. Brown smiled. "In high school. I was too slow to be a running back, so they put me at guard. I didn't have a guard's heart. I never could get my mind and body to work in sync toward being the best guard I could be, so in the middle of my senior season, I decided to quit and focus on wrestling. That brought me a scholarship, so I came out of it okay, but quitting football was a trauma.

"The biggest shock was to my family, especially my parents, but siblings and friends took it hard, too. Not my teammates, though. If anyone knows when you're really unhappy with the game and what it can do to you, it's your teammates. They know before anyone else does."

That, too, was true. This guy knew his stuff.

"The core issue for football players," he went on, "and what I was telling Pete when you arrived, is deciding how you want to live the life you enter after you quit, whether that's in high school, college, or even pro. For most young people, it's extremely difficult to look ahead, especially far ahead. However, for college football players that difficulty increases exponentially because for a decade or more, half of your life, football is all you've known as an expression of your core identity, of who you feel you are.

"If someone asks you to define yourself, 'football player' is always at the head of the list. Nothing else compares with it, not even close. Not son or brother, friend or enemy, student or artist or musician, or any other interest or hobby you might have. What are you? You're a football player, first, last, and always. Right?"

Tom, Pete, and I nodded dutifully, even though I hadn't been able to honestly say that for three years. In my mind and in my heart, as long as I stayed closely attached to the team, I remained a member of it, a player of sorts.

"For any human being, it can be difficult beyond imagining to give up something as precious and meaningful as your identity. Yet that *is* what we're talking about losing, isn't it? The only real *identity* you've ever known for yourself. Superficially, there can be nothing tougher to give up than that . . . until you stop and think about it."

We were now hanging on every word. This guy wasn't just good, he was eerily on target.

"What we all bring to the party—what I brought, too—is our body, the skills our body provides, our intelligence, our passion for the game, and our spirit, which overrides everything and makes us all who we are on the field.

"When your spirit is whole and firm, you're invulnerable, you can't be touched by anything. Nobody can cause you to doubt yourself. You can't be defeated. You can be beat on the scoreboard, but not defeated, never defeated, if only your spirit can stay intact. This, I think, is what football coaches never seem able to grasp."

He faded into his own thoughts, giving us an insight into what his own high school experience must have been like. But then he gathered himself and continued.

"The absolute most valuable thing any young player brings to the game is his spirit. If his spirit is sound, he is sound. If his spirit is weak or broken, he can't be a fraction as competitive as he might have been. Yet, invariably, coaches set out to do what the military readily acknowledges doing: they try to destroy every individual spirit, to shatter it into pieces that they think makes it easier to manipulate people to do what they want them to do.

"That, of course, does make their jobs easier because they're right; it's *much* easier to manipulate a player with a broken spirit than it is to deal with one who hasn't been thoroughly tamed yet. It goes back to the cowboys, really. The first thing they did to a headstrong stallion or mare was to break them down, break their spirits."

"No," Tom interrupted. "You're wrong. They treat us a *lot* worse than most cowboys treat their rankest horses."

Tom grew up in the country on his family's ranch, so he knew his animals, especially horses.

"Horses are a metaphor," Dr. Brown explained. "I'm sure you get the gist of my meaning."

Tom nodded. "I get it."

"My point is that a team full of unbroken spirits would be unbeatable, even in defeat. They'd come back the next week as if the previous defeat didn't happen. Unbroken spirits won't wilt under any kind of adversity or pressure."

We all nodded agreement with that wisdom.

"From what Pete says about his situation, I can assume he has the kind of spirit that annoys coaches instead of heartening them. They'd rather he have a broken spirit.

"They're way past caring about his spirit," I put in. "They're going after his body—tomorrow."

Pete stared at me. "It's for sure? Quit drills?"

Tom and I both nodded somberly.

"What are quit drills?" Dr. Brown asked.

Tom deferred to me on that one. "When a guy won't take any other hint that his scholarship needs to be returned, quit drills are arranged. They're specifically designed to hurt, and hurt seriously. Usually just knowing they're coming is enough to make a target quit. Sometimes, though, they're hardheads about it, or they think they're invincible and can be the one person to survive them."

I glanced at Pete to see if he might be imagining himself as magically endowed. His eerie pale eyes didn't blink, his gaze never wavered. I couldn't tell what was going on in his head, but I wanted to be certain he heard me.

"You can't win this, Pete; you can't even put up a good fight. All you'll do is end up seriously hurt, something you don't need to happen when it's so easily preventable. All you have to do is give the damn coaches what they want."

"It's suicide to go through with it," Tom added.

"No, gentlemen," Dr. Brown put in. "Socrates faced real suicide when the Athenian government sentenced him to death. Then his friends bribed his guards to arrange his escape, and he could have gone that route, but he didn't. He stayed and drank hemlock rather than let the bureaucrats of his day force him to renounce who he was."

"I hope you're not suggesting I take poison!" Pete said with a tight smile, trying to lighten the room's grim mood.

"It's another metaphor," Dr. Brown said. "But in a sense, Socrates' choice is yours, too. Escape with your friends," he nodded at Tom and me, "or drink the hemlock."

Rather than harden, as did Tom's expression and mine, Pete's turned inquisitive. He leaned toward Dr. Brown. "Why would I—or Socrates—choose to drink hemlock?"

"I can't speak for you, Pete," he replied. "Nobody can. But in the dialogue with Crito, Plato tells us that Socrates chose death rather than continuing his life under the restrictions he'd be forced to accept. For him, life wasn't worth living if he had to live it according to the rules and restrictions laid down for him by his persecutors."

"He didn't want his spirit broken," Pete said.

"That's one way to look at it," Dr. Brown agreed.

"Then it's a broken body or a broken spirit," Tom put in sourly. "A helluva choice to have to make."

Pete focused on him with a dead-level stare. "A broken body will heal. I'm not sure about a broken spirit."

That was all I could take. "Don't be stupid, Pete!" I snapped, with a lot more heat behind it than I intended. "A broken neck *won't* heal! A knee like mine *won't* heal!"

"Maybe not," he said agreeably, "but that's a risk we all take every time we suit up . . . every single day."

"Yes, but if you suit up tomorrow, you'll be *asking* for it!"

"If I don't suit up, I could carry the emotional equivalent of a broken neck inside myself for the rest of my life. I don't think I want that. I wouldn't want to live like that."

Tom looked at Dr. Brown with a pleading expression. "Please, Dr. Brown, talk him out of it if you can."

"I can't and I won't," was his reply. "It's Pete's decision to make, and he should consider *all* aspects of it."

Pete nodded acceptance of that obligation, then spoke.

"I'm new to classical philosophy, but eastern masters, our *sensei,* teach that fear is the greatest weakness in life because it's the greatest obstacle to true happiness.

"Yanaguchi teaches that it's good to know fear, to be aware of it and sometimes to wrestle with it. But it should not be allowed into one's inner circle of power. If fear lodges there, it's a burr that clings and resists being removed."

He paused to gaze at all three of us, making it clear how seriously he was taking this. "I have to admit, in all honesty, that tonight I truly am wrestling with fear."

"Let it win," Tom said. "Please. Let it lodge. Better that than what those bastards might do to you."

Pete suddenly rose from the bed, indicating it was time for us to go. "I want to thank you all for coming over tonight. It's been very instructive for me. Now, though, I'd like some time alone to meditate and think it all over."

We said hurried, uncomfortable goodbyes, and in a few minutes Tom and me and Dr. Brown stood awkwardly in the dorm's elevator. Tom punched the button for one floor down and waited in silence until the doors opened.

"See you tomorrow, Sage," he said, then turned to Dr. Brown for a last word. "And you . . . thanks for nothing."

Dr. Brown and I remained silent for the final five floors, then the doors opened and we walked toward the point outside where we'd go separate ways. Finally, he spoke to me.

"Tell me, Larry, do you feel the same as Tom?"

"Yes, I do. I think that Socrates crap swung him toward suiting up, which could be a disaster if he does."

"Maybe in the short term, but you and Tom wouldn't have visited him tonight if you didn't think he's as special as I do. Ones like him come along very, very rarely. When they do, they have to be nurtured and preserved."

"You're not trying to preserve him!" I snapped.

"I am, but not in the way you want me to because I don't think of him as the football player he is now. I see him as the great scholar and teacher he'll be a decade from now."

"But what if they blow a knee, or tear up a shoulder, or, God forbid, break his neck? Can you live with that on your conscience? With knowing you egged him on? And how would he live with it, knowing it didn't have to happen?"

He stopped walking, so I did too. "No matter what injury they inflict on him, he'll leave the game with his pride intact. But you and Tom . . . you're asking him to leave with his tail between his legs. Is that *really* a good idea?"

"Are you saying it's better to *limp* away from football, maybe permanently injured, than to *walk* away from it?"

"In the right circumstances, yes, it could be better."

It was all I could do to keep from punching him. "You don't know what you're talking about, you stupid asshole!"

Then I turned and left him, as conscious of my own slight limp as I had ever been in my life.

MONDAY

The first day of the regular-season practice schedule meant I didn't have to bother with any more early wake-ups. It was also the first day of the fall semester, my last, so 9:00 a.m. found me starting my final crip course as an undergraduate, the Romantic Poets—Keats, Byron, and Shelley—seated next to Big Dick.

I asked him how he and Rabbit made out in their new accommodations last night. There was no way for them to sleep in their room with the car in it, so Don gave him the spare key to the room Stanton and I shared *in absentia.*

Big Dick smirked. "About like any other night until the dipthongs arrived. Things picked up a little after that."

"How did *they* find out?"

"Around midnight, Tom called them and said a guy had a car parked in his room. He had to use three different voices before they'd believe it enough to come over and check it out. When they got there and found it was the truth, they reacted like you'd expect. Tom told them we were sleeping in your room, so they came down, rousted us both out of bed, and raked Rabbit over the coals."

"They blamed *him*?" I exclaimed in a hushed whisper so our new semester's classmates wouldn't hear. "They thought *he* put his own car in there like that?"

Big Dick smirked again. "Geeze, Tom, dipthongs can't figure the instructions for a roll of toilet paper."

"Point taken. So what happened then?"

"When they started hollering at him, Rabbit just stood there sputtering, spraying spit, trying to get some coherent words out, so they got even madder at him because they thought he was being a wise ass. And the more they hollered at him, the more Rabbit panicked and choked up, until I had to step in and explain it for him."

"What did you say?"

"I told them it was an evil trick someone played on us for some reason. They know a lot of crazy pranks go on around here, especially starting a new semester when students have free time before the grind starts. But then, to top it off, I told them Rabbit's old man had arranged to have two mechanics come over from Mobile. I promised them it would be back on the street in a couple of days."

Rabbit's father owned, among many other things, four or five automobile agencies in his home state of Alabama, so Tom knew from the inception of the car caper that in the end there would be no real problems caused by it.

"Did the mechanics get here yet?"

"His father told him they'd be here by noon."

Suddenly, an idea struck. "Maybe you could find out from those guys the how and the why behind Rabbit and his scholarship. There *has* to be an explanation for why he's here, and for why the coaches never hassle him."

"Tom and Heape already suggested that," he muttered as our professor walked into the classroom.

***

As lunch aproached, everyone on the team wanted to see if Prosser would show up. If he was quitting, he'd do it before classes started, so he wouldn't be here for lunch.

As Tom and I feared, he came in and chose food like the rest of us, then sat at a table with three other suddenly uneasy guys looking to see who might be looking at them.

For my part, I couldn't imagine how he could eat anything. It was like the last meal before an execution. How could he possibly have any appetite? Yet, he did eat.

We all stole furtive glances at him until Big Dick leaned over to me and spoke softly but intently. "Today is my first day back in pads. You think they'll make me take part?"

I knew he and Prosser were becoming buddies due to their shared interest in motorcycles. Even so, I had to tell the truth. "They'll say you're rusty and need extra work."

His expression soured, which was understandable because, for as bad as quit drills were on the receiving end, the giving end was no better if you had normal feelings.

"What do you think they'll start with?" Grant Heape asked, keeping his voice low so Prosser couldn't hear it.

"They'll never get rid of him with two-on-ones or three-on-ones," I said softly. "Those would be a waste of time."

"That's right," Butch Colley agreed. "He's like a damn *vapor* out there. You never get a solid shot on him."

"You will today," I assured them, wishing it wasn't true but knowing it couldn't be avoided.

I went to the equipment shed to "dress out" for practice. For managers like me and Stanton, that consisted of putting on an official Cajun State polo shirt with the Fightin' Crawdad logo on the left breast pocket. All of those shirts were white, and we were given three each to wear as cleaning requirements dictated. Our pants and shoes were always our choice. Nobody cared.

There were no lockers in the equipment shed, just hooks along a wall with your name hand-printed on a piece of athletic tape stuck to the wall above it. That made it easy to remove and swap it out for someone else taking your place. In football, at every level, the whole system was set up so that people were *easy come, easy go.*

"Some of your boys dodged a bullet today," Cap'n said to me and Chris Stanton as we got ourselves ready.

Stanton was like me, an ex-player with a blown knee. I got mine in a pileup, which was common enough, but he got his on a crackback block from a flanker, which was *very* common; so common, in fact, that there was talk of actually outlawing it as a legal block. Nobody would be happier about that than linebackers and defensive ends. They were the crackback's victims 90% of the time.

"What kind of bullet, Cap'n?" Stanton asked. He was a pre-law major, definitely on his way to making an impact somewhere. He was smart, minded his own business, and always got his work done without complaint or quibbles.

"That car in the room business," Cap'n replied.

"I had nothing to do with that," Stanton said, while I remained suspiciously quiet.

"Well, whoever it was," Cap'n went on, "they almost got themselves in a load of deep trouble. Darryl's father was pretty damn hot about it. He called here wantin' to offer a ten thousand dollar reward to tell him who did it."

That caused me to speak up in a hurry. "Ten grand! Why did he take it so hard? It was only a joke!"

Stanton muttered, "Guess nobody told him."

"Coach Anderson talked him out of it," Cap'n went on. "Said it would be too much of a distraction for the team. So Darryl's dad simmered down and agreed to let it go."

"A distraction?" I repeated.

That was odd. Tom and Heape and Colley and Big Dick were not essential cogs in our team. They could easily be sacrificed if there was any reason important enough to do so. Ten thousand dollars sounded fairly important.

"Not so much a distraction," Cap'n said. "They figured it must have taken ten or twenty guys to get it up there, and they couldn't afford to lose that many people, even if it was nothing but redshirts. They figured at least a handful of the varsity had to be involved . . . right?"

Cap'n was baiting us, fishing for insight, but I didn't fall for it. "No idea, Cap'n. Chris and I don't even live in the dorm, you know that. We have no clue who did it."

Stanton played along. "Nope, no clue at all."

"Well, whoever it was," Cap'n concluded, "they sure did dodge a high-priced bullet today."

Tom and the others would be relieved to hear that, but the coaches' retribution was still a legitimate concern.

"What do you think Anderson will do about it?" I asked. "Surely he has to do *something*."

Cap'n shook his head. "I don't think so. They all figured it was pretty damn funny. I think they're not even gonna mention it . . . just pretend it didn't happen and move on."

"You sure about that?" Stanton asked, with good reason. It didn't sound like the coaches we worked for.

Cap'n nodded. "It's what I hear from the front office."

A Monday practice usually consisted of looking over the offensive and defensive sets of next Saturday's opponent, but this Monday would be devoted to basic work. The varsity players had seen Texas sets since spring training, and by now each of them knew every variation of every formation Texas ran in all of last year.

A game against the defending national champions was a prestige event for second-rate hackers like us, so the entire athletic department was going all-out in the hope we'd make a decent showing against them. They felt a good effort would sell tickets in the future, and also might establish some carry-over respect for our team around the country. No one expected a victory, or even close to it, but there was a driving urgency to avoid a fiasco.

"Men," Coach Anderson said, beginning his traditional Monday pre-practice speech, "today's the day we start getting *serious* about Saturday night. You'll be digging in against number one in that game, and every football fan in this country will take the trouble to find out how well you performed. It's a golden opportunity for each of you, and I urge you all to not let it slip through your fingers for lack of mental or emotional preparation.

"The investment you have to make is simple. You have to devote every waking minute to thinking about what you should do in every conceivable situation you might face. There's no way to half-ass it; you have to pay that price. If you do, you'll walk off the field Saturday night with your heads high and the crowd cheering for you. If you don't, I guarantee those Texas boys will shame you so badly you'll wish you were born in another country.

"All right, now, I want us to get after it today and start building some *momentum!* Let's have a good, crisp practice with *no* missed snap counts, *no* busted plays, *no* dropped passes, and *no* fumbles! What do you say, men?"

Tense players let out a collective yell that was more relief than assent. Anderson had a flair for browbeating a team into getting serious about an opponent, and our players were much tougher mentally since his arrival as head coach. Of course, their bodies were still the same.

"All *right,* then!" he roared, raising his right fist as a sign for Chris Stanton to blow the airhorn.

BRRRRRAAAAAAAKKKKKK!

As Monday practices went, it was B-minus. The adrenaline Anderson stirred up lasted over an hour, and only near the end did things start to wind down. The reason, of course, was that minds were shifting off Texas and onto Prosser, who would meet his fate when practice ended.

Though he knew what lay ahead, Prosser gave no hint that he cared. He broke two fairly long runs against the varsity defense, but mostly contained himself to the redshirt standard of into the line and onto the ground.

It was an inauspicious ending to what might have been a truly great career.

***

After Coach Anderson concluded his post-practice pep talk, a beaming Coach Hackler made the announcement.

"Redshirts stay out for some extra work. Biggs and Thompson stay out, too. Everyone else, in."

Quink's name caught most by surprise, but I expected him to be singled out along with Big Dick. Quink tried his best to play kiss-ass the way the coaches wanted, but his independent spirit had a way of coming to the surface at odd times, like Friday morning's green gold incident.

I knew Soupbone watched those cups like a hawk to prevent double-dipping, so no doubt he saw what Quink did and passed the word up the chain of command. This was the coaches' way of telling Quink that if he didn't put a stop to that kind of behavior, he might be next to go.

Quit drills were the kind of travesty that could lead to legal problems if not handled very carefully, so only necessary and trusted people were allowed to be present. By the time Hackler was ready to address the redshirts, only Trainer Hanson, me, and the old truck were left outside the stadium. We were like the body-disposal unit at an execution, with Hanson responsible for first aid and me there to help load the body and carry it away.

"Okay, men," Hackler began, "we're gonna find out who wants to play football, so let's start with a defensive drill. Give me a defense lined up on the standing dummies."

The standing dummies were seven padded uprights that looked like canvas-covered oil drums stuck on huge springs. They stood in a row on the stadium-side end line, representing an opposing offensive line. Eleven redshirts arrayed themselves across the south end zone, taking up normal defensive positions facing the dummies.

"All right," Hackler continued as he took a position opposite the defense on the end line side of the dummies. "I need a running back here with me. Prosser, you'll do."

And so it began.

***

Rather than jog as required, Prosser walked to Hackler—slowly, deliberately—but Hackler only smiled tolerantly. Vengeance was about to be his, so he could afford to be magnanimous. He told Prosser to stand ten yards from the middle dummy in the row of seven, then pointedly handed him a football with his casted right arm.

"Now, son," he said, as smarmily benevolent as he could make the words sound, "the object of this drill is to give the defense a good workout. I'll wave my hand at them and say, *left!* and they'll shift left, and I'll say, *right!* and they'll shift right. I'll do that a few times and then say, *run!* When I say *run*, I want you to run as hard as you can in either direction to give them a good workout. Understand?"

Prosser ignored Hackler's question. He stood casually, holding the ball on one hip, staring straight upfield. The silence was deafening as Hackler's bemused expression clouded over. He turned from Prosser to face the defense.

"All right, gentlemen, nobody on the defense can stop until everyone makes contact with the runner—*everyone!* Readyyyy . . . Left! Right! Left! Right! *Ruuunnn!*"

As Prosser took off to his right, Hackler muttered just loud enough to be heard. *"Run,* you arrogant cocksucker!"

Even a player of Prosser's wondrous talent had a snowball's chance of going more than a couple yards upfield with no blockers against eleven opponents. I'd seen this drill before, and the results were nearly always devastating. The runner got straightened up by the first man to hit him, speared with helmets by the next two or three, then trampled under the cleats and crushed by the weight of the remaining seven or eight defenders.

Prosser, though, was as intelligent as he was talented. Instead of heading upfield in the normal way, he made straight for the defensive end and dove toward his ankles. The end had no choice but to dive back at Prosser, but Prosser was lower. He wound up on the ground with the end lying on top of him, and the onrushing defenders had no choice but to pile onto their teammate's back. When it was over and the pile untangled, the defensive end was rubbing his lower back, while Prosser seemed none the worse for lying under all that weight.

Hackler was livid.

"Goddammit, Prosser! I said I wanted you to give those people a workout! How the hell can they get a workout if you keep diving into the ground like a fucking pussy? I want you to *run* the damn ball! Go out for the swim team if you want to dive! Now get up there and do it again!"

This time Prosser went left, a little wider than before, but he cut back into the flow and again dove into the first pursuer's ankles. The results were the same as the other side. Prosser walked away unhurt, while one defender held a sensitive wrist and another had a bleeding shin.

"Prosser, you turd!" Hackler yelled. "You're the most chickenshit motherfucker I've ever fucking seen! If you have parents or friends, which I doubt, I wish they could see you now! You'd make them as sick as you make me!"

Prosser held his position staring blankly upfield, as if he didn't even acknowledge Hackler's presence in the universe, much less on earth. Prosser somehow made it seem as if his body was there, but his mind was somewhere else. It was a neat trick we all would have liked to emulate when a coach was berating us like that.

Hackler gave up getting a rise out of him and turned with crimson rage to shout at the defense.

"Everyone line up, single file, over there!" He indicated an area just left of the dummies. "I want you, Prosser, to go over there, and I want you to run into each man, one right after the other, and don't stop until you go through the whole fucking line! I'm gonna teach your chickenshit ass how to take a lick like a goddamn man!"

Prosser did the teaching. Hackler's stupidity led him to pick a quit drill designed to get rid of linemen who knew nothing about protecting themselves by slipping direct contact. Prosser made it through the line twice before

Hackler realized he was dealing with a genius of sorts.

Though clearly getting tired, Prosser was holding up better than any of us expected, but the worst was still to come as Hackler quit wasting time and got down to the nub of it.

"All right!" he finally shouted. "That's enough of that one! Everyone come over here with me."

He walked to the twenty yard line and indicated a left side hash mark. "You redshirts stand behind that hash mark." Then he walked fifteen yards farther and pointed to the thirty-five yard line's left side hash mark. "Prosser, you stand on this one." He then planted himself at midfield between the hash marks, the three positions establishing a fifteen yard equilateral triangle on the field.

"Here's the way it works, gentlemen," Hackler said as he took his place. "I want you, Prosser, to run right at me and I'll throw the ball at you. All you have to do is catch it. Now, those are very simple instructions, so you shouldn't have any trouble carrying them out.

"Redshirts, you take turns playing pass defense. I want you to come at me in the same way Prosser will come from his side, but I want you to *stop* him from catching the ball. Do you understand? *No* completions."

Hackler smiled amiably to let the implications sink in. This was the dreaded "Buster Kidney" drill, the number-one decimator—king of quit drills. Prosser would be running forward and to his right while the defenders would angle left to intercept him. The ball would always be thrown high so Prosser would be forced to fully extend himself to reach it, which would leave his right-side ribcage and vital organs unprotected by any padding and directly in line with the defender's onrushing helmet.

There was no way to avoid serious injury short of refusing to do it, which meant quitting and loss of your scholarship. Even Prosser had to know this was hopeless.

"Thompson up first," Hackler commanded.

Quink moved uneasily to the head of the line.

"Okay, Thompson, show me what you can do."

Hackler counted on Quink to do his best to stay on the varsity by going all-out against Prosser.

"Go!" he shouted, and the two rivals at tailback began moving on their collision course.

The ball flew high over Prosser's head, but he made the required leap for it. Quink could have broken him in half if he'd driven hard through the tackle, but he held back and allowed Prosser to fall easily onto his left shoulder pad. He even kept his body under Prosser as they fell, cushioning his impact down to almost nothing.

"Thompson, you turd!" Hackler screamed. "That was the worst fucking tackle I've ever seen! You're gonna be taking his place in this drill if you're not careful!"

Quink hung his head and jogged back to the end of the line. He could be pushed only so far, and if the coaches didn't figure that out and leave him alone to play the game on his own terms, they'd lose another good contributor.

"Biggs!" Hackler yelled. "Get your ass up there!"

Big Dick hesitantly stepped to the front of the line. My heart went out to him because this meant he had to try to hurt his new mortorcycle buddy. His right hand was clearly shaking as he buckled his chin strap into place.

"If you don't tackle this pussyfooting cocksucker like I *know* you can," Hackler added, so everyone could hear, "I give you my word you won't letter this year. Understand?"

Big Dick clamped down on his mouthpiece, and we knew what was coming. It would be asking too much of him to give up his hard-won second team position for Prosser's sake. Besides, if he didn't do it, someone else would.

Prosser was fully extended in the air, reaching with both hands for the overthrown ball, when Big Dick's helmet smashed into the small of his back with a thumping wallop. Prosser's whole upper torso snapped backward so violently that his head nearly connected with his butt, and he cut loose with a blood-curdling scream of anguish.

My first thought was that his back might be broken, but as soon as he hit the ground he was writhing in pain. He'd lost his wind, so Big Dick was immediately over him, lifting him by the belt to help force air back into his lungs.

"Dammit, Biggs, get your ass away from there!" Hackler shouted. "Get back in line!"

Big Dick hesitantly moved away as Hackler approached. "Get up, Prosser, you're not hurt!"

Prosser somehow had the presence of mind to turn his face away, toward the ground, so his agony couldn't be enjoyed by the sadistic bastard standing over him.

"I said get *up!*" Hackler repeated, kicking Prosser hard in the same spot Big Dick's helmet struck.

Prosser groaned loudly, but it was clear he wasn't getting up no matter how many times he got kicked. Big Dick had truly hammered him.

"All right!" Hackler finally said, as his biggest smile turned his fat face into a pile of wrinkled jello. "That's enough for today. Good job, Biggs. Tomorrow we'll pick up where we left off. Everybody head on in now—*everybody!*"

That meant Prosser had to lie where he fell until he could make it in under his own power.

Trainer Hanson calmly watched that travesty he had witnessed several times before, and when it was over, all he did was join Hackler in the old truck for the short ride back to where it was kept under the stadium.

Big Dick, Quink, and I joined the rest of the redshirts jogging in bitter silence to their dressing room. No words were spoken, but helmets were slammed into lockers as we all took seats and sat in furious, helpless despair.

Each of us had seen fuck-overs on football fields before this one. They happened in high school, too; they were a part of football. But that didn't make this easier to accept.

Suddenly, a guttural roar shattered the quiet.

"*Arrrrrgggggghhhhhhh!*" Quink howled as he jumped to his feet, grabbed his helmet by the face mask, and

smashed it into the cement floor, sending pieces of it flying around the room like shrapnel from a bomb.

"Take it easy, man," Skid said quietly. "There's nothing
we can do about this, and you know it."

Quink stepped to the middle of the room and whirled
around it, seeking support from everyone. "Why the hell
not, huh? Why can't we get together and at least *try* to do
something? This shit makes me feel like an *accomplice!*"

Big Dick stood up with tears brimming in his eyes. We
all knew, and could clearly see, how profoundly bad he
felt about what he had been forced to do.

"We *are* accomplices, Quink," he said softly, "but Skid
is right. We either do what they say, when they say it, or
they'll get rid of us. We have no choice."

"There must be *something* we can do about it!" Quink
protested, tears of frustration brimming in his eyes, too,
as he looked to me for support. I had to shake my head.

"When you signed on to play football here," I reminded
them, "the coaches agreed to feed you and house you and
give you the chance to get an education. You're bought
and paid for, the same way a slave is bought and paid for.
They own you until you're fed up enough to quit."

The certainty of that knowledge sunk everyone into an
even deeper state of quiet depression.

Ten minutes later a few guys had stripped off all parts
of their uniforms, but most were still half-dressed when
Prosser opened the door. His face was whiter than usual,
and his expression was blank. He was clearly in shock.

"I feel . . . sick. . . ." he gasped as he pitched forward
into Skid's arms and passed out.

Anyone in shock shouldn't be down on cold cement,
so I helped Skid lay him out on the wooden bench that
circled the room in front of the cubicles.

Suddenly, Prosser gagged and began throwing up his
lunch. I held his head to the side so he wouldn't breathe
his own vomit. The convulsion slowly brought him back

to consciousness. He spit twice to clear his mouth, then asked the classic first question: "What . . . happened?"

"You passed out for a minute," I said, using a towel to wipe vomit off his cheek and chin. "How do you feel?"

"I hurt. . . ."

"Where?"

"My back. . . ."

"Can you get up?" Tom asked.

He made an effort but couldn't. "I need help. . . ."

Tom and I lifted him to his feet as gently as we could, then waited for him to stop weaving.

"Okay," I said, "you're doing fine. Now, just stand there for a few seconds while Tom and I get your uniform off."

As soon as we lifted his jersey, everyone could see the circular red welt covering the right side of his lower back, with a bruise line from Hackler's toe in the middle of it. Nobody said a word as we finished stripping him down.

"Can you get in the shower by yourself?" I asked.

Some of his color was returning as he nodded and said, "Yeah . . . I think so."

I went with him in case he fainted again, but he walked into the shower and toilet area with no apparent trouble. Instead of going into the shower, though, he moved to the porcelain trough on the opposite wall. This worried me.

"Don't force it out," I said. "Just let it flow."

Prosser glanced at me with a puzzled expression, and then his urine appeared. "My piss is pink," he marveled, more to himself than to me or those lurking behind us.

"Good news," I said in the most upbeat tone I could manage. "You have a bruised kidney. If it was red, that would mean it ruptured. This should heal by itself in a few days."

His head shook. "I don't have a few days."

"I'll speak to Trainer Hanson about it."

"No!" he growled. "Don't say anything to anyone."

He looked past me to see the other redshirts gathered at the door of the shower room. All of them were watching him intently, deep concern obvious on everyone's face.

"I'm going out there tomorrow," he told us, "to settle the score with that fat fuck. They may be getting rid of me, but they're going to remember I was here. Understand?"

Out of the stunned group who heard his threat, including me, Quink voiced what all of us were thinking.

"Ohhhh, *shit!* . . . You're not gonna *kill* him, are you?"

"No, but I can sure make him wish he was dead."

Smiles began spreading across every face in the room.

"Seriously, Pete," Big Dick said in a hushed, quavering voice. "You can do something like that to him?"

His underlying meaning was so glaringly obvious that Prosser walked slowly to him and gazed into his eyes.

"Listen, I hold nothing against you, now or ever. You're a friend, I know that. You only did what you had to do."

Big Dick's watery eyes looked relieved because he knew whatever could be done to Hackler could be done to him.

"If none of you tip anyone off," Prosser said, "I promise I'll go out of this place with a bang like you've never seen."

Quink wasn't satisfied. "If you can do it tomorrow, why didn't you do it today? Why'd you go through that shit?"

"I'm not sure you'd understand."

Quink stepped forward from the group. "Try me."

Prosser's dark contact lenses were still in his eyes, as was the bootblack he always smeared under them, which combined to give him an eerie, almost unearthly gaze.

"It's all about karma. If I did anything serious to him before he did something serious to me, it would be bad for my karma. Now that he's drawn first blood, I don't think it will hurt my karma to balance things out with him."

"You took an enormous risk out there today," Tom put in. "Sage and I tried to warn you. Why did you do it?"

"I try to hold my life in the hands of fate, Tom. If I was meant to be injured seriously, I would have been. The fact I wasn't tells me I have an important job to do tomorrow."

With that he turned into the shower and left us all to wonder what fate would have in store for Wade Hackler.

***

MONDAY NIGHT

After dinner on Monday nights, the varsity was obliged to watch films of Saturday's performance. During the season they'd be game films, but this night's were of the Saturday scrimmage that ended with Prosser's incredible run. Of course, as part of the process of erasing any trace of his presence on the Cajun State team, that piece of film would already be destroyed.

During the season, redshirts were excluded from these meetings even though the coaches believed they should be made to suffer as much tedious bullshit as could be devised for them. Two hours of watching film they didn't appear in was indeed tedious. On the other hand, they should also be humiliated as much as possible. Refusing to let them attend team functions served to point out their insignificance as players and contributing team members.

Given that choice, the coaches chose to humiliate them rather than bore them, but in this one instance it really was a sacrifice for the redshirts to miss it because they all got into the scrimmage at some point or other.

I'd arranged to meet Carla at the Hofbrau Haus, Cajun State's replica of an old-fashioned German beer hall. Its low, heavy-beamed ceiling, handcrafted wooden furnishings, stuffed animal heads on the walls, and dark, murky atmosphere all helped make you forget you were only in a basement section of the University Center.

When I arrived, Helmet was already there. His gregarious nature and German background made him a fixture in the Hofbrau Haus on Monday nights. Though technically required to participate in all team related activities, including the Monday night film sessions, in which he was usually our brightest star, he refused to attend.

He did go to it the first time the coaches told him to,

after which he walked out muttering, "Useless . . . this is too useless for me," and he never attended another.

That was when the coaches first understood they had created a kind of monster by suiting him up and letting him express his obvious talent to the world.

I bought a small pitcher of beer and found an empty table, and Helmet soon walked over to join me.

"I am glad to see you, Sagely," he said as he sat down. "I have been wishing to speak with you."

"About what?"

"My roommate, Peter. I went to see him after dining this evening. He is in much pain."

"He took a helluva lick out there today."

"So it happens again, eh, my friend? When will they discover a more civilized way to resolve these difficulties?"

"When lunatics aren't in charge of the asylum."

"But it is so absurd, the ruining of one such as Peter for the benefit of one such as Hackler."

"That's what you get when people like Hackler have authority over people like Pete."

"Truly, it would take the whole of tonight to explore the problems such a system generates."

"Yeah, it would, but it really doesn't matter in the long run. Pete will be gone after tomorrow."

"Such talent he has. What a pity to waste it."

"Football isn't the place for someone like him."

"Hello, you two handsome devils," Carla suddenly said, appearing out of nowhere. "Mind if I join the fun?"

Helmet sprang to his feet to assist her into a chair. "We can hardly wish for a more lovely addition to the table."

I could see Carla's blush even in the dim light of the Hofbrau Haus. Helmet always had that effect on women. With looks, manners, and charm, he was devastating.

We exchanged general chitchat for a few minutes, then Helmet graciously stood up to leave.

"Ahhh, dearest Carla," he said, taking her hand and kissing it lightly, "when will you overthrow this reprobate of a boyfriend you have so we may be together always?"

It was the perfect balance of comical disrespect for me and sincere appreciation of Carla's raven haired, sloe-eyed, stacked-to-the-ceiling beauty.

"When you, my dear, can no longer juggle five or ten others at the same time. At the rate you're going, that should be in about fifty years. Check with me then."

He laughed and said, "Take care, my friends. *Ciao!*"

He turned and walked to a table where three girls sat huddled in serious discussion. In five minutes he had them laughing, and in ten minutes they were his newest fans.

We watched him work his magic until Carla turned to me and said, "Why can't more of you be like him?"

"Men in general, or players in particular?"

"Players, ex-players, wish-I-had-been-a player. All the men I know fit in there somewhere, even my father."

"But Helmet *is* a player."

"Come on, Larry, you know what I mean. Helmet is on a football team, he's not a football player. My father hasn't put on a uniform for thirty years, but he's *still* a player."

She may as well have been talking about me.

"What I mean," she went on, "is that Helmet would be the same person whether he played football or not. He doesn't need football to feel like a man. He *is* a man—period."

"Now, wait a minute, honey. You have to remember one important thing about Helmet: he's not part of our culture. We measure ourselves as men in one way and his culture does it in another, but we're all cut from the same cloth."

"What do you mean?"

"The boomerang-shaped scar below his cheekbone . . . you have any idea how he got that?"

"I assumed an accident of some kind."

"Dueling."

Her shock was palpable. *"Dueling! How?"*

"With swords, sabers, rapiers. It's illegal in Germany,

which of course makes it very popular with young men, especially students. A dueling scar has become a prized status symbol for them, a red badge of courage.

"How do you know that?" she demanded.

"I asked him about it. He told me he squared off with another student, both flailing at each other with sharp rapiers, trying to cut each other somewhere in the face."

"Jesus!" she gasped. "What if they hit an eye?"

"That's a big part of what makes it so glamorous, the fact that you could get seriously hurt doing it."

"And I thought football players were crazy!"

"So does Helmet," I added. "Football makes as much sense to him as dueling does to us."

"Then what's the point of either one?"

"They're rites of passage into manhood. Men seem to need ways of proving to themselves that they *are* men, so certain levels of risk are required to make the tests valid."

"I'm glad women aren't like that."

"Maybe having children serves that purpose for you. It's difficult to do, it has a certain element of risk, and it clearly establishes credentials as a woman."

"If rites of passage are so common . . . if dueling with swords equals football . . . how do you account for the huge difference between Helmet and the other players? I mean, he's so together, it's like he's from another planet."

"Helmet and others like him undergo finite tests. Young native Americans did things like spending three days alone on a mountaintop. Australian aborigines endure a weeks-long walkabout. Helmet fought with a sword. The point is, there's a definite, limited goal for them to achieve. Once they make it, they can stop trying to prove themselves and move forward as men. Their rite of passage is over and—"

"Larry," Carla interrupted, "could we—?"

"Wait a minute, I'm not finished. I want you to understand this. In football, there aren't any finite goals. Instead of a few moments of swordplay, or a few days of exposure, football players commit themselves to *years* of mutual self-torture, with no hope of ever getting to the place where someone says, 'You can stop now, you've done enough. Today you are a man.' No matter how well you play, someone is always there saying, 'You could have done better; go out and prove yourself again tomorrow.' There's just no acceptable level of performance, and—"

"Please!" Her urgency startled me. "Could we talk about something else? You're making me very uncomfortable."

I suddenly realized how intense I'd become. "I'm sorry, honey. I guess I'm a little upset with football right now."

She took my hands in hers. "Why do you stay part of it, Larry? You don't belong to it any more than Helmet does."

"No, that's wrong. I'm a full-fledged product of the system . . . and I'm as hooked on it as anyone ever was."

We dropped football for a while, as she requested, but it didn't stay dropped long. As soon as I began telling her what happened with Prosser, she was all ears. I finished with his vow to take revenge against Hackler as his swan song, and her reaction was, "That fat bastard deserves it! But won't that leave Prosser open to an assault charge?"

I shook my head. "No way. They'd never press charges unless Prosser actually killed him. Anything less than that, even if he puts him in the hospital, they'll have to let it slide because they can't afford to expose quit drills."

"So Prosser has a clean, clear shot at him?" she asked.

"Anything he wants to do, as long as he doesn't kill him. We're all hoping he takes maximum advantage of it."

"From what you've said about him, I bet he will."

When we left the Hofbrau Haus to return home, a full moon hung directly overhead. Late summer smells and lingering warmth filled the night air, and occasional swirls of breeze ruffled the trees and bushes along our path.

"Let's not go straight home," she suggested. "Let's walk around the campus a bit. It's too lovely to go right in."

We walked and talked about the topics young couples

focus on, our hopes and dreams for our future together after I got into graduate school, when we could think seriously about getting formally engaged and then married.

Children, too, were on our agenda, though downstream a bit. That clock wasn't ticking loudly for Carla yet, even though Annie Slade's pregnancy was one of her greatest delights from the moment she found out about it.

During our roundabout route home, the stadium's hulking silhouette came looming through the haze of streetlights and moonlight. Struck by inspiration, I said, "Carla, have you ever been in the stadium with the lights off?"

"Don't they lock it up at night?"

"Sure, but I know how to get in. Want to try it?"

"Ohhhhh, yeah! That sounds exciting!"

We quickened our pace and were soon at the secret entrance: a hidden crack in the chain-link fence near the east side ticket office. We wasted no time slipping through.

"That was easy!" Carla said, breathing faster.

"Shhhhhhh! There's always a security guard patrolling at night. Keep your voice down."

I motioned her to follow me up an entrance ramp leading to the top of the stadium. We climbed many steps before reaching the south end, beside the scoreboard and the looming Fightin' Crawdad, who scowled down on friend and foe alike. Catching our breath, we were serenaded by the occasional clatter of the air vents cut into his outline so stiff winds wouldn't knock him over.

We gazed across the stadium's rim at the entire campus spread before us. The breeze had picked up a bit, and now whipped and swirled against the bulk of the stadium in addition to rattling the air vents in the Crawdad.

I looked up and noticed clouds starting to scud in front of the moon. The languid night of earlier was giving way to a weather front moving in. I hoped that didn't mean heavy rain coming because rain meant a lot of extra work for everyone on the team, from coaches to managers.

After a while, we turned to face the field below and the city's glittering carpet of lights beyond.

"This is absolutely gorgeous, Larry," Carla said. "Thank you soooo much for thinking to bring me up here."

An eerie emptiness filled the stadium's enclosure, while the moon overhead provided a soft, intermittent glow. I glanced at Carla and was mesmerized by her long black hair whipping around in the breeze. I couldn't recall any other occasion when she looked so awesomely beautiful.

I took her in my arms and poured my feelings for her into a long, deeply passionate kiss. By the time we broke apart, we were both trembling with unleashed passion.

"Let's go home," my surging hormones urged her. "We can come back here some other time."

"Ohhh, yes! Let's go, let's come back, *whatever!*"

She began leaping down the steps by twos, and I had to struggle to keep up with her bounding strides.

"Hey, take it easy! We'll get there!"

"Not soon enough!" she almost whimpered, her Italian blood boiling. "Hurry, *please!*"

We finally got down to the field and were headed across the southeast corner when Carla suddenly stopped and whirled around to face me. "Let's do it here, right now!"

"Here?" I rasped. "Right here on the *field?*"

"No, on the fifty yard line, right in the middle!"

At first, that seemed like a sacrilege far beyond the pale of reason . . . but it quickly became intriguing.

"What if the guard happens to see us? That's a full moon up there!"

"It's getting cloudy!" she hissed. "We just have to be quiet and take our chances. Come on!"

She took my hand and pulled me toward the center of the field. "Listen, think about it. When we're old and gray, watching games here on television, we'll always be able to remember the night we made love on the fifty yard line."

Sold! I had already unbuckled my belt and unzipped my pants when we reached the center of the field.

"Just drop 'em and I'll lift my skirt," she directed as she stepped out of her panties. "Best to make it a quickie."

She laid down directly on the fifty yard line, feet pointing toward the press box, legs spread wide. Then she looked up at me with incongruously wide-eyed innocence.

"Do I look okay? Am I centered?"

"Perfect!" I said, diving down onto her.

Suddenly, every light in the stadium came on, bathing our quasi-naked revelry in the glare of full exposure!

I heard Carla inhale, which meant she might scream reflexively, so I clamped my left hand over her mouth.

"Be quiet and don't move!" I rasped.

She was on her back, uplifted skirt now jammed between her legs. I was on my side at her side, bare butted, pants at my shins, scanning the field's four ground-level corner exits to see where the guard would appear.

No one showed themselves, so I checked each exit again. Finally, a movement caught my eye in the upper reaches of the stadium's west side, just below the press box.

"Don't panic!" I hissed as panic surged through me.

A lone stooped figure stepped out of an upper middle entrance with a clipboard in his hand.

"Jesus!" I muttered. "It's Soupbone!"

Carla yanked my hand from her mouth.

"Soupbone?" she hissed in my ear, turning to see him for herself. "What's *he* doing here? What does he want?"

One of Soupbone's duties was to check the stadium's lighting system before every home game, listing and then reporting every extinguished bulb to the maintenance crew so the crew could replace them before game time.

"I can't explain now," I said, quiet but urgent. "Just don't move and maybe he won't notice us."

"What do we do if he sees us?" she whispered. She was apparently gaining control of herself.

"Hell if I know. I think I can talk my way out of any trouble with him, but let's worry about that if it happens."

Soupbone examined each bank of lights towering above

the stadium's upper edge. Occasionally, his head moved down toward the clipboard to note a bulb to be replaced, but his face always went right back up to the lights.

Five minutes later, he turned and walked back down the entranceway, and two minutes later the lights went back out. As far as I could tell, he never bothered to look down at the field. This time, it seemed, Carla and I had dodged the bullet, and we heaved enormous sighs of relief.

We lay still, trembling in the covering darkness, until we were sure the coast was clear. Finally, I rose to my feet and pulled my pants back on as we began to laugh nervously, which soon built into something close to hysterics.

We hurried back to the apartment, and by the time we got there, we could hardly wait to finish what we started.

TUESDAY

I slept well knowing my concerns about Prosser would soon be resolved. Whatever he did to Hackler wouldn't be nearly enough to balance all the anguish that jerk had caused for who-knew-how-many players in his career.

Carla woke me with a bad weather report.

"It rained hard last night after we went to bed."

"Awwww, Christ! How's it look now?"

"Puddles everywhere and it's still drizzling."

I buried my head in the pillow as Carla went into the kitchen to start breakfast. I fleetingly thought of staying in bed all day, then reluctantly began dragging myself out.

Rain meant Stanton and I had to work our asses off at practice. The main problem was keeping footballs and the football handlers' hands reasonably free of mud, and though we always did our best to maintain a steady supply of towels, we could never satisfy the demand. Rain practices were always an exercise in futility for managers, and

I hated them as much as I could hate anything.

Of course, there was always a possibility the coaches would decide to hold practice indoors in Holt Field House. It all depended on how they felt the team was coming along in its preparations for Texas. If they felt the players needed more physical toughening, they'd send them out in the slop to pound on each other for two hours. But if they felt the team was more in need of mental sharpening, they'd go inside to work on execution.

I felt pretty sure we'd stay outside today. Texas was a big, physically aggressive team that did nothing fancy, so play execution wasn't an issue. We needed all the toughening we could get to hope to stay on the field with them.

The drizzle stopped well before classes started at 8:00, and although the sky was still gray and overcast, the clouds were fluffy enough to indicate that all their moisture might be drained. By noon it was clear the rain had indeed come and gone, so a decision was posted on the bulletin board at lunch: *Practice as usual, on the field.*

As far as I could tell, not one redshirt told any of their varsity friends what lay in store for Hackler at the end of today's practice. Like me, nobody wanted to jinx it.

I entered the equipment shed and Cap'n took me aside for a quiet word. "Soupbone told us he caught you diddlin' your girl on the field last night. The coaches know it, too."

I could only grit my teeth and plaster on a tight smile. "Yeah, we got a little frisky at the wrong time. Thanks."

I took a good bit of ribbing from everyone in the dressing room, and then in the training room when it was time to tape ankles. I kept wanting to focus on the upcoming conflict between Prosser and Hackler, but the interruptions were constant, even from Coach Anderson himself.

He came into the training room to confer with Trainer Hanson about Don's puffy knee and the Bull's swollen ankle, then he ambled over to where I was taping Heape's right wrist. "Hi, Larry, how's it going?"

"Fine, coach, just fine."

"Good, glad to hear it." Then, "Heard you and your lady-friend had a little trouble with the lights last night."

For as humorous as our indiscretion was, it fit well with the accepted jock image, and would be favorably viewed as a clear indication I was still a football player at heart.

"Yes, sir," I said, grinning sheepishly and ducking my head in the expected fashion. "We sure did."

"Then we'll have to make Soupbone post his schedule from now on," he said, raising his voice so the whole training room could enjoy his wit. "That way you both can do your business without getting in each other's way."

Everyone laughed, though a bit nervously, then Coach Anderson switched to his sincerest tone of voice, the one he used on parents. "You're doing a hell of a fine job for us Larry," he said, placing a fatherly hand on my shoulder. "Forget what happened and keep up the good work."

It was only the second time he had spoken to me as a person in the year I had already worked for him, but that wasn't unusual. The coaches who were here before him and his crew, the ones I initially signed to play with, were no more friendly than these. Coaches went out of their way to avoid relating with players on a personal basis, figuring such familiarity weakened their authority. That policy extended to even minor staff members like me.

"I'll try to, sir, don't worry." And I meant it.

Practice was typical for after a heavy rain. The field was soaked and soon became a quagmire. Players caromed off each other like giant mud-covered billiards, footballs squirted around like greased pigs, and Stanton and I wiped frantically at every ball or pair of hands around us.

Finally, Anderson whistled everyone to the tower as a prelude to the final stage of practice. As we gathered at the center of the field, I noticed Prosser slowly jogging along.

So far, practice had been fairly easy on him. It was hard to tell his back was hurt until he pulled up after a run, and even then he seemed only slightly stiff. He was able to keep a low profile because Hackler laid off him completely. There was no point in calling attention to him during practice, considering what everyone but the red-shirts assumed would happen to him when it was over.

Little did non-redshirts know how far the shoe was on the other foot—a foot well trained in martial arts. From my own limited experience with karate, I knew Prosser could do massive damage with only a few well-placed punches or kicks. I wondered which ones he'd choose.

"All right, men," Anderson intoned, "we've had a decent practice in these conditions, and I want you to keep up the good work through this last drill. It'll be a twenty-minute varsity scrimmage on the baseball outfield so you can get some decent footing. I know that's been hard in this mud, but the grass there is fresh and strong, so you all should be able to get good traction on it even though it's wet.

"Now remember, especially backs and ends, when you hear a whistle, *stop!* We don't want late-hit injuries when we're tired, and we don't want anyone piling up against those bleachers. Also, if you see yourself going into the fence, make a fist! Don't grab it. The wire in it can cut your hands if you reach out to grab it. Everyone understand?"

That was the signal to nod and stay silent.

"All right, then, get going before you cool off!"

That was a signal for everyone to start yelling like ban-shees as they jogged to where the drill would take place.

"*Craw*-dads! *Craw*-dads! *Craw*-dads!"

As I sloshed through the mud, my interest in the pend-ing Prosser/Hackler confrontation faded. My duties dur-ing this drill demanded total concentration. I'd handle the ball-cleaning and its placement, *plus* I'd keep track of down and distance. Practice on the baseball outfield also meant one additional responsibility . . . staying aware of those two sideline hazards Coach Anderson mentioned.

Whenever wet weather forced us to scrimmage on the baseball outfield, we kept the sessions short and confined them to the smallest possible area because football cleats could tear wet grass runners out by the roots. Our athletic director felt that since we weren't forced to dodge line drives when we practiced, we shouldn't make the baseball team work out on chewed-up outfield grass.

We scrimmaged in the far corner of left field, running plays from fifteen yards inside the foul line through foul territory and toward the track beyond. That gave us forty unobstructed yards to work in, which was all we needed when long passes weren't allowed, and we damaged only a fifteen yard strip inside the left field foul line.

Those restrictions were minor compared to what was just outside both of our sideline boundaries. Ten yards beyond the left sideline markers and twenty-five yards upfield from the initial line of scrimmage was a wood-and-metal bleacher extending along the left field foul line.

Any player running into it would almost surely break something because football pads offered little protection against hard edges. As a result, anyone heading that way was quick-whistled to a stop by me or assistant coaches.

The outfield's boundary was a ten-foot-high, chain-link "hurricane" fence placed five yards beyond, and parallel to, our right sideline. We were less worried about the fence because, unlike the immobile benches, there was a small amount of "give" in its fishnet construction. Players running into it would bounce off, and their pads gave good protection even when they hit the circular brace poles.

The fence's real threat was the one Anderson cautioned us about. Its fist-sized, diamond-shaped holes had crusted zinc coatings at the connecting joints, and those rough spots could easily cut skin. They were nothing like the jagged, inch-long bottom prongs that kept freeloaders from sneaking underneath into games, but we couldn't afford even small hand injuries just four days before a game.

***

I whistled the ball in play. "First down, twenty-five to go!"

In this drill, the first team offense had five plays to go twenty-five yards against the second team defense. Then the teams switched: second team offense against the first team defense. To be successful, quarterbacks had to make daring play selections. A close-to-the-vest series usually didn't score. A mix of traps, flares, sweeps, and play-action passes was needed to get anywhere. Consequently, in this exercise we often played some of our very best football.

The first team offense broke their huddle and lined up to run their opening play. I took my usual position straddling the line of scrimmage ten yards outside Denny O'Toole, the right end. O'Toole cheated out a yard as he took his stance, which put Loop Watson, the second team left defensive end, on the alert for something coming his way.

At the snap Gil Travers, the starting wingback, launched himself into a crackback block on Watson from outside, while O'Toole cut out on Big Dick at left cornerback.

The two defenders sensed what was coming, but the cross-blocking end and wingback had better angles of attack. Don Slade took the hand-off from Davis and moved to his right on a fullback slant, slicing between their four prostrate bodies. He gained seven yards before being drug down from behind by linebacker Corky Ames and others.

With the play whistled dead, I ran to retrieve the ball from the pileup where Don went down. He was still pinned beneath a couple of players when I reached him, but his mud-spattered face beamed as he handed the ball up.

"How'd it look?" he mumbled through his mouthpiece.

Players never dreamed of asking a coach for an instant critique of a play they'd made, but they often asked me. They knew I could evaluate them, and I'd tell the truth.

"Sharp," I said, reaching down to help him to his feet. "You picked the right hole and hit it hard. Good job."

I gave him a quick pat on the rump as he headed back for his huddle, then wiped the ball and respotted it.

"Second play, eighteen to go!"

The second play started off looking exactly like the first, which was common in football because misleading and misdirection were key parts of any offensive strategy. It was the same with the defenses, for that matter. At bottom, football was a chess game with living players trying to dominate each other to the extent they could.

This play, though it started out like the fullback dive of the previous play, was in fact a play-action pass. After O'Toole and Travers crossed and delivered brush blocks on Watson and Big Dick, they both took off downfield. Unfortunately, wet grass can be just as slippery as mud. They lost their footing making down-and-out cuts, which left Ronnie Davis, the quarterback, with no choice but to dump a flare pass to Don in the right flat.

Don tucked it away and headed upfield near the right sideline, where Big Dick was coming up from covering Travers. When they met, Big Dick delivered his usual hard shot, but Don's straight-ahead momentum carried him through that tackle and two more solid hits before he fell twelve yards downfield. It was a gritty, powerful run.

"Goddammit, Slade!" Coach Marshall bellowed. "That's the way to run the damn ball! Cram it down their throats!"

"Gotta stick 'em, defense! Need some *stick* out there!"

"Third play, six to go!"

The next play was a fullback dive straight up the middle, inches away from the right cheek of Jimbo Wheeler's butt. Wheeler threw a crunching forearm into the nose guard's earhole, and Don cut off his block for an easy score.

"All right, big offense! Bring on those Longhorn pussies!"

I was surprised at how strong we looked on that drive without the Bull in there at fullback. One of the hardest things to overcome when you lose a starter is the lack of faith in his replacement. Don was taking care of that problem by showing his teammates he could hold his own against anyone, and they were responding by going all-out for him. It seldom happened so quickly.

On the next series, the first team defense looked every

bit as impressive. They allowed the second team offense two incomplete passes, two short runs, and a sack, for a grand total of minus four yards in five plays.

The first team offense came out for a second series and lost no time taking up where they left off. John Lawrence, the starting tailback, swept left end for eight yards outside of another savage crackback block by Gil Travers.

"Goddammit, defense!" Hackler screamed. "Get your fucking heads out of your pussies and *hit* somebody!"

The second team defense started chattering and slapping each other on the helmets. They'd try hard to salvage their pride by ringing some bells on the next few plays.

"Second play, seventeen to go!"

I glanced behind my back at the players standing along the sideline in front of the fence. I knew they'd be pleased at Hackler's aggravation. I looked for Prosser, but couldn't single him out from the row of mud-covered look-alikes.

When I turned back to face the line, the ball was already snapped for the next play, and a fullback sweep was in progress. Don had taken a short pitchout from Davis and was heading my way behind Lawrence's escort. I started backpedaling out of their way, then noticed two thin tape streamers fluttering around Don's right knee as he ran. That meant the dampness had soaked through his leg bandage enough to loosen it, so I made a hasty mental note to caution him about it after this play ended.

As the sweep continued to develop, Big Dick and Watson began working to maintain outside positions. Their combined responsibility was to force Don inside toward the defensive pursuit, and they both knew Hackler would have their asses in traction if they failed. Watson started off with a hand-fight against O'Toole's scrambling crab block, but he got completely wiped out by a double-team crackback from Travers, who specialized in that block.

Big Dick was left all alone outside, facing a tandem of John Lawrence as a lead blocker for Don, and Don right behind him. Big Dick backpedaled until he thought he had a good angle, then he dug in and blasted Lawrence with a forearm shiver. Lawrence lost his balance trying to recover from the surprise of it. Don was forced to give ground in order to negotiate around Lawrence's sprawled body, which gave Big Dick time to regain his outside position.

Don now had the option of waiting for a pulling guard to come help out, or heading upfield alone and hoping to beat Big Dick one-on-one. His previous success on the safety-valve pass must have made him think he could go it alone, so he cut upfield without waiting for help and pointed himself straight at Big Dick.

Big Dick was not to be trifled with after being run over by Don a few plays earlier. He drove foward, legs churning, and plastered his face mask flat against Don's chest. Don's straight-ahead momentum neutralized the impact, leaving neither man with a clear-cut advantage. They continued to sweep outside, struggling for the best leverage.

It's always great fun to watch two quality players go hard after each other like that. Their legs churn and drive against the other's power and momentum, while their upper bodies remain fused together, and it seems as if they can only fall sideways from exhaustion. In this case, though, a closely staggered line of defenders was rapidly closing in on them to finish Don off.

I was still backpedaling away from the flow when the second defender hit into both men somewhere behind Big Dick. All three remained on their feet, moving laterally toward the sideline. Another pursuer added his weight to the rear, but Don obstinately kept his head high and refused to go down without a fight to the end.

I should have blown my whistle right then, but I held off in the hope that Don might luck out and break free. I'd seen pursuers knock their own men off runners countless times before, and it usually happened in exactly this kind of side sweeping situation. Suddenly, I heard several frantic shouts coming from behind my back.

"The fence! Watch out for the fence!"

The instant that warning registered, I blew my whistle and stopped moving backward to spin and gauge where the fence was: fifteen yards and closing fast. It wasn't critical yet, but players along the sidelines were already scrambling away from the hurtling group of bodies. More whistles began to shrill from all over the field, but nothing stopped . . . it went into a kind of slow-motion sequence.

I looked back at the combatants and saw that they'd drawn alongside me a few yards downfield. My new angle allowed a view of two more pursuers running in close tandem. They were so covered with mud I couldn't tell who they were, even that close, but I could see their eyes.

Their eyes told me they would neither hear nor react to our whistles. Those two were listening to the inner voices of all their coaches preaching football gospel—*Go for the ball! Punish the runner! Don't stop till he's on the ground!*—and they were beyond hearing anything else.

Tiny globs of mud flew out from the moving stack of bodies as those fourth and fifth defenders smashed into it. Don staggered as the first impact traveled into him through the three people already clinging to his body. Though still in Big Dick's tight grasp from the waist up, Don had managed to keep his legs free and churning until the fifth man delivered his blow. I saw, heard, and almost felt it happen, and my first thought was of Annie.

It was nothing more than a misstep on the wet ground. Don's left foot hit a slippery patch and failed to hold, which threw all the weight massed against him squarely over his bad right knee. It sounded like a short-shot .22 rifle when it snapped under the strain, breaking so cleanly and completely that his right hip nearly hit his right ankle when they all fell. I knew in that horrifying instant that Don Slade would never play football, or walk normally, again.

Don and Big Dick hit the ground together, with Big Dick's face mask still flush against Don's chest. Their fall sent a splash of water almost to where I stood. The other defenders swept forward and up over their bodies with a rolling motion that meant even more trouble for Don.

When a knee went like that, any twisting of the lower leg did even worse damage to the joint and made decent repair virtually impossible. Knowing that, I was running toward them, shouting, before the last man left his feet.

"Don't move! Don't move! Slade's hurt! I'll untangle you! Get up *slow!* Let me handle it!"

I didn't gain much on them at first because their combined mass skimmed along the wet grass like a huge, multi-part ball-bearing over oil. Still, those last two hits generated enough momentum to shift their motion from laterally along the line of scrimmage to somewhat parallel with the sideline. That put them moving more toward me than away from me, which meant I'd reach them that much sooner. Then came something I didn't anticipate: The whole pileup slammed into the base of the fence.

I was so intent on reaching them quickly, I didn't notice how far they slid. The two top bodies catapulted off the stack and into the fence, while the bottom four skidded only another yard before an abrupt stop surprised me. More surprising was the fine pink mist that went up as they slid those last few feet. That should have been alarming to me, but its significance didn't register right away. What struck me first was that Don wasn't screaming in pain from his shattered knee. I assumed he had the wind knocked out of him when they hit the ground.

I was two strides away when they stopped moving and one stride away when I saw and heard it. Just as I was about to repeat my warning to get up slow and easy, a bright red plume spurted up into the air accompanied by a sharp hissing noise, something like steam escaping from an iron. Someone had cut an artery on the fence!

The pileup still had to unstack itself carefully to protect Don's knee, but I also had to find that cut and get pressure on it. The blood had spurted from beneath the far side of the pile, apparently near the fence line, but I couldn't tell exactly where it came from. All that weight slamming into the fence had bent it out of shape.

A second plume shot up just as I reached the pile, smaller than the first. A third and fourth came up as I yanked the topmost body away. Their level continued to drop. I clutched the next man by the jersey when the fifth spurt came up only enough to clear his helmet. I threw him aside like a rag doll and saw what had happened.

"Oh, Jesus God!" I screamed. "Help me! For God's sake, somebody *heeeelllllpppp meeeeee!*"

On impact with the fence, Don's hard, smooth helmet had been jammed underneath the fence, burrowing below the serrated bottom edge. His shoulder pads prevented him from sliding through any further, so he was trapped at the neck like a fish in a gill net. He slid those last few feet beneath the fence like that, and now his throat hung in shreds along those jagged bottom prongs.

As I flung Big Dick away from Don, he blinked against the blood pooled in his eyes. I dropped to my knees and straddled his chest as he stared at me, wide-eyed, from the other side of the fence, seemingly studying me, my expression, looking for reassurance I couldn't give.

In total panic I tried to reach his wound by jamming my fingers into the fence holes to rip them apart. He could see the futility of my efforts and tried to say something, but no words came out of his mouth. His severed carotids were barely spurting by then, and only a pathetic gurgle came up from the ugly, blood-filled hole where, only seconds before, his throat had been. His eyes suddenly widened, very wide, and then rolled up into his head.

"He's dying!" I sobbed. "Somebody help me, *pleeeese!*"

Big Dick joined me trying to lift the fence, but its tension was stretched as far as it would go. Still straddling Don's chest, I yanked blindly at the prongs, in anger and frustration and horror. Then I felt his body start to twitch beneath me, and I knew at that moment he was dead.

"No!" I screamed. "No! No! No! *Nooooooo!*"

Big Dick grabbed me in a bear hug to pin my flailing arms. "Stop it, Sage! *Stop!* You're tearing your hands up! There's nothing more you can do!"

The rest of them arrived as Big Dick and I kneeled there in our bloody, horrified, weeping embrace.

"Oh, Jesus God!" someone yelled at their sight of Don lying under us. Several others reflexively gagged. Then we all howled and cursed and wept and wailed in our own ways as the finality of his death began to sink in.

I really don't remember much of what happened next. It's all pretty much a blur of tears and shock and vomiting and lashing out at the staggering unfairness of it.

My clearest memory of it then, as now, was gazing down through that blood-drenched fence and seeing the look in Don's eyes when he saw the look in mine.

I've never been able to shake that image, to blur it or even come to terms with it . . . and I know I never will.

AFTERMATH

My first awareness was of how tired and confused I felt. I opened my eyes and saw a bottle of clear fluid suspended above me to my left. A long plastic tube extended from the bottle to the crook of my left elbow. From my elbow I noticed my hands, covered with gauze boxing gloves, lying on top of a white sheet that stretched across my legs. I began to realize I was in a hospital room, but I couldn't understand what I was doing there.

As I continued to groggily survey my surroundings, I was surprised to find Carla and Dr. Jack Yarborough, our team physician, talking at the right side of my bed.

My first effort to speak was futile because my tongue felt swollen and heavy, and my mouth was incredibly dry.

After another failed attempt, I gasped out her name. "Carla. . . ."

She hurried to my bedside. "Thank God!"

"How do you feel, Larry?" Dr. Yarborough asked with quiet concern as Carla reached out to caress my cheek.

"Dizzy . . . I think." Snockered was more like it.

"We put you under for a few hours," he said, holding up a glass of water so I could sip from a straw in it. "You'll be woozy for a few more, but you'll feel much better soon."

All I could think to say was, "I have to take a leak."

Carla reached under the bed and pulled out a large plastic bottle. While I relieved myself into it, I began to remember bits and pieces of what happened, and those fragmented memories made me burst into tears again.

My stupefied brain still saw it very much as a bad dream, but somewhere deep inside I knew it was true, that Don had died under that horrible chain-link fence.

Carla comforted me as best she could, but her own red eyes poured too, while Dr. Yarborough turned away.

They let me cry until I couldn't any more, then Carla wiped my cheeks and blew my nose so I could talk again.

"What about . . . Annie?"

"Nobody told her until her parents were notified," Carla replied. "They drove into town and told her themselves."

My eyes focused on my hands. I lifted them up to study them as best I could, realizing that underneath the bandages they felt totally numb. "What about these?"

"Pretty bad," Dr. Yarborough said. "The flesh of both palms was ripped instead of cut, and several wounds had foreign matter, dirt and such, embedded in them. But I was with the surgeons who put them back together for you, and I've never seen men work harder to repair such damage. I honestly think that with good care and therapy, both hands should be as good as new in a year or two."

"A *year?* Or *Two?*"

"You shredded several main nerves, Larry," he said. "Nerves need about eighteen months to regenerate."

"Ohhhhhh, Jesus!" I muttered as I began to fully grasp what I'd done to myself. *Somebody has to feed me . . . shave me . . . help me pee . . . wipe me when I take a dump!* Then something else hit me, something that struck me as far worse than any of that. *I can't be a manager any more!*

For the second time in my life, I felt the gut-twisting jolt of facing life without football, but this time I was better able to deal with it. This time there were more important things to worry about than my personal concerns.

"How did Biggs come out of it?" I asked Dr. Yarborough, "I know he got cut, too. He did it trying to help me."

"Nothing like you. Twelve stitches on his left hand, twenty on his right He's already back in the dorm."

"How many stitches did I have?"

"Couldn't count 'em," Dr. Yarborough said. "Your cuts were so deep, the surgeons had to do a lot of double-layer and triple-layer stitching. I'm sure well into the hundreds."

"Ohhhh, geeze . . . !"

"Biggs had normal surface stitches," he said. "Each layer of yours was with extremely fine thread, the kind that dissolves as you heal. And they were laid extremely close together, like carpet stitching, so your palms will retain their proper shape as you heal. Also, you have extra large hands, nearly twice as large as Biggs."

"Tell me about it!" Carla muttered.

"Believe me," Dr. Yarborough added, "in the long run you'll be fine. The short run will cause you some problems, no question of that, but our commitment is to do what-ever it takes to get you back to where you were. Okay?"

"Okay," I said, wanting to believe it. "You're the doctor."

"That I am, and as a doctor I'm ordering myself to get some sleep now. It's way past my bedtime, so I'll drop in to see you first thing tomorrow morning. Keep resting."

When Carla and I were finally alone, she shifted from standing at my side near my head, to sitting on the edge of the bed near my right hip. She vaguely reminded me of my mother when I had appendicitis in the seventh grade.

"What about Mom and Dad?" I asked. "Who told them?"

"I did. They told me to give you their love and asked that I help you call them as soon as you feel up to it."

"Will they be coming down to see us?"

My parents lived in west Texas, and both had jobs that would be difficult to leave at a moment's notice unless the emergency was extreme, to the point of life and death.

"They both put in for emergency leave and should be able to get here by Sunday. That's your Mom's best guess."

I wanted to see them, but this was how it was when my knee got blown, too. In the end, I decided the delay was a good thing because it gave me time to adjust, to meet them with something other than tears and remorse.

"Where are we?" I suddenly thought to ask. "Memorial?"

Surgeries were usually done in Memorial Hospital, but Carla's head shook. "Your surgery wasn't complex, it was just tedious. They had everything they needed here."

I'd been to both, and the infirmary was much better— near home, near school, near friends. "What time is it?"

She checked her watch. "A little before 2:00 a.m."

That meant quite a while since the accident. The word about it was probably out far and wide by now.

"Do many people know what happened?"

"Larry, the whole *country* knows! It's been on every major news program since an hour after it happened."

It took me a moment to digest that, then a thought struck me. "Then how did Annie not hear about it?"

"They didn't release his name until her parents told her."

"Have you been able to see her? . . . to talk to her?"

For the first time since I woke up, Carla's composure showed visible cracks. "Yes," she said in a shaky voice.

"Can you tell me how it went?"

She closed her eyes. "Not without crying, and I just don't want to cry any more . . . not now . . . okay?"

I let that drop and asked something that had started gnawing at my memory, at my nagging guilty conscience.

"On the news shows . . . what did they say about it?"

"What a horrible tragedy it was that a wonderful guy like Don got killed. Mostly, though, they talked about you."

My heart sank like a lead plummet. That was what I was afraid of. I'd helped kill one of my best friends, and they put it on the goddamn national news! How would I ever be able to face anyone who knew what I did?

"You're a national hero, Larry," Carla went on, tears welling in her eyes as she patted my unbandaged forearm. "My very own All-American hero."

I thought I'd misheard her. *"What?"*

She seemed surprised by my reaction. "You're a hero, honey. You sacrificed your hands trying to save Don's life. The switchboard here lit up like a Christmas tree after the national news. Calls came in from all over the place."

I heard her words, tried to absorb them, but all I could visualize was Don's last seconds . . . every chilling detail—especially not blowing my whistle when I should have.

Guilt overwhelmed me and I struggled to hold back my tears, the way all strong men are supposed to do, but I didn't make it. Carla sat down on the edge of the bed and cradled my head in her arms, then she couldn't hold back any longer, either. We cried together, like a mother and an overgrown child, as she rocked me to sleep in her arms.

When I woke up the second time, the fluid bottle and plastic tube were gone, and a young nurse had replaced Carla. She sat in a chair beside my bed, and as soon as she noticed me looking at her, she got to her feet and pressed a button on a console at the head of the bed.

"Hello there, hero," she said. "How do you feel?"

Her well intentioned greeting reminded me of how rotten I did feel, but there was no reason to take it out on her.

"I'm fine," I answered on my first try. The anesthetic seemed to have worn completely off. "Where's Carla?"

"She couldn't sleep here, so at 5:00 we talked her into going home. She said to tell you she'll be back later today, and she loves you and can't wait to be back with you."

I couldn't help smiling at that. "What time is it now?"

"Almost 9:00. I just rang for a breakfast, in case you're hungry. You should be by now."

After she mentioned it, I realized I was and told her so. I threw up just before I passed out after the accident, and since it I'd had only a few sips of water. I was famished.

"Is there anything else I can do for you while we wait?"

"Well . . . if it wouldn't be too much trouble. . . ."

She smiled brightly and reached for a bedpan.

Nurse Kelley had almost finished feeding me breakfast when Dr. Yarborough walked into the room. She started to get up to leave, but he waved her down.

"Please keep your seat, I'll only be a minute. How do you feel this morning, Larry?"

"To be honest, I'm still upset about the whole thing."

"Well, try to pull yourself together. Coach Anderson is here and wants to see you as soon as you finish eating."

That suited me because I intended to ask to see him. Since waking up, I'd gone over every detail of the accident a dozen different ways, but every replay came out the same: Don's death was my fault. A quicker whistle could have prevented it. The "hero" had blown it, bigtime.

As soon as Nurse Kelly left with my tray, Coach Anderson came in. "Hello, Larry," he said somberly. "How are you feeling this morning?"

"Fine, Coach," I said, responding with those automatic, robotic words even though I was anything *but* fine.

"Good, good, glad to hear it," he said, equally robotic.

There was a pause, a brief moment of discomfort while he chose the tack to take in this unfamiliar situation.

"A lot of people have heard about what you did yesterday," he began, "and you can't imagine how many calls we've had since last night. All wanting to know about you, how you're doing. We have a stack of telegrams this high."

He spread his thumb and forefinger about two inches.

"Yes, sir, let me tell you" he went on, allowing himself a slight smile, *"Time, Newsweek, Sports Illustrated, Sporting News . . .* they've *all* called asking about you. You're the biggest thing to happen in these parts in a *long* time."

"What about Don?" I snapped, with more heat on it than I thought I intended. "What do they say about *him?*"

That immediately put Anderson on the defensive. "Well, they mention him first, naturally, but it's you they want to talk about and talk *to*. They can't talk to Don."

He said it as if he thought that was what I wanted to hear, that people wanted to talk to me about what happened. It wasn't. "It's *my* fault Don is dead, Coach. You know that; you saw it. So I don't want to talk to anyone about such a horrible mistake. I want to try to forget it."

Anderson seemed genuinely surprised by that. It literally rocked him back on his heels. "Now, wait just a minute, son. You don't know what you're saying. Don's death was an *accident*, pure and simple. Nobody's to blame for a thing like that, no more than if a lightening bolt hit him."

"A lightening bolt didn't hit him, Coach! I late-whistled them! You were there, you saw it! Everyone there saw it! How can I ever pretend it was like a lightening bolt?"

That gave him serious pause, which impressed me. When he finally spoke, it was with as much sincerity and honesty as I think he was capable of generating.

"Well, hell, son, if that's the way you want to look at it, I never should have had us out in that weather. Or I should have kept us on the practice field. That makes me as much to blame as anyone. And it's Davis' fault, too, you know. He never should have called that play. That situation called for a sweep the other way. And it's Biggs' fault for not turning the flow back inside. Shit, son, if you want to assign blame, I can make you a goddamn list!"

Tears of rage and anguish stung my eyes again. "Look, I appreciate what you're trying to do here, but it's not right!"

He moved over and sat on the foot of my bed, dropping his "coach" mask as much as he could. He spoke from his heart, man to man. "Listen to me, Larry, I'm going to tell you the one big truth that overrides anything you think *might* be the truth. And I want you to hold onto this.

"Yesterday afternoon you did one of the most courageous things I've ever seen in my life, and it's one of the most courageous things a helluva lot of people have heard about in a long time. Don't cheapen what that means to them.

"What I'm saying, son, is that there is very damn little dignity in dying, and especially not in the way poor Don died. But what you did trying to save him can gave his death a lasting value to everyone who witnessed it, and to everyone who will ever hear about it. What you did makes his death stand as a lasting symbol of something grand and noble . . . of the love one teammate can show for another in a moment of absolute, heart-rending crisis. I'd sure hate to see you piss something like that away."

His words got a stranglehold on me that I couldn't shake. Maybe he was right. He sure *sounded* right. Maybe it would be wrong to reduce Don's death to one stupid mistake.

"Now you listen to me, Larry," he commanded, quietly but firmly. "That accident was either nobody's fault, or it was a lot of people's fault, me among them. But no matter how you choose to look at it, no one person is entitled to *all* the blame for it. And if you'll please trust an older man's judgment . . . a man who's seen death in war on several occasions . . . if you try to take it all on yourself, you'll wind up right alongside Don. It will kill you, too."

Tears started gushing again, I just couldn't help it.

"That's the way life is," he concluded. "You can blame yourself to death for all the bad things in it, or you can take your lumps, however they come at you, and move on."

He was getting to me, no question, so I wiped my wet cheeks against my shoulders and nodded agreement. "I can see your point, Coach . . . I think you make sense."

"Good!" he said, clapping his hands and rubbing them together while getting to his feet. "Now, how do you feel, seriously? Are you up to a little excitement?"

"What do you mean?"

"Remember I told you how the people out there want to know about you? . . . how you're doing and so forth?"

I nodded again.

"Well, I didn't mean just people around here at Cajun State. I mean people all over the country. Reporters and television news crews have flown in from everywhere. We called a press conference for you at 10:00 this morning."

Ten! "Geeze, Coach, that's only about a half-hour from now, isn't it? I think I'd rather have more time to gather myself a bit more, to have more time to talk to Carla."

His head shook emphatically. "We can't wait, Larry. The evening editions of east coast newspapers will get left out if we do that, and that's not fair, is it? It has to be at ten."

I didn't like it, but I didn't know how to argue against it.

"Fine," he said, heading for the door. "They're setting up the lights and cameras in a big room down the hall. Stay here and rest until they're ready to get you ready for it."

I lay there in a daze, trying to figure out what was happening to me, when suddenly it occurred to me that this might be another one of Tom Everett's crazy pranks.

Sure! That's it!

Then a makeup lady came to shave me, comb my hair, and make me look presentable. I knew then it was for real.

MEETING THE PRESS

A few minutes before 10:00, I asked Nurse Kelley to dress me in the fresh clothes Carla brought for me last night. Everything I had on yesterday would have to be trashed, even if it wasn't covered with Don's blood. I wouldn't want any mementos of that event anywhere near me.

I guess out of sentiment, Carla had brought one of my three white manager shirts. Nurse Kelly explained that we'd have to cut the inside seam of both sleeves so my gauze-gloved hands could fit through the holes. I told her to go ahead, there were more like it where it came from.

Not long after that, a plump, bald, sweaty little man arrived in a highly agitated state. "Absolutely not!" he began. "You can *not* appear before the nation dressed like that! We're set up around a bed, for God's sake! America expects you to *be* in a bed, hands all destroyed. Can't you see what being dressed like this will do to your image?"

"Who are you?" I asked, as politely as I could manage.

"My firm has been retained to handle publicity for your team," he snapped, "so you'll do well to follow my advice."

"But I'm fine now," I protested, which was a bit of a stretch. I nearly fell off the bed when I first sat up, but the initial wave of dizziness passed and I felt okay again.

"That's not the point!" he insisted. "The point is that we don't want to look *contrived*, do we? Everything is set up around a hospital bed, and people will expect to see a *patient* resting in that bed, not some strapping brute with a red crawfish springing off his chest, for God's sake!"

I looked down at the tiny Fightin' Crawdad on my shirt.

"You really *must* allow us to put a gown and robe over your clothes. No one in that room will care, but you should always consider your public image, dear boy—image!"

He was fruity as a popsicle, but he clearly meant business, so I let Nurse Kelly—not him—put the gown back on me, then he tied it up so my shirt didn't show under it.

They offered to roll me in a wheelchair, but I knew I could walk it. Then, when I stepped into the hall, flashbulbs started popping and dozens of people waiting there started clapping, but I couldn't pick out a familiar face among them. It reminded me of our charter flights to away games, when strange faces came to lick the team's gravy, while freshmen, redshirts, and the injured were left behind.

Coach Anderson escorted me to another hallway lined with more people congratulating me and patting me on the back. He brought me into a wardroom with six beds in it. Bright lights sat atop a forest of thin poles extending around the foot of the right-side-center bed. Four television cameras were set up outside that perimeter, two at the foot and one on each side. They were small, portable models, like the ones used to film interviews at practice.

I began to pick out familiar faces in the room, local sports commentators and a few sports reporters. Then I saw Randall. I went over to him and spoke in a low voice.

"Man, am I glad to see you. I feel like a freak."

"You're doing great," he said softly. "I'll talk to you later."

A hand gently tugged by elbow. "Larry," the familiar voice said, "we haven't met. I'm Stan Jefferies." He was a big-time roving correspondent for one of the major TV networks.

"Hi," was all I could manage.

"I'm one of a half-dozen newscasters who want to interview you this morning. We drew straws and I got to go first. The others will introduce themselves later. Understand?"

"Yes, sir."

"We're about ready to begin my interview, so could I ask you to get in bed now? We need a light-meter reading."

I nodded and got into the bed.

"Now, Larry, Coach Anderson assures us that you're an articulate young man, so we won't waste time rehearsing. We're only going to ask simple, basic questions about the accident, and all we want are simple, basic answers. If you have any problems or make any mistakes, we'll cut those out of the tape, so no need to be nervous. Okay?"

He smiled, turned around, reached for a microphone, and said to one of the cameramen, "How do I look?"

The cameraman gave thumbs up and Stan Jefferies said, "Okay, then, roll it!"

The interviews went like Stan Jefferies said they would. None of the interviewers became ghoulish or maudlin, and the whole affair came off surprisingly well. When it was over, everyone thanked me and gave me a small ovation, then Nurse Kelley escorted me back to my room.

The crowd was much thinner on the way back, and many of those remaining stopped in briefly to offer personal regards and sympathies. After several minutes of that, Nurse Kelley ordered everyone out so I could get some rest. When they were all gone, I thanked her and sent her to get Randall. I was in bed when he came in.

"Well?" I asked him. "What'd you think?"

He shrugged and stuffed his hands into his pockets.

"What does *that* mean?" I asked.

"It means I'm not sure. I don't know what to make of it."

"Make of what?"

Randall scratched at his ear as he moved to the chair beside the bed. "This whole publicity bit," he said as he sank down. "I mean, is this something that *needs* so much attention? Is there no room left for dignity in death?"

"What do you mean?"

He nodded toward the room's big window. "What's out there, Larry, is an apathetic town as far as Cajun State football is concerned. You have a 50,000 seat stadium for a team that basically can't draw flies. Am I right?"

"Right."

"So what I see is a crappy football team that barely pulls its own weight, financially, if it pulls its weight at all, suddenly in a position to sell a lot of extra tickets if they play the sympathy card hard and fast. See what I mean?"

I balked at the outrageousness of his suggestion. "Do you *really* think they'd hype Don's death to sell tickets? I mean, even them . . . could they possibly stoop *that* low?"

"Well, so far, nothing has looked out of line. It's certainly a national-level news story, so there's no problem explaining all the attention it's getting." He paused a moment. "All I'm really saying, I guess, is that the *potential* for ugly exploitation is lying right there. It will take some very noble types to not pick it up and try to make the most of it."

I sank back in bed. "I think we both know about the nobility of coaches and school administrators."

"Exactly. . . ."

Just then a distraught Carla barged into my room and threw herself on the bed, into my arms. Randall could see he needed to leave and made silent motions to me that he intended to do just that. In seconds he was gone, as Carla wailed against my chest and I held her as lovingly as the clumsy hand bandages would allow.

"What's the matter, honey?" I said in a soothing tone.

"It's Annie!" she blubbered.

I couldn't help thinking it. She loved Don so much, the word *suicide* flashed through my mind. "What happened?"

"She lost the baby this morning!"

I couldn't help thinking this, too: *When it rains, it pours.*

I held her until she cried herself out, which gave me time to come to some kind of grips with it. This would put yet another gaping hole in a lot of Swiss-cheesed hearts.

Finally, I said, "You'd have been the best godmother a baby ever had . . . and your turn will come someday to return the favor to her . . . I promise."

She looked up at me, frantically. "I don't care what, our first son will be called Don. I mean it. Are you with me?"

I smiled. "Our team will produce about a hundred Dons over the next decade, honey, so sign me up for one."

A smile broke through her tear-streaked anguish. "I'm going to tell Annie that as soon as I see her. Okay?"

"Speaking of Annie, I want to see her, too. When can I get out of here? When can you sign me out?"

"Will they let you out so soon?"

"I don't see why not. I feel up to it, it's what I want to do, and I can't be held against my will."

"Don't bet on it," she replied. "The team has been confined to the dorm like on game days. The coaches sealed it off this morning so only authorized people can get in."

"What's *that* all about?"

"I don't know. Classes were called off for a day of mourning, and that's supposedly what they're doing—mourning."

Enforced mourning sounded like an overreaction by

the coaching staff. "Shouldn't it be voluntary?"

"Considering all you've told me about how the coaches operate, it just seemed par for the course to me."

"Yeah, I guess you're right. It would be par for them."

"So, anyway, they might not want you out, either."

"Listen, we're gonna walk out of here *right now*."

After a bit of quibbling and some paperwork, we did.

It was a long walk across campus, with countless people stopping us to offer quiet condolence or words of praise or thanks or whatever. I waded through it all as patiently and politely as I could because I was determined to see how the team was handling it, especially Big Dick.

Carla took a seat in the downstairs TV room while I went up into the men-only dorm. The assistant trainers were monitoring the lobbies of the two floors that housed the football players. Bud Ross was on the fifth floor and Ray Trent on the sixth. I walked up to Bud, chatted with him for a minute, then walked out onto the floor.

Loop Watson saw me first, and his face lit up. "Hey, Sage! Great to see you! You're lookin' good, man!"

He was chatting with Gil Travers, who turned around and smiled. "Hey, listen, Sage, we all wanted to come see you this morning, but the coaches locked us down."

"Yeah, I heard. What reason did they give for it?"

Watson smirked. "To stop us from going out carousing."

"You know we all feel like doing that," Travers added.

"Come on down to Tom's room," I said. "We'll talk."

We picked up a trail of others as we moved along. They all wanted to know about my hands, how I was doing, what the recovery and healing prognosis was, etc. I told them all they better hope they weren't anywhere near me over the next several weeks if I had to take a dump.

Just seeing I could make fun of myself about it seemed like a tonic for them. We ended up filling Tom's room to overflowing, with several left standing out in the hall.

***

When the conversation finally turned serious, Tom explained the lockdown as an attempt to control information. "They said it was to help keep our minds on Texas, but you know that's a pile of bullshit. If we didn't need to be locked down before today to do it, then why today?"

"They don't want you talking to reporters," I suggested. "The old 'no comment' routine. They're nuts about that."

Everyone associated with the team was never supposed to talk to anyone anywhere about team business, supposedly because of gambling influences; but we all knew it was only to allow the coaches to control the flow of information about the team, both outward and inward.

"Absolutely," Tom agreed. "At lunch today, the coaches brought reporters around to our tables and let them ask any of us any questions they wanted to ask, but they always stood right there, lurking near each of them."

"What about practice?" I asked, assuming it was cancelled.

"They made us vote at lunch," Tom said. "Anderson gave a speech about how it was entirely up to us, but he asked us to consider what Don would have wanted us to do."

"Like President Kennedy," Swede mumbled, recalling how most scheduled football games were played the weekend of his assassination, even high school games that very night! He was pronounced dead, and six hours later kickoff whistles blew all over America. Everyone justified it by insisting that was what President Kennedy would have wanted.

"They told us to vote only because of all the media people there," Wizard explained. "'Hackler went out with the ballots and came back in a few minutes with the result."

"Don't tell me," I said, "let me guess . . . it was unanimous. A split vote would make it seem like there are some chickenshit assholes on this team who don't want to honor Don's memory with a practice the day after his death."

"Well, I'm one of those chickenshit assholes," Tom said, quickly followed by a chorus of, "Me, too!" "Me, too!"

But, as always, the coaches called the tune.

***

PRACTICE DIRGE

I stayed with them about forty-five minutes, during
which players would drop by to say a few words to me and
then move on to let someone else in. I especially wanted to
see Big Dick, but they said he was finally napping after a
very long night of sleepless recrimination of the same kind
I was feeling. I decided not to wake him now, but I made
sure Tom would tell him I wanted to talk to him.

I left when I could tell they were starting to get nervous
about the upcoming practice. The accident would make it
a doubly tough mental strain, and each one needed to go
though their preparations in their own particular way.

I took a back route to the stadium, which took me into the
residential neighborhood where the campus was inserted.
Not many people noticed me or my injured hands, which I
hid by tucking them under my armpits as I walked.

Suddenly, a car with a couple of campus police pulled
up behind me and honked the horn once. "Hey, Larry,"
one of them called out. "We know who you are! Get in!"

I walked over to them. "Something wrong, officers?"

"Wherever you're goin', we're takin' you," the driver said.

"We're not takin' no for an answer," the other one said.

They drove me to the stadium saying nothing but kind
things to me, or about me, which made me feel bad about
all the crap Tom habitually dumped on them. I thought of
having a word with him about it, to tell him they weren't
so much dipthongs as just ordinary guys trying hard to
do a job that in many ways was thankless and mundane.

Then I remembered it wasn't my place to interfere.

I went around to everyone on the coaching staff and in
the front offices, letting them see I was okay, saying nice
things to them, letting them say nice things to me. None
of us kidded ourselves about my situation. I was on my

way out, and I had no choice but to say some goodbyes.

My last stop was the equipment shed, saying goodbye to Cap'n without actually saying it. He was a huge part of my life for the past three years, in many ways a surrogate father, and I'd miss him like a family member.

I also spent time talking to him about Sir Henry. Before yesterday's practice, I'd mentioned that Sir Henry would be a good choice for Stanton's replacement in the spring, when I'd be gone and his shoulder would be healed enough to let him do nearly all of what would have to be done.

Cap'n agreed with me because everyone knew Hank was a good guy, and smart, and motivated by his need to hold onto his scholarship in any form, even doing laundry. Now, though, if the job was going to be his, he'd have to come on board as soon as possible, well before his shoulder was healed. Cap'n told me not to worry about it.

"We'll get walking wounded to pitch in until he can take over. They just stand around with their thumbs up their butts most of the time, anyway. I don't mind puttin' a few of 'em to work while Hank gets well and gets trained up."

"Thanks, Cap'n," I said. "He's worth the extra trouble."

While I was in the shed, Big Dick came to pick up his roll. I saw his hands were bandaged very differently from mine, more like a boxer before they put the gloves on. His palms were covered, but all of his fingers were free to move, though three were wrapped with bandaids.

Even with limited use of his hands, he'd be dressing out in shorts and a T-shirt. That was the rule for all injured players who could do it—shorts and T's for every practice, rain or shine. If you were on the team, and your injury wasn't season-ending, you were expected to stay as much a part of it as possible until you could return.

Our eyes met and held in silence, but now with a bond that would hold us together like brothers for the rest of our lives. Without even a nod, with only instinct to guide us, we both moved away from the equipment shed, far enough to one side of it so we could talk in private.

"How you feeling?" I asked.

"Like shit," he replied. "You?"

"Shit squared, but I'm trying to be positive about it."

His eyes misted with tears behind his granny glasses. "How can anyone be positive about something like that?"

"We didn't do it, Ricky," which was the name he grew up with and what we called him in public. "It wasn't our fault."

"I didn't drop him, Sage. If I would have just dropped him with a cleaner, harder shot. . . ."

"It was a great tackle," I assured him. "He just fought you too hard for too long. It was an accident, no more or less."

He blinked hard. "Coach tell you the lightening story?"

I might have known! "Yes, as a matter of fact, he did."

"What do you think? Do you buy it?"

"It makes a good point. There must be any one of a hundred things . . . maybe a thousand things . . . that if any of us had done differently, it wouldn't have happened."

"But it *did* happen!" he rasped. "And I was right in the goddamn middle of it! How am I supposed to get over *that?*"

"Look, I blew a late whistle, so I'm more responsible for it than you were. You were doing your job . . . I didn't do mine."

He was clearly surprised to hear me say that. He wiped his cheeks with the backside of his bandaged hands and said, "Noooo, Sage, your whistle wasn't late. He was still struggling . . . he still had a chance to break away."

I shook my head. "No, Ricky, he really didn't. You had him in a locked-tight bear hug. He was as good as down . . . but I just *wanted* him to break away because he was my friend and I . . . I loved him . . . and. . . ."

He stepped forward to grip me in another bear hug, and we both started bawling like babies.

We both were embarrassed by our bloodshot eyes, but we walked into the varsity dressing room with our heads up. We weren't the only ones in there looking like hell, but I wanted them all to see we'd been crying together.

The real reason I joined him was that I couldn't let him walk in there alone, looking like that, as if he weren't man enough to stand the pain everyone else was feeling and managing to cope with. I didn't even know what it meant to *be* a man any more. I used to *think* I knew, but now I wasn't sure of anything in that area of my life.

In a way, I felt neutered.

I went around the room saying a few words to the guys I hadn't spoken to in the dorm. When I reached the locker of Jeff Rivers, he patted the bench beside him so I could sit down and we could talk quietly between ourselves.

Jeff was a second team tackle, a guy I came in with as a freshman, and someone I had battled with on the field during many freshman practices. I liked him, he was a good guy, but once you've fought over the same position on a team, there's always a thin veil of animosity between you, a lack of trust or confidence or some other vague emotion that can be felt but not precisely named.

"Listen, Sage," he began, "I want to tell you a story. When I was a junior in high school, my best friend was Ed Morgan. We did everything together, including lifting weights. So one day we're lifting in our weight room and we're sweating like pigs, dropping beads all over the floor. So Ed lifts a heavy load in a clean and jerk, and his rear foot slips doing the clean. He falls backward, straight back, holding the bar. He went down so fast, you can't believe it. Up, down, *whomp!* Just that fast."

I couldn't see where this was leading, but I said, "Got it."

"Well," Jeff resumed, "Ed doesn't say anything because he's knocked silly when his head hits the floor. He just lays there kind of groaning. My first thought is that the bar might have crushed his ribs, but we were using 25 pound plates, so there seemed to be enough room to clear his chest. That was how it looked at first glance, anyway.

"So I figured maybe he'd lost his wind and that's the worst of it. But it's not. Suddenly, I notice his left hand and wrist. It's bent back almost touching his forearm with the top of his hand. He's broken it clean. So then I wonder how his other arm is, and I see it's broken the exact same way. He's broken both arms clean, just above the wrist, because he was still holding the bar when he hit the floor."

Now it was clear. This was a story about how to deal with life with your hands out of action. I tuned in completely.

"You can see Ed had a problem exactly like you do now. He couldn't eat or shave or pee or crap without help, so at school when he needed to eat or had to hit the head, I was the only person he'd let help him until he could do it for himself. So I want to tell you, Sage, that any time you're near me—on campus, in class, anywhere—and you need help, I have a poop-load of experience with Ed, if you'll pardon the expression, and I'd be honored to help you."

I looked at this smiling, friendly guy who, at bottom, I had never bothered to get to know really well. To me he was just another player on the team, no better or worse than most of the others. A kind of place holder in my life, a guy I'd never contact again after my graduation in a few months. Now he was offering to be a central character for me in the new life that was shaping up for me.

"Thank you, Jeff," I said. "I can't tell you how much that means to me. And, to be honest, I could pee right now."

His big round tackle face smiled wide. "Let's do it!"

After peeing, I left the varsity locker to spend the rest of the pre-practice wait with the redshirts. As always, they needed as much support as the varsity, but never got it, so I knew I could find ways to be more useful with them.

I also didn't want to seem like a martyr seeking sympathy, because once you lose your "active" status, you're expected to keep a certain distance. It's another way of isolating the unfit, of keeping the losers from the winners.

Among the redshirts there was another undercurrent of concern that only they, and I, knew about—Prosser and what he'd vowed to do to Hackler. Don's death would mean no quit drills this week, and probably not next.

We'd be awash with unfamiliar media people until the novelty of our tragedy wore off, and quit drills couldn't be held in an atmosphere like that. So now Prosser was on the team at least for the first couple of games, maybe more. Eventually, though, Hackler would be able to get things back on the track they were on yesterday.

Coach Anderson called the team together for a pre-practice speech, surrounded by a group of out-of-town journalists and cameramen busily recording his words from outside the team perimeter. Their presence clearly inspired him.

"Men," he began, "yesterday we went through a tragedy that will stay with each of us for as long as we live. There's no point in me moralizing about what happened, beyond saying that it's hardest to accept when you're young and strong and healthy. But now it's over and we have to put it behind us, and this practice is where we have to start.

"We'll expect dropped passes and missed snap counts and busted plays today, that's only natural. But we still have a game to play this coming Saturday night, and we can't use Don Slade's death as an excuse for giving up. *He* wouldn't give up *one inch* without a dogfight for it!"

Anderson's tone had risen, and a film of tears glistened in his eyes, as his voice dropped to a raspy growl. "And we all know . . . each and every one of us who were there, who saw it happen . . . we all *know* that's why he died. *Because he wouldn't quit when the average person would have!* That's the kind of man he was, the kind of man we'll remember him as, and by God that's the kind of men *you* have to be to honor his memory on Saturday night!"

Dramatically, he searched the earnest young faces crowded around him as he drove his message home. He let the silence build for several long seconds, then he spoke out again, his voice rising in a slow crescendo.

"Dammit, men, the University of Texas Longhorns are coming here to whip your butts! Are you gonna let 'em do it?"

That brought a rousing chorus of, "Hell, no!"

"Then get out there today and show me something!"

Anderson's speech was masterful, and for one crazy moment even I felt like our team could beat anyone. Then practice started and we all came back to reality.

The starting horn was blown by a lightly injured freshman who'd been assigned to assist Chris Stanton in my absence, and now that job would rotate among the lightly injured until the arrangements were made for Sir Henry to take his place as the new assistant manager.

With or without any second thoughts, Stanton assumed my role as senior manager, but nothing he or anyone else could do would help to get this practice on track. The spark was missing from the moment calisthenics began.

Superficially, everything looked the same: uniformed bodies performed routine exercises to the same cadences they used hundreds of times. However, I knew the spirits inside those bodies, and I could see they'd been terribly damaged. Each player has his own rhythm, his own level of energy, and neither measuring rod was the same.

I don't know if they were physically gun-shy or simply heartbroken, but practice was bad, even for us. They ran like sleepwalkers, blocked like clowns, and tackled like wimps, but the coaches kept up a constant patter of compliments and encouragement. Everyone gave it their best.

With nothing for either of us to do but watch, Big Dick and I gravitated to each other along the west sideline. We didn't say much, and when we did speak, it was only technical comments about what we were seeing. We certainly didn't want to say more than that in case it would trigger another round of crying in either or both of us.

"Goddammit, Jensen!" Hackler suddenly shouted, delivering the first harsh words of the day. "Play to the outside when they come at you like that! Never get sucked inside!"

On the field still mucky from yesterday's rain, Prosser

stutter-stepped Will Jensen on a slant run, drawing him inside, and then skirted around him. But then, in typical redshirt fashion, he cut directly into Corky Ames' pursuit and let himself be stopped for only a three yard gain.

"What do you think they'll do about Prosser now?" Big Dick asked. "And what about tomorrow's two-minute drill?"

The only serious hitting in a Thursday practice came at the very end, when the varsity offense and defense ran a series of two-minute drills against a freshman defense at one end of the field, and the redshirt offense at the other end. It was the only time both the freshmen and redshirts could play real football, because there was no stopping to re-run a play that made the varsity look bad.

The whole point of the drill was to track the ball's movement against the clock more than the opponent, so it was here that freshmen made their best impressions for the upcoming spring and the following season. Redshirts, on the other hand, were inviting later retaliation from Hackler if they embarrassed his defense more than an occasional play that could be attributed to luck rather than talent. However, even though they were under extreme pressure to give sub-par performances, they still managed to get in some solid licks, whether Hackler liked it or not.

Last year, Tom Everett guided his truly inferior redshirt team to several last-second scoring drives against Hackler's finest. He may have lacked option-running ability, but Tom was a brilliant tactician and an excellent passer, the two qualities most needed by a successful two-minute quarterback. In fact, when he was allowed to call his own plays, Tom was the best quarterback we had at using his personnel, the clock, and field position. It was just a damn shame he didn't play for a pro-spread team, because there he might have been a starter.

This year's redshirt squad was considerably stronger than last year's, despite the loss of Sir Henry. A good freshman had been moved into his spot, while Gene Skidmore was an excellent blocker on runs or passes, and

Heape would have been on the varsity if not for Rabbit's charmed existence on it. But Prosser was the *real* difference this year, and everyone knew it. If he wanted to, he could run crazy wild in a wide-open exercise like Thursday's two-minute drill, which the coaches would dread.

"They'll find a reason to keep him out of it," I said.

Big Dick nodded solemnly, then a few seconds passed before he said openly what had to be on everyone's mind. "Those bastards would've been happy to see Prosser under that fence. Hackler would have danced a jig on his body."

As horrible as that was to imagine, it might well have been true. No, actually, it almost certainly *was* true.

Big Dick and I drifted near a three-quarter-speed half-line drill. There was no tackling, and Prosser was doing nothing unusual, but little moves here and there . . . a juke, a feint, a mercurial stop and go . . . showed his true skills.

"What about this idea?" Big Dick said. "Now that Don is gone and the Bull's ankle will be iffy at game time, do you think they'd consider dressing Prosser out? Not to start, or anything like that, but to play when the going gets tough?"

I shook my head. "They can't, even if all of them except Hackler wanted to. He's made such a big personal deal out of getting rid of Prosser, he's painted himself into a corner, not just with us but with the other coaches, too."

"What do the other coaches have to do with it?"

"It's the old blackball system. If a coach gets down on a guy, and it's personal the way it is with Hackler, the others are obliged to get down on the target just as hard. They never override each other about who to get rid of because, while it's Hackler's personal vendetta this time, the next time it might be their own, and they want to know their fellow coaches will back them up on it."

"So even if other coaches wanted to use him . . . Marshal or Anderson . . . Hackler's vote would keep him down?"

"Not exactly. Anderson can override anyone's vote, but he won't undermine coaching principles or loyalty to his assistants unless the ground is cracking under his feet."

"You make it sound like a closed case."

"It is. Even if Prosser had support among the assistant staff, which he might for all we know, it won't help. Only Anderson and Marshall carry real weight against Hackler, but they won't use it if there's any way to avoid it."

"I'd sure like to see what Prosser could do in a game."

"So would I, but Hackler won't let it happen."

A few minutes later I noticed Randall Webber walking my way. I muttered to Big Dick, "I need to talk to this guy," then I moved down the sideline to meet him halfway.

"Feeling any better now?" he asked me.

"Better than I was," I replied, "but still not too good."

"Me, either, but we have to deal with the realities. I just heard that Don's funeral will be tomorrow at 1:00 p.m. The team will go as a group, of course, but since you'll be with Carla, I thought you might like to ride with me."

The word *funeral* jolted me. Images flooded through my mind . . . Don's eyes, his throat, spurts of his blood. . . .

"Sure," I managed to squeeze out. Then something else intruded on my thoughts. "How'd you know about Carla?"

"I talked to her for long time last night at the hospital."

"You did? She didn't mention that to me."

"She talked to a hundred people she didn't know last night while they were operating on you. You should have seen how she took charge of that madhouse at the hospital. She was amazing. You'd have been very proud of her."

"I'm *always* proud of her."

At the end of practice, Coach Anderson huddled everyone together for more than his usual wrap-up.

"We had a good practice today," he lied, "and I'm damned proud of you for putting yourselves through it under these terrible conditions. I think it shows the kind of character we have on this team. We're going to surprise a lot of folks come Saturday night . . . you can bet on that."

I was sure a helluva lot of gamblers would.

"Now, I hate to bring this up, but it's something we all have to face. Don will be buried at his home in Libertyville tomorrow, and we've arranged for the team to ride up on buses as a unit. Does anyone have any objections to that?"

What fool would have spoken?

"Good. The service is scheduled for 1:00 p.m. so lunch will be at 11:00, and the buses will pull out at noon sharp. Dress is dark slacks, ties, and team blazers. Questions?"

Again no one spoke.

"Good. Now, gentlemen, let's have one minute of silent prayer for Don and his family, then take it on in."

I went home and watched myself talk about Don on all the major news programs. Carla kept switching channels so we could see how each one handled the story. A local sports announcer insinuated that Don's death might fire us up enough to beat Texas. It would have bothered me more if the announcer wasn't a low-brow dimwit who spent most of his program reporting horse racing results.

After cooking and feeding me dinner, Carla drove me to the infirmary to meet Dr. Yarborough. A small blood spot had seeped through the bandage on my right hand, and when Carla called about it, he told her to bring me over.

"Ahhh *hah!*" he exclaimed when the bandage came off. "There's the culprit."

When I saw my hand free of its bandage, I almost gagged. It was a bloated purple and yellow color, with ugly red gashes twisting all over the palm and fingers. The thin black thread of the outermost stitches held them all together like the stitching on a baseball. All but one of those stitches seemed to be cutting through the surrounding skin. Carla turned away.

"It looks horrible!" she yelped, which was exactly what I was thinking, then she asked exactly what I wanted to ask. "Are you *sure* those hand surgeons fixed him up?"

"Except for this stitch right here," Dr. Yarborough said, pointing to a black string with an untied knot at the base of my thumb. "It just came loose, that's all. Nothing serious. Again, trust me, those guys did a fantastic job for you. A week from now it will be half this size, and two weeks from now we can think about taking off the bandages. You'll be surprised how fast the skin heals."

"But not the nerves, eh?" I asked.

His head shook. "No, I'm sorry . . . not the nerves."

When we got back to the apartment, the phone was ringing. Carla rushed in to grab it. It was Tom, so she held the phone up to my ear to let me talk to him.

"Where have you been?" he asked peevishly. "I've been trying to get you for an hour."

"I popped a stitch and had to get it fixed. What's up?"

"I know you must have watched the news shows, so you know about the rumors going around that Don's death might motivate us enough to beat Texas."

"Yeah, I saw it. What a bunch of morons!"

"Techno says the line has been near forty all summer, which is standard for one-sided games. But it's already heading south at a good clip. Now it's thirty-seven."

Techno was one of the smartest guys on our squad, a second team wide receiver with good speed, good hands, and an astounding grasp of math and all mathematical principles. For obvious reasons, football betting systems were an abiding interest for him. He could read a point spread like a road map, and chart fluctuations in it like a seismograph. He'd be one of the first to know about it if people were actually taking us seriously.

"He says it'll be thirty-five by tonight," Tom added.

That meant bookies all over the country would soon be accepting bets with Texas as 35-point favorites over us.

"He says that's not out of line considering what's happened with us. He'll know a lot more by tomorrow night, but he expects it to level off. People aren't *that* stupid."

I could only agree. The spread in a game like ours could only drop so far. As money poured in on us, driving the spread down, other money would pour in on Texas, driving it up. The issue was where the balance point would be reached, and would it be a reasonable margin going into the game? In the shape we were in now, Texas could beat us by fifty points, easily. The bookies would clean up.

"What about the gate?" I asked. "How's that looking?"

Tom said, "Looks like we'll break the attendance record."

THURSDAY

Libertyville was a bit less than an hour's drive from the city, and Carla and I did take Randall up on his offer to ride with him. I asked Carla to call Coach Anderson's office and tell whichever secretary answered that I felt I'd be more comfortable driving there in a car. She was careful, of course, to avoid saying which car it would be.

I knew the coaches would be pissed if they realized I went with a reporter they didn't have a firm lock on, but my worries about what they thought of me were already easing. My connections to the team were being severed as completely, and in some ways as raggedly, as the nerves in my hands.

The feeling was how I imagined an ocean liner would be when leaving the dock for a long voyage to a strange land. The ropes holding me fast were being loosened, and soon the tugboats would come to guide me out and on my way. I could feel it happening, slowly but surely, and now, with no choice about it, I was buoyed by the sensations.

We arrived shortly before the team buses, but not before a crowd of reporters and television camera crews. They swarmed the car, asking for comments as we made our way into the church. I answered as best I could until we wedged into the front door, and I realized that was as close as I'd ever come to feeling like a movie star or rock star.

***

For me, and I suspect for Carla as well, Don's death finally became reality when we viewed his body in the half-opened casket. His skin was ghostly-white, whiter than Prosser at his palest, and his scattering of farm-boy freckles had somehow disappeared. His closed eyes were sunk deep in their sockets, and they were ringed by large, dark circles he never had in life. Only his reddish-blond hair looked the same as two days ago.

I glanced down at his hands to avoid looking at the terrible place below his chin. They were neatly folded across his stomach, and were as white as his face. I noticed a scraped knuckle on his left hand. The skin was knocked off during that last practice, maybe during that last tackle, and the raw wound was covered by a pale cosmetic.

I finally mustered the courage to look at the turtleneck sweater that covered what used to be his throat. I couldn't help wondering what they stuffed the hole with, because the concealment was perfect. The turtleneck, I think, was a pale yellow color, but I can't be sure. My eyes kept filling with what they saw under that blood-drenched fence, and, finally, there were too many tears to see any more.

I turned away and went into the small antechamber set aside for Don's family. The first person I noticed was Annie, sitting in a wheelchair, which startled me at first until I remembered yesterday's miscarriage. Her blank, vacant stare went past me as I stepped through the room's entrance, but somehow, someway, she recognized me, and both hands flew to cover her mouth.

She rose unsteadily as two girlfriends tried to make her stay seated, but she shook them off and determindly weaved her way toward me. I stepped forward to meet her in a state of near-shock myself. She looked so much more wretched than I could ever have imagined, nearly as changed as Don. Her face was drawn and pale like his, though her eyes were beyond red and allergy puffy.

"Ohhhh, Luurie," she slurred, making it clear that she

had been heavily sedated, "it's sooo . . . I'm sooo. . . ."

She fell into my ham-handed embrace, and we stood holding on to each other for a long, awkward moment of unparalleled anguish for me. People in the room glanced away as Annie tried to fight through the haze of drugs.

"Whut hap . . . happened?" she mumbled. "Can you . . . tell me . . . please . . . whut *really* . . . happened?"

Despite the drugs addling her brain, in her own way she was doing what we all were doing in our own ways. She was fighting against the absurd illogic of finding someone to love, someone who is a perfect compliment for you, and then to lose them to such a capricious twist of fate.

How could she accept it as that? It had to be much more; there had to be a reason behind it with value and purpose on a grand scale. Otherwise, the fickle arbitrariness of it was too much to bear. And yet, there was nothing else for any of us to do except call it what it really, truly was:

"It was an accident, Annie," I whispered, repeating the same useless words that by then she'd heard countless times from others. "A terrible, terrible accident."

I felt her weak grip loosen on me. "Thass whut . . . everyone says . . . a turrible . . . askadent. . . ."

Carla stepped in and gently but firmly took Annie into her embrace, steering her back to the wheelchair. Annie directed a few incoherent words at Carla before sinking back into the stupor I found her in, vacant and staring, not really there, not really anywhere. For the duration of this funeral, she would be as gone as her husband.

A few seconds later a large, ruddy, middle-aged man approached me, and I recognized him as Don's father.

"Son," he began very quietly, "I want to thank you for what you tried to do for Donnie. This whole town appreciates what you gave up to try to help him. Mrs. Slade and me . . . we want you to know . . . we want you to. . . ."

He couldn't go on, letting his chin sink to his chest as he bought his right hand to his eyes to stanch his tears.

It was devastating to watch such a powerful-looking man reduced to emotional rubble. I replied quietly to him.

"Donnie would have done as much for any of us, sir. He was a wonderful young man. I loved him like a brother."

That was the absolute truth.

My mind was nearly a cinder by the time I found myself standing in front of Mrs. Slade. She was a small, gray-haired woman who sat staring straight ahead while tightly clutching a single white rose in her lap.

"Mrs. Slade, I can't tell you how badly I feel for you."

"That's quite all right," she said as a tight little smile twisted across her otherwise frozen features. "I understand perfectly, perfectly. Have you met my other sons?"

She motioned to her left side where a young man older than Don and two younger boys sat with bowed heads. "That's Doug and Mike and Steven here next to me," she went on. "Say hello, boys. Mind your manners."

They looked up at me and nodded desultorily, clearly wishing this was over. Then the oldest, the one she called Steven, put his arm around her and said, "Take it easy, Mom, take it easy. Everything's going to be all right."

No, Steven, it isn't . . . not ever again.

After Don was laid to rest, we stood around outside the cemetery waiting for the buses to pull up to take the team back to campus. Nobody said much. There wasn't much to say. The ceremony at the graveside tore our hearts out, and I could tell from looking around that a piece of every member of our team was down in that coffin with Don.

When the team started loading into the buses, Carla asked if she could stay behind with Annie. It was clear Annie needed help, but it was also clear she had many friends she grew up with who would care for her and see her through the worst of it. I urged Carla to come back the next afternoon, when Annie would be more lucid.

***

On the way home, Randall said, "How do you think the funeral's going to affect the team? I saw some pretty shook-up guys when they lowered him into the ground."

"If it makes them feel how I feel," I said, "I doubt they'll be able to dress out for practice when they get back."

"They don't have any choice," he replied. "All the real heavyweights are coming to cover this. *Sports Illustrated* and *Sporting News* are planning cover stories on the game, and their men are due in town today. I heard they made a courtesy stopover in Austin yesterday to get the Texas side of things, but it's your guys they have to figure out as soon as they can. It isn't every day a runt school like Cajun State supposedly challenges a defending national champion."

"That's ridiculous!" I snapped, still trying to cope with emotions I had no experience feeling. "We aren't challenging anybody! We'll be lucky to get through it without a rout."

"Rout or not, a lot of money is swinging in behind you. Bookies are starting to rub their hands in anticipation."

"Why?" Carla asked.

Randall turned to her to explain it. "If enough money flows in on our guys, the spread gets driven down and Texas has to beat us by fewer points to cover the spread. So whenever a game like this happens, where one side is a heavy underdog but there's a lot of 'sympathy' money bet on them, then gamblers always clean up—big time."

"So we have no chance to beat the spread?" she asked.

"Not unless we fall into a parallel universe," I put in. "And with the way things are going, we can't rule it out."

As Randall dropped us off at the apartment, he said, "You want me to pick you up in a while for practice?"

"No, I can walk, thanks just the same. See you there."

Carla and I then went inside, and with hardly a word passing between us, she fixed and fed me a sandwich. She didn't push me to talk, not even afterward, as she washed the dishes. I stayed sitting at the kitchen table, feeling numb and wasted, until she finally came over and straddled my lap so she could face me and drape her arms across my shoulders. "Funeral got you down, right?"

"Yeah, but those media people covering it got to me, too." I held up my bandaged hands. "These things are like walking around with a kotex on my head."

She didn't smile. "They'll be gone before you know it, and you'll slip right back into your well deserved obscurity."

She was right, and I did know it, but there was more to my problem than what was showing up on the surface.

"Please don't feel guilty anymore, darling," she said softly. "You did all anyone could possibly have done. And wherever Don is, I'm certain he knows that, too."

I looked back at her and realized exactly what and how much she meant to me, and what an incredible person and partner and lover she was. I could not imagine being without her, much less losing her like Annie lost Don.

I eased her off my lap, sat her down in her chair, dropped down onto my good knee, and took her hands in mine, holding them as best I could inside my big gauze mitts.

"Carla Biscotti, I love you more than anything, and I know I will *always* feel this way. Will you marry me?"

Her eyes misted over and she choked on whatever she meant to say. Then she slid down out of her chair and knelt too, pressing herself against me, wrapping her arms around my neck, clinging to me, whispering in my ear.

"If this took you much longer, I was going to ask you!"

REGAINING BALANCE

The team arrived back on campus at a little before 3:00, giving them about an hour break before they'd have to head to the stadium for the 4:30 practice. In the ground floor lobby of the dorm, I had just punched the fifth-floor elevator button with my elbow when I heard someone shout from outside it: "Hold up! Hold the 'vator!'"

I quickly pressed the "hold" button and the already clos-ing doors snapped back open. Heape and Colley stepped in with me, both nodding solemnly. They looked at me, then at each other, as if trying to decide something.

"What's up?" I said.

"We just heard some weird news about Rabbit," Colley said. "Come with us to Tom's room and we'll fill you in."

I smiled. "That's where I was going."

When we arrived, Tom's room was already filled with the usual suspects, who had been alerted that something serious was in the wind regarding Rabbit. Tom, Swede, Wizard, Skid, Big Dick, Quink, and the Bull were there.

Heape and Colley looked at each other as before, but something in Colley's manner gave Heape the floor.

"We just got the goods on Rabbit," he began.

Everyone in the room became extra attentive.

"You know those two mechanics who've been working on the car? We've asked them several times to tell us more about Rabbit, but each time they blow us off and don't say anything about him. Well, they just finished putting it back together out on the street, and Butch and I got a chance to talk to Terry, the young one, alone.

"Curly—the older one—was a real hard-leg, but he had to go call Rabbit's old man to tell him they were finished, get final instructions, and all that. Butch and I happened by just after he left, so we struck up a conversation with Terry. It turns out he actually played football with Rabbit in high school, and he knew the whole story. Naturally, he swore us to secrecy because he said they'd sack him if anyone found out he told, but he felt he could trust us not to get him in trouble. Right, Butch?"

Colley flashed his lopsided grin. "He may know cars, but he can't judge character worth a damn!"

"So, anyway," Heape went on, "Terry confirmed what we always suspected about Rabbit being a bit wacko. It's for sure now. He was under a psychiatrist's care for years as a kid. Terry said Rabbit's older brother was a bona fide stud in high school, and he played college ball on scholarship at Alabama. He said Rabbit got overpowered by his reputation and cracked up in junior high trying to be like him. He's supposedly never been the same since."

"He tried to kill himself with pills," Colley added.

"Right. So the psychiatrist told Rabbit's old man that before he could form his own identity, he had to come to grips with his brother and what he represented to him. I guess it has to do with all that ego and id stuff that teachers yap about. Anyway, it turned out that all Rabbit *really* wanted was to be a football star like his brother was. The psychiatrist found out that the reason he tried to kill himself in junior high was because he was afraid he'd disgrace his brother's hotshot reputation."

"Man, that is twisted shit!" Quink muttered.

"It gets better," Colley said, taking over from Heape. "After the psychiatrist told the old man about Rabbit's problem, he solved it the way any smart rich man would— he bought his way out of it. He owns most of the area where Rabbit went to high school, so he was able to arrange for the local offense to be structured around Rabbit. Terry said that no one ever found out exactly what strings the old man pulled, but he did make Rabbit the big gun on his team. Of course, Rabbit was never *really* good like his brother, but it got him through high school."

"Which brings us to the interesting part," Heape said, taking back over. "Once Rabbit was stabilized by getting to be a star in high school, the old man had to put him in a major college because his brother played at Alabama. The brother never started because he was injured a lot, but he was on the varsity, on their kick cover teams, which meant Rabbit had to do at least that much. Right?"

We all nodded, fascinated by this unfolding tale.

"So then," Colley resumed, "the old man put out feelers about buying Rabbit's way in somewhere, but he found out money wasn't the answer at topnotch schools like 'Bama and Auburn. They blew him off and told him to find a less prestigious, smaller program, which brought him here."

"Why here?" I wondered. "Why not Vanderbilt or SMU?" They, too, were smaller schools with doormat reputations.

"The coaching change a year ago," Heape said. "He got wind our athletic department wanted to bring in a topflight coach like Anderson, but they were short on inducements. The old man offered to help if the department would sign Rabbit to a scholarship and keep him on the varsity as long as he stayed uninjured and wanted to be on the team. He asked that the coaches play Rabbit in games if they could—which explains putting him at safety on our kick-off team—and for that he keeps his part of the bargain."

"Which is," Colley said with a flourish, "those brand-new Pontiacs the coaches get free each year! Those come courtesy of Rabbit's old man, working through the dealer here in town that gets all the credit for supplying them."

"Wait a minute," the Bull interrupted. "Those cars are loaned to the coaches for promotional considerations. Hell, we've all seen the ads they do for that agency. And let's face it, coaches everywhere get freebies like that."

"Coaches at major schools get them," Skid said, "not at places like Cajun State. That's apples and oranges."

"Skid's right," I said. "The old staff here didn't have them. They came when Rabbit came, but I never put it together."

"It makes sense," Tom said. "All the old man has to do is juggle his books a bit to have those cars come out of his Alabama agencies with no one the wiser. The local agency plays along to get all that free advertising, and it's a sweet deal for everyone. We have to give his old man credit."

Everyone nodded agreement. It really was a clever deal.

"Well, then," Tom went on, "we can either expose what happened and create a huge stink around here . . . or we can just sit on it and let nature take its course."

He paused for feedback, but got none. Finally, he looked at Grant Heape, since Rabbit was all that stood between Heape and his dreams of glory as a varsity wingback.

"What do you say, Grant? You're the person who'll be impacted the most by what we decide."

"If it was anything other than risking him committing suicide, I'd be happy to lower the boom on him. But since that *is* the kind of risk we seem to be talking about, let's lay off for now and see what happens for me next year."

Everyone in the room breathed a sigh of relief. Nobody wanted another death on our team, not even Rabbit's.

The back dressing room was usually loose and full of energy before a Thursday practice because the week's hard work was nearly over. The only serious hitting exercise would be the two-minute drill held at the very end.

Ordinarily, redshirts prepared themselves for those last-minute drives the same way varsity players prepared for Saturday games, which explained why they often made the varsity look inept. The redshirts peaked for the two-minute drill, while the varsity just wanted to get off the field with no injuries and take their showers.

Today, however, was no ordinary Thursday. Today the redshirts would perform for a dozen media heavyweights and dozens of curiosity-seeking fans. They all recognized it as perhaps the only time in their careers when a good performance might have some lasting value. Even Prosser seemed keyed up. He sat in front of his locker, head down, idly flipping his helmet around in his hands. That was a notable, almost glaring exception from his usual calm.

"How's it going?" I said, sitting down on the bench beside him. "We haven't had much chance to talk since Don."

"I think we've all been in a kind of daze since then."

"Are you okay? Are you dealing with it?"

"Me?" He forced a smile. "Sure, I'm fine. I mean, I'm heartbroken, but that goes for all of us, doesn't it? At least I'm still alive and my hands are still in one piece."

He said it looking at my bandages, so I knew what he was thinking. "They'll be gone in a couple weeks, but the hands won't be back for a year or two. It'll be a challenge."

He looked up at me and I saw his eyes already had those dark contact lenses in because practice would start soon. "Do you think they'll let me play in the two-minute drill?" he asked. It was the first time I'd seen him show anxiety.

"I don't know, Pete. This is such an unusual situation, I have no experience of it to fall back on. I'd be guessing."

"I'd like to play," he said. "It might be the last time I ever get to really show what I can do on a football field."

That was a surprise. It sounded like he'd decided to quit soon. "Are you planning to quit without nailing Hackler?"

"Ohhh, no way, man! The more I think about that, the more I come to believe my karma *requires* me to square things with that worthless sonofabitch. So I absolutely intend to wait for the next quit drill. But the thing is. . . ."

He paused to fashion exactly what he wanted to say.

". . . .the thing is, I'd really like to actually *play* the game one more time, the way it's supposed to be played . . . the way I know how to play it . . . before I give it up for good."

"Today may be your day," was all I could think to say.

He nodded. "I sure hope it is."

Unfortunately, he didn't have a snowball's chance.

As the redshits gathered their gear prior to moving out onto the field, Teekay Junior came into the room. He was young, only two years older than the oldest of us. This was his first coaching job, and without his father's influence, he wouldn't have it or anything close to it. From a coaching perspective, he was the equivalent of Rabbit. He had no business being in the profession. He was pathetic.

We quieted as he snapped his clipboard up to where he could read it. At times his father used that same motion, and when Teekay Junior spoke, his delivery was often a bizarre imitation of Teekay Senior's authoritative tone.

"I have some announcements to make," he said.

We all kept straight faces. I pretended respect out of habit, the redshirts did so out of fear. Teekay Junior called nearly all plays, except for the two-minute drill, and he could make life miserable for anyone who crossed him.

"First, it's been decided that *every* team member—redshirts included—will dress out for Saturday's game. This is a one-time honor that's a part of our tribute to Don Slade. Freshmen can't suit up, of course, but they'll stay together as a group in special seats along the sideline."

He paused for an apparently expected cheer, but the redshirts were too stunned to speak. Realizing applause wasn't forthcoming, he went on. "However, redshirts will *not* be granted free tickets to the game. That's strictly a varsity privilege, and it will remain that way."

NCAA rules allowed athletes only $15 per month for laundry money and pocket change, an absurdly low amount. Thus, most athletic departments—including ours—got around that restriction legally by utilizing the ticket exchange. All varsity players were granted four tickets per game, which they could sell back to the ticket office for face value. Most did exactly that, even if their families came to see them play. Being able to pick up that extra cash was one of the very important side benefits of making the varsity. So for the redshirts, this was just one more of many insults they were required to tolerate.

"Finally," Teekay Junior concluded, clearly anxious to get out of the room, "you can keep and use the Friday night movie passes if you want to. Any questions?"

Whenever Coach Anderson said, "Any questions?" nobody ever asked any, but doofus Teekay Junior was always bombarded. Several redshirts started chattering at once until Tom stood up to speak for the room.

"Are you saying Friday night's practice and meeting are optional for us this week? We can go to that *or* a movie?"

"No," he said, flushing a bit, "that's not what I meant. You still don't practice tomorrow night, or go to the meeting, so you may as well take the passes and go to a movie. You're only dressing out for the game, nothing else."

"What about uniforms?" Tom said. "We haven't been fitted for game uniforms. And where will we dress out?

The visiting team always uses these two back rooms, so where does that leave us?"

"All that will be worked out later," Teekay Junior said, becoming more flustered. "You'll be notified about everything. Just do what you're told and you'll be all right."

He spun around, fast, and scuttled out of the room.

We sat in silence for a minute, then suddenly the tension broke, and a slow-rising tide of laughter began until everyone was whooping it up at Teekay Junior's inanity. Suddenly, he was back in the doorway, crimson faced.

"I forgot to mention," he gushed in a nervous bleat, "that today's two-minute drill has been cancelled. The coaches don't want to risk any more injuries before the game."

When he left this time, no laughter followed him. We all sat stunned as the message, and its import, sank in.

"They're afraid," Tom finally said. "They know what we can do to the varsity, so they're cutting us off at the pass."

I glanced across the room at Prosser, and his expression clearly revealed the depth of his disappointment.

"Gotta hand it to 'em," I said. "They don't miss a trick."

THURSDAY PRACTICE

The redshirts understood that they'd been outflanked and, as usual, couldn't do anything about it. Still, even Tom, the most militant, realized the coaches were doing the right thing. Ordinarily, a poor varsity showing against the redshirts was at worst a slight embarrassment, leaving any number of rationalizations open to them. Not so for the reporters and fans who would be on hand today.

"You know," Tom said as we walked from the dressing room out to the field, "I can understand what the coaches are trying to do, and I can't blame them. But I sure wish there was some way we could pressure them into having the drill. I'd love to see Prosser put their feet to the fire."

"Me, too, but I think it's too late. His turn has passed."

I drifted along the sideline for awhile. The funeral's sadness, if anything, seemed to have sharpened concentration. It looked as though Anderson's gung-ho strategy was working. Execution was good and mental lapses were few. Emotions were subdued, though, so it was a surprise when a cheer rose from over near the standing dummies.

I glanced at the defensive line's work area and saw them clapping and raising clenched fists. Then nearby defensive backs joined in the ruckus, and soon the commotion spread to all the groups as a lone figure trotted into view and headed across the field to report to the offensive backfield unit. Even with a noticeable limp in his stride, the Bull left little doubt that he intended to play.

He spoke briefly with Coach Mayhue, the offensive backfield coach, while everyone returned to work and spirits seemed to lift across the entire field. Shouts of ridicule, encouragement, and frustration began to pepper the air.

The Bull watched his group drill for a few minutes, then jogged onto the track and began slowly, carefully, making his way around it. He completed a lap and a half before coming back onto the field near where I was standing.

"How about it?" he said, puffing hard. "How do I look?"

"Like you're already out of shape."

"Never was in shape . . . to run that far. . . ."

"Just be thankful you can run at all. How's it feel?"

"Not bad . . . considering,"

He took a last deep breath and exhaled loudly. "Man, I needed that! I've been feeling like a scorpion in a bottle."

We stood side by side near the field's southeast corner, watching the double line of media people winding along the west sideline, some drifting one way and some the other.

"They're going to see the fence," the Bull said, nodding

to our right on the field's opposite side. Twenty-five yards beyond the outer edge of the track was where it happened. "They're probably looking for a puddle of blood, but there's nothing to see. Maintenance already changed the bent section." He was quiet for a moment, then resumed.

"How are your hands coming along?"

"Doc says they'll be as good as new in a year or two."

"You're right, I *am* lucky. My ankle should be okay in a *day* or two. It won't be great for Texas, but I can play on it."

"How'd it feel out on the track just now?"

"Okay on the straights, murder in the turns. I'll try low-speed cuts tomorrow and see how it goes. I've been living in the training room. If it doesn't hold up, it won't be from any lack of trying. Diathermy, whirlpool, elevation, ice; diathermy, whirlpool, elevation, ice. Man, I am *sick* of it."

"I don't blame you."

We stood in silence again while he flexed his injured ankle, then he looked at me and smiled. "Not bad. . . ."

Toro! The Bull was back.

Practice ended with extended skeleton drill sessions, followed by practice for kickoff returns. This was a key part of every game for us because we were scored on so often. John Lawrence, our starting tailback this year, was our kickoff returner last year and finished in the national top twenty. He ran back more kicks than anyone else.

A two-minute drill was normally the closer, but not this day. This day they simply stretched out kickoff and punt returns, and that ended it. There was no hitting at all.

I stopped by the equipment shed on the way to the front dressing rooms to check with Cap'n about what the redshirts would wear and where they'd be dressing out.

"It's a problem," he admitted. "We have five spare varsity uniforms and fourteen redshirts, so nine get left out. They'll have to wear uniforms from two years ago."

"The ones with the crappy looking green satin pants?"

He smirked. "I don't pick 'em, son, I just hand 'em out."

"I know, I know. It's just that the darker green ones we wear now will make quite a contrast, won't they?"

Cajun State's team colors were what was called "swamp green and boiled orange," to honor our Crawdad mascot. That allowed us to wear one of the most colorful—some would say garish—uniforms in college football.

"How about jerseys?" I asked, giving the pants up for lost.

"We got plenty white jerseys," he said. "Only difference will be the numbers and the stripes on 'em."

The old white jerseys we wore for home games had our standard swamp-green numbers, the color of duckweed, with two red-orange bicep stripes, the color of boiled crawfish. The new ones still had the swamp green numbers, but with thick boiled orange UCLA type shoulder stripes. Cap'n was considerably understating their contrast.

"Who'll get the new uniforms and who'll get the old?"

"Don't know. They said they'd send me a list later on."

"Why don't they put *all* the redshirts in old uniforms instead of only ten? That way they at least look like a unit."

"I don't reckon the coaches will think of somethin' that simple," he said with a sly wink, "but if they get all busy and forget to send me a list, that's what I'll do for 'em."

"Thanks, Cap'n, I'd appreciate it." I was already turning away when I remembered my final question. "By the way, where do you suppose they'll dress out?"

"No one told me, but I bet it'll be the weight room."

The weight room was a dark, dank, cramped anteroom adjacent to, but not connected to, the rear of the training room. On game days, it was the only unused place in the south end of the stadium.

An outcast room for our team's outcasts.

I went in the half-empty varsity dressing room to confront the usual post-practice effluvia: odors of sweat, tape remover, deodorant, talcum powder, and antiseptic, mingled with steam from the shower; scattered on the floor were damp towels, tape cutters, tape and gauze bandage shreds, orange rinds, and dirty uniforms; players were positioned around the room in various stages of dress and undress. Only habitual stragglers were left behind by now, and I spoke to a few of them as I moved along.

"How's it going, Quink? You doing all right?" Don's death and Prosser's reprieve left Quink safely on the varsity.

"Yeah, I'm okay. You?"

"I'll get by."

I moved down to Wheeler. "How about it, Jimbo? You feeling pretty good?"

"I'm ready," he said. It was all he ever said, whether he truly believed it or not. "I'm gonna give it all I've got."

I had no doubt he'd do at least that much.

THURSDAY EVENING

I went home to have dinner with Carla and was surprised to find Helmet at our apartment. He was his usual polite self as we exchanged the usual polite chitchat, but Carla seemed uptight until she came to the point.

"Helmet got a threatening phone call this afternoon, Larry, and he doesn't know what to do about it."

Neither did I, so I sat down and asked for a beer.

"Did you hear what I *said,* Larry? Helmet got a threatening phone call today!"

"I heard you, yes." I turned to Helmet. "Tell me about it."

"The person says to me, 'Muddle'—he does not say my name correct—he says, 'Muddle, you must not kick so well Saturday night. You will make very many people very unhappy. If you do that, they may hurt you.' That was all."

"I wouldn't take it too seriously," I said. "We're all going to be targets for jerks until things settle down around here."

"A friend told me," Carla said, "you'll also be targets for

gamblers." She was much more upset than Helmet.

"I worry not so much about the caller's intention," Helmet said. "I am asking what should be my response. You are my good friends, and this has never happened before."

"Go to the police," Carla said. "That's what I'd do."

"Let's not go off half-cocked. It could cause more trouble than we have already if cops start swarming around us."

"Then tell the coaches," she said. "At least do that much."

"Tell you what. Helmet stays here to have dinner with us, then he and I walk over to the dorm and discuss this with some of the other players. We'll completely air it out, and then do whatever the group collectively decides. Okay?"

Helmet smiled cheerfully. "I do not like our coaches, and they do not like me. This way will be much better."

Seeing he was okay with it, Carla nodded. "Okay, good idea. Now, how do you two feel about red beans and rice?"

Helmet explained his situation to Tom and his group, then Tom said, "I just can't believe professional gamblers would do something that might bring in federal agents."

"I agree," said Swede, Tom's roommate. "We're hardly the favorite in this game, even with the hype from Don's death. So I think it's just some kook getting his jollies."

"Is that the consensus?" I asked, suspecting Tom and the others were downplaying it for Helmet's benefit. "Forget it?"

"Not exactly," Tom said. "I think we should wait to see what develops. We have two more days to get help if it starts to look like Helmet needs it. A move right now would be premature. But any more calls and we'll tell. Okay?"

Helmet slapped his palms on his knees and got to his feet. "If this is what you feel, this is what I shall do. Now, I leave you to your affairs, but I thank you sincerely for your help. I will, as you say, keep you posted. *Ciao*."

As soon as Helmet was out the door, I turned to Tom. "What do you *really* think?"

"I seriously doubt he's in any real danger."

"Why not? He's the team's only consistent point maker,

so they only need to rattle him to affect the spread."

"Sage is right," Swede said. "A lot rides on Helmet, and serious gamblers don't have to worry about the law. From what I understand, they keep a lot of it on their payroll."

"That's true," Tom admitted, "but I do think it's way too early to make a move that might freak him out."

"But what if you're wrong?" I persisted.

"Look, they'll call Helmet again, or they'll call Davis or Wheeler, or one of the others who handle the ball a lot. We'll know if it's a real threat. Right now, we're guessing."

There was a knock on the door and Techno walked in. He was our resident math whiz, so Tom had invited him in for a chat about the spread. "What's the latest?"

Techno was a rangy guy from the Tennessee hill country, where both his parents worked in the nuclear arms industry. Like Prosser, he always seemed calm and collected, on the field and off, and he was as precise in running his pass patterns as in his school work.

"It's down to Texas by four," he said casually.

In unison we all erupted. "*What!!!*"

"Touchdowns!" he quickly added. "Four touchdowns, twenty-eight points. I thought you'd know what I meant."

We needed a few seconds for our hearts to start beating properly again, then Tom said, "That's not like four points, but it's still a pretty healthy drop, don't you think?"

Techno's head shook. "There's nothing else it *can* do right now. Since that rumor went out about us having a chance, the betting action is unreal. The spread will probably get down around twenty before things stabilize."

"We shouldn't be on the board with them," Tom said.

"You know that, I know that, and every serious gambler in the country knows that," Techno agreed, "but the great sea of fish out there doesn't know that. All the fish know is what they read in the papers and see on the tube."

"And so the suckers are going for it?" Swede asked.

Techno nodded. "By the millions, because twenty to thirty points is a huge edge for a team that's supposed to be psyched-up enough to play close to even. It's perfect bait for the fish, and as long as their money keeps flowing in on us, and the spread keeps dropping, the gamblers' kitty gets larger and the bets get surer. In the end, all those fish go belly up and get flushed down the toilet."

We looked at each other, nobody saying anything. What *could* we say? It was surreal being a part of something skewed so badly out of whack by the quirky hand of fate.

"Gotta go," Techno finally said. "Gotta lay a heavy bet."

At the door he stopped and turned back to confront a half-dozen flabbergasted expressions. Then he roared with laughter, the first guffaw any of us had heard in days.

"Gotcha!"

FRIDAY MORNING

Classes resumed, and I soon learned what a hardship the new semester would be without the use of my hands. I couldn't write and wouldn't be able to for the next few months, until the nerves I'd severed started coming back to life. That wouldn't be until well after the semester ended, so my first instructor kept me after class to talk about it.

The class was advanced auditing, and the instructor was Gerald Robinson, a man who taught me in two previous classes. We knew each other well, and I trusted his advice.

"Larry," he began, "nobody admires what you did more than I do, but now I have to tell you some grim facts. You won't be able to perform satisfactorily in this class this semester. If you want to stick with it, I'll cut you every break I can, but you need to confront your limitations.

"You won't be able to take your own notes, you'll have to count on the notes of others who might not be as good at it as you are. Then you won't be able to take tests or write extra credit reports. We can try to set up a system where you do everything verbally, but that nearly always results in a couple of letter grades lower than you'd make if you weren't handicapped in this way."

"Do you think that will be true in every class I have?"

"I'm afraid so, especially basket weaving and pottery."

He waited for it to sink in, then we laughed together. He really was a good guy and a first-class teacher.

"Seriously," he resumed, "I want to suggest that you consider dropping out for this semester, and maybe the semester after that, too. If your financial situation can tolerate it, I'd say you should focus to the extent you can on getting therapy for your hands, to get them back working for you as soon as possible. From where you are right now, therapy seems more important than classes."

I thought it over for a few seconds, then mentioned what I felt was an important point. "I have a 3.8 GPA right now. Graduate school requires at least a 3.5 GPA. What are the odds that this one semester could sink me below 3.5?"

He shrugged. "I've no idea, but you've worked too hard for too long to gamble on how close you can shave it to the minimum you need to get in. You want to go into graduate school carrying a GPA with room to spare, and you want to go in with all cylinders running properly. It could be a very serious mistake to try to just scrape by."

He was making sense, but now I had Carla to think about. We had unofficially talked about getting married for months, but now that it was official, I felt a whole new sense of responsibility. I had to stop being a student and become a wage earner as soon as possible because she would be chomping at the bit to start our family by the end of my stint in graduate school.

"I'll think about it, Gerald, I really will. Thanks."

At lunch, Carla was her usual supportive self, assuring me that we'd find a way to work these difficulties out.

"Larry, I love you. You're the man in my life, the one who owns my heart. You've been that almost from the moment

I met you. So these are small problems, really, compared to what Annie and her family have to deal with now."

Annie was on her mind because she'd arranged to drive up to Libertyville to meet with her this afternoon.

"If I drop out for a year to let my hands heal, what kind of work can I do? How can I bring in money?"

"I make enough for us to live on," she said. "That's all we need for now. You'll make it up once you're a stockbroker."

"Maybe I could start playing the market on the side . . . do a little day trading . . . learn the ropes that way."

"Using whose money?"

"Well, uh . . . our money, I guess."

She gazed at me, thinking it over, pursing her lips. "We can spare twenty dollars a week for you to play with. Not a penny more. If you lose it, it's gone for that week. Fair?"

I couldn't help beaming at her. "More than fair!"

It felt like a mountain lifted off of me. *Twenty bucks a week to play the stock market!* It sounded like a fortune.

The Friday afternoon before any home game was structured by the coaches to be as boring and uneventful as possible. The team was isolated in the dorm under the same procedure as Wednesday, so that Bud and Raymond could keep unwanted "friends" and "cousins" away from the players. At the same time, players had to give legitimate reasons for leaving the dorm, and usually they went with an escort. That policy was to keep the horses in the paddock until the big race—and no fillies allowed.

Naturally, the redshirts were subject to those varsity restrictions even when they would not normally dress out for the game. That was in keeping with the coaches' philosophy of making them endure as much inconvenience and tedium as possible. Tom's counter-philosophy was to subvert every such strategy by making the best of each bad situation. That was why he usually spent the empty Friday afternoons entertaining his troops with hoaxes and pranks, keeping everyone distracted from their lowly status and the approaching game they had no role in.

Normally, I spent home-game Friday afternoons in the dorm with Tom and the rest, but I no longer felt a part of that routine. An invisible curtain had dropped between me and all but my closest friends on the team, and very soon even they would be forced to abandon me. I lost my functional status the moment I wrecked my hands.

It's difficult to describe the experience of being washed up on the beach of football has-beens. You're suddenly sprung from a comfortably rigid world with a frozen, one-dimensional lifestyle that—while occasionally difficult to maintain—was seductive as hell. Losing the predictability of it could make you want to crawl in a hole and hide.

The scars could run deep, too, with the depth usually depending on when you were knocked out of the game. If you tapped out after high school, or early in college, you were more likely to reorient yourself to get a degree and prepare for life in the real world. The later you tapped out, the more disadvantaged you were likely to be relative to your peers outside football. The ones like that tended to end up selling cars or insurance, even though they had the brains and moxie for something better. They came to think of themselves as failures, and they acted it out.

A common slogan was that "football builds character," and it often did. But at the same time, when nobody was watching, it could also shatter self-esteem. Fortunately, I had already been through one separation from the game, which left me living in a kind of halfway house as a manager, weaning myself off its powerful narcotic. Now I knew pretty well what to expect of myself and the system.

I made up my mind and headed to the University Center to visit the team's "brain coach," Dr. Keith Westrum.

Dr. Westrum greeted me with his usual good cheer.

"Fabulous to see you, Larry, and let me say how sorry I am about what happened. I know everyone is telling you that, but I want to add my heartfelt sentiment to it."

"Thanks, Dr. Westrum. I appreciate you saying that."

He was a devious man doing a devious job, but he had a useful asset for the work he did manipulating his portion of our lives—a wonderfully reassuring smile.

"So, tell me, Larry, what can I do for you today?"

"I need to know where I'd stand with the athletic department if I dropped out this semester and finished up later on. I know you'll see me through all my therapy costs, but can I get any kind of extention to the grant-in-aid I have right now? Can we suspend it for a year?"

His smile didn't waver. "A kind of redshirt year, eh?"

"I guess that's one way of looking at it."

He paused to consider, then nodded. "Normally, I have to admit, this request would probably be considered out of bounds. But since it's you, and because of what you now mean to this team, and to this university, I can't imagine you'd be turned down for any request you'd make."

"No offense meant, but I need more than your opinion. I need something in writing that I can take to the bank."

A small muscle twitched in his right cheek. These guys were known for making all kinds of promises they never intended to keep, so I had to be sure this wasn't one, too.

"Tell you what," he finally said. "If you'll step outside and wait a few minutes, I'll try to track down the director and Coach Anderson and discuss this with them."

"Sure," I said, rising to leave. "I'll be right outside."

He rose as well, to open and close the door for me.

I shot the breeze with Bernice, his secretary, for about ten minutes before Westrum came out to join us. He was all smiles, so I figured I probably had it sacked.

"I talked to the director," he said, rubbing his hands together, "and it's all squared away. Whenever you're ready to finish your last semester, it's on the house. You'll have the paperwork in your mailbox in about a week."

"That's terrific news," I replied, trying my best to match his cheesy smile. "The next time you talk with him, please tell him how much I appreciate his generosity."

I turned to leave Westrum's office, but he spoke again before I reached the door. "One more thing, Larry. Coach Anderson wants to talk to you. Can you go right over?"

"Hi, Larry, good to see you," Coach Anderson said. "Have a seat. I hope it wasn't much trouble for you to stop by."

"No, sir," I said as I sat in the proffered chair in his spacious office. "No trouble at all."

"Good, good." Dead air hung between us for a moment, then he said, "How are the hands?"

"Fine, coach, as good as they can be right now."

"Good, good, glad to hear it. Say, did you see yourself on television? We all thought you did a hell of a good job."

"Thank you, sir."

He picked up a pen from his desk top and began rolling it between his hands. It reminded me of Captain Queeg and his little steel balls. "I understand you've made plans to watch the game from the stands with your girlfriend."

"She's my fiancée now, sir, and yes, that's true."

I was surprised that he could already know that. Carla and I discussed the matter briefly only last night, and I mentioned it to maybe a dozen of the guys. Word traveled damned fast on our team's convoluted grapevine.

"Well, that's a problem for us because a lot of people coming to this game will want to see you, too, and see that you're still as much a part of this team as you ever were."

I stared blankly at him, not quite understanding this sudden change of protocol. When a player was as hurt as I was, he could stay on the sidelines during a home game, dressed out in slacks and a jersey to show he was still part of the team. Managers were not the same as players. We had no jerseys to wear, and given the shape I was in, I shouldn't have any place on the sidelines.

"You're a symbol of our team now, Larry. You're representing us to the entire country, and doing a damn good job of it. So I know you don't want to let anyone on the team down after all we've been through together this week."

"No, sir, I guess not." I was beginning to get his drift and was rapidly recovering my composure.

"Good! Now, let me offer my personal invitation to you to take part in everything leading up to and including the game, just as if nothing ever happened to your hands. Can we count on you to do that for us?"

I twisted my face into what I hoped looked like a mask of indecision. "Well, I don't know. . . ."

"If there's some problem with your hands, I'm sure we can work out anything you need."

"It's not that. I promised Carla she wouldn't have to sit alone for this game. Now I have to break my word to her."

"Would it help if I talked with her? I'd be happy to. We can't put her on the sideline, but I'll get her a box seat on the first row if that'll keep her close enough to you."

"I don't think that's necessary, Coach. I'm sure she'll understand this unusual situation, and I'm equally sure she'll make the best of sitting where she usually does."

Actually, Carla had a group of friends she enjoyed sitting with, and *I* was the one not looking forward to watching from the stands. However, I couldn't see any harm in making it seem like a degree of a sacrifice on my part.

"Well, I hate to cause problems for you two young people, but I'm sure you see how important your presence is to the team and the fans. I'm being frank with you about this matter, Larry, and I hope you understand my position."

"Yes, sir, I believe I do."

"Tell you what," he said. "How about we arrange a nice steak dinner for you two after the game? How about that?"

I smiled sincerely. "That should make it up to her."

"Good! Then I guess that's all I have for now." He put the pen back in its holder and moved to the door to open it for me. "Thank you again for all you've done for this team."

"You're welcome, Coach. It was my pleasure."

And it was . . . it really, truly was.

***

FRIDAY NIGHT PRACTICE

Every Friday before a home game, practice was held in
the stadium under the lights to accustom everyone to nighttime conditions. It always started at 8:00, and consisted
of little more than breaking a sweat doing routine things
like running down under punts and kickoffs. Our opponents usually arrived in town at mid- to late-afternoon
and went through a similar light workout at 8:45, so our
routine seldom lasted more than half an hour.

If a team wasn't ready to play by the day before a game,
additional work wouldn't make much difference.

My original Friday night dinner plan was to meet Randall at an off-campus restaurant. Someone had to feed me,
and I felt comfortable enough with him to ask him to do
that. When Carla called to arrange it, she said he sounded
truly delighted that I thought to invite him.

Carla would still be with Annie in Libertyville, so that
made a dinner date necessary. But then Coach Anderson
told me to feel free to remain an integral part of the team,
and I was as delighted as Randall to take him up on it.

I asked Tom to call Randall for me to break our dinner date, then we walked to the sewer. I always enjoyed
Friday's early dinner because the air began to be electric
on Fridays, giving off the first little sparks and sprinkles
of the flood of energy that would inundate the campus
tomorrow and be slowly siphoned off into the stadium.

The talk of dinner was that both Helmet and Ronnie
Davis, our starting quarterback, received calls toward the
end of the afternoon, saying their arms and legs wouldn't
work too well if they had good games Saturday night. The
local FBI was notified, and agents were now scheduled to
meet with both players after dinner.

"Helmet's taking it pretty well," Tom said, "but we don't

know about Davis. He hasn't been around any of us."

"I'm not sure Helmet really understands the situation," Colley put in. "Does Germany even have gangsters?"

"They're everywhere, in every country!" Heape snapped. "Geeze, don't you ever read anything besides porno?"

"Easy guys," Tom said. "No sense getting worked up about it. Let's just wait and see what the feds say."

Another focus of conversation was that even though the redshirts were officially dressing out tomorrow, they would not dress out to participate in tonight's workout. There was no point in it since none of them would play, so they were told to use their free passes to a local movie house to remove them from the *real* players on the team.

This night, though, would be different. The redshirts decided to go as a group to sit in the stadium to watch our team run through its light workout, and then watch Texas run through theirs. That would be much more germane to them than watching any movie. They wanted to be more of a part of what was developing, even if only a widely peripheral, heavily disdained part.

Freshmen were normally excluded from everything the day before a game, and on game day. Like the redshirts, they were given free movie tickets and were expected to make themselves scarce until Monday's practice. But when they heard that the redshirts were attending this practice as a group, they felt pressure to do the same, so the thirty that were still on the team gathered on seats high up and close to the press box. The redshirts sat low down, in the southeast corner, near the exit in case one of the coaches told them to leave.

Redshirts could take nothing for granted.

It was right at 8:00 when I joined the team to gather at the southwest corner exit chute. The players were yelling and carrying on, psyching themselves up, while the coaches seemed too focused on those players to notice the freshmen or the redshirts. Finally, at Anderson's shouted signal, they sprinted out onto the field, chanting:

"*Craw*-dads! *Craw*-dads! *Craw*-dads!"

For this practice they always dressed out in their game uniforms, but without the shoulder, hip and other padding. It wasn't to focus on how they looked, but how they felt, and the unpadded uniforms gave them a sense of game reality while helping to establish the sense of passing a point of no return. Game uniforms meant business.

Calisthenics ended and I found a place on the sideline under the press box. The workout started badly when, on the first snap from center, Davis and Wheeler bungled the exchange. Under normal circumstances that was hardly news, but in this case it caused a chorus of muted groans to erupt from everyone watching it.

Ronnie Davis was a steady, reliable player who, though he lacked exceptional size, arm, or foot speed, handled our roll out offense better than anybody else we had. It was doubtful his back-up, Dee Kimberly, could do the job adequately if Davis got rattled by his threatening call.

Eventually, we all felt better because Davis didn't miss another snap during the rest of the workout. In fact, it seemed likely that first fumbled snap was Wheeler's fault. Wheeler was far more high-strung than Davis, and whoever made those calls to Helmet and Davis showed an intimate knowledge of the inner working of our team.

They seemed to know that Jimbo Wheeler was already more unsettled by the persistent specter of Kevin Stoner than he would be by a message from a burning bush, much less by a mere threatening phone call.

Helmet was in typically good form, booming kick-offs and field goals in his inimitably stylish fashion. I didn't accept the theory that Helmet didn't fully understand what the threatening calls might mean, but it certainly looked as if he wasn't letting them get to him.

We especially focused on the Bull. His ankle would make all the difference in our running game the next night, and our run game—such as it was—had to consistently keep the ball away from Texas to give us any chance to hold the score down. Ball control, with an occasional third and long pass, was our only hope of preventing a rout.

The Bull ran like a champ. He had a hard time going left, but he fired out of his stance reasonably well and seemed to have little trouble moving to his right. If he and Helmet could play well tomorrow night, we might well be able to hold Texas to below a four touchdown margin.

We knew that wasn't very likely, but it *could* happen.

After thirty minutes, Coach Anderson gathered the team around him for his final few words of wisdom, the words he always left the team with before a game. Like all coaches, he had a set of preferred images that he liked to use in certain circumstances. One of his favorites was to tell his players to go out and "stand like tall pines," which he used again this time. However, this time there was a difference.

Helmet, who stood fairly close to him, raised his hand and then his voice. Since he was the target of threats, we thought he might be wanting to say something about that, because it was *verboten* to interrupt the head coach when he was addressing the team in this way.

"Coach An-dare-son," he said in his accented English, "for such a critical game, can the team not, for a change, stand like the stout oaks instead of the tall pines? They are too easily knocked down when they stand as tall pines. Perhaps they should try to be more like the stout oaks."

Helmet complimented his words with a few body gestures indicating stout versus thin, which were as funny as his words. We all struggled mightily to stifle our giggles, and some of the assistant coaches hid their faces under their cap brims to keep their amusement from being obvious.

All of our coaches, Anderson included, considered Helmet a disrespectful Kraut knucklehead. Two of them fought the Germans in World War II, so they felt extra animosity toward him. But what angered them most about him was his firm refusal to take football as seriously as they did.

Anderson glared at him for a long moment, then continued on as if he hadn't spoken. In a peculiar way, I felt sorry for Anderson. Helmet, and much of the world outside the stadium, was simply alien territory to men like him.

When the team left the field, I walked over to the stands and climbed up several rows to where the dozen redshirts sat. Prosser was notably absent, but that didn't surprise me. His status as the team's main outcast made everyone uncomfortable around him, especially in public where the coaches could see the association, which he had no trouble recognizing. So he didn't inflict himself on them any more than absolutely necessary—at meals and at practices.

When I arrived at the group, Tom wasted no time getting to the heart of the matter. "What's the word from inside?"

I knew what he meant. "Turns out the feds say threatening calls are strictly routine around big games where a lot of money rides. They cover hundreds every year in pro and college ball, and no one's ever been hurt for playing full out. Naturally, they don't publicize those calls for the obvious reason of not wanting to give assholes ideas."

The range of expression among them went from stunned disbelief to calm acceptance, as if they were saying to themselves, *Yeah, I figured it was something like that.*

"Guess what else?" I went on. "The feds asked Stoner to come over and personally tell Helmet and Davis about all the threats *he's* received. Davis said he was a really nice guy who worked hard to put them at ease about it."

Grant Heape, always with his nerves on edge because he knew he should be on the varsity, made a guttural scoffing sound. "It's enough to make you believe in Santa Claus."

"Or the sandpaper fairy," I added.

They all were confused by that quip. "*What?*"

"Ask the Bull. He knows her quite well."

We stayed in the stands to watch the Longhorns work out, but we should have left when we were ahead. As they gathered in the northwest corner exit before taking the field, we saw several who filled their jerseys without the benefit of pads. Stoner's number "50" stretched across his back without a wrinkle, an awesome physical presence.

They stormed onto the field with a roar that seemed to vibrate the wooden planks we sat on.

"I changed my mind," Tom suddenly said, standing up to start moving away. "I don't really want to watch this."

As usual, he spoke for us all, and we all went with him.

The redshirts went back to the dorm to settle in for the night. On Friday nights they were under the same 11:00 p.m. curfew as the varsity, though this night they went back knowing that tomorrow they'd be dressing out, too.

I left them to return to the apartment to join Carla, long since returned from visiting Annie. That was the first thing we talked about because she was so clearly upset.

"I don't think I've ever done anything harder in my life than holding that poor girl and crying with her as she tried to make me understand how she feels about what happened. Don . . . the baby . . . it was just awful!"

"Does she have good friends there, shoulders to cry on?"

Carla nodded. "Plenty. You know how everyone around here loves her? She's like that there, too. It was like people standing in line to comfort her. I practically had to take a ticket and wait my turn. She's a super special person."

Everyone knew that from the first time Don brought her to a team function. She was our age, but she always came across as the fun older sister we all wished we had.

"Did you tell her I popped the question?"

Carla's long hair swished. "I can't do that yet."

That surprised me. "Why not?"

"It's not part of female etiquette."

"What do you mean?"

She paused, uncomfortably. "You, ummm, can't really brag about it until you have the ring on your finger."

That took me aback. "Ahhhh, so a ring is necessary?"

Her head shook. "Not to *ask*, but to make it *official*."

"Okay, then," I said, flashing a devil-may-care smile, "my fault. But that's easy to correct. Let's just start eating Cracker Jacks regularly, and sooner or later. . . ."

She punched me on the shoulder, hard. "You better not, you rascal!" Then she paused to consider. "On second thought, why not? Sure! Make it a Cracker Jack ring!"

I laughed with her, but I was already scheming about how to pay off what I owed on the ring I had on layaway.

SATURDAY

I spent the morning watching cartoons on TV because I had nothing else to do. Carla had to teach, and most of the players had to attend classes, so I was left with an empty dance card until lunchtime, when she returned to feed me, shave me, shower me, and help me use the toilet. After that, for the first time since the accident, we assembled enough of our shattered libidos to make love.

Our life was slowly, steadily, returning to normal.

I left the apartment to join the team for the late-afternoon pregame meal, the official starting point of the pressurized rituals leading up to kickoff. Because the meal for each player was always centered around a healthy chunk of filet mignon, usually only those dressing out for the game were allowed to attend, so my invitation from Coach Anderson to be a part of it was truly a bonus.

It began with a short wait in the lobby area outside the dining hall. Everyone stood around while the food was laid out on the tables inside, then the doors were opened when everything was ready. The pre-game meal was the only one served that way—all others were cafeteria style—because it was the only meal where a known number of people ate a special meal at a specified time.

Ordinarily, Stanton and I would be inside helping the cooks set the tables and lay out the food. Today, I stood with the redshirts in a far corner of the waiting area, feeling as lost and out of place as them. With the exception of Heape and possibly Prosser, none of us felt we deserved to be there. We tried a few jokes and quips to loosen each other up, but only in hushed tones so the somber varsity players wouldn't hear our irreverence and be offended.

Suddenly, the coaches strode into the lobby and Coach Anderson spotted us across the room. He pointed a forefinger at us, and Hackler nodded at that subtle but obvious instruction. He waddled his fat gort over to us.

"What are you assholes doing here?" he demanded.

I knew the others would be even more afraid to speak up than I was, so I gave it a try. "We, uhh. . . ."

"Not you, Larry," Hackler interrupted, "You're supposed to be here. I'm talking about these other ungrateful pussies who try to take a mile when you give them an inch."

Every redshirt except Prosser stood momentarily stunned into inaction, but he didn't miss a beat. He was on his way out the door by the time Hackler finished speaking, and the others quickly followed his lead.

Tom valiantly tried to offer an explanation by saying, "No one told us not to come, Coach."

Hackler roared back, "Who the hell told you *to* come?"

Tom turned to slink away with the others.

The rest of the team saw and heard what happened, but they made the required effort to pretend it hadn't. Redshirts were humiliated like that on a regular basis, and it was merely part of the curse of being one. Also, incidents like that were designed to have a specific effect on varsity players—it forced them to be constantly vigilant against letting their play slip below acceptable levels.

When Tom was finally out the door, Hackler turned to me and a vaguely threatening smile split his porcine face.

"Looks like you've been keeping bad company lately, but for now . . . for now you're still welcome at our table."

I felt a powerful urge to say something sassy to him and walk out to join Tom and the others, but I knew if I did that I would, in that moment, become *persona non grata*, bad hands and all. I wanted to join them, very much, but I wanted even more to stay with the team and be a part of this game. Besides, I knew the redshirts would find food and then come back to dress out for the game. That felt like the most I could comfort myself—and them—with.

The pregame meal of any college football team was a wonder to behold, at least for young men who had only, maybe, heard the term "filet mignon" before they sat down to eat the first one they ever saw with their own eyes. And an eye-opening experience it could be, too.

When my freshman team first saw those thick circular cuts of meat, we couldn't wait to dive into them to see why the varsity players kept raving about those incredible steaks. Then we cut into ours and found out the cooks were instructed to cook them *very* rare, so they'd digest slowly and provide energy throughout a game.

One of our team was a cowboy-boot-wearing nose guard from Amarillo with a heavy Texas twang. When he cut into his and saw the bluish-pink meat inside, he yelped, "Gawddd-*damn!* I seen cows *hurt* worse'n this get well!"

Anyone with a mouthful at that moment strangled on it.

I nearly strangled on some of this meal, too, trying to choke it down through the fury and shame surging through me. I was furious with Hackler and the coaches and the injustice of life as a redshirt, and I was ashamed of myself for choosing to serve my own needs over theirs.

When I was a manager it never seemed to bother me like this. I had a job to do, and that job always allowed me to look the other way whenever I wanted to or needed to. Now, without that excuse to fall back on, I was feeling the pinch of having to face up to certain moral obligations.

The only thing levening this was my new good friend Jeff Rivers as he fed me. His experience with his broken-armed buddy in high school showed itself in a number of unexpected ways, not least being the rollicking good humor with which he handled even slight aggravations.

The more I got to know Jeff, the more I found myself liking him, and I realized what a shame it was that our early competition for a slot on the team had created an imagined wall between us that endured even after our competition ended. It made me wonder how many other guys like him were on the team, guys who for whatever reason never connected with me in the ways others did.

Not only was I no longer sure about what was required to be a man, I wasn't sure about being a friend, either.

After the meal, everyone had about an hour in the dorm, where all routine taping of ankles and such was done on a couple of tables set up in the sixth floor lobby. The early routine taping eased the jam-up that would come in the training room later, when the team was dressing out and serious taping of the major joint injuries would get under way. It also gave them all an early taste of the rituals that went into preparing them for the upcoming combat.

I found most of the redshirts—again minus Prosser—in Tom's room, trying to figure out what to do now. They had been told they were dressing out with the varsity, so they reported for the varsity's pregame meal and were turned away from it. Now they had to worry about reporting to the stadium to dress out, and being turned away from that, too. It was a genuine, legitimate concern, and I couldn't blame them for sweating it out.

"Tell you what, Sage," Tom said to me. "To put our minds at ease, would you please go to the stadium and check with Cap'n to see if we actually *are* dressing out?"

I held up my hands. "I can't go out there by myself with all those fans on campus. I'd need an hour to get through them. But I can do something just as good."

They all looked at me expectantly. "I know Cap'n's private phone number, but I need help making the call."

"Cap'n, are the redshirts dressing out for sure?"

"Yep," he said, matter-of-factly.

"That's good," I said, so the redshirts standing around me would know things were moving in the right direction. "Did the coaches ever send you the list about them?"

"Yep, a little while ago. All four backs and the tight end get the spare new ones, everyone else gets old ones."

That caused me a twinge of resentment. Backs and ends were always favored over linemen. It seemed automatic.

"Thanks, Cap'n. I'm glad to hear it's squared away."

"It's not squared away for Everett," he replied.

I glanced at Tom, frowning. "Oh? Why's that?"

"When they sent the list, I called Coach Anderson to remind him I had three back numbers, one end number, and a guard number. That's all. I asked if he wanted to name a guard instead of one of those backs, figurin' he'd put Prosser in an old jersey and reward Duggan and Everett and Heape for their good work. But, no, he said to give Everett the guard number, so tell Tom he'll be wearing 67. I don't want him gettin' here and bein' upset with me for makin' him look like a clown. It's not my fault."

"Okay," I said, trying to figure out this odd twist of the screw. Then another alternative popped into my head.

"Hold on, Cap'n, what about Don's number?" That was number 33, a fullback number. "Could his be used?"

"Haven't you heard? They announced it's being retired. They'll present it to his family just before the kickoff."

"Are you sure? His family is a wreck. I saw them."

"He had three brothers, you know. They say the oldest one is sharp like Don was. He'll be coming to get it."

I was glad to hear someone on the staff had the presence of mind to think of expressing that gesture of permanent respect. "The blind hogs found an acorn, eh?"

"They're under a ton of pressure to do things right for a change," Cap'n said, letting his true feelings show in an uncharacteristic moment of candor. "I'm glad to see it, too."

"So am I, Cap'n. Thanks for the heads-up."

Tom lowered the phone from holding it to my ear, then I told him and the redshirts gathered in his room the gist of my conversation with Cap'n, covering every aspect of it.

They heard me out, then Tom said, "It doesn't make much sense, does it? Except for retiring Don's jersey. I'm surprised any of them had brains enough to think of it."

"Good ink," Dave Duggan pointed out. "They'll go all-out for as much good ink as they can wring from this game."

Duggan was the redshirt fullback, and now that Don was gone, he should have been moved up to third team behind the Bull and Roger Johnson. That he had not been moved up was a sure sign the coaches were thinking of moving another running back—most likely Quink, who had a body for it—to fullback, or maybe moving a linebacker over from the defense. Dave was a good player, a hard worker, and a fine guy; he was just too damn slow.

"Yeah," Tom agreed. "It doesn't take a genius to figure out that good ink is behind a helluva lot of what they've been doing this week. But that still doesn't explain why you, Dave, and Heape and Prosser and Vin dress out for real, while I get stuck in a guard's uniform? Why not dress us all the same, or at least give my jersey to a guard?"

"That would make too much sense for them," I said.

"I bet it's because you talked back to Hackler at the pregame," Heape pointed out. "They all hate it when anyone does that to them, but Hackler especially hates it."

Every head nodded, realizing it might well *be* a punishment. On the other hand, Tom's protocol breach was extremely slight, nowhere near deserving of this nuclear-level payback. There seemed to be more to it, but what?

None of us could figure that out.

***

GAME PREPS

At 6:00, the team and its attending personnel gathered in the dormitory's ground-floor lobby for the traditional quarter-mile walk to the stadium. Lined up like a military unit—twenty ranks of four abreast—we moved across campus for what was usually a six or seven-minute trip through sparse crowds that were a mockery compared to the thick walls of fans that major powers like Texas would move through on the way to their home stadiums.

Today, though, that walk was very different for us. An incredible number of fans and well-wishers lined our route, clapping for us, offering advice and encouragement.

"Give 'em hell, guys!"

"Kick some Longhorn *ass!*"

Redshirts formed a short line in front of the equipment shed to pick up their uniforms, while the varsity players poured into their dressing room. Varsity uniforms were laid out in every player's cubicle before a game, including a towel rolled over an under-pad half T-shirt, socks, and jock. The displaced redshirts had to shift for themselves.

Before each home game, they and the freshmen cleaned out their lockers in the "back" dressing rooms to make space for the visiting team coming in. They'd put their equipment—helmets, shoes, shoulder pads and other pads—in a laundry bag with their name on it, which was then handed in at the equipment shed and kept until Monday, when they would retrieve them. So now, to dress out, they had to retrieve their equipment bags, along with a towel "roll" and the uniforms Cap'n set aside for them.

It was an awkward, uncomfortable business all around, but one-by-one they graciously accepted whatever Cap'n handed them. From there they walked fifty feet to the door of the weight room, where they'd dress out by themselves and prepare to make a humbled entrance onto the field.

I went in the varsity dressing room and looked around. There was still plenty of time left for them to get ready, which was important because they all needed a certain amount of personal, individualized pregame ritual before Anderson's order to "strap it on" and prepare to play.

I was conspicuously aware of being the only person in the room without a specific reason to be there, so I eased back out and turned to face the equipment shed, which gave me a different sense of isolation. I saw Cap'n and Stanton scurrying around inside it, gathering and arranging the spare-part tray that would be carried to the sideline in case it was needed during the game.

Preparing that tray used to be one of my old jobs.

There was only one place I could go and not stick out like the sore thumbs I now carried. I walked to the weight room door and rapped on it with my elbow. Someone pushed it open, allowing me to step in and ask the obvious question.

"What happened to the lights?"

"This stinkhole doesn't *have* lights!" Heape snapped in obvious frustration. "They're fucking us over *again!*"

The weight room was indeed a converted storage area with no lights of any kind. I didn't spend much time in it, so it was easy to forget that. And it was small because using weights was not a common activity for our players. Only a few linemen ever used the facility, but without real regularity. Our coaches didn't make it even close to mandatory because most of them were convinced that lifting weights turned those who did it into musclebound oafs.

"We can make do with the outside light coming in through the windows," Skid said quietly. "That reflects off the mirrors, and your eyes get used to it pretty quickly."

Other than having no lights, the weight room was a small, barren area with two Universal weight machines bolted into the dirty concrete floor. The top two feet of the western wall consisted of two long windows, and a palisade of mirrors lined all four walls. That combination made lights unnecessary on even the cloudiest days, and since the stadium was always locked at night, nighttime facilities weren't normally an issue to deal with.

My eyes did adjust to the dimness, and I saw that most of them stood motionless with blank expressions, not yet reconciled to the baseness of their temporary quarters.

"Standing there staring at it won't change anything," I reminded them. "Why don't you all just dress out?"

Another problem quickly became apparent—no chairs. It was a weight room, with nothing to put anything on, including the clothes they were wearing. They were all holding their gear in both hands—helmets, shoulder pads, hip and girdle pads, knee and thigh pads, and shoes in the sacks in one hand, and jersey, pants, and roll in the other—but no indication of where to put it, much less where to put their clothes when they took those off.

Vin Newbert, the tight end, suddenly noticed another problem. "This place has no hooks!" he muttered angrily. "We have to leave our clothes on a filthy goddamn floor!"

"Fold them and put them on your shoes," Skid advised.

"Jesus, Skid!" Heape barked. "Don't you *ever* get mad?"

Most redshirts had reached Heape's level of frustration, and I couldn't blame them. Whether by design or not, they were being humiliated to the point where dressing out lost all emotional value. It was like handing over a canteen full of water to someone dying of thirst, but leaving the lid screwed on so tight that it couldn't be opened.

"What are we supposed to do after we get dressed, Sage?" Tom asked, trying to move beyond the impasse. "Do we go sit in the varsity room or stay here or what?"

It was a shame they hadn't been told at least that much, but I was grateful for the chance it gave me to be useful.

"I don't know, but I'll be happy to go find out for you."

"Good," Tom said. "And if you see the concierge there, I'd like a word with him about these accommodations."

***

The coaches were holding their usual pregame meeting in Trainer Hanson's office, off to one side of the training room. I'd have to hang out in the varsity locker until one appeared. I glanced around the room, noting the various stages of pregame preparation, and I wondered if the atmosphere had ever been more saturated with tension.

Step one: remove street clothes and hang them up in your individual locker. Next, unroll the towel, hang it up, and put on the jock, socks and the half T-shirt that fits under the shoulder pads. Next came hip pads, whether the old strap-on kind with better protection, favored by linemen, or the new stripped down girdle pads favored by running backs and wideouts, or two additional knee pads taped over the hip bones with nothing over the tail-bone, favored by cornerbacks and safeties.

Pants followed, with knee and thigh pads positioned in their holding pockets. Few players had the nerve to play without thigh protection, but some defensive backs disdained both, swearing it let them run faster. I never understood that, but I'd come to be particular about knees.

Shoes came next, together with the endless rituals that went with them. A football player's shoes were one of his few safe outlets for a little individualism. Players clung to distinctive taping patterns, or shining methods, or lacing techniques as mute self-assurance that they still existed as individuals in their otherwise look-alike uniforms.

The final piece of the basic pregame waiting uniform was the game jersey, with its crisp, green numbers and garish shoulder stripes, put on as it was in the Friday practice session, without shoulder pads underneath.

Players stayed that way until forty minutes before kick-off, when Coach Anderson came in and told them to "strap it on." That meant to put on the shoulder pads and helmets, and get ready to take the field for warm-up drills.

The sound of someone throwing up in the toilet area meant quantum time had kicked in full-bore.

***

The varsity dressing room was long and relatively narrow, with the toilet/shower area jutting from the side wall opposite the player's cubicles. Two alcoves were on either end of the shower/toilet complex, with quarterbacks and tailbacks in the one nearest the training room, and marginal players in the far alcove. A portable blackboard was always in the quarterback alcove prior to games, and I was standing near it when Steve Merritt, the receiver coach, came out of the adjacent training room.

"Coach Merritt," I said, moving to block his path, "what are the redshirts supposed to do when they get dressed? Do they come in here to wait before warm-up, or what?"

He looked genuinely puzzled and said, "Can I get back to you on that, Larry? I don't know a thing about it."

Merritt wasn't the worst of coaches, and in fact was reasonably honorable, so I said, "I'll check with you later."

I rejoined the redshirts in the weight room, reporting to all of them about what happened.

"Great!" Heape spat angrily. "I bet those cocksuckers completely forget about us and we spend the whole damn game sitting on our asses in this dump!"

I waited with the redshirts until they were all dressed and ready to go. By then it was less than an hour before kickoff, so I knew two or three assistant coaches would be in the quarterback's alcove going over last-minute details on the blackboard. Sure enough, Coach Merritt was there with two others, so I caught his attention.

"Tell the redshirts not to worry about warming up," he said. "Coach doesn't want those old uniforms making it look like a Chinese fire drill out there. Tell them we'll send for them just before we take the field for the kickoff."

That seemed reasonable. Two different uniforms *would* look strange, so it made sense to minimize their exposure.

"What about the guys in the varsity uniforms?" I asked. "They're dressed out like everyone in here."

Merritt shrugged in exasperation. "Suiting them up was

Coach Marshall's idea. If he wants them out there, I'm sure he'll let them know. Now, is that all?"

It was obvious I was pushing him too far. "Yes, sir!"

The redshirts were certainly disappointed, but not surprised, about having to miss the pregame warm-up. We all wondered, though, about Coach Marshall's reasons for dressing out Duggan, Heape, and Prosser like the varsity. Everyone had an opinion on the matter.

"It has to be because of Duggan," Tom said to the group. "With Don gone and the Bull on a gimpy ankle, they need insurance at fullback. Dave's a good player, a solid blocker, and he never blows assignments. He's smart."

"I think it's because of Heape," Duggan said. "Coach Marshall respects talent, and everyone knows if it wasn't for Rabbit being there, he'd be the third team wingback."

"So you think," Heape countered, "that he's dressing me out in a varsity uniform tonight as a gesture of . . . what? Encouragement so I don't get chapped and quit?"

Tom nodded. "That would be good strategy on his part."

"Okay," I said, "that may explain Grant. How about Vin?"

Newbert pointed to his jersey with an 87 on it. "I think it was dumb luck. It's an end's number, and I'm an end."

Prosser's number 25 was the next focus of attention. Everyone else was standing up, but he sat on the floor against the far wall, his legs stretched out in front of him and his eyes closed, as if he wasn't even in the room with us. Earlier I watched him put his dark contacts in, so he probably couldn't see any of us clearly in the dim light.

"The same holds for Prosser as for Vin," Tom said. "The other spare number was for a running back, and he's our running back. It wouldn't fit a lineman, and the only other person who could wear it is me, and I'm being punished with this clown suit—" He gripped its front and pulled its extra-large size away from his average body, making him look like a child playing dress-up. "—for speaking to dickhead Hackler without being spoken to."

That was actually a very stupid move by the coaches. If there was any player on the redshirts they should favor, it was Tom. It was always difficult to find ex-high school stars willing to submerge their own style of play to try to imitate each week's opposing quarterback. And even when coaches did find someone like Tom, it was almost impossible to keep them around for more than a year. Nearly everyone got discouraged and quit after a season of such thankless work, yet Tom was now starting his second tour of duty as the redshirt leader.

"I have an angle on Prosser that maybe none of you have thought about," I suggested. Pete opened his eyes to listen to me. "Since we know the whole thing started with Marshall, what about the idea that he did it to get back at Hackler for injuring the Bull's ankle in goal line drill?"

"Hackler definitely deserves a major payback for that," Tom said, and even Prosser nodded agreement. "He had no business calling that stack on the goal line—period."

"So break it down into its most basic components," I went on. "Inside the coaches' offices, it would come down to Hackler not wanting you to suit up because he hates you, and Marshall pushing for it to stick a cobb up Hackler's ass. Based on what I know, I think Marshall has more throw-weight with Anderson, so Marshall trumps Hackler."

"Makes sense," Skid said. "Marshall's not the kind to let something like that pass without a counterpunch, and this is a great way to annoy the hell out of Hackler."

"Absolutely," I said. "If you think coaches rag you to death, you should see how they treat each other. It's all in fun, kind of, but they love to gig each other if they can."

"And nothing would piss Hackler off more than seeing some of us suited up in varsity uniforms," Heape finished. "Especially Prosser. He must *really* hate to see that."

Everyone except Prosser nodded in agreement, so I said to him, "What do you think, Pete?".

"I think it'll be a long night for all of us."

***

PREGAME

Anderson, Hackler and Marshall spent their pregame quantum time in Trainer Hanson's office in the training room. Players didn't feel comfortable going through pregame rituals, or revealing pregame jitters, in front of the head coaches, and the coaches knew it, so they made themselves scarce and let the assistants handle everything.

Unlike the redshirts, varsity players were still without shoulder pads when I got back up front, but I knew Anderson would soon leave Trainer Hanson's office to tell them to get ready, so I made a last quick tour of the room.

"How about it, Ken? How's the ankle?"

The Bull, chewing furiously on his mouthpiece, looked up and nodded. Words weren't necessary.

"Quink? How's it going?"

"I'm taking Don's place in the wedge," he said gloomily.

That meant he'd be one of three up backs on the kickoff receiving team, positioning himself between our six front linemen and two deep backs. It was trench duty on the bomb squad. "Who's in the center?" I asked.

The center man of the wedge would be the point of fiercest attack for opponents, and he usually got the holy crap knocked out of him by big linemen hurtling downfield specifically to break up the wedge. "Johnson, thank God."

Roger Johnson had been our third team fullback and now would back up the Bull. This news could explain Coach Marshall's desire to have Dave Duggan in a varsity uniform. If Johnson was injured doing wedge duty, Duggan was the most likely person to fill in for him.

In fact, Duggan would be a better choice than Johnson as the middle of the wedge. He was a burly guy, a solid blocker, though slow, and totally expendable. But he was a redshirt, and while coaches were quick to move a player down to that group, once that decision was made, once the stigma was applied full-force, they were notoriously reluctant to move anyone back up to the varsity.

"How's it going, Swede? You ready?"

"You bet!" he said loudly, then he whispered in an aside only I could hear: "As long as I don't get sent in!" His position as a third team end didn't make that likely.

Wheeler, like many of the others, was lying on his back on the floor below his locker. "How's it, Jimbo? You ready?"

Of all the players to be tested tonight, everyone knew Wheeler faced the toughest challenge. His efforts against Stoner would largely decide our success up the middle, and if we couldn't control the middle occasionally. . . .

Wheeler looked up at me with widely dilated pupils and spoke in a very low but urgent tone. "I took speed."

Oh, shit! I squatted down by him so no one could hear. "Have you ever done it before?"

I knew several guys on the team would take amphetamines for a boost, but they always got the feel of the drug at practice before they tried it out in a game. I never knew Wheeler to take anything stronger than coffee.

He shook his head. "I just couldn't stand the thought of facing him without some help, Sage . . . he'll rape me!"

"Do you know what to expect from the speed?"

"They say I'll feel really strong, and I won't get tired, but I may be a little confused at first. Is that the way it is?"

I nodded. "Yeah, that's it. . . ." *Jesus!* He'd be lucky to find his butt with both hands once it got a grip on him.

He took a deep, shuddering breath. "Wish me luck."

I tapped a bandage on his shoulder. "You got it, big guy."

Coach Anderson's voice rang out behind me.

"All right, men, strap it on!"

Within five minutes, everyone was dressed for war. Players banged fists on each other's shoulders and heads, all the while emitting prehistoric roars and growls of intimidation. It could be a terrifying scene if you didn't recognize it as the ancient male posturing routine that it was.

Players pushed and shoved, crowding together at the exit door, as if unable to wait another second before leaping out to devastate everything in their path. The whole display was orchestrated to benefit the coaches, who needed a final dollop of reassurance that their team was *ready*.

As soon as Anderson said, "Okay, everybody outside!" the volume level dropped by half as players simmered down to carefully file out the door so no one got hurt.

On the walk from the dressing room to the entrance chute, the cool, clean evening air struck you first. Then the noise of steel cleat-caps scraping on concrete drowned out everything else. You rounded the corner and entered the area under the stands, and the fans down there began to see you and cheer for you. Some called out a favorite player's name; others offered boisterous encouragement.

As the first players entered the chute, people in the stands began to notice. A cheer went up, followed by more cheering as more people realized what was happening. You looked up from the chute and saw thousands of people, an ocean of them, and you stood awash in the thrilling sound. You soaked it up and swelled with it, feeling you were at the core of whatever brought them together.

To be a part of that core—no matter how insignificant your role—was football's great addictive power. Take away those heady moments of overblown self-satisfaction, and you couldn't get lobotomized gorillas to take part. But *with* those moments, you had every man (and probably many women) in the stands wishing there was some way he (or she) could be there among you, at the heart of it.

Standing in the chute, looking around, feeling the familiar adrenaline rush, I realized how much I'd miss it all.

At Coach Anderson's signal, the team streamed from the chute, into the end zone, under the goal post, and onto the field. Tom wasn't far off the mark when he predicted a record crowd. I jogged out onto the field behind the team, trying to spot empty seats in the stadium's upper reaches; there were none to be seen. And the crowd noise! Not even pro games I had attended produced that kind of pandemonium. 360 degrees of loud cheering produced vibrations you could literally *feel*, all through your body.

I took a position near Trainer Hanson as the team lined up for calisthenics. He shouted something at me, which I couldn't hear over the din, so I bent down to put my ear close to him. I still couldn't hear above the crowd's roar.

Suddenly, he grabbed my forearms and pushed my hands up over my head, and the noise level went even higher! Then I understood what he was trying to say— that a lot of the noise the crowd was making was for *me*.

I felt stripped naked, nearly overcome by a crazy urge to run out of there. Finally, Hanson dropped my hands and the noise subsided, but within seconds there was another roar and my heart started racing again with the strange sensation I had just experienced.

Then I spotted the Longhorns making their entrance down at the northwest chute, and I was taken over by a chilling realization: my own shot at the brass ring was past me now. I was lucky enough to enjoy one last personal thrill on a football field in front of a big crowd.

I felt I could walk away from it now, contented.

During the warm-up drills, Davis looked sharp and confident in his movements at quarterback. Wheeler showed no ill effects from the speed he took—yet. The Bull refused to limp in front of his opponents. Meanwhile, Helmet boomed kicks from fifty yards out, while the Longhorns stole furtive glances at our only pro-level-talent star.

Our players likewise tracked Stoner and McElwee, their All-American split-end, and the other players they knew they would soon be facing head-to-head. It had to give all of them the same kind of pause it gave me. Those guys were just damn *big* . . . big and fast and powerful.

***

The warm-ups ended at 7:45, and both teams quickly went back to their respective locker rooms, leaving the field to the half-dozen babes known as the "Crawdettes." They were athletic cheerleaders who could tumble and twist and turn in the air, keeping everyone hyped up.

Inside the dressing room, the final few minutes before returning to the field were spent in a flurry of last-minute equipment adjustments and trips to the toilets. I went down to the weight room to prepare the redshirts to leave their hovel and join the varsity when it was time to take the field for kickoff. Then I went back to the varsity room to monitor things there, and I walked in just as Coach Anderson began his final words of encouragement.

"Men," he began soberly, "I know you've all probably gotten pretty sick of me saying how important this game would be for us, for our team, but all you had to do was look up in those stands tonight to see how right I was. I hope you appreciate what that means. It's a once-in-a-life-time opportunity for each of you to make your mark, and I can only hope you're willing to take advantage of it.

"Now, you're as thoroughly prepared as any team can possibly be for a game like this. You *are* ready to play, whether you feel like you are or not. I've been in this business for a long time, and I *know* when a team is ready. You've had some hard knocks this week—as hard in one instance as I hope you ever have to endure—but you've come all the way back from that blow, and now you have a golden opportunity to turn it to your benefit.

"Yes, we all know I'm talking about Don Slade, so let's bring it on out in the open. Don is what this whole game is about. Don Slade put those people in the stands and those reporters in the press box, but now the burden passes from him to you. Each and every one of you has an obligation to him to sacrifice yourselves the way he would have sacrificed if he were still with us today; and each of you will be ashamed the rest of your lives if you don't—just this once—give yourselves up totally to the great cause of dedicating this game to his memory.

"Now go out there, play good, solid football, and come in here at halftime with something Don would be proud of. What do you say, men? Will you get after 'em?"

Anderson did it just right. I'd never seen anything like it. After three or four seconds of stone cold silence, a roar erupted from every person in the room, even the coaches and trainers. Players leaped to their feet and went crazy, pounding themselves, each other, the walls, anything in their way. I had never seen a team emotionally higher.

I had the foresight to take up a position near the door, so when the team finally gathered its senses enough to start heading for the field, I was the first person to step outside. I hurried down to kick the weight room door so the redshirts would know to come out and join their teammates. I hadn't mentioned the redshirts to anyone since I last spoke to Coach Merritt, so I wasn't sure whether the coaches had assigned someone to go fetch them or not.

I wasn't taking any chances.

Regardless of what was intended for them, the redshirts blended smoothly into the stream of varsity players that poured out of the dressing room. Even the ones wearing the old uniforms were in the chute and visible to the crowd by the time the coaches joined the team for that quick jog to the sideline. As far as I could tell, the coaches were too preoccupied to care who was with them now. Everyone's focus was, and should be, elsewhere.

The ceremony for Don was simple and moving. Our athletic director presented his older brother, Steven, with the number 33 jersey Don would have worn, and the letterman sweater he would have won. He then announced that for the rest of the season, after this game, our team's jersey's would have a black left sleeve bearing Don's number.

Steven then spoke to the crowd on behalf of the family, explaining that neither Don's parents nor his wife were recovered enough from the shock of his death to attend the game, but he thanked everyone for coming and promised to relay to the family the emotion everyone expressed.

A heartfelt prayer followed, then 50,000 people became respectfully silent for sixty seconds. The whole thing was tastefully done, and I could find no fault with it.

When you stop and think about it, though, a jersey, a sweater, and a minute of silence weren't much consolation for what Don's family lost, or for what our team lost.

It certainly didn't plug the gaping holes in our hearts.

KICKOFF

We lost the toss and elected to defend the north goal because a light breeze was blowing in off the lake from that direction. Conditions were ideal. The field had great drainage and was immaculate, the air was cool and clean, and the stadium was a tense sellout. When the "Star Spangled Banner" played, I shivered with anticipation.

It may seem like a boring, routine ritual on television, but it's hard to describe what it's like from the floor of a packed arena seconds before combat begins. The energy generated by those thousands of bodies pours down onto the field and suffuses everyone with an otherworldly feeling of lightness and grandeur. You seem to drift outside yourself, to become more than you actually are, and for those few addictive moments you feel like Superman.

Our kickoff unit took the field and lined up as the referee handed the ball to Helmet and Rabbit did his head-count with a flourish. The least demanding position on our team was safetyman on the kickoff unit. For other teams, this was a position of responsibility because kickoff safetymen trailed down the field behind their teammates as the last line of defense when the other side broke a return.

In our special case, Helmet put ninety percent of his kickoffs in the opponent's end zone, so Rabbit would have few returns to deal with this season. It was a situation designed by the hand of God to satisfy his old man and keep the coaches riding in their new Pontiacs.

The whistle blew and Helmet approached the ball with his sidestepping soccer motion. There was a solid *thunk!* as his foot made contact. The game was under way.

Two Texas deep backs stood on the goal line to receive the kick. The left side deep back, number 37, caught it near the back line and wisely elected not to run it out.

Texas' ball, first and ten at their twenty.

Their first drive needed four minutes and eighteen seconds to score, and I was surprised it took that long. They executed their plays so well, it seemed as if we hardly got in their way. That smoothness and crisp efficiency showed why they were number one, and it showed the kind of night we could expect against them.

While the Longhorn drive was in progress, I wandered up and down the sideline, tense, excited. After the Texas score, I went back to midfield and found myself next to Wheeler as the Longhorns lined up to kick their extra point.

"How about it, Jimbo? How you feeling?"

"Only 4:18? Only 4:18? It seemed like *forever,* didn't it?"

"Yeah, right, but how do you feel?"

"Fine, fine, I'm okay! I feel strong and solid, but everything is so damn *slow!* I want to get *out* there!"

The ball went cleanly through the uprights and our kickoff return unit took the field.

"All right!!!" Wheeler screamed almost hysterically into the heavens. *"Let's go, big offense!!! Let's take it to 'em!!!"*

I didn't approve of using speed to increase stamina, but now that Wheeler had done it, I hoped he could handle it.

Travers and Colter were our deep backs on kickoff returns, and Travers took that first one at the five with a full head of steam. He got right behind the wedge and the three of them plowed out a respectably wide path for him out to the twenty-seven, where number 89 for Texas stopped him cold with a jarring head-high tackle.

Hackler gathered the defensive line around the communications table, and I eased over while the offensive unit took the field. The communications table was located at the fifty and stood five yards from the sideline. It was covered with microphone headsets so the coaches could maintain contact with observers in the press box. Hackler had a headset on and was shouting into its mouthpiece.

"Goddammit, Burt, did they seal or pinch on the inside traps? That's all I need to know!"

There was a delay, then Hackler glared at Craig Bonham, the left defensive tackle. "He says they pinched!"

Bonham steadfastly shook his head. "It was a seal on both plays, Coach, I'm sure of it."

Hackler tore the headset off and flung it onto the table. "Fuck it! Play inside if they give you air either way! Cheat it! They won't go outside till we stop 'em up the middle!"

Our first offensive play was always called in the dressing room before the game. This one would be a slam-dive between left guard and center, with Wheeler and the Bull double-teaming Stoner, while Lawrence followed on their blocks with the hand-off. Much depended on who could establish initial dominance in the line, but an extra measure rode on dealing with a player of Stoner's caliber.

At the snap Wheeler fired out hard and, just as he said he'd do, he drove his face mask squarely into Stoner's broad chest. Stoner met his charge with a thudding forearm shiver that got under Wheeler's breast plates and hit his abdomen, while the Bull slammed into both of them to carry out his part of the block. Though not really moved out of position, Stoner was neutralized by his two blockers, and Lawrence blew by him for five yards.

"All right, offense! Way to hit in there! Way to stick it!"

The sideline went wild at the success of our first offensive play. Then we saw Wheeler weaving back and forth on his knees, trying to struggle to his feet.

"Hancock!" Coach Marshall called out, whirling around frantically to find him. "Hancock, where are you?"

Sandy Hancock was last year's starting center, but as is often the case, someone with a bit more talent and a bit more enthusiasm for the game had come along to roll him off first team. Though much depended on how badly Wheeler was hurt, Hancock was being given one of those rare chances to reestablish his credentials as a starter.

Wheeler was on his feet by the time Trainer Hanson made it out to him. Hanson's special pride in being the picture of controlled calm, never making a hurried movement to help anyone, was why all our players religiously wore mouthpieces and dreaded collisions violent enough to make them swallow their tongues. They knew they'd be turning blue by the time Hanson arrived to try to help.

Hanson broke an ammonia cap under Wheeler's nose, and he soon jogged off the field. Coach Marshall met him at the sideline. "What happened, son?"

"Knocked . . . my wind out," Wheeler replied shakily.

"Okay, then," Coach Marshall said as he patted him on the rump. "That was a good block, we got five off it. Shake this off and go back out for the next series."

Wheeler nodded and headed for the bench.

First-play injuries always had an impact on any team. You go into the game focused and prepared, then right out of the gate, one of your starters gets hurt. If it's serious, it can flatten you, take the wind right out of your sails. But if it's minor, the effect could be galvanizing.

In our case, Wheeler had endured days of steady taunting about what Kevin Stoner would do to him when they met, and Wheeler had absorbed it all before going out to meet his fate against the monster. Now that he had done it well enough to leave the field under his own steam, it somehow rendered the Longhorns less invincible.

We scraped out a first down at the thirty-eight, then they measured for another at the forty-eight. We were grinding it out so slowly that the referee was reaching for a delay-of-game flag each time Hancock snapped back to Davis. Nevertheless, we were getting just enough of our blocks, and they were missing just enough of their tackles, to let us pick up three or four yards per play, with the Bull and Lawrence and Davis running hard inside and outside.

On first and ten after the measurement, Davis took the snap and moved left. Stoner took an immediate cross-step to his right because up to that point we'd been running straight hand-off dives. As soon as Davis pivoted back and handed it to the Bull up the middle, Stoner must have known he'd been had. He made a lunging backward move attempting to refill the hole he'd vacated, but Hancock was already there sealing to the inside. Hancock fired into Stoner's off-balance position and knocked the monster flat on his back. The Bull bolted over center, cut left around a hard-charging safetyman, and picked up nine yards before a closing cornerback nailed him.

The beauty of the play got to us, as did seeing Stoner knocked down for the first time. Not only were we looking like a real football team, we had second and one at the Longhorn forty-three! Moving into their territory on our first drive was an achievement none of us dared to hope for.

Anderson grabbed Del Stevens, a second team guard, and yelled above the noise, "Screen right! Everybody *block!*"

Stevens sprinted out and relayed the call to Davis. The Bull faked a play similar to the one he just ran, and Stoner held his ground up the middle. Lawrence, meanwhile, swung out to the right on a fake pitch, which left him alone in the right flat to receive the screen pass.

Davis threw the ball out a little high and behind him, but Lawrence's good hands snared it. He looked upfield and found Stevens and Mike Watterman, the two guards, ahead of him, and Moe Polaski, the right tackle, on his way to help. The Texas cornerback and safety were closing fast from upfield, so Stevens took the cornerback outside, Watterman took the safety inside, and Lawrence was left with nowhere to go but between their blocks.

Stoner had moved into the pursuit flow as soon as the Bull came through the line empty handed, and was now bearing down on Lawrence with all the speed his muscular bulk could generate. Polaski, our biggest and best offensive lineman, planted his near equal bulk directly in Stoner's path to seal off an outside alley for Lawrence. Polaski was well positioned to meet Stoner's charge.

Stoner clearly sensed being set up, because instead of evading Polaski's block in an attempt to make the tackle, he grabbed the initiative and became a blocker himself. He blasted into Polaski's chest in a move that was totally unorthodox and unexpected—and utterly successful.

Polaski had prepared himself to deliver a blow instead of receive one, so the impact knocked him backward and into the air like an enormous piece of kindling off an ax blade. An incredibly loud *"Uhhh!!!* went up from the crowd as Polaski's flying body cut Lawrence down at shoulder height, like a scythe blade cutting a shock of wheat.

Lawrence had already turned his attention away from Polaski's assumed block, which left him unprepared for the crunching blindside blow he received. The ball popped from Lawrence's stunned grip and bounded into the Texas secondary, where their offside safetyman had no trouble falling on it for a successful fumble recovery.

As Lawrence and Polaski untangled themselves and shook away the cobwebs, their confused look symbolized for all of us the certain knowledge that Stoner was indeed a breed apart, and he deserved all of his accolades.

The magnitude of that level of disaster took more than a moment to sink into any victim's consciousness. While the recovering team bounded around gleefully and quickly made its way off the field, the offensive victims staggered off in a kind of coitus interruptus shock. Tremendous levels of frustrated energy had to be dissipated on the sideline instead of in combat, and the defense was thrown equally out of sync. They had to reenter the battle with little or no chance to gear up emotionally, and that inverted state often led to a follow-up disaster for them as well.

If a 2:38 drive for a score can be seen as a disaster, then Lawrence's fumble led to one for us.

STEMMING THE TIDE

We were down 14-0, with less than five minutes left in the first quarter, when Wheeler went back in at center for our second offensive series. Hancock had done an admirable job against Stoner on the first drive, but protocol gave Wheeler the right to reclaim his starting role. No one ever lost their jobs due to a minor injury like his.

Our first play of the second series was a trap over center. Davis faked a dive to the Bull over right guard to pull Stoner to his left, then he whirled back and handed off to Lawrence up the middle. Wheeler and Watterman cross-blocked, with Wheeler knifing left to trap Watterman's man, while Watterman pulled right to cross-block Stoner.

Stoner took the Bull's fake and stepped left. Watterman kept him from refilling the hole while Lawrence headed into what looked like a good opening. Unfortunately, Wheeler only half-completed his block, and number 64 for Texas reached out and nearly stole the hand-off. Lawrence was tackled for a two yard loss and the coaches blew up.

"What the hell happened?" Marshall screamed into a headset. "Was 64 offside?" He waited for an answer from the spotters up in the press box, then looked at Anderson. "Wheeler barely hit him, Coach . . . slow off the ball."

Anderson kicked the ground, then composed himself.

"All right!" he shouted between handclaps, "This is the one! Let's get 'em this time!"

The next play was a fullback sweep right, the same play that killed Don. The Longhorns were playing second and twelve a bit loose, so the Bull got seven yards before he was tripped up. Wheeler got a barely decent cut-off block on the guard who beat him on the previous play, but it seemed to appease the coaches for the moment.

On third and five we tried a play-action pass, but Texas blitzed Stoner. Wheeler completely missed Stoner's charge and let Davis get creamed for a four yard loss that would have been worse if Stoner hadn't hit him so quickly.

As the punting team went on and the offense came off, Anderson and Marshall closed ranks to confront Wheeler.

"What the hell's the matter with you, Jimbo?" Coach Marshall demanded. "Are you scared of those boys?"

Wheeler hung his head and seemed not to understand the full extent of what was happening to him.

"Answer him, son!" Coach Anderson said, with threatening menace in his tone. "Are you afraid?"

"No, sir!" Wheeler insisted. "I can't seem to get off the ball right. I can *see* what's happening, and I *know* what I'm supposed to do, but I can't make my body work right."

Anderson and Marshall exchanged arched eyebrows. Players never gave truthful replies to explain failures, normally answering accusatory questions with, "Yes, sir," or "No, sir," and let the chips fall where they may. Wheeler's honest answer emphasized his degree of befuddlement.

"Sit it out till halftime," Anderson said curtly.

Even though the score denied it and most observers would never realize it, we played some of the best football I'd ever seen us play through the next few series of downs. We suffered the standard isolated screw-ups that most teams endure on every play, but our patented wholesale disasters were being kept to an absolute minimum. We were playing this game as well as we possibly could.

Texas also revealed something interesting throughout that first period. They seemed determined to avoid looking like complete assholes by stomping us into the ground. Their coaches knew they were in the national spotlight right along with us, and it wasn't hard to calculate how many ranking votes they'd lose by running the score up on us. After all, how impressive would it be it to pile insult on a bereaved family struggling to get over a tragedy?

At any rate, after notching touchdowns the first three times they had the ball, Texas put their second team in the game and left them there. Ordinarily, even their second teams would be more than a match for our first units, but for as long as we played so far over our heads, this looked like it could turn out to be a decent contest.

Late in the second quarter, with the score at 21-0, the Longhorn substitutes put on a drive that seemed sure to score again. I stood near midfield as they crossed our thirty, and just after that I noticed Coach Marshall grab Coach Anderson by the arm. Marshall motioned toward the communications table and indicated a headset, so I casually edged over and back to eavesdrop.

"If they score this time, we ought to put him in," Marshall said with intent determination. "Upstairs says their kicking team is loafing now, and he can break one for us."

Coach Anderson didn't acknowledge that comment as he listened to the report from upstairs in the press box. Then I heard the headset go down on the table followed by Anderson's voice. "Tell Wade to come here," he said flatly.

In seconds Hackler joined them, and they stood talking only a few yards behind my back. Normally, everyone on the team gave the coaches plenty of space when they huddled up like that. It was part of football protocol to let them speak in private. But I ignored that rule and hovered within the distance I needed to be able to hear them, while keeping my visual attention focused on the field.

"Wade," Anderson began, "I want you to hear this from

me. If they score this time, I'm putting him in. We'll be down 28-zip, and it will only get worse if we don't do something to fire our people up. We all know he can break one for us."

"Dammit, T. K.!" Hackler shot back, "playing him is a *mistake!* It'll be just like that fucking Kraut! He'll undermine respect for us with the others, and we won't be able to touch him. So, *no!* It's not worth that sacrifice, I don't care *how* you and Paul try to rationalize it."

"Look, Wade," Marshall cut in, "we know how strong you feel about it . . . we know he took you down on purpose and broke your wrist. Even so, we're outvoting you."

I wished I could have turned to see Hackler's expression as Anderson finished him off. "We played it your way as far as we could go, so now I expect you to play it our way. We're in a unique situation here, Wade, and principles or not, we have no choice. Do you understand me?"

I heard a growl of frustration followed by a noise that sounded like someone kicking a bench or a table or something else. Then I heard nothing from them for several seconds, so I risked a quick glance to my left. Marshall and Anderson were several yards away, moving to where Prosser sat on the far left side of the bench.

They'd tell him to warm-up so that if Texas scored on this drive, he'd be ready to run their kickoff back.

Hackler was down at the other end of our sideline, yelling at his defense to keep Texas out of our end zone.

Texas was at our fifteen, with a second and seven as I hurried into position alongside Tom. I jabbed him with an elbow and motioned for him to move back away from the sideline so we could talk in relative privacy.

"Can it wait?" he asked. "I don't want to miss the score."

"No, it can't."

He shrugged in resignation, keeping his eyes on the field as he stepped back with me. "This better be good."

"If they score, Prosser goes in for the kickoff return."

Tom's head nearly snapped off its hinges as he whirled

to his left, his face a picture of disbelief. *"What?"*

"I overheard Anderson, Marshall, and Hackler talking. The gist of it is that the score is getting out of hand, the whole country is watching, and they know Prosser can break a return and give our guys a shot in the arm."

"Oh, that's perfect!" Tom said as the logic of it began to sink in. "If they only use him as a specialist—like Helmet—it's less of a concession to his attitude. Why didn't we—?"

His words were drowned out by the crowd's roar as Texas fumbled at our eight and we recovered.

"Awww, *shit!*" Tom and I blurted without thinking.

We were upset because we knew Prosser might have lost his shot with that fumble, but several guys near the sideline in front of us turned around to give us dirty looks.

I could only think to smile weakly at them, but quick-witted Tom was on top of the situation. "Sorry, guys! From back here it looked like Texas recovered!"

As our offense hustled out to take possession and the defense came rollicking off the field, Tom looked at me.

"Do you think he goes in, next score, no matter what?"

I shrugged. "We'll have to wait for the second half."

HALFTIME

The offense worked the ball out to our forty-five by the time the half ended. The crowd gave both teams a polite round of applause as they jogged off the field, but a pall had hung over the stadium since the middle of the second quarter. Although by our standards we were playing inspired football, Texas was ahead by three touchdowns, and no amount of crowd encouragement could change that.

The redshirts faced the problem of where to spend the halftime. Should they return to the grungy weight room and endure that humiliation, or go into the varsity room and risk Hackler dumping another load of crap on them in front of their teammates? It was a genuine quandary.

"What do you think?" Tom asked. "What should we do?"

"The weight room has no toilet, and they can't expect you to pee in your pants. Go in the varsity room and stay in the far alcove. Just keep your heads down and try to stay out of their way. You should be okay doing that."

"Thanks!" he said, and I could feel his sincerity, which was odd because I had no more reason to be in the varsity locker room than they did. We were *all* outcasts.

"Don't worry," I countered, "I'll be right there with you."

Halftime procedure began when the players filed into the dressing room and found ice-cold cans of soda on the floor in front of their cubicles. They came in, relieved themselves as they needed to, then sat down and drank their sodas while waiting for the whole team to file in and get settled in a similar fashion. Talking was allowed— boisterous if we were winning, subdued if we weren't— until the coaches made their appearance.

This time when the team assembled in the dressing room to wait for the coaches, it was evident that most players felt no sense of gloom. Except for Wheeler and a couple other victims of misfortune, they were pleased by their first-half performances. The 21-0 score took second place to the high quality of their efforts, and I was glad to see they hadn't lost their capacity for self-appreciation.

In the first several minutes of the twenty-minute break, the coaches stayed outside to analyze the team's first-half effort, trying to coordinate opinions about what they saw, trying to help Coach Anderson form a strategy for his half-time speech. Unfortunately, coaches perceived any game from an entirely different standpoint than players, so they were seldom able to give sound advice about the mood of the team. Thus, no matter what emotional stance Anderson chose when he stood before the team at halftimes, he was nearly always on the wrong wavelength.

This time was no different. The coaches stormed into the locker room wearing frightful scowls of anger, apparently convinced that what the team needed to close the twenty-one point gap was a tongue lashing. That approach was as incongruous as it could possibly be, but coaches were not known for the subtlety of their temperaments. Thus, they got what they expected from their players. Smiling faces went blank, and heads dropped in feigned shame.

In an effort to leave no doubt about his calculated-for-effect mood, Anderson hit on a dramatic illustration. He spotted an unopened soda can still resting on the floor, and savagely kicked it toward the other end of the room, forty feet away. Whatever his proposed halftime strategy was, however he meant to berate the team, he lost all hope of making it work when he kicked that can of soda.

In the far right-side corner of the dressing room stood a large round metal container where players put all manner of trash. Sure enough, whether directed by existential will or sheer coincidence, the soda can tumbled end over end all the way across the dressing room and landed squarely in the container with a metallic clatter that was astonishingly loud in the otherwise silent room.

Every eye was on Anderson when he kicked, and every eye followed the soda can as it spun across the room and disappeared in the garbage container. Naturally, players in the target area maintained the closest watch until they were sure it would land in an unoccupied zone, but without doubt the takeoff, flight, and landing held everyone in the room mesmerized—everyone, that is, except Helmet.

Helmet just happened to be one of the two players sitting next to the garbage container when the can rattled home. Without missing a beat, he leaned over and looked inside as if to officially verify the sanctity of what we all just witnessed. He then calmly looked back out over the room and, with every eye locked on him, he threw both arms upward in the classic referee's signal that a kick has been successful. It brought down the house.

A wave of choking and sputtering swept the room as we all struggled to keep from laughing out loud. Coaches were even more on the spot than players, turning away to keep their reactions from being interpreted as disrespect toward Anderson. Those efforts were unnecessary, though, because as soon as Anderson's initial astonishment faded, he burst out with a full-fledged belly laugh. That immediately gave everyone permission to guffaw as loudly as we wanted to, so we all cut loose.

Anyone outside the dressing room must have been amazed to hear a team down 21-0 laughing so hard.

After a minute or so, we began regaining our composure, so Coach Anderson raised a hand for silence and our chuckling rapidly faded. Looking at us now, he'd clearly dropped all pretense. What was the point? Everyone's emotional momentum had swung in a direction none of us were used to expressing in the dressing room, but he was a good enough coach to recognize that and utilize it.

"Men," he began, "I'm glad we were able to share that moment just now because it highlights something we, as coaches, tend to forget. Football is supposed to be *fun*, which we need to be reminded of now and then because if you don't have fun at something, you just can't do it very well. That doesn't take away from the value of winning, but it gives our situation here tonight a different perspective than I'm used to admitting, much less accepting.

"We can't kid ourselves about what's happening to us tonight. We're getting beaten by a better team, plain and simple. The score proves that. But the important thing, as far as I'm concerned, is that we're a damn sight far from getting our asses whipped! We're playing the very best football I think it's in our capacity to play, and I'm extremely proud of you for that—proud of *all* of you."

He said that with a nod toward Helmet, who beamed happily in return, possibly aware—but just as possibly unaware—of the magic he had just created.

"I had intended to come in here and tell you that since Texas scored twenty-one and held you to none in one half, there was no reason why you couldn't go out there and do the same to them. Well, I'd still like to see that happen, but let me just ask you to go out there this half and play as hard and as tough as you played the first half. Do that and I'll be as proud of you as I am right now, you'll be as proud of yourselves as you are right now, and Don Slade, wherever he is, God rest his soul, will be proud of you.

"Now, get out there and do what you know how to do, and I guarantee the final score will take care of itself."

That was the best halftime speech I ever heard.

The final few minutes of halftime were spent going over technical details with individual coaches, while anyone too tense to relieve themselves immediately after coming in could do so now. I looked over and caught Jeff's eye and nodded toward the toilet area. He nodded back and came to help me, as he'd done several times by then.

As we stood at the urinal getting me squared away to pee, Wheeler came in and knelt down in front of a commode. He stuck a finger down his throat three times trying to empty his stomach, but nothing solid came up.

Jeff shook the dew off my lily and zipped me up, then we went over to where Wheeler knelt, on the verge of tears.

"You okay, Jimbo?" I asked.

Wheeler nodded disconsolately, got to his feet, and went over to the sink to rinse his mouth. He then sucked in a deep breath and let it out before turning around to face us.

"That pill ruined me," he finally said. "I wanted to get it out of my system if I could so I can get back in the game."

He was too late on two counts. First, the speed got into his bloodstream soon after he took it, and now the best he could hope for was rapid dissipation of its effects. And second, he'd already lost his first team job to Hancock, and he had no chance to get it back unless Hancock was injured.

No matter Wheeler's excuse, he folded when the chips

were down and Hancock came through. Now his only hope was to stay second team until Hancock graduated at the end of the year. He'd have to be lucky, though, to have any chance of working himself back up in the spring.

Coaches had long memories for guys who let them down.

Right on schedule, the referee stuck his head in our dressing room door and said, "Five more minutes, Coach."

Everyone stopped what they were doing and gave Anderson their full attention. For the last time before rejoining the battle, he went over the routine trivia of our game plan—a litany that coaches everywhere recited constantly.

"All right, men," he began, "what are the things we want to always remember out there? We want to go all-out on every play and give one-hundred-and-ten-percent effort at all times. We want to be first off the ball on both offense and defense; we can't be winners sitting on our dobbers. We want to drive through our blocks and lock our arms on every tackle. We want to punish the runner and not stop hitting him till he's down or the whistle blows. We want to play the *ball* on pass defense—not the man. And, lastly, we want to concentrate on all phases of the kicking game because *it's there the breaks are made!*"

That last quote was a staple throughout football, and with basis in solid facts, so Coach Anderson always gave it special emphasis. This time it led into the blockbuster announcement he planned earlier out on the field.

"Now, speaking of the kicking game, we receive this half, and we've made some changes in our return formation and personnel. Coach Marshall has the details. Coach. . . ."

Marshall stood at the blackboard and drew a diamond pattern of zeroes, while the players exchanged furtive glances. Changing a basic formation was nearly always the result of an injury to a key player, or back-to-back screwups, and our return unit suffered neither. Consequently, everyone except Tom and me had a right to be confused by such an unexpected change in procedure.

"All right," Marshall said as he turned from the black-board to face the room, "we're changing from the two-three box we've been using to this one-deep, three-up configuration. We want a seven-man front line with Rodriguez added in the middle. Miller, Johnson, and Thompson stay as the wedge . . . and back here in the key is Prosser."

Prosser! Is he serious? Holy shit!

Football players were trained to accept any dictum from coaches with no outward sign of reaction. However, as Marshall went on speaking, who could resist sneaking peeks at Hackler staring bullets at Prosser on the other side of the room, and Prosser's dark eyes glaring back.

"Do any of you have any questions about how to carry out the one-three diamond return?" Marshall asked.

Everyone knew how to run it because it was the most common return formation at high schools, where they usually wanted one stud running back handling kickoffs.

With no questions offered, Marshall concluded his remarks. "We're making this change because we think we have a good chance to break one and get back in the ball game. The spotters upstairs tell us Texas is loafing down on their coverage, so let's go out there and cram this first one down their throats! What do you say, men?"

The team sent up a roaring, *"Alllll riiiiight!"* and then clambered out of the dressing room with what seemed like even more noise than before. They knew that if an opportunity to break a kickoff return against Texas did exist, no one had a better chance to seize it than Pete Prosser.

I stood watching the team file out, fired up by its new enthusiasm, wondering if Randall and Carla would appreciate Prosser's chance for vindication as much as the redshirts did. And because I was one of the last people out of the room, I know Hackler did *not* appreciate it.

My fondest football memory will always be the look he gave me when I passed him on my way out and asked:

"Coach, you think his sore back will slow him down?"

***

SECOND HALF KICKOFF

Back out on the sideline, I saw Wheeler sitting on the bench, his head in his hands. He'd been told about being permanently demoted, so I wished there was something I could do for him, but there really wasn't. He had to come to terms with it by himself. Besides, the kickoff teams were lining up, and I didn't want to miss the return.

In this quarter we defended the south end, so I looked to my right to see Prosser and the others preparing to receive the kick. As soon as the team was back on the field, Prosser went through a rush warm-up session along the sideline, but now our number 25 was in position along with everyone else on the return team. Even the mighty Crawdad, staring down at his back from his post beside the scoreboard, seemed to smile with anticipation.

I wished everyone there could know what we knew.

The Texas coverage unit lined up across the field along their thirty-five yard line as their kicker placed the ball in the tee at the forty. All kickoff units—Texas included— covered kicks from the same basic ten-abreast-with-one-safetyman pattern. The field was divided into straight-ahead lanes, and each player was responsible for protecting his own lane until the ball carrier committed himself to a specific direction, at which point they all left their lanes and converged to make the tackle.

Opposing the coverage unit was the return unit's front line and its rear wedge. The front line members tried to disrupt the pursuit pattern by knocking holes in it, while the wedge was responsible for trying to clear one or more adjacent lanes in the middle of the field. Even when kicks were deliberately returned down the sideline, the wedge would stay in the middle initially to act as decoys.

Wedge members would drift back under the kickoff and

then come together several yards in front of the deep back setting up to receive it. They then had the unenviable job of turning upfield to try to knock holes in the pursuing wall of linemen after they passed through the front line's initial attempts at blocking them. Because everything on kickoffs was well out in the open, with plenty of room to maneuver, most defenders got through the first wall by dodging and weaving their way past its blockers.

Those defenders roared downfield under full throttle, and in turn were trying to flatten the onrushing wedge in order to stop the runner tucked in behind it. That situation created the most consistently violent collisions in all of football, so it was no wonder that Quink, Gene Miller, and Roger Johnson twitched and paced nervously as the Texas kicker raised his left arm to signal he was ready.

Prosser stood centered on the five yard line, bent over at the waist, hands on his thigh pads in the classic "prepared" stance of running backs. Then the referee's whistle blew, and he dropped into a slight, coiled crouch as the kicker moved toward the ball to loft his kick.

With the wind at the kicker's back and a good foot into it, the ball carried to our goal line. Prosser drifted back under it while Quink, Miller, and Johnson drifted back at the same ratio of speed so they could keep their relative positions fifteen yards in front of him. All three were proficient blockers, which was why they'd been chosen for the wedge, so Prosser had a decent array of firepower leading him when he gathered it in and headed upfield.

The wedge turned and plowed straight down the middle of the field as Prosser hit the ten yard line and veered sharply to his right. It seemed a senseless move because only about twenty yards separated him and the Texas defenders when he bent away from his escort.

What was he thinking?

True to form, as soon as Prosser moved to his right, the Longhorns began to sweep in that direction. The ones nearest him broke their strides to get under control so he couldn't blow past them, while the ones on his left began stretching out in an attempt to hustle over to him. When it seemed certain he had blundered into an inescapable trap, he knifed back to his left and hit his afterburner.

When Prosser cut to his right, the Texas defenders to his left naturally let up a bit, and that moment's relaxation created gaps in their assigned lanes, with some rushing ahead of others, while some bent too sharply toward the ball. As soon as Prosser stepped back into the teeth of their sweep, the gaps were apparent to everyone. A gasp went up from the crowd as they recognized the moment of possibility. Then Prosser picked his spot and shot through it before the gasps could turn to cheers.

While the wedge and everyone else blocked for it up the middle, Prosser streaked toward, and reached, the sideline in front of our bench, with nothing but seventy yards and the Longhorn safetyman in front of him. We were all going absolutely crazy—even the coaches—even *Hackler!*—jumping up and screaming and marveling at the brilliance we were watching at work this fine night.

In our minds, in our hearts, we were already viewing the completed run, the scoreboard lighting up on our side, the cheering, the Crawdettes doing cartwheels. We automatically discounted the Texas safetyman, even though his trailing position gave him an unbeatable angle on Prosser. Why worry? We all knew, without the slightest doubt, that Prosser couldn't be stopped one-on-one in an open field.

That's why we were so shocked when he was.

The safetyman headed straight to the cut-off point, which we all saw would be somewhere near the Texas thirty, and Prosser met him there as cordially as could be imagined. No wrinkles, not one fake—just two people running to the same spot and then colliding.

Prosser got up and calmly jogged back to our bench listening to scattered booing and catcalls. Coach Marshall met him in an absolute rage, demanding to know what the hell he was trying to prove. Prosser didn't say a word to him or to anyone else. He jerked his arm from Marshall's grip, brushed his way past the rest of us, sat down on the bench next to Wheeler, and proceeded to concentrate on nuances in the ground beneath his feet.

There wasn't much time to dwell on Prosser's actions. We had first and ten at the Longhorn twenty-eight, which was by far our deepest penetration of the night, and we seemed certain to get at least a field goal out of it.

To everyone's amazement, Texas stayed with its second team defense while we went all the way for a score in seven plays. The Bull would not be denied and looked tremendous on the drive, slashing and hammering for those tough goal-line yards. We could hardly believe it when Helmet kicked the extra point and brought the score to 21-7.

Our satisfaction at having scored on an opponent was characteristically brief. After our kickoff to Texas, they put their studs back in on offense, and those Longhorns lost no time starting to cram it down our throats again. I was wondering if we'd be able to hold them for even four or five minutes when I felt a tug at my elbow.

"What's with Prosser?" Tom asked.

"He tanked it."

"I *know* he tanked it! Do you think that's all he'll do?"

"Can you blame him?"

"You're damn right I can! Let's go talk to him."

Prosser was still on the bench where he went after his run, but Wheeler had moved away. He was staring out at the action on the field as Tom sat down to his left and I moved in on his right. He started to get up, but Tom frimly yanked his arm to hold him in his place.

"We want to talk to you, Pete."

"Don't bother, guys," he said with a hint of threat in his voice. "I'm giving the coaches what they want. Do it wrong the first time, remember? Into the line, onto the ground. That's what they want, so that's what I'll give them."

"Listen," Tom said, "you have every right to pay them

back for how they've misused you. No one can blame you for that. But just remember one thing. You're doing what you're doing as a *redshirt,* so whether you like it or not, you're representing redshirts *everywhere* here tonight.

"What you do, and how you do it, will reflect on *all* of us in tomorrow's papers, and for those of us who hold onto the dream of someday moving up the way you are in this game . . . well, you won't leave us much to hope for."

Prosser gazed back at him through those eerie dark lenses. "I don't owe you or anyone anything."

"Bullshit, Pete!" I snapped. "The redshirts on this team are the closest things to friends that you have right now. They've been in your corner, blocking their asses off for you, since the first day of two-a-days! So, go ahead, screw the coaches if you think that serves your karma, but just remember, you'll be screwing your friends, too."

His eyes stayed locked on the field, so Tom opened his mouth to try another tack when Prosser suddenly spoke.

"Save it," he said softly. "I heard you."

"Then you'll think about it?"

He said something that was drowned out by the roar when Texas scored again. We couldn't press him about it any more because, like everyone in the stadium and along the sidelines, we watched him put his helmet on to start warming up so he could run back the next kickoff.

When any coverage unit has a long kickoff return broken against them, they become extra careful the next time out. Heads roll after back-to-back long returns, so the Texas defenders were understandably determined to maintain rigidly proper lanes as they swept downfield.

The ball dropped in at the ten, several yards to Prosser's left, allowing him to gather it in with a fair degree of forward momentum. He then cut sharply to his right to go get behind the center wedge, but instead of stopping when he got behind his escort, he continued driving to his right in an apparent repeat of his earlier effort.

The Longhorns on that side reacted as before, breaking stride and bringing themselves under control, but the offside defenders didn't repeat their mistakes. Instead of lengthening their strides unevenly as they moved toward Prosser, they maintained proper spacing and alignment as they bent toward him. As a result, when he cut back left as before, he faced a solid wall of defenders ready to repay him for their earlier embarrassment.

He was also ready. He took three steps left before he again cut back right, and that movement brought him into centered alignment behind the flying heels of the wedge. A quick burst brought him directly behind his convoy as it blasted into the three Texas defenders who were left to guard the middle by their flank-conscious teammates.

Again, the crowd's reaction was only moments behind the action on the field. A huge groan went up as the contact took place near our thirty, but the anguish just as quickly turned to joy. Quink and Prosser survived the collision and were still on their feet, with Quink in the lead and Prosser clinging to the back of his jersey. You couldn't tell if Quink was pulling or Prosser was pushing, but they thundered like tandem stampeding horses toward the retreating Texas safetyman.

By the time the safety backpedaled to the fifty, he could see there'd be no angles to play this time. Whichever way he committed himself, all Quink had to do was block him and Prosser could cut the other way and be gone.

The safety had a hole card, though, which he played brilliantly at the forty-five. Instead of taking Quink on an angle and hoping for the best, he faked left and then dove at Quink's ankles. Prosser, unfortunately, had stayed too close to Quink's protective back, and the safetyman's move caught them both by surprise. As Quink tumbled over the prostrate safety, his feet slashed back and knifed Prosser's legs out from under him at the Texas forty-four.

All three bodies lay sprawled together.

***

The abrupt termination of that apparent touchdown run brought new groans of dismay from the stands and the sidelines. Still, this fall was much less clearly Prosser's fault, and he gave us good field position for the second time this half. We all realized that could have happened to anyone, but we also knew Pete Prosser wasn't just anyone.

As Prosser jogged off the field, Coach Marshall looked to Coach Anderson for guidance about how to handle the situation. While Anderson was deciding, Prosser reached out to Quink and gave him an encouraging pat on the back of his helmet, as if to say, "We'll get it next time."

Anderson stuck his hand out, palm down, and wiggled it at Marshall in an unmistakable universal language.

Leave him alone.

LAST QUARTER

Our drive was stopped at the Longhorn twenty-seven, at which point Helmet came through with his first field goal of the season. Actually, I was relieved we only got three points because it meant Texas might still leave their studs on the bench with a 28-10 lead.

As we lined up to cover our kickoff, Texas shifted their return to the one-back, three-up diamond we used against them the last two times. It looked like they intended to give us a dose of our own medicine, but instead they ran a reverse that caught several of our guys out of position.

In typical fashion, Rabbit failed to react normally to what they were doing, so he didn't bite on the fake and wound up in perfect position to make the tackle. The last thing I could see was Rabbit sailing waist-high into the Texas return-man near our sideline at their thirty-five.

Everyone beside me was shocked by the crisp efficiency of Rabbit's tackle, so we looked at each other in disbelief instead of down where Rabbit and the Texas man tumbled out of bounds. By the time we refocused on the field, someone was calling for a stretcher where they went out.

Normally, I was the person responsible for handling such requests during a game, so I was particularly attuned to that word. The stretcher was always folded and lashed up under the communications table, where Stanton was busy ripping it loose from its bindings as I came over.

"What happened, Chris? Who needs the stretcher?"

He yanked it loose with the surge of panicky energy I had felt so often when it was my responsibility. "Rabbit hit a down marker . . . broke his ankle. Gotta go!"

I hurried to check for myself. Sure enough, Rabbit was down on the ground three yards outside the sideline, with a blanket thrown over his legs and his left arm covering his eyes. Trainers enforced that because shock often wasn't as severe if a victim wasn't allowed to focus on his injury.

Bud, the assistant trainer, told me what happened. "The chain man didn't get out of the way in time. Somehow the down marker replanted when they hit into it, and Hayden's ankle wrapped around it when they went down."

"How bad is the break?"

"Bad. Broken, dislocated, and twisted backwards. My guess is, he'll have to hang it up like you did."

I wandered back to midfield to tell Tom about it. He expressed the natural shock, then said what everyone on the team would be thinking. "Wouldn't you know it would happen to him the one time he does something *right*?"

"Yeah, if only he'd taken the fake and been out of position, like everyone else with good football sense."

"What about the coaches?" Tom added with a wry grin. "Does this mean they lose their Pontiacs?"

I stifled a laugh and nodded toward Grant Heape, now in his own kind of shock. In that one momentous play for Rabbit, a play he could live on and talk about and stand up to his brother with for the rest of his life, Heape had finally achieved his well-deserved varsity status.

"As one career ends," I said, "so begins another."

As we all hoped, the Texas second team went back in on offense after Rabbit's score-saving tackle, but we were no longer able to hold out against them. We had given it all we had for nearly three quarters, but we were finally running out of steam. Their second team drove down the field as efficiently as their first, and they scored with the same apparent—and by now routine—ease.

The only light at the end of that tunnel was the prospect of another kickoff return by Prosser. "You think we should go have another chat with him?" I said to Tom. "I couldn't tell if he tanked that last one or not."

"What good would it do? He already knows how we feel. Besides, they won't kick it anywhere near him."

Sure enough, the Texas coaching staff took no chance on another long return by Prosser. Their kicker laid the ball flat on the tee and kicked a squibber that barely reached our wedgebacks. Quink tried to scoop it up on a short hop, bobbled it, then fell on it at our thirty.

Prosser didn't get close enough to it to throw a block.

Texas started substituting even more frequently when it became apparent we'd shot our wad. We played against their third string the entire fourth quarter. It wasn't a dull quarter, really. Both sides made some good plays, we saw a few adequate drives, and even standout individual efforts, but Texas was content to let the score stand at 35-10.

We could only be grateful for their charitable intentions and we were happily preparing to celebrate a bona-fide "moral victory" when Lonnie Fulton, a second team linebacker, shook everything lose with a jarring tackle.

There were :37 seconds left on the clock, and Texas was grinding out one last drive against us, when it happened. They had third and five at our forty, so their quarterback decided to try to pick it up on a quick slant to the flanker split left—an easy, routine pass play over the middle.

The flanker took two driving steps off the line to get our

cornerback, Andy Ferragino, moving backward, then he cut sharply to his right, executing a routine down-and-in pattern, and looked for the ball. The pass was on target but high, so just as in the Buster Kidney drill, the flanker had to leave his feet and stretch out to get it.

Lonnie arrived exactly when the flanker's feet touched back down, and he didn't flinch or lower his head. His face mask hit squarely on the ball as he smashed into the flanker's chest. The impact noise went up into relative quiet, because people had started filing out midway through the previous quarter. When the two players collided, only about thirty thousand were left in the stadium, but they sent up a deafening roar as the ball popped high into the air—as much as fifteen feet up.

None of our players were close to it except Lonnie, sprawled on the grass. The Texas tight-end, though, had run a clearing pattern from right to left, which put him in position to continue his route and recover the fumble in full stride. He caught the ball as if it were intended for him, then he knifed between our out-of-position safeties and set sail for a thirty-five yard cruise to our end zone.

If the Crawdad could feel anything, he had to feel miserable as he guarded the scoreboard's 42-10 embarrassment. On the other hand, it meant Texas had to kick off one more time, though we all knew they'd do what they did last time. For as long as Prosser played football, he'd probably never see another kickoff directed his way. No team would risk what he could do to them by putting it directly into his hands. The same would be true when we started using him to return punts. Twice burned was enough for any team. He'd made his point and everyone would get the message that he was not to be trifled with.

Even so, we could use a few counter-strategies. As our kickoff return unit went back out on the north end of the field, Prosser moved up to the fifteen and the wedge moved forward accordingly. Then the Texas kicker laid it flat on the tee, and we knew another squib kick was coming.

The clock read :17 seconds and the score was 42-10 when the Longhorn kicker signaled ready. The whistle blew, and he sent it twisting and bounding to our three up backs in the wedge. Again Quink was there to stop it, but this time he got a good hop and fielded it cleanly.

With no hesitation, looking as if he'd practiced it all his life, Quink turned and shoveled a perfect spiral lateral ten yards backward, into the hands of a surprised Prosser. No one expected him to get another opportunity to run, probably least of all him, yet there he stood, stock still at the twenty, with Texas defenders barreling down on him.

At first, Prosser seemed unable to decide what to do. Because it was a squib, the return pattern was thrown off its timing, so he had no organized help to speak of. He took a tentative step right, but the Longhorns on that side promptly geared down and got themselves under control. He stepped back left, and that side geared down just as quickly. He took one more stagger step to his right and could see what all of us could see: he was trapped.

Prosser headed straight upfield in an apparent effort to squeeze as much yardage as possible from a hopeless situation. Two big rangy defenders pinched in on him from either side, and he didn't even bother trying to fake them. He just ducked his head and drove forward as the two men plowed into each side of him at the same instant.

Surprisingly often, the physics of a collision allows a runner to undergo a violent impact with little damage. When the two Texas defenders slammed into Prosser from opposite sides, he crouched directly between them. As their bodies crunched into his and their helmets met just above his back, the combined force they created was enormous. It criss-crossed through his body and knocked both of them off him as if they had touched a thousand volt cable.

Because each defender hit him with near equal impact, Prosser's body became a conductor of straight line physical forces. Of course, if their heads had collided *with* his torso instead of over his back, he would have stood free for a moment and then slumped forward, probably with some broken ribs. As it was, though, both players simply bounced off him, which left him stumbling forward through the first wave of Texas defenders.

Even though Prosser came out of that collision on his feet, there wasn't much to be said for his prospects. Miller was down after throwing a block, Johnson was in the process of throwing one, Quink was out of the play after fielding the ball and lateraling it, and the frontline seven were scattered about after attempting their first blocks.

Despite all of that chaos, Prosser somehow found a gap to his right and started heading straight for our bench.

FINAL STAND

One of the interesting things about football is that occasionally everyone sees and reacts to a situation in the same way, at the same time. In this instance, we all saw number 24 for Texas coming up from the left as Prosser drew a straight-ahead bead on the sideline trail man. We immediately started shouting above the crowd noise:

"Blind side left! Blind side left!"

Prosser heard us because he turned his attention from the trail man in front to number 24 at his left. He had only a second to react because number 24 had already lowered his head for contact. Just as he did to Colter several days earlier in the half-line drill, Prosser jumped high enough to let number 24 pass beneath his feet, and at the same time he spun 180 degrees to wind up facing the center of the field instead of toward our sideline.

The Texas defenders had swept toward our bench when Prosser committed to that direction, so his dramatic mid-air twist left him facing directly against the grain of their flow. That put them all in the same vulnerable positions he exploited on the first return. Only the safetyman, who proved his abilities when he stopped Quink and Prosser in the open field, maintained a perfect defensive position.

Just as before, Prosser hit the ground and sped into the teeth of the coverage, but this time there was no opening wide enough to slip through. Number 72 had him bottled upfield to his right and number 63 had the lane to his left, and neither seemed out of control in pursuit. Prosser saw it, slowed abruptly, then turned upfield toward 72.

Five yards from 72, Prosser suddenly grasped the ball with both hands and faked a lateral directly across his path. It was a child's playground trick, the hokiest fake imaginable, which is probably why it worked. Number 72 instantly reacted by accelerating his speed and jerking his hands out to intercept the bogus pitchout, and that automatic reflex created all the room Prosser needed.

The giant Longhorn went steaming by completely out of control, only inches from Prosser's right side. It reminded me of a bullfight, with Prosser's skill and courage indeed comparable to a matador toying with an enraged bull. And by leaning in so close to 72, he also escaped the outstretched arms of number 63 on his left, which put him free at our forty-five with only the Texas safetyman, number 10, between himself and the goal line.

Prosser bolted straight at number 10, who reacted by drifting into the controlled backpedal he had used twice before. He obviously wasn't the type to plant his feet and leave himself open to a fake, so Prosser sized him up for a few strides more, looking for an opening of some kind.

Suddenly, Prosser cut to his left and accelerated, and 10 mirrored the move by cutting to his right. As soon as 10 took his cross-over step, Prosser cut back to his own right, and 10 had no choice but to mirror that move, too.

The gap between the two was rapidly closing, so that when Prosser cut *back* left again, he was no more than five yards away from 10. As 10 turned back to his own right to counter Prosser's move, Prosser darted forward and performed his most outrageous maneuver of the night. He grabbed the back of 10's jersey the same way he grabbed Quink's on the earlier run, and for a moment it looked as if 10 were leading interference for his opponent!

The safetyman's surprise could not have been greater than ours. All of us thought we knew what Prosser was capable of, but we were wrong. We were seeing a genius perform on this field tonight, a creative wonder who could orchestrate his own careening motions, and the motions of others, and turn those freewheeling skitters to and fro into splendid works of visual art. I felt truly honored to be there on the sidelines, watching it with my own eyes.

From the stands it might have seemed more like luck than talent, but every player and every coach on both sides of the field knew the brilliance of what they were seeing. As soon as 10 realized what happened, he whirled to his right, but Prosser shifted left behind his back. He twisted left, Prosser shifted right. And all the while Prosser was shoving him and guiding him toward the Texas goal line, which they were rapidly approaching.

Finally, 10 wrenched to his right in an apparent repeat of his first futile effort, but halfway through the move he dug his heels into the ground and shoved backward into Prosser. He was on his own twenty-three and facing his own end zone when his splendid countermove caught Prosser as unprepared as he was when Quink cut him down.

When 10 slammed backward into him, Prosser was in the middle of a corrective cross-over step, which made it impossible to avoid a collision. The only problem for 10 was having no way of locking his arms around Prosser's legs to seal the tackle. He scrabbled desperately behind his back for something to hold onto as he fell, but Prosser's luck held. He was able to bounce back a step and keep his feet away from 10's frantically thrashing arms.

It sounded as if every person in the stadium was screaming in alarm as Prosser staggered to regain his balance.
The Texas defenders and several of our guys maintained
a steady pursuit of the two men well out ahead of them,
and their collision delayed Prosser long enough to give
everyone a reasonable chance to catch him. All that remained was a twenty yard dash to the end zone.

It quickly became apparent that Prosser was running
out of gas. The pursuit pack's lead dog was number 42,
and when Prosser hit the ten it was certain he'd be caught
from behind. I started cursing bitterly as 42 reached out
his right arm and dove at Prosser's back, and there were
thousands of groans as contact was made.

Maybe it was possible from the stands to see what was
happening as Prosser bent away from our sideline toward
the far corner of the field. I know that from the bench,
there was no way to see what was developing in front of
the screen of players strung out behind him. At any rate,
whether he deliberately set it up or not, I don't know, but
Prosser somehow managed to lead 42 into Quink's path.

Quink had crossed the field and circled from the offside to try to intersect the pursuit angle, and that effort
made it possible for him to pick 42 out of midair just as his
arm was about to hook Prosser's neck. As the two bodies
crashed to the ground behind him, Prosser had only five
yards to go, which seemed about all he could manage.

When he did cross into the end zone, our sideline went
crazy, screaming with joyous relief and incredible pride
that one of *us* could do something so magnificent. Even
though it was reflected glory, it damn sure *was* glory, and
we *all* felt it, I'm sure, even the coaches. We all found it
hard to believe, much less accept, that one of our own
could have completed such a highly improbable journey.

Few of us on the sideline could see what happened immediately afterward on the field because of all the leaping
and screaming and pounding going on among the players. I was forced to move back away from it to protect my

hands. Later, I found out Prosser dropped to his knees in exhaustion, rolled the ball to a trailing official, and then was smothered by his deliriously happy teammates.

I'll always regret not getting to see that part.

When the sideline calmed a bit and the field started clearing for our extra-point attempt, number 10 jogged over to Prosser and offered his hand in congratulation, certifying that Prosser's ability was as far out of the closet as it could get. Prosser looked at his opponent in surprise before giving the hand a shake and patting his helmet in mutual congratulation. Then Prosser turned to jog to our bench, and thunder roared from the stands. I couldn't help wondering what he must have thought about it all.

Because time ran out sometime during his run, there was nothing left of the game except Helmet's extra-point attempt, which he laced through with no trouble. Final score: 42-17. For as bad as that seemed, by any other measure it was a tremendous "moral victory" that none of us dared to hope for, and none of us would ever forget.

I can't recall my exact thoughts as I jogged out onto the field along with the team and the fans pouring out of the stands. I do know several images will always be with me

I'll always remember all those people, more than I ever saw come on the field after a game, all of them wanting to somehow be a part of it . . . to take something of it home with them, if only the memory of being there . . . because it was so incredibly, awesomely, monumentally special.

I'll also remember the scoreboard's lights, shining like beacons through the stadium's upper-level haze of mist and smoke. And the mighty Fightin' Crawdad, surely smiling at what he saw down on the field where he had watched so much mediocre football during his tenure as our mascot.

I'll never forget Coach Anderson embracing the Texas head coach at midfield, obviously happy, relieved to have it all over at last. And then his efforts to graciously accept congratulations from the Texas assistant coaches, who all knew how hard he had worked to ensure that this miracle never happened. I'll remember that, too.

But most of all, I'll remember Prosser surrounded by dozens and dozens of kids screaming for his autograph, begging for his chinstrap, doing anything to get near enough to touch him. It quickly got to be too much, the crush around him was dangerous for everyone, so Pete called for help from several of his teammates. Tom waded into the crowd and jostled his way to Pete's side, where he was joined by Quink and Heape and Swede and even Big Dick, bandaged hands and all. They formed a phalanx around him and then hustled him off the field before he was mobbed to a point where some kid might get hurt.

I wished I could have been in on that, too.

The varsity dressing room was like no loser's dressing room I ever saw. It was as if we just won the biggest victory of our lives, and no coach dared pretend it wasn't so. There were no big postgame speeches or prayers or anything like that, but Coach Anderson did, as always, quiet things down to make a brief summary statement.

"Men, you gave it all you had and I'm as proud of you as I can possibly be. They were the best out there tonight, and they deserved to win, but you have *nothing* to be ashamed of. Go out, have a good time tonight, *no curfew!* Practice will be at 4:00 tomorrow in sweats. Come out prepared to loosen up and get ready for Mississippi State!"

Cheers shook the walls and rattled the high windows as Anderson moved into the training room to begin his post-game sparring with reporters. He'd have a helluva lot of explaining to do about Prosser—particularly to all the Texas reporters—and I'm sure he knew that. I couldn't imagine how he planned to try to make it all sound plausible, but I was confident he'd find a way. He always did.

If he did one thing well, it was bullshit the media.

***

One reporter Anderson wouldn't be able to snow was Randall Webber, who saw me in the locker room and came my way, beaming like a kid on Christmas morning.

"You should have seen it from up in the press box! As soon as they put him in, I started telling anyone who'd listen that he could do incredible things, and he *did!*"

"Did he ever!"

"And the high rollers!" Randall yelled over the commotion. "Those bastards had heart attacks at the end!"

"Why?"

"You beat the spread!" he yelled. "It got down to twenty-six, and they only beat you by twenty-five! So you won!"

Helmet's extra point did them in. *Gotcha!*

I turned and headed for the weight room, where the scene was nothing like the varsity's brightly lit hubbub. The redshirts stood in the dim light talking with subdued voices. There were no shower facilities, so most of them were already dressed in their street clothes, waiting for the final few to finish. Redshirt policy, as always, was to hang together rather than risk getting hung separately.

"All right," Tom said when the last straggler finished. "This one's done, so let's give these monkey suits back to Cap'n and split. Nobody told me, but I assume most of us aren't invited to the post-game buffet at the sewer, so let's keep away from that and not have another scene like this afternoon at the pregame meal. Anyone object to that?"

Tom's question was aimed at Prosser, who'd earned the right to attend; Heape, who'd move to the varsity because of Rabbit's injury; and Duggan, who remained a long shot.

The door swung open to reveal Teekay Junior framed in the outside light. He made his announcements with no preliminaries: "Prosser, be up front in five minutes to have interviews. Prosser, Heape, and Duggan are welcome at the buffet tonight. All three of you should report for practice tomorrow afternoon. You're on the varsity now."

***

There should have been congratulations for the lucky
three, but that could have been interpreted as disrespectful to the unlucky ones, especially Tom Everett. So after
Teekay Junior left, everyone quietly gathered his uniform
bundle and began moving out the door. Prosser hung
back in an apparent effort to avoid flaunting his exorbi-
tant success in the faces of his teammates.

I stood with Tom at the end of the equipment check-in
line as he waited for Cap'n to take up his laundry sack of
gear, and his separate uniform and the pieces of his roll.

"Jersey, pants, jock, shirt, socks, towel." Cap'n checked
each item in a bored monotone across the shed's counter.

Tom and I were the only ones left in line when suddenly
we heard a clatter behind us. We looked back to see Prosser deposit the entire mass of his gear on the counter top.

"It's all there," he said to Cap'n. "I quit."

Tom and I heard his words distinctly, but we couldn't
make ourselves believe them. We stood in numb shock.

"You can't mean that, son," Cap'n said. "Not now."

"Yes, I do, Cap'n," he said, reaching a hand out to shake
a goodbye. "It was a pleasure working with you."

"No!" Tom finally exclaimed. "Not after breaking through
like this! You have it *made* now! Stick with it!"

Prosser's blond head shook and a grin flashed his white
teeth as we walked several steps away from the shed so we
could talk in private. "Actually, you two convinced me that
it's better to walk away from this game than limp away."

I didn't say that to Prosser, I said it to his friend, Scott
Brown, who must have passed my comment on to him.

"That was before!" I yelped. "Now you have everything
going for you, everything lined right up!"

"It won't last, guys," he said, calmly, confidently. "They
used me tonight, but eventually they'll use me *up*. I don't
need to end my career like that . . . I don't *want* to."

Neither Tom nor I could think of anything to say to him.

"The more I thought about our chat the other night," he
went on, "the more I realized you two were right. I've taken

what I can from the game, what it was willing to give me free and clear, but now, to keep doing it, I'll end up having to pay a very high price, a price I really don't want to pay. It just isn't for me any more. I think I've grown out of it."

"Are you sure, Pete?" Tom asked. "Absolutely 100% *sure?*"

He nodded resolutely, his pale eyes holding steady above the black smudges he hadn't been able to shower off.

"What about Hackler?" I asked. "What about paying him back for all the crap he laid on you?"

Pete smiled. "Whenever anyone asks, I'll always say I quit because of him. That should follow him for a while."

"Have you done everything you wanted to do?" Tom asked. "You're really ready to walk away from it?"

"All I wanted was to play once more, so I could pay close attention to how it felt—so I can remember it. I'd have been happy to do it at practice, but I was able to do it tonight, which made it beyond special. I'll always remember this."

So would Tom and I. We looked at each other and Tom smiled, a flicker at first but then it widened, and he said, "You know, I think I should take my own advice."

He turned to look at the equipment shed window, which now had other people, players and nonplayers, milling in front of it, probably trying to absorb the word from Cap'n that Pete had just quit. He turned back to Pete and me.

"You two should go ahead without me. I need to have a few words with Cap'n, then I'll catch up with you. Okay?"

I looked at Pete, who smiled wryly and turned to Tom. "Are you sure? Absolutely 100% *sure?*"

Tom smiled back. "Touché."

"Seriously," I added. "Nobody's pushing you to quit now."

His head shook. "No, Sage, you're wrong. They've been pushing me since we changed to a roll out offense. Making me wear that clown suit tonight was the last straw. It made me realize I should quit while I still love the game."

The three of us looked at each other and realized there really was nothing more to say.

***

EPILOGUE

I was born in 1946, the year after my father and millions of men like him returned from World War II to begin
sprouting families. 1946 put me and my infant peers on
the cutting edge of the soon-to-be-recognized Baby Boom.

The millions of us born in that golden year were mostly
sprung from the loins of battle hardened but psychologi-
cally damaged young men, and innocent young women
who joined them in lives they could manage no easier than
their parents managed in the Great Depression. Veterans
of war—especially war on that scale and of that duration—
inevitably brought home another kind of depression.

After the war, those men poured back into the country looking for jobs, and they found them in every corner
of American life. However, four years later, from 1950 to
1953, many of them went back to join with a new crop of
young men who missed out on the "glory" of World War II.
They found themselves bogged down in the embarrassing
stalemate that turned out to be the Korean "Police Action."
Looming ahead for their sons and daughters would be
the assassination of President Kennedy, the catastrophe
of Viet Nam, and the resignation of Richard Nixon.

Among the memorable traumas to America's national

psyche was another one that was definitely noticed at the time it appeared, but it wasn't recognized early on as the turning point it became. As those emotionally scarred war veterans began finding their way onto whatever paths would take them through the course of their lives, many became football coaches. One man in particular shaped the game like no other coach before or since.

But first, a bit of football history.

In the 1920s, the most famous and revered football coach in America was Knute (Kah-nute) Rockne, who died in a plane crash in 1931, aged 43. Prior to his untimely demise, Rockne's brilliant career imposed on the game his particular vision of how it should be organized, played, and most of all, coached. He believed it was the greatest game in the world, and it built solid character.

Rockne preached and believed football was, and always should be, good clean fun for good clean boys, everything the University of Notre Dame—where he coached—should and did stand for. Adolescents turned into young men playing four or five years for Knute Rockne, and they were his top priority. Winning was a close second, he loved to win, but if it threatened one of his players to do so, the player's health and welfare should and would always come first.

Rockne was able to be a consistent winner because his university, Notre Dame, was attractive to a large number of a small pool of very talented athletes. His on-the-field success and superstar popularity insured his methods and techniques were copied by other coaches everywhere, through every aspect of the game, trying to emulate his personal style and to match his statistical results.

One man who continued Rockne's legacy that a football player's welfare should always come before winning was Bobby Dodd, an assistant coach at Georgia Tech who took over as head coach in 1945. When World War II broke out, Bobby Dodd was already 33, so he continued coaching at Georgia Tech during the war years.

Younger men, like 28-year-old, gravel-voiced Paul "Bear" Bryant, went into service. Bryant did his hitch with the U.S. Navy, joining when he was already a seasoned football coach. Soon his experience landed him a coaching job for the football team at a large Naval base, and that career move gave him an entirely new slant on coaching, a slant that changed an important aspect of the game.

In 1945, ex-servicemen like Bear Bryant began to flood into, or back into, the coaching ranks of football at every level—high school, college, and professional. As they did, differences began to develop between them and coaches like Bobby Dodd, who still clung to Knute Rockne's tradition of putting a player's welfare first. The new "war" coaches came to, or returned to, the job with very different ideas about the inherent value of their players.

Those men had spent four bloody years watching the war machine chew up and spit out hundreds of thousands of young men while serving the ultimate goal of winning the war. For those coaches, winning was not merely a desired outcome, it was *essential*, at any and all costs. To them, football became a metaphor for—and in many ways an extension of—the highly addictive drug of war.

Many of them personally felt the exhilaration Winston Churchill spoke of when he said: "There is nothing more thrilling in life than to be shot at—without result." In their eyes, and in their hearts, they saw their players as no different from what they themselves were during their four years in service to the highest need of their country and, indeed, of the world itself—*expendable*.

In 1954, a year after the Korean War ended, fourteen years after expendability of resources became a way of life in the U.S., the leading voice in the "expendable" camp of coaches emerged as the new icon replacing Knute Rockne.

Bear Bryant's brutal coaching methods put Kentucky

football on the map, but when the team's boosters re-
warded him with an expensive watch instead of a new
Cadillac—which they bestowed on legendary UK basketball coach Adolph Rupp—Bryant took his injured pride
and hurt feelings to the Texas A&M Aggies.

In Aggieland, Bryant set about marking his territory.
He took a group of ordinary players to a "boot camp" at
Junction, Texas, which is now a famous book and movie
called *The Junction Boys*. They were the few who survived
one of the most sadistic winnowing processes any coach
ever inflicted on a football team. It was so ruthless, in
fact, that Bryant scaled it back considerably in later seasons, but the die was cast for coaches everywhere.

In 1955-56, Bryant's draconian techniques seemed to
be validated as he forged the Aggies into a winning team.
He produced the Heisman Trophy winner in 1957, John
David Crow. At the same time, he ruined the college career
of Ken Hall of Sugarland, Texas, whom many still consider
the greatest high school running back of all time.

In later years, with the advantage of an old man's hindsight, Bryant supposedly said his greatest regret was how
ineffectively he dealt with Ken Hall's truly superior talent.

(Hall was an offensive specialist who could run rings
around Crow, but he seldom played defense in high school
and couldn't tackle well. Bryant handled him the way he
handled all poor tacklers—he drove him off the team.)

In 1958, Bear Bryant's alma mater, the University of
Alabama, lured him from Texas A&M. At Alabama, Bryant
settled into becoming the coaching icon of his era, an era
that included Bobby Dodd at SEC rival Georgia Tech.

Coach Dodd didn't approve of Bear Bryant's oppressive
coaching methods, and Bryant considered Dodd's "player
first" coaching style to be what it was rapidly becoming—
an artifact from a bygone era. At only five years older
than Bryant, Dodd was a dinosaur on his way to extinc-
tion. They were five years and one ideology apart.

***

I began playing organized football in 1958 as a seventh grader in Amite, Louisiana, a small bump in the north-south route between New Orleans and Chicago. My peers and I were 12 years old, entering puberty, and about to go through the primary rite of passage for young males of many generations—walking into a locker room for the first time to be given your first real football uniform and told to dress out in it. As was often the case, a few of us couldn't figure out the subtle intricacies of a jockstrap.

By sheer luck, my junior high and high school coaches were good men steeped in the Knute Rockne and Bobby Dodd tradition of treating players with respect, always willing to sacrifice a win if it meant jeopardizing a player's health or safety. Of course, they lived in the same community with the parents of their players, and they had to create an inviting atmosphere for their younger brothers, so brutality was never seen or allowed at our school.

I loved my high school coach, Jack Pope. He was the best surrogate father any boys like us could ever have, and all of his ex-players were distraught when he died young.

Coach Pope showed us the game could be played hard, clean, and fair. He made practices fun, so games were fun. He established a winning tradition at Amite that has remained intact for forty years. Its teams are routinely in the Louisiana state playoffs for schools of its size.

That long train of success began when Coach Pope joined our school as my peer group teammates and I were becoming sophomores. Two years later, 1963, our seniors brought Amite its first-ever State Championship on a cold, muddy December night at our home field.

Life didn't get much better than that.

On our 1963 team were fifteen seniors, and six of us went on to sign scholarships to play football in college. Astonishingly, the entire backfield went to major universities: quarterback Fred Mixon to LSU, fullback Russell Thompson to Arkansas, and left halfback Lloyd Pye and right halfback Weldon Russell both went to Tulane.

Tackle Fred Carpenter came to Tulane with Weldon and me, while end/linebacker Nic LaBarbera went to a small college in north Louisiana. Those were the six who signed on, although our center, Marty Crowson, could easily have played in college, too. Instead, he accepted an academic scholarship to Tulane. And our other end opposite Nic, Steve Catha, could also have played football in college, but he chose to accept a track scholarship as a hurdler.

In any football league of any era, this was quite a coup. Normally, the largest, most outstanding high school programs produced only three or four seniors, at most, who could compete in college. For a small, dominantly rural community like Amite, with a combined senior class of eighty-three (nearly all born in 1946), putting the entire backfield and two linemen into college programs was far beyond exceptional, it was a certifiable miracle.

Coach Pope fully prepared us to play the game of football, but he didn't begin to teach us how to cope with the coaches we confronted in college. The game he knew as a young man had changed, and the men who coached it had changed. The Bear Bryant philosophy had developed a stranglehold on the college game, and its influence was expanding into high schools everywhere.

It reached Amite after Jack Pope died, but then it took root there as effectively as in most other places.

When we arrived at Tulane as an entering class of 44 freshmen football players, we received a welcoming speech from a grizzled coach who informed us that, statistically, only 11 of us would stick with it for four years. He told us to look around the room and decide if we expected to be in that final group of 11. I was an undersized running back and receiver, an inch shy of six feet and 160 pounds after a good meal, so I didn't give myself much chance.

I was the next-to-smallest player in that room, and I soon developed a bad feeling about the prickly attitudes of every coach I met. None were anything like Jack Pope. These were not friendly, confidence-inspiring men; they were serious and dour in every word and gesture.

What I know now but didn't know then was that I, and several others, had washed up on a special kind of blacklist. Assistant coaches then were heavily invested in the success of players they signed. Whenever a player failed to develop into a contributor, that naturally cast doubt on the acumen of the coach who recruited him.

The assistant coach who signed Weldon and Fred and me, among others, to our scholarships was very shortly thereafter hired away by another team. That left each of his signees as "orphans" at Tulane, with no coach looking out for us to protect his own interests.

After two years, only two players from my high school team were still playing in college—me and linebacker Nic LaBarbera. Nic played four years for Northeast Louisiana, a small college in Monroe, and I managed to become one of the—sure enough—11 of those 44 freshmen who began together at Tulane, and who made it through four years of playing each season to graduate in 1968.

Seven years after I graduated, I began writing a book based on my experiences during my redshirt season at Tulane. I novelized the story I created to protect the innocent as well as the guilty, but it was—and it remains—a fact-based, thinly disguised roman à clef.

What led me to write it was a bestselling nonfiction book by Gary Shaw called *Meat On The Hoof* (1972), which harshly criticized the University of Texas football program of the mid-1960's, the same time I played at Tulane.

He was written about in major periodicals and reached the top rung of sports celebrity of that time—an interview by Howard Cosell. His entire book was read into the Congressional Record by a legislator intent on crafting changes in the way young men like Shaw were being treated at "football factories" like the University of Texas.

This was a noble piss against the wind that Shaw himself knew would never fly. He wrote: *To attack football is to attack the major exhibit of the masculine view of the world; it would be much more strongly resisted than an attack on the church or most other American institutions.*

Gary Shaw was persecuted in his home state of Texas for driving a stake of truth through the heart of Longhorn football, and football everywhere. Because if, as the legislator suggested, things were so bad at Texas, then surely they were similar at other major football powers.

That was true. But what the legislator didn't know, and what I knew for a fact, was that the horrors Shaw exposed at powerhouse Texas were very close to what I had experienced at dinky little Tulane, known as the "Harvard of the South" because it steadfastly preferred—then as now—academic excellence over football excellence.

Brutality had become the coin of the realm.

Gary Shaw's success with *Meat On The Hoof* convinced me that I could write a book similar to his, to verify his story as fundamentally true, and to establish my name in the writing career I was then starting to envision. However, he limited his range of expression by writing a strictly nonfiction, wholly true account of what happened to him. He simply couldn't write a page-turner.

I felt a fact-based novel could provide me with the best of both worlds. I could recount many aspects of the truth about what I had experienced as a player, while crafting a more entertaining, and a more gripping, story. I could be creative where Shaw could not, so I should be able to deliver a book that was easier to read through than his.

It would be a challenge, but I felt up to it.

I began writing it in 1975. When I reached the halfway point, I needed to know if I was wasting my time or proceeding on the right track. I lived then in Washington, D.C., where renowned writer Larry McMurtry owned an equally renowned used bookstore in Georgetown. One day I barged in on him and told him what I was doing.

Incredibly, he was sympathetic, promising to read the first half of my story and tell me what he thought of it. He later called to say that what he read struck him as good enough for mainstream publication, and if I could finish it as well as I started it, he'd help me find a publisher.

That was one of the happiest days of my life.

My new book's core theme was the plight of being a redshirt on a college football team. Redshirts were called by various upbeat euphemisms to make their lowly status sound less demeaning: Go Squad, Spirit Squad, Scout Squad, etc. But no euphemism could disguise their roles as living, moving dummies for blocking and tackling.

On our team, redshirts ran the offensive plays of the team the varsity would face on the upcoming Saturday. They pretended, within their limits, to be opposing players so the varsity could become familiar with how the upcoming team ran its offensive schemes. During the season, every aspect of practice was geared around that primary goal—to prepare for the next game's opponent.

During practice, if any member of a redshirt squad did anything remotely effective against the varsity players they opposed, no coach blew a whistle to congratulate the redshirts for a good play. They blew their whistles to berate the varsity for *allowing* a successful play, and coaches' reactions were universal: "All right, line up, run it again—same play, same count—and this time, varsity, *get it right!*"

Nothing chilled a redshirt's blood more than to hear those angrily barked instructions, because it meant all eleven guys lined up opposite you knew exactly where the play was aimed, and they knew the snap count. They could afford to simply tee off on your head and drive straight to where the play called for the ball to arrive.

Coaches understood that this created a grossly unfair advantage, but it was a crucial part of their strategy. A mistake made on the practice field by varsity players had to be quickly erased and made good, so no "bad habits" (read "doubts") would infect the mental attitudes of "contributors." Redshirts could not be allowed to make varsity players look bad in any fashion and get away with it.

The psychological cost might be too dear.

With protection of varsity egos a topmost coaching concern, redshirt egos were totally expendable, as were their bodies. In those days of the 120 scholarship limit, if a player was injured there were always more where he came from. It was a numbers game. Football powers could easily afford to recruit and sign 50-plus freshmen each season, then see which ones panned out as contributors.

Scouting combines did not exist in those days, no professionally trained men finding out if, indeed, a young man seemed to have what it took—physically and emotionally—to play college football. In the 1960s, a college coach came to watch you practice one time, or play in one game, or even only watched one game film of you, then he'd make a decision about granting you a full scholarship.

Thousands of quality athletes missed out on playing in college because of a bad practice or a bad game when a coach was evaluating them. Likewise, other thousands slipped in the back door by playing far over their heads at exactly the right time. Luck figured into everything.

Another route in required massive *cojones*. When one guy on our team was in high school, he wrote to our coaches asking if he could send them a film of himself in action. They agreed, so he sent it in and told the coaches to watch the number of the *other* tackle on his team, a true stud with no hope of passing the academic requirements at Tulane, which our guy could do in his sleep.

The coach assigned to watch the film had no trouble establishing that the player in question was a bona fide stud. Thinking they knew the truth about who they were watching, they sent a scholarship by return mail. Our guy signed it and was in for a free ride for as long as he could hold out. He made it through his freshman and redshirt years before getting hurt and quitting.

Recruiting was so slipshod in those days, no coaches ever tried to assess a player's emotional makeup or the quality of their character, which today is a huge part of recruiting efforts. All of us were assumed to be from the same Great Depression, obey-all-rules-without-question mold that produced the coaches, along with our parents.

When any of us proved to be resistant to that kind of regimented thinking, we were removed from the barrel so we wouldn't spoil the other obedient apples. That ruthless policy could be enforced because coaches knew that many more players were readily available to choose from.

There was an endless stream of wannabes.

At the time I played in the SEC, its teams and coaches voluntarily abided by the 120 scholarship limit before it became mandatory. They were trying to avoid the official limits later imposed by the NCAA, which has steadily reduced 1-A teams down to the present 85 maximum.

That had no bearing on walk-ons, ordinary students at a school who took nothing monetary from an athletic department, thus paying for the privilege of becoming the cannon fodder for the varsity that all redshirts were.

Teams could have as many walk-ons try out as wanted to make the effort. All any walk-on needed was enough resources to enroll in school on their own, a strong desire to play football, and a modicum of talent. If that trifecta was in their resume, they were welcome on most teams.

Walk-ons tried out at the start of two-a-days, and again in spring training. However, as the difficulty of what they signed on for began to sink in, they tended to give up. It was nothing like high school. In high school, football could actually be fun; in college, it was invariably all business.

The scholarship and walk-on situation of that era was why the coaches saw to it that their attrition rate was a severe 75% (the exact rate that panned out for my class). The dead wood had to be cleared out, and forcing them into a difficult—and sometimes barbaric—sojourn as a redshirt was a grimly efficient way to get it done.

With room for "only" 120 scholarship athletes on any one team, and with 50 or more freshmen coming in each season, something had to give. Not all of those boys could be allowed to keep their scholarships for the entire four years of the commitment the colleges made to them.

Yes, that was the deal with all teams: *If you sign with us, we'll see to it that you get your full college education, even if you're hurt too seriously to play any more, even if you try your heart out but can't rise above the redshirt team, and even if we made a terrible mistake by giving you a scholarship in the first place. If you sign a grant-in-aid with us, it's yours for as long as you don't do one thing:*

For as long as you don't quit.

Quitting was the greatest bugaboo in football at every level that I played the game, and I'm sure it remains that way today. If boys and young men can't be stigmatized into avoiding quitting at all costs, the sane and rational among them would never stick with it when the handwriting became clear on their particular wall.

If things weren't going their way, they'd do the smart thing and quit, then move on to a different life away from football. It sounds so simple, but it's almost impossibly difficult because by the time you face the wall where your name is written, you're usually in much too deep.

You've played football since grammar school or junior high. You define yourself *as* a football player; it's how you're identified in your world. You're a hero, a demigod, the most blessed of the blessed. And, most importantly, chicks dig you. It's all about esteem—of others and of self—and such esteem is a drug of enormous power. In my case, I needed ten full years to kick it. Some never do.

***

Regardless of magnitude, no star of the game, when faced with the day he can no longer play, feels like anything other than a quitter. This is true whether a career ends at high school, college, or the pro football Hall of Fame. You feel a sense of profound, gut-wrenching failure, of giving up the fight, of quitting. That is how painfully deep this one stigma is driven into our psyches.

I'm confident that was true for Knute Rockne's teams in the 1920's, I'm sure it was true in the 1960's, and I suspect it's still every bit as true today as it's always been.

Without the stigma against quitting, football as we know it, and have known it, would be in jeopardy. But with that stigma in place, as functional as ever, football will remain the gold standard of spectator sports in America.

In late 1976, I finished *Do It Wrong The First Time,* its title being the redshirt motto describing how they had to play the game to keep coaches from jumping down everyone's throats. If they ran a play wrong the first time, they didn't have to go right back to the line to run it again. That motto crystallized the story's main theme of life on the bottom rung of college football's ladder.

Larry McMurtry approved its final half and helped me find an agent to represent it to publishing companies in New York. By sheer coincidence, that same year a shocking book hit stores and created a mild sensation. *The David Kopay Story* was about the first professional football player to come out of the closet as gay.

The scandal rocked the sports world, but especially the football world. It also sold books, so the man who published it, Don Fine of mid-sized Arbor House, promptly sent word out to literary agents that he was looking for another "hot" football property. My agent sent him my manuscript, and a deal was done by March, 1977.

The book was slated to come out in the first part of September, in time for the upcoming football season.

***

Don Fine believed *Do It Wrong The First Time* would only confuse browsers in bookstores, so he lobbied for a more "vanilla" title to appeal to a broader spectrum of readers. I made it clear I had no intention of changing it, so without my permission he changed it to *That Prosser Kid,* and told me, in effect, I could like it or lump it.

He knew the situation with young first-novel writers like me. You had hocked everything you owned to get the money to pay for the time you needed to write the book, so you wanted it out and into readers' hands as soon as you could get it there. Thus, my choice was to let things proceed with his title on it, or buy it back and start over.

I decided to try to like it, but I never did.

That Prosser Kid was far from a bestseller, but it did reasonably well for a first novel. It was resold as a paperback and optioned as a movie, though no movie was ever made. I've always felt it would have done much better with its original title, or if it had been published by someone who actually understood football. However, all of that is now water under a very dim and distant bridge.

When planning this new revision of the old story, the matter of the title came up with my wife, Amy, and my cover artist, Daniel Huenergardt. Both felt we might do better giving it a less confusing title than *Do It Wrong The First Time*. I hated to give it up, but Daniel hit on what felt like a winner when he suggested *A Darker Shade of Red,* which provided a perfect double entendre for *redshirt,* while hinting at the darker aspects of what it meant to actually be one. I gladly accepted his gem.

This revision is still the same basic story I published at Arbor House in 1977. I've taken the opportunity to apply thirty years of writing experience to make it read much better in many places, and a little better in most places. On balance, it's quite an improvement over the original.

Naturally, the world it describes will, in certain ways,

be as unfamiliar to fans and players of today as certain aspects of Knute Rockne's game were to me in the 1960s. But in every era, football is football. The basics remain.

No fan or player of today will fail to recognize the heart of the story, which—when you move beyond the timeless essentials of blocking, tackling, catching and running—is really about the macho rituals that create many nebulous notions regarding "manhood." Those were core issues when I played, and I'm sure they will remain central forever.

Another component today's readers will notice is that no African-American players are introduced. They didn't make inroads into the college football teams of the Deep South for another few years after my graduation in 1968. We were products of our time and place, and we played under those conditions, so that is how I present it.

Also, freshmen were not eligible to play on the varsity in those days. The freshman season consisted of four games with other freshman teams in the general area. The rest of the time, at least on our team, they played the upcoming defense against the varsity's offensive teams.

For that year even their skilled players, the ones who would move directly to the varsity the next season, were in a fashion redshirted, and their motto was also "do it wrong the first time." However, coaches always cut freshmen vastly more slack than they did for real redshirts.

If you found yourself on the redshirt team, you were no longer considered to have good—or even possible—prospects to make the varsity. At that point you were merely holding a scholarship the coaches wanted back to give to a new freshman with more potential, and the skids were being greased for your imminent departure.

Hair length was another non-issue in my era, even though the Beatles exploded on the world in the fall of 1963. Long hair didn't appear on football fields because coaches forbade it, clinging to the culture of buzz-cuts and flat-tops they grew up in and, apart from the bald ones, still lived in. Not until Joe Namath led the New York Jets to a Super Bowl victory in 1969 did long hair become inevitable on football fields across America.

When Broadway Joe made long hair fashionable for football players, coaches could no longer ignore its existence as a social fad. But that came in 1969, the year after my class graduated in 1968. When Tulane played Alabama, led by Namath, in the fall of 1964, he sported a head of hair that was as close-cropped as the rest of us. Of course, he was playing for Bear "The Tyrant" Bryant.

An oddly related aspect of hair length was, of all things, Gatorade. Somewhere along the line of human ignorance, someone got the idea that drinking liquids during strenuous physical activity led to cramps. With iced liquid that might have been true. Maybe someone somewhere was working hard, sweating buckets, and someone brought them a big glass of iced tea and they cramped.

Maybe. But however it came to pass, it became gospel, making all liquids forbidden—other than your own sweat scraped off your arms and legs with your fingers and then licked off them. And those were not clean limbs or digits.

That being the case, you did all you could to keep yourself as cool as possible during practices in the hot-climate areas of the Deep South and Southwest. Nothing would raise your body temperature more than a thick mop of hair pressed against your head by a football helmet. The shorter your hair under a helmet, the cooler you were.

That axiom happened to be true.

The no-liquids-during-football-practice axiom was not, which Gatorade proved in a big way.

Gatorade was actually developed during the four years of my career at Tulane. We were part of the cadre of teams asked by scientists at the University of Florida to test various blends they would concoct, trying to find the best one.

I discuss this in detail in the novel, so I'll cut it short here. Suffice it to say that with Gatorade in your belly, you could afford to have long hair under your helmet.

Thus, football players started wanting to wear their hair long *exactly* when Gatorade came into their lives, and it allowed long hair on football players. Gatorade first appeared in supermarkets in the summer of 1968, and Joe Namath led the Jets to the Super Bowl six months later. It doesn't take a genius to see that connection.

Also, of course, I must mention "performance enhancing" drugs. Today they are a common malady in virtually all sports, reaching as far down as junior high schools, but the football players of my era didn't know what steroids were. In fact, only a few of us ever lifted weights.

Another of those testaments to human ignorance was the idea that lifting weights made athletes musclebound and cost them their agility. If weightlifting was taken too far, or done improperly, that would be true, and since almost nobody knew how to do it properly in those days, the vast majority of us tended to avoid weight training.

However, that tide was already well into turning when I arrived at Tulane in early September of 1964.

In 1957 (the year John David Crow won the Heisman Trophy for Bear Bryant at Texas A&M), a player at LSU named Billy Cannon was a sensation as a sophomore running back. The next year, 1958, he was an All-American, leading LSU to an undefeated season and an undisputed national championship. His senior season he led LSU to another top-ten finish, and capped his college career by winning the Heisman Trophy in 1959, the second Louisiana native to win it in three years. (Crow was from tiny Springhill, while Cannon was from Baton Rouge.)

Much was made of the fact that Billy Cannon had lifted weights since junior high school under the careful supervision of Alvin Roy, a gym owner and trainer in Baton

Rouge. Roy put him on a program designed to increase his overall strength and stamina, without moving him into the musclebound inflexibility of bodybuilders.

It worked. As a senior at Istrouma High School in Baton Rouge, 6' 1", 190 pound Billy Cannon ran a 9.7 hundred yard dash *and* he won the state's shot put championship! His combination of speed and power was on a par with the best running backs at the professional level, so at LSU he was very much a man playing among boys.

Naturally, this was trumpeted far and wide within and outside the sport of football. It was quickly picked up by coaches of related sports in foreign countries, as U.S. failures in the next few Olympics made abundantly clear. But it was not initially appealing to the coaches of most U.S. sports, the vast majority of whom were quite comfortable staying within their status quos.

Football coaches were especially vulnerable to sitting on their hands when faced with radical innovations because they were extremely conservative men working in a highly competitive field. Thus, they tended to accept major changes with grinding slowness after enormous resistance due to a consistent, widespread fear that the next big change might be more than they could handle.

Only the bravest and boldest among them would break ranks to try things like forward passes, single wing over flying wedge, winged-T over single wing, face masks, foreign placekickers, spread formation, I-backs, and all the innovations the game has seen since its inception.

So, too, with weights, which didn't catch on until Hank Stram hired Billy Cannon's old trainer, Alvin Roy, to create a weight training regimen for his Kansas City Chiefs.

When those Chiefs made it to Super Bowl IV in 1969, the NFL was still smarting from the loss to Joe Namath's AFL Jets the previous year. But whereas the Jets won it with superior guile and technical skill, the Chiefs needed a different edge. Their quarterback, Len Dawson, was no Joe Namath. He was more of an anti-Namath, not daring or artistic, but precise and methodical.

If the Chiefs were to have any chance against the Minnesota Vikings, a physically dominant team if ever there was one, they had to find it elsewhere. And, as the game showed, the Chiefs had what they needed in the strength and stamina imparted to them by Alvin Roy's training regimen. They simply wore the Vikings down.

The success of the weight-trained Chiefs finally turned the tide. By 1970, nearly every pro team and most college teams had installed extensive weight-training facilities for their players. What started as a football heresy by one young man in Baton Rouge in the 1950s, was common knowledge in the sport by the 1970s.

This is a lesson in progress in far more areas of life than football. So much of what we think we "know" at any given moment turns out to be colossally, blindly, even stupidly wrong, and so it was with the prohibitions against ingesting fluids at football practice and lifting weights.

Social drugs were—and remain—a very different matter. While this story's events unfold in the middle of the notorious 1960s, social drugs were rarely an issue for football teams of that era. Crack cocaine didn't exist, and marijuana and LSD were things "hippies" were only just beginning to experiment with in large numbers. Athletes, for the most part, left them alone. Alcohol was enough.

Social drugs did not begin to impact heavily on football players until late in the 1960s and into the early 1970s, for good reason. Today, it's almost forgotten that the 1960s of sex and drugs and rock-and-roll fame did not hit full stride as a social phenomenon until the gathering at Woodstock galvanized young people worldwide in 1969, the year after I graduated, and the movie came out in 1970.

We of the Baby Boom generation *initiated* the sixties as we began to assert ourselves during our college years

(1964-1968), but our younger siblings actually did the heaviest lifting during the 1970s and beyond.

Those of us at the leading edge always had to grope our way along, zigging and zagging toward, and then through, our newly forged freedoms. Those a few years behind us travelled a much easier path in our wide wake.

For all of us, though, it was a crazy wild ride.

The framework of this book's story is filled with irony. In 1963, Gary Shaw's first year at the University of Texas and my State Championship senior year of high school, Texas won the National Championship, going 11-0 under Head Coach Darryl Royal and chief assistant coach Jim Pittman, who in 1966 left Texas to be Tulane's head coach. The Longhorns "ran the table," as the saying goes, and were universally acclaimed the #1 team in the country.

Like most topnotch 1-A football teams of that era, they preferred to begin their seasons with a "warm-up" game against a "patsy" they could easily beat. That was Tulane's role in the SEC, until we dropped out after the 1965 season to become an independent. If you wanted a team to offer a respectable fight before going belly up, Tulane was always a good choice, so top teams competed to schedule us as their first, second, or third game. Texas worked for and won our coveted "first game" slot for several years in a row, just as they hit the peak of their power.

In 1963, they came into New Orleans and beat us 21-0, allowing their second and third teams to play most of the second half—a perfect "warm-up" for their championship run. In 1964, defending their national championship, they opened up by walloping us, 31-0, at Austin.

The next year, 1965, my redshirt sophomore season, they were scheduled to come again to New Orleans to play us in the old Sugar Bowl stadium, then the largest steel girder stadium in America, officially seating 81,000, though 85,000 could be crammed in for Sugar Bowls and, starting in 1967, games of the fledgling New Orleans Saints.

(The Sugar Bowl lacked a parking facility, so fans had to park on the streets of nearby neighborhoods surrounding Tulane. If not for that terrible inconvenience to fans and residents alike, it might still be standing and the world-famous Superdome might never have been built.)

Because football seasons in the 1960s were only ten games long, the first game usually kicked off in the third week of September. The 1965 game was slated for the 18th. However, that was the year Hurricane Betsy struck New Orleans, and therein lies a relevant tale.

Betsy was similar to Hurricane Katrina in many ways. Like Katrina, it was a ferocious Category 3 storm that struck the city hard. The lower Ninth Ward, still devastated today from Katrina, was also flooded by Betsy. It killed 76 people and did a billion and a half dollars worth of damage, the first hurricane in U.S. history to top that mark, earning it the nickname "Billion Dollar Betsy."

It struck New Orleans the night of September 9. My teammates and I were near the end of two-a-day practices, getting ready for the opener with Texas nine days later. Even with the hurricane bearing down on us, our coaches made us practice and wouldn't let us evacuate or go home to be with our families. Not even guys who lived *in* New Orleans were allowed to ride out the storm at home. We were a *team*, by God, and we'd practice and play and face this potentially devastating storm as a team.

This makes it harrowingly clear that the Bear Bryant philosophy of player expendability had saturated coaching mentality at every level. It didn't seem to *occur* to our coaches, not even as an afterthought, that they were putting us in serious danger by forcing us ride out a severe hurricane in a 12-story dormitory that was long enough, high enough, and narrow enough to be blown over by strong winds hitting it flush on either of its broad sides.

Everyone was lucky the wind direction didn't turn out to be directly on it. For Betsy's duration of several hours, it slammed against the blunt, relatively narrow edges of Monroe Hall, which rocked and swayed for most of the night the storm passed over the city, leaving massive flooding and devastation in its wake.

No game could be played in the Sugar Bowl in nine days, so the venue was switched to the Longhorns' home field at Austin. We missed one day of practice before getting back to it, but the players were shell-shocked by what happened to those around us. Our team flew to Austin and we were pounded out of the game early, finishing at the same score as the 1964 game, 31-0. We were lucky it was that low.

The 1965 Texas game became the frame around which I built my novel, though I treated it more like the 1964 game that was not marred by Hurricane Betsy; and I set it as a home game at mythical "Cajun State," whose equally mythical "Fightin' Crawdads" now stand in for Tulane's far less aggressive sounding "Green Wave."

The story covers the week leading up to the big game, and then the game itself. Naturally, not as many defining moments could occur in one week. I culled four years of events to choose those that fit best in the story's time-frame and in the context of its narrative. However, in one way or another the core parts of the story are based on truth, either as I knew it or knew it to be.

For me, with the hindsight of thirty years, it provides a fascinating glimpse back in time. It's no longer the novel I wrote at thirty, when I boiled over with the same youthful angers that drove Gary Shaw to write *Meat On The Hoof.*

Now, for me, it's a stroll down a memory lane holding many things I cherish and remember fondly, along with things I wish never happened—not to me or to my team-mates who endured those "doormat" seasons with me.

In the thirty years since *That Prosser Kid* was published, I have been contacted by several dozen ex-redshirts who wrote to tell me their experience closely mirrored mine, in the same way I wrote the late Gary Shaw to tell him my experience mirrored his. We belong to a unique fraternity.

That said, the world I describe is largely unknown to players with enough skills to never endure the indignity of a redshirt season, who joined a college team and moved directly to being a major contributor on the field.

Stars who read my book may well be perplexed by it because it bears little if any resemblance to the football experience they enjoyed. But that makes the redshirt experience no less real, or painful, for those who did endure it.

This book also spoke to, and it still speaks to, young men who desperately wanted to play football but could not, or did not, for reasons specific to each individual. Every now and then I hear from one of them, too, and—believe it or not—I heard from one, Paul Feinberg of Santa Monica, CA, while I was writing this introduction.

This is what he wrote to me:

"Are you, by any chance, the same Lloyd Pye who wrote a novel about college football called *That Prosser Kid* about 30 years ago? I read it in high school, and it remains a favorite of mine. I'm 99% sure there is still a copy of it in my parents' house (where I grew up).

"It's interesting to me that even though the book is three decades old, it remains remarkably current. You could base a film on that book and set it in the present if you wanted to. Naturally, many details would have to be changed to make it conform to the game now.

"I'm a writer and I've been a sportswriter, and I always liked the sportswriter character—Randall, I think, was his name. If you are a different Lloyd Pye and you have no idea what I'm talking about—sorry about that. Someone with your name wrote a book that meant something to me at one time. If you are the same Lloyd Pye—great work. It was/is a memorable book."

I wrote back to Paul to thank him for writing me, and to tell him that by a remarkable act of providence he was contacting me precisely when I had decided to write and publish a thirty-year-anniversary complete redraft of it.

I told him I knew things were very different now due to scholarships being restricted to 85, and the great amount of professional evaluation of high school players, winnowing each year's crop of seniors down to those with the best chances to play and thrive in college. Of course, mistakes in judgment will always occur, so there will always be players that coaches would rather be rid of . . . *always*.

This was how, in part, Paul responded to that:

"I now have kids who play football. I try to guard them against taking on the notion that once you're a player, you have to always be a player, and to not develop, or hold onto, feelings that you can't leave the game because of ideas about manhood and the rest of it. (Doesn't the girlfriend in your book have a line like, *My Dad is still a football player?*) I never played football beyond Pop Warner, but I 'get it' because later in life I studied psychology, and men's issues were a part of my studies. As a sportswriter, I dealt with material like that on a regular basis.

"I guess what was important about that book to me— beyond its outstanding craft and memorable characters and scenes—was that on a meta-level it said a great deal about 'maleness,' and what it means to be a 'man' in our society. I haven't read the book in a long time, but as you can tell, it still resonates with me very strongly. I hope it finds a much wider audience this time."

So do I.

Printed in the United States
94399LV00003B/191/A